SOUTH COAST SHENANIGANS

Jeff Crook

The Book Guild Ltd

First published in Great Britain in 2021 by
The Book Guild Ltd
9 Priory Business Park
Wistow Road, Kibworth
Leicestershire, LE8 0RX
Freephone: 0800 999 2982
www.bookguild.co.uk
Email: info@bookguild.co.uk
Twitter: @bookguild

Copyright © 2021 Jeff Crook

The right of Jeff Crook to be identified as the author of this
work has been asserted by him in accordance with the
Copyright, Design and Patents Act 1988.

All rights reserved. No part of this publication may be
reproduced, transmitted, or stored in a retrieval system, in any form or by any means,
without permission in writing from the publisher, nor be otherwise circulated in
any form of binding or cover other than that in which it is published and without
a similar condition being imposed on the subsequent purchaser.

This work is entirely fictitious and bears no resemblance to any persons living or dead.

Typeset in 12pt Adobe Jenson Pro

Printed and bound by CPI Group (UK) Ltd, Croydon, CR0 4YY

ISBN 978 1913913 090

British Library Cataloguing in Publication Data.
A catalogue record for this book is available from the British Library.

Foreword and Acknowledgement

In the course of my career, I have witnessed fascinating developments in the maritime world, such as engine room automation and advances in offshore technology. With a natural interest in these subjects, I began to contribute to trade magazines after leaving the industry. I should like to thank Kim Jackson, editor of *Petroleum Review* (published by the Energy Institute in London), for publishing the most recent of these articles. These articles were intended for energy professionals. But in 2016, I felt the urge to write in a more light-hearted manner.

This novel is fiction, with imagined characters, but some events did occur, and are well known to the maritime community. The first submarine to employ fuel cells sailed on its maiden voyage in April 2003[1], the *Kursk* disaster cost the lives of 118 Russian sailors in the year 2000 and Type 45 destroyers suffered power problems. These problems were discussed at a parliamentary defence committee hearing, but not as described in this book.

---

1 Howaldtswerke-Deutsche Werft AG (HDW) issued a press release on 7 April 2003, reading: "The world's first submarine with a fuel cell propulsion system starts its maiden voyage on 7 April 2003. 'U 31' the first of the four 212 A Class submarines to be delivered to the German Navy, is now beginning its sea trials in the Baltic Sea following extensive port tests."

The story features some familiar landmarks, such as Plymouth Hoe and the Old Town of Portsmouth, but most of the action takes place, in Whitebait Cove and Leighton Hollow, which are imaginary. The naval officers behave in an outlandish way. It is unlikely that naval officers would be permitted to act in this fashion. I hope to write a sequel in which the renegade officers are brought to book.

It was a long struggle to write this novel, so I would like to thank my friends and family for their patience. My special thanks go to Rosemarie Gibaud, who showed great interest in the project, right up to her 100th birthday; to my friends Tony Reynolds and David Chiang; to my friend Kim Philpott; and to my sister Hazel Haughton, and her friends Anne Arabian and Anne Mehlmann. I would also like to thank all the competent engineers that I have worked with over the years. They will know who they are – they are the ones that keep the lights on! I should also like to thank the editorial staff at The Book Guild for correcting and improving my manuscript.

Contents

Chapter 1	Shipmates Are Drawn into a Cloak-and-Dagger Scheme	1
Chapter 2	Martin Beckwith's Story	26
Chapter 3	Lieutenant Anne Dexter	42
Chapter 4	Anne Seeks Commander Woods	65
Chapter 5	Anne Dexter's Tea Party	84
Chapter 6	A Trip to Whitebait Cove	104
Chapter 7	The Admiral Pulls Strings	120
Chapter 8	A Texan Takes Charge	144
Chapter 9	The Admiral has a Score to Settle	168
Chapter 10	Steve Lured into a Team	187
Chapter 11	Steve collects debts and fishes with Mark	217
Chapter 12	Mark Hosts a Fishing Trip	245
Chapter 13	Mark Joins the Gang	271
Chapter 14	The Heist is Planned	286
Chapter 15	Steve Sounds Out his Old Shipmates	306

Chapter 16	The Conspirators Gather	315
Chapter 17	The Heist Gets Underway	323
Chapter 18	Steve in Bother, not Scotland	347
Chapter 19	Turmoil at Whitebait Cove	360
Chapter 20	The Shipmates are Introduced to the Dredging Business	377
Chapter 21	Detective Smells a Rat	393
Chapter 22	A Botched Investigation	422
Chapter 23	Steve Briefs His Team	450
Chapter 24	Tweak his Tail	483
Chapter 25	Portsmouth Outing	512

Chapter 1

Shipmates Are Drawn into a Cloak-and-Dagger Scheme

Shortly after losing his wife to cancer, Bill Prior was astonished to receive an invitation to a shipmates' reunion in Plymouth. On the face of it, there was nothing unusual about this. But he was in two minds whether to accept. The reason for his hesitation was that the event was organised by a studious fellow called Steve Jones, who was not regarded as a particularly sociable member of the crew. Little did he know this would lead him into a bizarre cloak-and-dagger world.

Bill decided to accept the invitation when he learned that Alex McKay was to attend, because it would give them a chance to catch up. The cantankerous Scotsman had a fractious relationship with the event's organiser. *With luck, there will be fireworks*, mused Bill gleefully. Bill was also looking forward to a tour of a boatyard where both he and Alex had worked before returning to sea. By some quirk of fate, Steve had become boss of the boatyard, so the weekend reunion did make some sort of sense.

In years gone by, the boatyard was run by a character called Sam Wheeler, who was a legend among the yachting fraternity. Sam had passed away a couple of years earlier and was greatly missed. While Bill and Alex studied for their Board of Trade 'tickets' at a technical college in Plymouth, they worked part-time at the boatyard. After receiving their qualifications, both engineers signed to the *Sea Ranger*; Bill acted as the senior-second engineer and Alex as third engineer.

Steve Jones joined the ship as a high-flying graduate cadet; Bill took the somewhat callow youth under his wing to teach him the ropes, and acted as a father figure. It soon became apparent that the lad was not cut from the same cloth as other members of the engine-room staff. The engineers were a raffish bunch, by and large. Most were headstrong, boisterous, and heavy drinkers, while the cadet was a serious bookish type.

While Bill respected Steve's intellect, he found the lad conceited and did not really care for him. It irked him that after teaching the youngster his job, the high-flyer would be quickly promoted over his head. His latest role as chief executive of the boatyard was a sign that he had enjoyed an extremely successful career. So Bill approached the reunion with a mixture of emotions.

At Steve's suggestion, they arranged to meet in the Nautical Inn. Bill recalled a shabby, tobacco-stained establishment that enjoyed a spectacular position overlooking Plymouth Sound, but he arrived to find the tatty old pub had been transformed into a gastropub with an upmarket clientele. Smartly uniformed staff served young professionals. The building had been renovated, with light woodwork and stylish light fittings replacing the gnarled old beams. There were few signs of the old-timers who used to prop up the bar.

Despite his misgivings, Bill found the staff friendly, and he was pleased to see that the real ale was served in proper 'jugs,' if so required. So he ordered three pints of the local beer and carried the scallop-indented jugs through French windows to a terrace that had been neatly paved with flagstones. The pub was quiet during the afternoon lull, so he sat on a bench attached to a stocky wooden table. The table was shaded by a tightly stretched cream awning and provided a panoramic view of the harbour.

Bill's journey to Plymouth had been uneventful, and he had checked into the guesthouse without any difficulty. But he disliked being cooped up in his small saloon car and was in urgent need of a drink to unwind. Sitting on the quiet terrace, he felt content for the first time that day. It was a nice spot to relax on an early-spring afternoon, with a light breeze to ruffle the few remaining strands of hair that graced his temple. While thick brown hair sprouted from the sides of his dough ball-shaped head, he was almost bald on top.

The rocky Hoe dominated the shoreline, with grassy promontories extending out on either side. Seagulls wheeled above, and the sun glimmered off the sea. A fishing boat chugged by, leaving a white-water wake. A warship swinging at its mooring reminded him of the strategic importance of the harbour. There was barely a ripple on the sea, thanks to a breakwater extending part way across the bay that formed the harbour entrance.

For Bill, the scene brought back memories of his college course. The qualification he gained at the technical college allowed him to take charge of machinery on board diesel ships. It was on this course that he met the cantankerous Scotsman. Both engineers went on to serve as engineer officers on a ship called the *Sea Ranger*. It was an unusual ship which carried a complement of 150 passengers, together with a large cargo of chilled meat.

As an officer, he was able to mingle with the passengers. Bill appreciated this because it was a chance to get to know interesting people, and this helped to break the monotony of the long ocean passages, but not all of his colleagues shared this benign view. There was a rougher element of the crew who regarded the passengers with something approaching contempt. This led to rows in the officers' bar on occasions. But one attractive feature of the ship was that it spent long periods loading cargo along the New Zealand coast.

Some of the ports in remote parts of this country lacked cranes to load the consignments of meat. So carcasses were carried up the gangway by the local Maoris, before the meat was stowed away in the cavernous refrigerated holds below decks. This time-consuming procedure allowed the engineers to explore the scenic coastline, while their fellow deck officers were busy supervising the laborious loading process.

Bill's ruminations were disturbed when a portly man tripped over the frame of the French windows, stumbled onto the terrace, and flung his holdall on the bench seat. "Where's my pint then, you softy Southerner!" demanded the angry-looking fellow. The new arrival was sweating profusely thanks to the heavy weatherproof jacket he was wearing.

Bill took the insult in his stride. "You should blow the moths out of your wallet, you tight-fisted sod!" he responded jovially as he pointed to the second pint pot. "What on earth do you need that jacket for? You must be boiling!" His old pal scowled and slumped down on the bench seat. The battered holdall thrown down on the seat beside him was covered in airline stickers. This was evidence that the new arrival was a seasoned traveller.

It soon became apparent that the new arrival, Alex McKay, had suffered delays and train cancellations on his rail journey down from Scotland and was fuming after a frustrating journey. After gulping down some beer, Alex extended a hand to his old pal and began to show a tentative interest in their plans for the weekend.

"Steve's not here then?" asked the Scotsman with a sour expression.

"No sight, nor sound," replied Bill brightly. "I haven't got a clue what he is planning. I've not heard from him in years, and doubt that he wants to talk about our time on the *Sea Ranger*. All I know is that he wants to show us around Sam's yard – you know that he runs the boatyard now?"

"Yes. I've heard that," replied Alex with a disdainful expression. "Can't imagine how he got the job! Sam must be spinning in his grave."

As they waited, Alex griped about the collapse of the railway system, the evils of gastropubs and his scorn for 'obnoxious college kids'. It was clear that the Scotsman was in a rancorous mood, and so Bill anticipated fireworks when Steve arrived to join them. The remarks were aimed, obliquely, at the young high-flyer who had sailed with them.

Steve was the blue-eyed boy of the Boston Line, when he joined the *Sea Ranger*. At the time, he was regarded as an elite member of the engineering community. This was an era of change, with the advent of liquid-gas carriers, containers and automation. The new ships demanded seagoing staff with knowledge of electronics and computers. Steve was part of this new wave of engineers.

But it had been a huge disappointment for the high-flying college graduate to discover that he had been relegated to an old rust bucket, rather than one of the modern ships. It later turned out that this seagoing appointment had been an administrative error. The error might have ended Steve's career had Bill not taken him under his wing. As mentor, Bill encouraged the cadet as best he could. But Alex did little to make life easy for Steve, judging the young graduate to be a 'conceited young puppy'.

As they got to know one another, the older engineers knew that the cadet would soon be promoted over their heads. As the industry changed, the Boston Line, like its competitors, had a policy of fast-tracking the promotion of graduates. After leaping the old generation, the cadet might, with luck, become a superintendent engineer by his thirtieth birthday.

Steve's golden prospects caused envy, particularly among the 'hairy-assed thirds' whose career prospects were blighted by poor academic qualifications. This raffish element of the crew found the young graduate aloof, standoffish and not really one of the lads. He rarely joined them on their shore trips. Instead, he would stay on board, using his spare time to study. But the studious cadet did eventually win the respect of the senior officers, as he showed he was prepared to knuckle down and take on tough jobs.

Bill and Alex had finished their first pint when their young shipmate appeared, though they scarcely recognised him. He had retained the athletic slim build of his youth, but he had matured. He looked quietly confident as he bounded up the steps, approaching them from a back entrance in the garden. He was dressed in a well-cut suit and looked the model of a successful young entrepreneur.

"Hello, you two, really glad you could make it. I bet you were surprised to hear from me!" he said with a fetching grin, and shook them both by the hand.

"Yes, thought you had forgotten us by now!" replied Bill with a friendly smile. "Hope you like the local bitter," passing him the remaining pint.

"Yes. Bitter is fine," replied Steve somewhat doubtfully as he dusted some tree pollen from the bench seat with a copy of the *Financial Times* before taking his seat. He sipped his pint diffidently. They had the appearance of an ill-assorted group. After the usual pleasantries, the conversation petered out, and there was little sign that they had anything in common. It seemed unlikely that they would rekindle the camaraderie as shipmates.

Bill recalled some anecdotes. But the conversation waivered and followed a desultory path. The atmosphere soured when Steve declined Alex's offer of a second pint, mumbling something about 'drink driving'. Things got worse when office workers refused to give way when Alex tried to make his way to the bar. Alex abandoned his attempt to buy his second pint in disgust. He had played little part in the conversation to that point.

The disgruntled trio became increasingly isolated as a gaggle of boisterous young salesmen spilled through the French windows onto the patio where they were sitting. They became hemmed in by office workers celebrating the end of their working week. Alex's temper boiled over, and he stared daggers at the encroaching rabble and his empty glass. To make matters worse, Steve put the cat among the pigeons when he recalled a story about a crankshaft repair job on the *Sea Ranger*.

The story was enough to push Alex right over the edge. "Why do you want to bring that up!" demanded the Scotsman angrily, staring pointedly at his empty glass. "You were damn all help. You just took the piss from the sidelines!" After all the frustrations of the long rail journey, this was a chance to vent his spleen. "What's your game anyway? You brought me all the way down from Scotland to rake over some stupid incident that took place more than ten years ago? Shove your reunion. I'm not staying in this dump!"

Why on earth has Steve dredged up that unpleasant affair? wondered Bill. The placid engineer had vague memories of the event. It all started when Steve tried to ingratiate himself with some 'hairy-assed thirds'. This unwholesome gang lounged round the duty mess in oil-stained overalls recovering from heavy drinking sessions and boasting of their sexual conquests. That was a familiar problem among some engineering staff of that era.

An undercurrent of discontent arose when capable engineers failed to pass the academic qualifications needed to secure promotion to senior positions. Knowing they had reached a glass ceiling, some of these men became troublemakers who took out their grievances on young recruits, like Steve. On some ships, this created a rift between the responsible senior engineers, like Bill and Alex, and unsavoury louts in the lower ranks.

The malign influence of these malcontents became evident when a diesel generator on the *Sea Ranger* developed a defect that threatened to leave the ship 'dead in the water'. In a desperate attempt to resolve the problem, Alex devised a tool to machine the crankshaft. While the Scotsman was hard at work, Steve mocked the 'Heath Robinson' device, in an effort to curry favour with the subversive gang of hairy-assed thirds. This was a serious mistake, not least because the contraption worked and the repair was completed. Alex never forgot the jibes and bore a grudge to this day.

Some days after this unfortunate affair, the *Sea Ranger* docked close to the entrance to the Panama Canal. With the prospect of a trip ashore, some unsavoury louts ribbed the nervous young cadet by saying that he had never 'had a woman'. They offered to take him ashore to 'make a man of him'. This was the one and only time that Steve fell into that trap. In a way, the bunch of no-hopers achieved their stated aim, but not in the way they envisaged. Bill had warned the young cadet not to come under the influence of the gang, but his warnings were made in vain.

The unruly gang set off in high spirits when the ship berthed at a bunkering station on a sun-baked quay. After a quick wash and brush-up, they waltzed down the gangway to hail a cab. The ringleader instructed the taxi driver to take them all to a 'Jolly Jack' bar. The smiling taxi driver took them on a torturous route through the shanty town surrounding the docks to a dreary single-storey building standing out in the wilds. They were ushered inside by a sleazy character who directed them to a dank, dark room.

The gang chortled as they urged the young recruit to sit up close to a raised platform that passed for a stage. When the lights were dimmed, the small audience was presented with a lewd display by a couple of unappealing young women with gaudy make-up. Steve was disgusted with the display and lost any sense of sexual desire. His lack of arousal became apparent when a young hostess grabbed his genitals.

But he was not the only member of the gang to be embarrassed by the affair. Despite boasting of their sexual prowess, none of the other members of the gang felt inclined to take advantage of the services offered by the women. It was an ignominious affair and none of the gang spoke about it again. They departed from the seedy brothel in silence and were forced to walk a long way before they could find a taxi to take them back to the ship. Steve learned who his real friends were that night. It was a lesson he would not soon forget.

"Look, Alex. I know I was wrong to mock your crankshaft repair tool, and it's been on my conscience, and I want to apologise to you after all these years," declared the young executive in a conciliatory way. "But that job showed how good you are at finding practical solutions to technical problems. We need someone like you for a new project. It's a complicated story, but I'll try to explain if you come to the boatyard tomorrow. I might be able to offer you a job that is just up your street."

"You must be joking," replied Alex, who was boiling with rage. "Sam Wheeler was a good man. A proper boat builder, he built proper wooden boats. You probably build plastic boats for upper-class twits, so what can you possibly need with my experience?"

"Look, I'm sorry if I have upset you," replied Steve as he struggled to make himself heard over the hubbub of the now crowded bar. "I really appreciate you coming all the way down here, and I am sorry the pub is crowded. But come and see me at the yard tomorrow, and you might see things in a different way – our business is complicated, and we do not build fibreglass yachts for upper-class twits. It's much more interesting than that. But it's too much to explain tonight."

"Well, I might think about it, but I don't want any of your executive bullshit," snarled the angry Scotsman. "I've enough problems as it is and don't need any more aggravation." At that, he lifted his pint pot to his lips to drain the last dregs in an ostentatious manner and picked up his holdall. "You coming, Bill?" shouted the Scotsman towards his pal, who remained rooted to his seat, sitting in shocked silence.

"I'll be with you in a minute," shouted Bill towards the fast-retreating figure. "Meet you outside." Swaddled in his waterproof jacket, the Scotsman used his weighty holdall to batter a path through the crowd, like a rugby forward forging his way over the line for a touchdown. But he met little resistance. The chattering office workers divided like the Red Sea in the Old Testament, to allow the human battering ram free passage to the exit.

The remaining pair sat transfixed. They were both familiar with Alex's volcanic temper and knew he would calm down in due course. Bill looked at the smart young executive with a bemused expression and said he would do his best to persuade his pal to join them at the boatyard at nine o'clock the following day. He then followed his pal to the rear entrance, hoping to catch him before he had gone too far. Looking dejected, the young executive strode off towards his sleek sports car, which was parked at the bottom of the garden.

When Bill caught up with his pal, the pair decided to move on to the Feathers, which they both remembered as an agreeable public house, more suitable for their generation. The public house was one of their regular haunts when they attended college, but it lacked the stunning view or gastronomic food of the Nautical Inn. The pub was located on a cobbled lane, in the Barbican area, opposite the fish market. "We can have a proper chat in the Feathers. You can't hear yourself think in that place," said Bill in a conciliatory gesture. If truth be known, he would have preferred to stay in the Nautical Inn and wait for the crowd to abate. But he did not want to offend the volatile Scotsman.

In sullen silence, they trudged towards the Barbican area, which was normally thronged with revellers at that time on a Friday night. Alex was in a foul mood as they passed the fish market and aquarium, on to a swing bridge. "Ach, he's a cheeky wee laddie, that Steve!" bawled Alex, reverting to his native brogue as his frustration boiled over. Alex's Glaswegian accent had softened after many years working with foreign crews.

"Yes. He's a bit cocky… but you must admit he's done well," replied Bill as he tried to smooth things over, as diplomat. "Best to listen to what he has to say, tomorrow."

"What do we know about plastic boats?" retorted Alex indignantly. In his pent-up rage, he had persuaded himself that the 'young laddie' was building glass fibre yachts at the old boatyard. "So why does he want to see us old-timers?"

Bill was going to say, *Who said anything about plastic boats?* but thought better of it – he did not want to inflame the situation. Alex was a capable mechanic, but his temper could be his own worst enemy. When riled, he rubbed people up the wrong way. The sad truth was that the Scotsman was born in the wrong era. He might have been a famous engineer if born a century earlier. But times had moved on and there was no longer a great demand for his old-fashioned mechanical skills.

Seagoing engineers monitor machinery from the comfort of an air-conditioned control room, on most modern ships. But Alex had an aversion to electronics, and things of that ilk. As a result, he was condemned to work on old rust buckets owned by disreputable foreign companies and registered under a flag of convenience. With little in the way of pension, he now faced a bleak future. He was part of a lost army of ships' engineers who struggled to maintain the old rust buckets, with few tools or spare parts.

Alex blamed his ill health on the conditions he endured on board these old ships. As he approached his sixty-fifth birthday, it was time for him to retire. But with much of his career on foreign ships, it would be a struggle to survive on a modest Merchant Navy pension. It was for that reason that he was seeking consultancy work. But there was little demand for people with his chequered service record. It was Steve's vague hint of employment that had persuaded him to Plymouth.

They fell silent again as they snaked through the Friday-night revellers on the final leg of their journey to the Feathers. This pub had been a regular when they attended the local technical college. It was run by a petite landlady, with close-cropped blonde hair, called Jackie. Unlike the upmarket

Nautical Inn, the Feathers attracted a polite clientele of business people, who understood pub etiquette. A couple of regulars stood aside when the pair approached the bar. "Well, well. Look who's here!" cried Jackie, as she hopped over an open hatchway to serve them. "Usual then?" she asked with a welcoming smile. One of the bar staff had opened the hatch to change a barrel of real ale.

"Yes, thanks," replied Bill with a sudden surge of well-being. It felt like returning home.

"Sorry to hear about your wife," said Jackie as she handed over the drinks. Bill was touched by the condolences for his wife, who had died of cancer some months earlier. He felt piqued that neither of his former shipmates had thought to raise the subject.

The bar was a hotbed of gossip, and that was one reason why the customers stayed so loyal to the establishment. Jackie's role as landlady put her at the heart of the local community, so she had an encyclopaedic knowledge of her customers' private lives. With a network of informants, she had learned that Bill's wife had passed away, just before Christmas, after a short illness. Jackie had always had a soft spot for the good-natured engineer and knew how much he adored his wife.

News of the terminal illness had been a devastating blow to Bill and caused him to resign from his job as a senior manager of a large corporation, to nurse his partner. His employers offered him a leave of absence. But with no dependents, Bill saw little point in carrying on – he did not need the money. So he took early retirement. He was now starting to regret that decision. Without a job, or children, he lacked a real purpose in life.

It was the first time that Bill's loss had been mentioned that weekend and it was typical that the landlady should be the one to bring it up. The remark left Alex feeling slightly guilty. The Scotsman muttered his condolences and offered to pay for the next round. Like many seafarers, he was uncomfortable discussing the family life of his workmates. Alex was single and had few friends in his home town. He was rather lost ashore, despite the hardship of his life at sea.

The amiable conversation was cut short when Jackie was called away to serve another customer. So, taking their drinks, the pair moved to a corner table to chat. As the evening progressed and the beer flowed, they shared jokes, gossip and banter with other regulars. With his good humour restored, Alex grabbed his holdall and set off to the guesthouse. It was the end of a long day for the Scotsman. Bill had already booked into the guesthouse and so the pair agreed to meet at breakfast the following morning.

Bill arose early on Saturday with a slight hangover after his night out. There was no sign of Alex in the hotel lobby, but the girl at the check-in desk confirmed that he had checked in the previous night, so Bill knocked gingerly on his friend's door to enquire whether he wanted to visit the boatyard, or not. He was prepared for a rant about plastic boats but was instead greeted by a thumbs-up signal from a steaming shower cubicle tucked away in a corner of the room. So Bill sent a text message to Steve saying that they would both be over to see him at around nine o'clock. He waited for Alex in the breakfast room.

Bill was keen to avoid another tirade about plastic boats and college boys, and neither did he want to be drawn into a morbid conversation about the death of his wife, so he flicked through a tabloid paper in search of a light-hearted topic that would entertain his truculent Scottish pal. This strategy worked, and they chatted in an animated way about the antics of a football star as they each chomped their way through a full English breakfast.

After breakfast, they climbed into Bill's hatchback and set off through some rather dreary suburbs to the boatyard. The traffic was heavy as they crossed the Tamar. But there were few other vehicles when they reached picturesque open countryside beyond. Approaching their destination, they climbed a small rise that overlooked the small hamlet of Whitebait Cove. The panorama was a shock – a modern housing development covered much of the land that the old boatyard used to occupy.

"What did I tell you!" said Alex contemptuously. "Those college kids will wreck the country, given half a chance."

Although Bill did not agree, he kept his views to himself. In his opinion, the new housing blended well with the landscape. The houses were tastefully designed with a wide range of architectural features. The buildings complemented the meadows and woodland that extended down to the waterside of the estuary. It was an improvement on the ramshackle boatyard that Sam Wheeler struggled to keep tidy, with its dilapidated sheds and rusting machinery.

As they drew near, they saw that the new marine business occupied only a fraction of the original site. The 'boatyard' was, in fact, a small industrial compound fenced off on the far side of the residential development. Both men were familiar with vast shipyards in the Far East with state-of-the art facilities occupying an area the size of a golf course. They had few expectations for this boatyard. But Bill was, nevertheless, impressed with what he saw.

It soon became clear that the old boatyard site had been divided into industrial and residential areas. On the western side of the site, the housing was set back, to provide public access to the waterfront. The modern industrial compound occupied the east side. The compound was surrounded by a high wire-mesh fence with a security hut at the entrance. A modern office building could be seen beyond the gate, flanked by a pair of metal-clad workshops. Two shabby portable cabins stood in the car park and spoiled the otherwise neat and tidy appearance of the site. A small ship was moored at the quay.

After following some brightly painted signs, Bill stopped at the security hut that stood by the entrance to the compound. The cheaply built wooden hut was out of character with the stylish modern office block within. A guard lounged in the hut and pointedly ignored them while he munched a sandwich. Eventually, the surly character ambled over with a clipboard and tapped on the passenger window.

As he watched the burly figure wander over, Bill had a nasty feeling that he had crossed swords with the guy in a nightclub the previous evening. But his memory was dulled by alcohol and a poor night's sleep. "I think I know that chap," he muttered as they sat waiting for the barrier to be lifted. When Alex opened his window and gave their names, Bill leaned over to take a closer look but still could not place the man.

"You are expected. Go on through. Use the visitors' space in front of the main office," grunted the guard officiously as he raised the barrier. He waddled back to his hut where he watched Alex park his hatchback in the visitor space next to Steve's sleek sports car. The foyer of the office building was faced with a smoked-glass window decorated with the stylish logo in flowing white script. The car park was otherwise deserted, suggesting that the yard was closed for business on Saturday morning.

After a few moments, Steve emerged from the foyer to greet Bill. His fresh, relaxed smile and fresh appearance belied the heavy burden of responsibility weighing on his slender shoulders. Casually dressed in jeans and a finely knitted woollen jumper, he appeared every bit the successful entrepreneur. Reading Bill's sour expression, Steve could see that he had received a hostile reception at the gate. "Did our friend give you a hard time?" he inquired sympathetically as he pointed towards the entrance.

"Not the friendliest reception we've had," replied Bill euphemistically. "Where did you get that gorilla?"

"Don't worry. We all have the same problem," commented Steve. "We don't normally employ guards but our client wanted some men to guard *The Normandy*. He pointed to the small ship that was berthed at the quay. "The navy is testing a new type of submarine. I'll tell you more about it later. The guards upset our staff. Sometimes it feels as though we are hostages in our own yard," he added with a sigh.

Then shaking off that depressing thought, he continued in a more cheerful manner, asking what Bill had done the previous evening. "We went down to a pub called the Feathers," replied Bill. "It's a nice old pub down by the fishing harbour."

"Yes, I know it. I sometimes go there myself," replied Steve to Bill's amazement.

Steve's failure to acknowledge Alex during this friendly exchange was as a slap on the wrists for the Scotsman's rude behaviour the previous evening. But the thick-skinned fellow ignored the snub. He had other things on his mind. The Scotsman was appalled that no boats were being built at the once-famous yard, so with little regard for their conversation, he butted in to ask: "Where do you build the boats?"

"We don't build boats!" Steve retorted with a sigh of exasperation. His patience was wearing thin with the cantankerous Scotsman. Then after composing himself, he turned to address Alex, adopting the calm, precise manner of a parent admonishing a naughty child: "We build control systems for the military and offshore industry." Having made his point, he turned back to Bill to continue their private conversation.

While it was obvious that Alex had got the wrong end of the stick about 'plastic boats', Steve resisted the impulse to rub salt in the wound. He needed the Scottish engineer's help with an undercover operation, and so he would have to put up with his tantrums. He braced himself to cope with further childish tirades before the day was over.

"Come on through. There is some coffee in my office," he suggested as he led them through the entrance lobby. They passed an empty reception desk and climbed up the polished oak stairs to an office on the first floor marked with an engraved sign saying *Chief Executive* on the door.

"Wow. You've really fallen on your feet here!" said Bill, who was really impressed by the magnificent surroundings.

"Glad you like it," replied Steve proudly. "We deal with some senior people from the Ministry of Defence and offshore industry, and they expect to receive VIP treatment. They sometimes call in to see us at short notice, so we need to keep them happy. But the yard is closed on Saturday, so we should not be disturbed today."

Bill loved the room and envied his young friend. He draped his sports jacket over the back of a chair standing by a conference table. Then he wandered round, examining the ornaments. A collection of model ships and nautical instruments was housed in a glass case behind the main desk. There were some sepia photographs on the wall, showing the early days of the yard. After completing a circuit of the room, he stepped through some French windows onto a balcony which provided a sweeping view of the estuary. From there, it was possible to scan the scenery with a brass telescope, mounted on a swivel stand.

The Scotsman was still swaddled in his weatherproof jacket and seemed uneasy about stepping foot into the immaculate room. After stepping gingerly inside, his gaze fixed on an old sepia picture of the boatyard hanging beside the door. After standing in silence for a few minutes, he murmured disparagingly, "Sam Wheeler must be turning in his grave. He didn't need a posh office. All his staff turned up for work on Saturday morning! It must have cost a fortune to build all this!"

The yard had a proud history. It became famous during the Second World War for building fast air-sea rescue boats. Then after the war, it gained a reputation for building bespoke wooden yachts. The yard boss, Sam Wheeler, was a wily character, who ran the family-owned business in an autocratic way. When Bill and Alex helped out at the weekends, they were fascinated to watch the craftsmen at work. But as the years passed, it became evermore difficult to find good timber, and the yard was unable to compete with fibreglass builders. When Sam finally retired, at the venerable old age of eighty-six, the business was close to bankruptcy, so the family decided to sell the valuable waterside property.

A family-owned Dutch conglomerate bought the entire site and appointed Steve Jones to run the marine business. The corporation had interests in property development, offshore construction and shipping. "We bought the boatyard five years ago and sold most of the land for housing development," explained Steve in response to Alex's barely audible remark. "The sale provided enough cash to build the new offices and workshops.

"If you would *like* to take a seat, I'll tell you what we are up to," he remarked as he poured three cups of coffee from the percolator. The sharp inflexion of his voice was reminiscent of a vicar rounding up a wayward group of churchgoers. Bill showed little inclination to move, because he was happily engrossed with the telescope on the balcony. Alex stood like a statue in front of the picture showing the glory days of the once-famous yard.

"Why don't you build wooden boats?" demanded Alex bluntly as he grudgingly turned around to acknowledge the young executive. Steve bit his lip in an effort to ignore the provocation.

"There's no money in building wooden boats these days," he replied patiently. "Other yards have switched to fibreglass. You can call them plastic if you like. It makes no odds! But we decided to follow a different route.

"We supply high-quality equipment for the navy and offshore industry," he explained. "Every job is different. That sometimes means working with exotic materials, so we have invested in sophisticated machine tools and welding equipment. We have just finished a project to build the fuel cell system for a midget submarine. It's the biggest job we've had so far. I'll take you down to have a look at it later on. We make a wide range of components for subsea industry and electronic circuit boards."

Steve pushed a company brochure across the conference table to tempt the pair to join him. After dragging himself away from the telescope, Bill reluctantly abandoned his observatory and moved to the conference table. After picking up the brochure, he studied it with admiration. Alex finally succumbed and grudgingly took his place. Once seated, he fiddled with his hot mug of coffee and grumbled under his breath that there were no biscuits. But something was stirring in the Scotsman's mind. The mention of machine tools had whetted his appetite. Alex was a keen model engineer and had a fully-equipped workshop in the garden in the house that he shared with his mother in Glasgow.

Alex spent little time ashore. But when home, he stayed in his family home, in a suburb of Glasgow. The terraced house was kept in immaculate condition by the feisty old lady. His father had died prematurely, but his mother was fit and well.

The elderly lady had a sharp tongue and had retained all of her faculties. Alex appreciated his workshop, where he could take refuge from the old woman. She nagged him about his failure to find a partner and bring her grandchildren.

"It all looks double Dutch to me!" retorted Alex as he thumbed idly through the glossy brochure.

Although the words were spoken in a disparaging way, Steve detected a slight thawing in his attitude. "Just bear with me, Alex," suggested the young executive. "You never know, you might just learn something today." They finished their coffee in silence, and neither Bill nor Alex had anything significant to say about the brochure, so Steve led his visitors on a tour of the yard.

The tour got off to a dull start, as far as Alex was concerned. The Scotsman had little interest in the circuit boards, insulated wiring and instruments that were all neatly laid out on the workbenches of the first workshop unit they visited. But as they made their way to the second workshop, the Scottish engineer started to show some enthusiasm for the tour. This workshop was equipped with wide roller doors, with neat yellow lines to delineate the different work areas on the cleanly swept concrete floor.

An ultra-modern, digitally controlled milling machine stood in one corner, flanked by a pair of sophisticated lathes. "The milling machine is the only one of its kind available in the West Country," declared Steve proudly. The tour party then inspected a complicated spider-like mechanism that was being assembled near the roller doors. Steve pointed to some TEG welding equipment and told them it could be used to weld titanium and exotic aluminium alloys. The high-quality craftsmanship appealed to Alex, reminding him of the scale-model steam locomotive that he was laboriously assembling in his garden shed.

As he slyly watched, Steve noticed the Scotsman's enthusiasm, but they could not dally, because he had more important things to show his former shipmates. So, dragging Alex away from the sophisticated machine tools, he led his shipmates smartly across the car park to the small ship that was berthed at the quay. "*The Normandy* is an old offshore supply vessel," explained the young executive. "It was operating in the southern North Sea, off the coast of East Anglia, before it came here. The navy chartered her as the base for trials of a new form of midget submarine."

With the deckhouse squeezed up towards the bow, the ship had a long, flat deck for cargo handling towards the stern. This cargo flat deck was surrounded by a bulwark. "I'm afraid that we cannot look round the whole ship, because it did not belong to the yard," explained Steve, "but there's something that I want you to see on the stern deck."

After checking that no one was watching, Steve led his party up the gangplank, and they then made their way furtively towards the stern. The young entrepreneur lifted the corner of the tarpaulin and shone a touch into the dark interior. As they peered into the gloom, they saw the outline of a strange craft. Bill thought that it resembled a huge insect trapped inside a cave. But as their eyes became accustomed to the dark, they could see a tangle of pods and tanks surrounding a cylindrical body. The craft was supported by a steel cradle, riding on eight wheels. A transparent plastic bubble covered the end of the cylinder.

"This is the first British submarine to use fuel cells rather than batteries for propulsion," explained Steve proudly. "The navy has just finished the sea trials and it performed much better than expected. It can stay submerged for longer than normal battery-powered craft. The plan is to fit hatches so it can be used for submarine rescue operations. It is designed to fit inside a container, so that it can be transported anywhere in the world by road, rail or sea."

Alex looked bored. He had a jaundiced view of the navy and refused to take an interest in any of their projects. But his pal was intrigued and wanted to take a closer look.

"Can we look inside?" asked Bill enthusiastically.

"Not today," said Steve. "The navy is touchy – this cost a lot of money to build, so they are very protective." He went on to explain that the body of the submersible was built of a special titanium alloy at the submarine yard in Barrow. "We supplied most of the systems needed for propulsion and life support. It can dive to a depth of 600 metres of water using its own power. If they decide to use it for rescue work, the yard will fit hatches that allow it to dock onto a disabled submarine and evacuate survivors back to the surface."

Just at that moment, a battered saloon car skidded to a halt in the car park. The driver had not faced the humiliating security rigmarole that Bill had endured at the security barrier. It was apparent that the security guard knew the driver, because he saluted the car and raised the barrier without bothering to check any documents A tall, lean bearded figure emerged from the vehicle and strode purposely towards *The Normandy* with his head down. The man's angry expression showed his intent on a confrontation.

"Whoops. Trouble coming!" exclaimed Steve as he looked uneasy for the first time that weekend. "Please don't say anything – just leave the talking to me."

"Another of your sightseeing tours, *Mr Jones*!" shouted the new arrival angrily as he bounded up the gangplank, two steps at a time. The man's eyes bulged from their sockets, and the skin of his face glowed in an unhealthy shade of purple. His tone suggested that there had been a long and bitter feud between the two men. Clearly, this was not the first time that

Steve had been found leading an unauthorised party around the small ship.

"Thought you had gone back to London," replied Steve sheepishly.

"Sorry to disappoint you!" said the bearded man with a hint of sarcasm. "Who are these people?"

"Let me introduce you," stammered Steve in an attempt to humour the angry fellow. He knew he was in the wrong and wanted to butter up the belligerent figure. "This is Bill Prior and that's Alex McKay. We sailed together on a Boston Line ship called the *Sea Ranger* back in the 1970s. They both worked at the yard when Sam Wheeler ran it, so I thought that I would show them how the yard had changed."

Then turning to his former shipmates, he adopted a fawning attitude. "This is *Dr* Martin Beckwith who is head of the recently established Marine Special Projects Agency. He is the project manager for the submarine rescue project," he explained in a gushing manner. Alex had a problem keeping a straight face as he watched the 'young pup' doing verbal somersaults to extract himself from embarrassing imbroglio. Bill was having a similar problem, although he did have some sympathy for his former protégé.

"It's a *very* impressive craft," said Bill in a placatory way, as he attempted to pour oil on troubled waters.

The angry bearded guy did not buy the soft soap. "Thank you. But this is none of your damn business, and the project is classified!" snapped Dr Martin Beckwith in reply. "So please get off *my* ship, before I call the security guard and have you thrown off." With that, he turned on his heels and set off in high dudgeon towards the security hut.

"That's torn it! We best get back on dry land before he comes back with the security guy!" declared Steve as they scuttled ignominiously ashore. The once cocky young executive looked acutely embarrassed. "Look, I'm really sorry about this. It's best if we talk somewhere else. Perhaps we could meet in the Feathers for lunch. That will give me time to deal with our friend," he stuttered.

This was the first time during the weekend that the pair had seen Steve nonplussed. Alex was tickled pink to watch the 'young pup's' ego deflate like a burst balloon. He decided that the weekend would not be a total washout.

"Okay" said Bill, "see you at two o'clock in the Feathers – after we've had our lunch." With that, Bill and Alex departed, sniggering like a pair of naughty schoolboys.

Chapter 2

Martin Beckwith's Story

Bill and Alex had little idea of the significance of the confrontation that had taken place on *The Normandy* during their tour of the boatyard, or the intrigue that lay behind it. The story could be traced back to the birth of a boy in a Salisbury hospital on Christmas Day in 1968. The auspicious birthdate was seen as an omen, and the proud parents had high hopes for their newborn son, whose name was Martin Beckwith.

The parents ran the village post office in a desolate part of the countryside, on the fringes of Salisbury Plain. The hard-working couple were reasonably affluent and pampered the little boy, showering him with gifts. But as conscientious post office employees, they spent long hours working behind the counter of their small store and struggled to find time to look after their offspring. To make matters worse, the parents had no roots in the rural community.

With no friends to play with, the lonely child spent his time shut away in a bedroom, reading books and magazines.

It soon became clear that he was intelligent but lacking in physical ability. A primary school teacher recognised the family's predicament and suggested that they should send their child to a boarding school. The bright young lad won a scholarship without undue difficulty. Although the overworked parents were reluctant to send the frail child away, they could see no alternative.

Things did not turn out well. The gangly, ill-coordinated lad was ill-suited to the rigours of a boarding school with a sporting ethos. To make matters worse, their son was argumentative and complained about the spartan conditions. With few friends among staff or pupils, he became a target for bullies. He gained a reputation as a 'swot'. Then to compound these difficulties, he reported his tormentors to his housemaster. In doing this, he broke the unwritten code of silence that is observed by all public school pupils.

As a result of this transgression, he was ostracised by staff and pupils alike. No one spoke to him for several weeks after his betrayal of his fellow pupils. To add to his woes, the gangly lad fared little better during school holidays; he was ridiculed by the village kids for his 'posh' education. This miserable period of his upbringing was to have a significant influence on his character, and colour his opinions.

A school prefect, called Richard Walters, felt sympathy for the lad's predicament. The prefect was one of the few people who refused to turn a blind eye to the bullying culture which was endemic at the school. As a prefect, the older boy was in a position to help the young lad. But his efforts were spurned, and he found it difficult to warm to the obnoxious youth. In the end, the prefect lost patience when the younger boy fell into bad company.

To escape his tormentors, the young Beckwith joined some rebellious misfits who sneered at the school's strict rules. The gang bunked off sports in the hope of meeting girls on the bank of an abandoned canal which ran alongside the school grounds. The ringleader of this gang was the son of a crooked businessman. The lad's father was being sued for embezzlement at the time. This spoiled tearaway was given a lot of pocket money by his doting parents.

Under the malign influence of the gang, Beckwith developed a rebellious streak and visceral hatred for the 'establishment'. The fallout from this period of his life would come back to haunt him. The gang leader splashed out his pocket money to win the affection of wayward teenage girls who played truant from the nearby secondary modern school.

One of these schoolgirls had a knowing nature and took pity on the shy, gangly lad. It was with this temptress that he lost his virginity at an early age. The sordid encounter took place in a concrete bunker that was built as part of a line of defence during the last war. The bunker provided shelter from the wind and rain while the school truants smoked illicit cigarettes.

But it was a sordid affair. The floor of the bunker was covered in droppings from the cattle that grazed in the surrounding fields, and the walls were covered in graffiti. The furtive groping in insalubrious surroundings had a profound influence on him, and in later life, he was drawn to nubile young girls. This was unfortunate, given the duty of care that he had for students in his role as university professor.

Under the influence of the subversive gang and the youth culture of the era, the young Beckwith rebelled against his hard-working parents. "You are slaves to the establishment who care more for their precious post office than their own flesh and blood," he declared in one outburst. With a jaundiced view of family life, the precocious teenager felt little sadness when his father died prematurely from a heart attack. After the funeral, the adolescent boy persuaded his mother to sell the post office and move to a more civilised part of the country.

His mother acquiesced to this request and mother and son settled in a two-bedroom flat in North London. The new home allowed young Beckwith to attend a comprehensive school. It was a relief for the teenager to escape the spartan boarding school conditions. Removed from this repressive regime, the teenager blossomed. In more congenial surroundings, the budding academic developed a circle of like-minded friends, and his hatred of the establishment was entrenched.

As an able student, the teenage Beckwith had little trouble gaining a place at Cambridge University, where he chose to study engineering. Once he found his feet, he was drawn into student politics and wrote outspoken articles for the university magazine. In one of these polemics, he blamed the nation's industrial decline on the malign influence of the 'old-boy network' and the 'establishment'. These views won him praise from left-wing activists. As these allies rose up the political ladder, they helped to advance Beckwith's career.

After post-graduate research and short spells in industry, Beckwith was appointed professor of shipyard management. In that position, some political allies asked him to investigate naval procurement. His task was to discover why naval procurement contracts were plagued with cost overruns and delays. After studying the problem, he recommended that a new agency should be established to procure warship construction. This agency would employ a novel form of project management which had been successfully pioneered in the North Sea. His arguments chimed with the progressive thinking of politicians and businessmen of that era.

As a result of Beckwith's recommendations, the Marine Special Projects Agency (MSPA) was established to work in parallel with the other longer-established defence agencies.

The purpose of this new agency was to apply innovative project management techniques to large naval projects. But there was also an unspoken desire to foster new technology. But this role was never publicly acknowledged for fear that it would upset the research agencies that were already linked to the military.

After his appointment as chief executive, Beckwith ensured that its supervisory board of the agency was dominated by people who supported his 'progressive' views. There were eight people on the board, with one member appointed by the government. At the outset, four members of the board, including the government appointee, were supporters of Beckwith's views. The remainder were 'committee fodder' who were happy to support the status quo.

The MSPA was established shortly before the *Kursk* disaster, in the year 2000. The disaster attracted a great deal of press attention. The horrific nature was laid bare when divers finally broke into the hull of the wrecked submarine and found a disturbing handwritten letter. The document had been written by the officer who was in charge of the stern compartment as he waited patiently for his death. It revealed that thirty crew members had survived the massive explosions which tore open the bows of the submarine. The officer knew that the desperate efforts to rescue them were likely to fail. It later emerged that the escape hatch was jammed shut and it was not possible to reach them before they died of suffocation or hypothermia.

The Russian high command was reluctant to ask the West for help with the rescue effort, at first, despite knowing that western navies had stockpiles of rescue facilities at strategic locations. These facilities were maintained by contractors and could be quickly transported anywhere on the globe. Britain and Norway were eventually asked to assist with the rescue attempt but, by that time, it was too late. When Norwegian divers broke into the hull, all they found were dead bodies of the crew. With the media spotlight on these harrowing events, Beckwith saw an opportunity for his fledgling agency.

Jumping on the bandwagon, he lobbied the government to allow his new agency to build a revolutionary form of submarine rescue vehicle. The lobby effort was supported by a media campaign designed to promote his plan and denigrate the naval high command. A friendly journalist wrote an article entitled: *Kursk disaster highlights need for improved submarine rescue capabilities.* That was the opening salvo in a high-profile media campaign directed by the artful academic.

The article appeared in a reputable maritime journal. While accurate in certain respects, the text was carefully slanted to give the impression that some crew members of the *Kursk* might have been saved if the navy had improved rescue facilities. The arguments were picked up by the tabloids (with the academic's help) and prompted questions to be tabled in parliament. A poorly briefed government minister failed to respond in a satisfactory way, and the resulting media storm laid the ground for the academic to make his case.

Under his scheme, Beckwith proposed that the MSPA would raise capital to build a new submarine rescue vehicle with loans underwritten by the government. In promoting his plan, he played on the prejudices of the left-leaning politicians who were in government at the time. The proposal emphasised the humanitarian and industrial benefits of the scheme. One of the main selling points was that the rescue vehicle would employ newly developed fuel-cell propulsion, rather than 'old-fashioned' battery power.

Fuel cells had been used as part of the hybrid propulsion system for a new generation of German submarines since the start of the millennium. But this technology had never been used in a British submarine. Beckwith argued that the adoption of the technology would allow British firms to compete with its German counterparts. In his media campaign, Beckwith reminded people that the first of the German submarines had been described as 'one of the most advanced "non-nuclear" submarines in the world', when it set sail in 2002.

In public speeches, Beckwith criticised the naval high command for dragging its heels over the introduction of this new form of propulsion. This was picked up by the popular press, who portrayed it as a 'David and Goliath' struggle with the navy top brass. But Beckwith's motive was personal advancement. To him, the project was simply a way of boosting funding for his Marine Special Projects Agency.

It took a couple of years to gain official approval for the project. As part of an official review, a distinguished naval officer called Commander Woods was appointed to assess the proposed scheme. The commander had been decorated as a war hero in the Falklands conflict, so his opinion was held in high regard both within the service and in government. The conclusion was that fuel-cell propulsion was not suitable for rescue missions. The reasoning was set out in detail. But the confidential nature of the report allowed it to be interpreted in various ways. As a result, people manipulated the conclusions to suit their own ends.

This allowed Beckwith to paint the decorated war hero as a Luddite who was resistant to change. This view was reinforced with a public relation blitz. Rather than attack the Falkland war hero directly, the artful academic set out to smear the navy 'top brass' as 'technical dinosaurs' in the popular press. This took place against the fiery backdrop of the Scottish independence referendum.

In his public relations campaign, Beckwith found an unwitting accomplice in a gullible political journalist. He fed the journalist a question that would be awkward for a politician to answer. The journalist posed the question at a press conference whose purpose was to outline the government's position on the nuclear deterrent, should Scotland vote to leave the Union.

"Why doesn't the British navy use fuel-cell propulsion as an ecologically clean alternative to nuclear power?" asked the journalist at Beckwith's suggestion.

The badly briefed minister tried to dodge the question. "The British navy uses the best available technology," declared the minister in a pompous manner.

"If fuel cells are good enough for use by the German navy, why does not the Royal Navy follow suit?" retorted the journalist, in a sharp follow-up question.

This exchange set the press pack on a feeding frenzy, and it did not take them long to discover that it was not only the German navy that was using fuel cells in submarines, but that German yards were exporting the technology to other countries. Articles began to appear in the tabloid press to give the false impression that the British navy was lagging behind Germany in this ground-breaking technology.

Had the minister been better briefed, he might have observed that the fuel cells only formed part of a hybrid propulsion system fitted on the German submarines. In these vessels, the fuel cells were integrated with diesel generators and lead-acid batteries. But even this sophisticated arrangement could not match nuclear power for underwater endurance. But with the press pack in hot pursuit, tabloids joined in the hue and cry, branding the naval 'top brass' as a bunch of 'technical dinosaurs'.

Having smeared the navy, Beckwith used a friendly press contact to place comments from 'well-informed sources' about the 'foot-dragging of old buffers in the Admiralty.'

Several journals carried glowing tributes for his fuel-cell scheme alongside damning commentary about the 'technical dinosaurs'. This crafty twin-pronged public relations campaign achieved its aim. Beckwith was given funding to build a prototype submersible craft, by a credulous left-wing government.

Although there was funding to build the midget submarine, the arrangements for operating it were never finalised. Under Beckwith's proposal, the MSPA would retain ownership of the rescue vehicle and build a base where the rescue vehicle could be stored. The rescue vehicle would be maintained ready for deployment in return for lease payments. This was somewhat similar to the commercial arrangements for the existing rescue vehicles. It was also in line with private finance schemes used by the government for building schools and hospitals.

Beckwith had devised this arrangement to provide an ongoing role for the MSPA. It would also allow the agency to use the rescue vehicle as a test-bed for innovative new forms of fuel-cell technology. This was a mouth-watering opportunity for the scheming academic. The only problem was that the arrangement was not agreed with the navy. It ignored the fact that the navy had reservations about using fuel cells for a rescue vehicle. So, in an attempt to resolve the impasse, it was decided to put the prototype submarine through stringent sea trials by a navy team when it was complete. If the sea trials proved successful, the government would lean on the navy top brass to accept the leasing agreement proposed by Beckwith.

Sensing the public mood, left-wing politicians began to talk up the project, boasting that it would allow British industry to 'catch up' with its German counterparts. Their enthusiasm was also fuelled by the belief that the armed forces should focus their efforts on humanitarian work. These politicians made great play of the fact that the new submarine rescue craft would be available to friend and foe alike. "This is an opportunity for us to reach out a hand of friendship to our Russian comrades," declared one left-wing politician.

While Beckwith was up to his skulduggery, a group of forward-thinking naval officers were studying unorthodox solutions to maritime threats. Their focus, at the time, was the need to protect merchant ships from hijackers. But there were also worries that submarine cables might be sabotaged by midget submarine operations. These fears were stoked by worrying news of covert underwater operations being carried out by our adversaries in the Baltic. The fears were heightened by news that the Iranian Revolutionary Guards intended to build a fleet of midget submarines at a time of rising tension in the Gulf of Hormuz.

The officers were lobbying for funding to build a fleet of midget submarines to tackle these 'asymmetric' military threats. But after building two huge aircraft carriers, the government's coffers were bare, so the naval officers looked jealously at Beckwith's midget submarine, wondering whether it could be repurposed for a military role. When they put out tentative feelers, their approach was firmly rebutted by the government of the day. They were told in no uncertain terms that the midget submarine would be dedicated to rescue work.

This left a feeling of resentment among the naval officers, because the benefits of fuel-cell propulsion were well known to high-ranking officers. Evidence of the benefits of fuel cells was provided in a press release issued when a new submarine was christened during May 2013. The ThyssenKrupp press release included a passage stating: *On the way to participate in naval exercises in the USA, the boat (German Navy U-32) produced a new record for non-nuclear submarines with 18 days in submerged transit without snorkelling.*

This submerged endurance was a truly impressive performance and was just what was needed for covert surveillance along hostile coastlines. It so happened that the naval officer leading this group was the school prefect who tried to help the young Beckwith when he first arrived at boarding school. That school prefect had since risen in the ranks of the navy and gloried in the title of Rear-Admiral Sir Richard Walters. Commander Woods, author of the report that questioned the use of fuel-cell propulsion for rescue work, was subordinate to the admiral.

Both officers had doubts about the real benefit of using fuel-cell propulsion for submarine rescue purposes. Both officers felt that Beckwith's craft would be an extremely useful asset for covert surveillance. But the cunning old fox played an underhand game to lay his hands on the revolutionary craft. His first move was to give Beckwith's proposal his (measured) support in the hope that he would be able to get his hands on the craft by some cunning ploy. The commander knew nothing about this double-dealing.

After paving the way for Beckwith's project to go ahead, the admiral made sure that his trusty subordinate was placed in charge of the diving trials. This would provide him with leverage. To further cement his influence over unfolding events, the admiral ensured that the commander performed a liaison role between the navy and the project team. But for the time being, the admiral resisted the temptation to confide in his trusted subordinate about his yet unformed plans to lay his hands on this valuable naval asset.

Blissfully ignorant of the machinations taking place behind the scenes, Beckwith embarked on the project in high spirits. The academic had unfettered control over the project because the supervisory board of the Marine Special Projects Agency was filled with placemen who supported his views.

Had he known that a former school prefect at his boarding school was taking an interest in his work, he would have been more circumspect in the way he acted.

To further bolster his authority, Beckwith established a 'technical advisory team' to oversee the project. The team were made up of former students who owed him allegiance in one way or another. They were an eclectic bunch, with each member bringing specialist experience. The team were based in the project office in Portsmouth, and their first task was to draw up an outline specification for the midget submarine.

The new rescue craft was to be modelled on those that were already in service, and would make use of standard military equipment for docking with a disabled submarine. But the design of the midget submarine incorporated important innovations. In addition to the fuel-cell propulsion, the craft was to use a titanium alloy for the pressure-resisting hull. While this tough material reduced the weight, it created fabrication difficulties. The size of the rescue craft was restricted by the demands for rapid transport to any part of the world. So, it was designed to fit within a standard 40-ft-long container.

The design team were keenly aware that working within the cramped confines of the hull would present a challenge. So, to reduce the quantity of internal work, the craft was to be built with five separate hulls sections. Each was to be fitted with equipment, piping and wiring before the sections were welded together to form a single watertight hull. It was inevitable that some cables would extend beyond individual sections, so these wires were to be routed to junction boxes, with multicores, cable looms or cable harnesses to make connections over the length of the entire craft.

The pilot's control position was located behind a transparent acrylic dome in a hemispherical bow section; a second control station was to be located in the cylindrical midsection; with another hemispherical section to house the fuel tanks, emergency batteries and power generation equipment at the stern. Two simple tubular sections would be provided to form the passenger compartment that runs fore and aft of the mid-section.

In the bidding process, three contractors were paid a fee to produce a detailed front-end design (FEED) for the rescue vehicle. The FEED fleshed out the design, providing details of special features and performance predictions. The technical advisory group assessed these documents before the final contractor was selected.

During these early halcyon days, the only small cloud on Beckwith's horizon was a bitter feud with the naval liaison officer, Commander Woods. The commander was puzzled that the project had been allowed to proceed, being ignorant of the admiral's underhand plans, so he took every opportunity to criticise the submarine rescue scheme. This enraged Beckwith. But the feud was also fuelled by personal animosity.

In their feud, Beckwith called the commander a 'clapped-out old warhorse'. In response, the commander called the academic a 'sandal-wearing peacenik'. At first, Beckwith tolerated the barbs as an elephant would regard a mosquito bite. But then some storm clouds gathered to threaten his comfortable position. The first serious blow was a change of government. This resulted in the removal of a political ally from the supervisory board. Then, to further weaken his position, another friendly board member suffered a heart attack. These setbacks hardened the academic's attitude and the feud with the commander became personal.

With the loss of two key supporters, Beckwith feared the supervisory board would take more notice of the commander's critical views. In other circumstances, he would have smeared the 'old warhorse', but he dismissed that idea, realising that he was dealing with a decorated war hero. So his next wheeze was to recruit a naval officer to his technical advisory team who would be sympathetic to his progressive views. He thought he had found a suitable candidate when he read a post-graduate research paper written by a female naval officer, called Anne Dexter. The insightful nature of her work suggested that she might be amenable to his views. Beckwith hoped that she would act as a buttress against the malign influence of the 'old warhorse'.

It so happened that Beckwith was friendly with the academic who tutored the female naval officer during her post-graduate research. The colleague knew of Beckwith's lecherous nature and misread his intentions. "Why on earth are you interested in her?" he asked incredulously. "She's built like a Sherman tank and I don't think she has ever had a boyfriend. We used to call her Starchy Knickers." But after explaining his predicament more clearly, the colleague was able to assure Beckwith that he had made a sensible choice.

The plan to recruit a female officer met with widespread approval. It gave the impression that the academic had adopted a more conciliatory attitude towards his end client. But Beckwith's real intent was to embroil his new recruit in controversial decisions about the design of the rescue vehicle. In this way, he sought to play off the two naval officers against one another. As he prepared to spring this trap, he relaxed his attitude towards the commander, asking his views about the internal layout of the midget submarine.

The commander was surprised, and gratified, at Beckwith's unexpected request. Shortly afterwards, a huge stack of drawings arrived on his desk. When taken together, the drawings provided the location of equipment within the confines of the hull. But it was quite difficult to visualise the interior from the disparate drawings. Despite the difficulty, however, the commander asked for one small change. The drawing showed the circuit breakers fitted at the stern of the passenger compartment, close to the power generation unit.

That arrangement could create problems, argued the commander, because electrical failures sometimes occur on submersibles due to seawater ingress into the connectors. The resetting of the circuit breaker would have to be carried out by a second crew member, unless the pilot left his seat to move to the rear of the passenger compartment, so he suggested that the circuit breakers be fitted closer to the pilot's seat. In his reply, he added that the internal layout needed to be closely studied by experienced submariners.

To allow for sensible discussion, the commander suggested that a physical mock-up should be built of the most congested sections of the midget submarine. This solution had been adopted for warship design and allowed the crew to get a feel of different layouts before the warship was built. The mock-up could later be used for training. Beckwith thanked the commander for the circuit-breaker comment. But he rejected the suggestion to build a physical mock-up, claiming that the same result could be achieved, more cheaply, with a virtual reality model.

Beckwith argued that virtual reality would allow naval personnel to 'walk through' the hull to get a feel for the layout. It would later emerge that his motive was to provide work for a newly formed business in which he had a financial interest. The start-up business had been established by some of his former students. It later emerged that these students had offered more than they could deliver.

Although the virtual reality model was Beckwith's idea, he gave the impression that the plan had been adopted to satisfy the commander. To further embroil his adversary, he made sure that copies of all virtual reality documents were sent to the commander's office, knowing that the busy commander barely had time to read all the papers in his in-tray. The commander had thus fallen into the carefully prepared trap. His failure to keep up with the flood of paper was to prove his undoing.

Chapter 3

Lieutenant Anne Dexter

Martin Beckwith should have known better than to become entangled with a female officer who came from a family with a proud naval heritage. At an age when other children were lulled to sleep with fairy tales, Anne Dexter was listening to the tales of the derring-do of her ancestors. The little girl was brought up on the (sometimes) fragrant island of Hong Kong, where her parents were pillars of the establishment. At the end of his distinguished career, her father was stationed on the island, where he was ably supported by his wife.

Anne had a brother, Mark, who was seven years her senior. After training at Dartmouth, the brother now served as the weapons officer on an aging aircraft carrier. But this was set to be the ceiling of a somewhat disappointing career. In his parents' eyes, the brother was to be the torch-bearer to maintain the family's proud naval tradition. Neither parent ever suspected that their daughter would rescue the family honour, much to the chagrin of her older brother.

When her parents retired to the West Country, Anne burned with ambition to join the senior service. The robust, outdoor-loving teenager excelled at sport and made her mark in the Sea Cadets. She was bright, and she went on to win a naval scholarship to university. The officer training scheme combined a university degree with sea service as a midshipman. During one of her voyages, her father died. After that sad loss, Anne received little family support for her career. Her widowed mother thought it unseemly for women to serve on ships.

After graduating, Anne continued with her post-graduate degree. Her research paper on control theory was influential in the development of guidance systems used for submarines. This led to a posting with the naval team overseeing submarine construction at a shipyard in Barrow-in-Furness. After a short spell with the team, she was promoted to the rank of lieutenant and her career followed a traditional naval path. As she approached her thirtieth birthday, she was given command of a River Class patrol boat.

The forty-five crew members of the 80-metre-long patrol boat were kept busy dealing with people smuggling, drug trafficking and illegal fishing. The vessel was permanently based at Portsmouth, which allowed Anne to spend time at her bungalow, which stood on the brow of a hill overlooking the naval port. She shared her home with her widowed mother and two pet Labradors. Although her mother was a strong, independent character, she had become frail, so Anne became increasingly worried about leaving her alone while she was away on patrols.

As one of the first female officers to command a warship, Anne found some of the older hands reluctant to obey her. But she had winning ways and gained the respect of most of the crew during her first nine-month tour of duty. During that time, she was able to improve morale on board the busy ship. But an engine room artificer became a thorn in her side. He was ringleader of a subversive gang that caused her some bother.

The artificer was, in fact, an extremely capable technician with ambitions to serve on one of the modern frontline warships that employ aero-engine derived gas turbine machinery for power and propulsion. The non-commissioned officer had applied for a transfer to one of the new frigates which was about to enter service. He was confident that he would be able to help sort out the teething problems that had plagued these 'all-electric' warships. But the artificer suffered from a poor disciplinary record, and his transfer request was denied.

So, instead of serving on a prestigious warship, the talented mechanic was relegated to the patrol boat whose old-fashioned diesel engines placed few demands on his technical ability. His frustration at being relegated to an 'old tub' was compounded by his irritation at taking orders from a female officer. Like many of the longer-serving sailors, he was a chauvinist at heart, whose old-fashioned views about women at sea echoed those of Anne's mother.

The disgruntled artificer knew the rule book inside out and had a reputation as a 'barrack room lawyer'. The rogue devised various cunning pranks to taunt the skipper and held court with a bunch of malcontents in the crew mess, where he boasted about his exploits. Anne knew that she would have to nip this in the bud if he was not to undermine crew morale. An opportunity arose when she was scalded with boiling water while taking a shower. At first, she thought this was a system's glitch, but that notion was dispelled when she heard raucous laughter emanating from the crew's mess.

After taking senior officers into her confidence, she set out to turn the tables on her crafty reprobate. The episode began when she was forced to spend a long night in the wheelhouse navigating through busy waterways. But before exacting revenge on the wayward artificer, she had another score to settle. She achieved this with a light-hearted comment. "Take the wheel, Number One," she commanded. "If you see anything bigger than us, try not to hit it!" It was a poor imitation of *The Navy Lark* radio comedy, but it served its purpose.

This caused a ripple of amusement, tinged with embarrassment. There was a serious point behind her words. This comment was intended as a shot across the bows of a couple of mischievous ratings who liked to mimic the characters of *The Navy Lark* to mock her when they were left alone on the bridge. The mimicry was part of the regular banter that took place when the officers were absent. Anne wanted the wheelhouse crew to know that she knew what was going on behind her back.

After looking sternly around the bridge personnel to stifle any laughter, she added in a more serious tone, "I'm going down below to clean up. Call me if you have any problems." The news that the skipper was going down to 'clean up' was duly signalled to those on the mess deck. As soon as the artificer heard this news, he gathered his cronies to a spot on the deck where they could hear what was taking place in the officers' washroom.

On previous occasions, they had been able to hear officers skipping around in their shower cubicle trying to avoid the scalding jets. The artificer was prepared with a plausible excuse, in case there was an inquiry. At first, all went well, as the malcontents listened gleefully to the commotion in the officers' washroom as the artificer fiddled with valves down in the engine room. Cackling with laughter at their wicked deed, they returned to their mess room to gloat over their victory.

As expected, the artificer was summoned to the bridge to explain the hot water problems to the duty officer. The artificer managed to keep a straight face as he delivered his carefully rehearsed response. His version of events was accepted by the duty officer, and the artificer smirked as he scuttled from the bridge, impatient to boast about his exploits to his pals who were, by that time, waiting in the mess room below. He was particularly pleased that he had managed to target the skipper on this occasion.

But this was his downfall. Anne had arranged for one of her subordinates to take a shower, while she slipped quietly down to the galley area, adjacent to the mess room. She used the pretext of an unscheduled galley inspection to hover within earshot of the mess room. Some junior ratings noted her presence and tried to signal the danger to the hapless prankster as he bowled into the mess room, impatient to boast to his mates.

The stocky artificer was full of bravado and was in full flow, recalling his exploits, as Anne calmly emerged from the shadows. As his predicament dawned on him, the artificer froze. He realised that he had been caught red-handed and could face serious disciplinary action. Anne held him with her eyes as he squirmed with embarrassment. Then, without a single word, she turned in a dignified manner and retired slowly from the mess. Following Nelson's example, she turned a blind eye to what she had witnessed.

The artificer was left deflated in front of his mates, just as Anne planned. The mockery of his peers would be a more effective deterrent than disciplinary action, she thought. This was the last of his pranks. While he continued to cause difficulties as the 'barrack room lawyer' who quoted the Queen's Regulations at every opportunity, his disciplinary record improved. As a result of his improved record, he was offered the transfer to a modern frigate that he craved.

The transfer would not have been possible if Anne had chosen to follow the rule book and taken the appropriate disciplinary action. The rogue acknowledged his thanks when he broke ranks to shake her hand during the formal parade to mark the end of the patrol boat's tour of duty. It was yet another breach of regulations, but one that Anne found rather touching.

After the shower incident, Anne was dubbed 'Madame Zelda' by the crew, for her almost mystic powers of perception. The female officer's reputation was further enhanced by an incident when she led a boarding party onto a Spanish trawler on a dark and stormy night. After they clambered onto the rusty trawler, the boarding party was faced with the drunken skipper and surly crew. It could have been an ugly affair had Anne not dealt with the situation with calm authority. In the search, they found illegal fish and drugs; several fishermen were arrested. The incident passed off in a peaceful way, thanks to Anne's capable leadership.

Commanding the patrol boat was the fulfilment of Anne's childhood ambition. She enjoyed the camaraderie on board the small ship and the range of challenges they faced every day, and had no wish to serve on a frontline warship. But events conspired to set her career on a different path. The first sign that her life was to change was a terse message saying that a civilian wanted to speak to her when she next docked at Portsmouth. This was to be her first encounter with Martin Beckwith, a meeting that she would grow to regret.

It all started in an innocent way, when a tall bearded figure pedalled onto the quay on a battered old pushbike. The man's clumsy efforts to lock the bike to a bollard and remove his bicycle clips caused titters of amusement among the crew of the pristine patrol boat. This became ribald laughter when the clumsy landlubber tripped over the raised coaming on his way to the officers' quarters. Dressed in corduroy trousers and grimy jumper, the scruffy visitor looked out of place on the immaculate patrol boat, with its polished brass and smartly uniformed crew.

There were many things to attend to when a warship arrived in port, and Anne was irritated by the intrusion into her busy routine. She greeted her visitor in a brusque manner. Her first impression was that the scruffy guy was a social science lecturer from a provincial university, most likely carrying out some form of survey. But she was disarmed by his self-deprecating manner. "Sorry to trouble you," said the visitor with a beaming smile. "I don't want to get in your way. But Harry Lofthouse said I should speak to you." This last remark caused Anne to pause for thought, just as the artful academic intended.

Harry Lofthouse was little known outside of Barrow, but he was a legendary figure within the shipyards. The portly fellow would bustle about the yard exchanging ribald remarks with pals while sorting out snarl-ups and problems. No one knew precisely what position he held; some believed he was a manager in the planning department. But whatever his official position, he had a reputation as the 'go-to man' to solve a problem. Most people called him 'Lofty', as an inevitable consequence of his diminutive stature and portly build.

"You know Lofty, then?" asked Anne. The name brought back some happy memories of her time in Barrow.

"Not well," answered Beckwith evasively. "But he has a very high opinion of you!" This was typical of the soft soap that the academic used to influence people.

Having captured Anne's attention, Beckwith asked subtle questions to draw her out. With occasional prompting, Anne spoke about her life in Barrow. As she reminisced, describing quirky characters in the shipyard, her visitor listened solicitously. Their conversation had the appearance of a priest listening to a confession. Then realising that her tongue had run away with itself, Anne checked herself. "What can I do for you?" she asked, rather belatedly.

Beckwith explained that he had assembled a team of specialists to design a novel form of submarine rescue vehicle and that he was looking for someone with specialist knowledge of submarine control systems. He thought that this was just up her street. Anne balked at this. She was happy commanding the patrol boat and had no desire to return to construction, recalling the suffocating bureaucracy at the submarine yard in Barrow-in-Furness.

"Thanks for the offer, but I'm happy where I am," she replied with a charming smile.

"Well, no harm in trying," said Beckwith jovially, then removing some papers from his pocket, he added, "if you change your mind, here is my card and the job description. Give me a ring sometime. We could use your help."

"Thanks," replied Anne as she reluctantly accepted the papers and bade her visitor farewell. Then as the academic approached the gangway, he turned with a forgetful expression. "By the way, I forgot to mention that the job is based at an office near here." The comment was made in an offhand way, as though it was a matter of little importance. But the artful guy knew that the comment would clinch the deal. When she looked back on this exchange, many months later, Anne realised that the academic used many tricks, including flattery and name-dropping.

The brief encounter left Anne with turbulent emotions. She was naturally curious to know more about the submarine project and slightly flattered by the job offer. But as she reflected, she came to see that beneath the superficial charm, there was something rather creepy about her visitor. Perhaps it was the way he stared at her. It reminded her of the way that a spider eyes its prey. She did not entirely trust him.

Anne's intuition was accurate. In preparing to lure the high-flying naval officer to his team, Beckwith had done his homework. He had trawled around his network of colleagues and former students, searching for nuggets of information that could be used to snare her. The name Harry Lofthouse had come up during this effort. To ensure success, he had looked into her personal life and learned of the dilemma that Anne faced over caring for her elderly mother in her bungalow near Portsmouth. He had also learned of her love for dogs. This intelligence allowed him to frame his approach in a way that would play on her vulnerable side.

After completing her dockside duties, Anne had a few days' leave, and this allowed her to consider the job offer more seriously. The more she thought about it, the more attractive it seemed. A short-term secondment in Portsmouth would enable her to look after her mother, without endangering her naval career. So, Anne phoned her visitor and they agreed to discuss his offer in a coffee house in Portsmouth town centre early the following morning.

As they chatted, Anne mentioned the dilemma she faced over her elderly mother. Beckwith sympathised with her and responded with a harrowing tale about his own late mother's last days in a care home. Anne later learned that while this story was true in parts, it had been greatly embellished. However, the ruse served its purpose, forcing Anne to reflect on the grim prospect of committing her mother to a care home. So, after pondering the offer for a couple of days, Anne reluctantly decided to accept. Her decision was swayed by the thought that she could remain in Portsmouth for a couple of years and return to the service.

Before accepting the offer, Anne looked into the secondment arrangements to make sure that she would not lose her position in the navy. In doing so, she discovered that the government was encouraging military personnel to seek experience in the commercial world. But her senior officer did not share that benevolent view. He was reluctant to release her. But, after some difficult negotiations, Anne was granted a leave of absence, with the understanding that she could return to her present rank, once the submarine rescue project was completed.

Anne had no inkling of the minefield she was walking into. Fortunately, she took the trouble to record day-to-day events in a notebook. She had adopted this habit while working on the nuclear submarine programme, after a lawyer told her that 'contemporaneous' notes could be used as evidence in a court of law.

On her first day in her new role, Anne reported to the project office housed in a converted warehouse in an industrial area of Portsmouth. The office was conveniently located near a slipway to the motorway. She arrived at nine o'clock sharp on Monday morning. It was a hot August day. She wore the blue jumper and slacks that formed part of her naval uniform, but dispensed with the epaulettes that indicated her rank. Beckwith greeted her in a friendly way and she was shown to her desk.

Among the stack of documents on the desk was a heavy bound volume entitled *Submarine Rescue Vehicle – Design Study*. Her new boss said that he would answer her questions after she'd had a chance to study the massive pile of information. This comment drew a wry smile from a slim young guy, who was busy sorting papers at a neighbouring desk. The apparently friendly young man was the only other person present in the office and introduced himself as Simon, the project administrator.

Over the next half-hour, a stream of scruffily dressed college types drifted into the open-plan office with little apparent interest in time-keeping, manners or personal hygiene. When they were all present, Beckwith summoned them to an informal meeting and introduced his new recruit. "Our latest team member was the first female officer to command a warship," he proclaimed.

Anne did not think it wise to correct him on this point. It would sound pedantic to say that she was 'one of the first'. Beckwith went on to describe her career in flattering terms, speaking at length about her experience of submarine construction at Barrow, and ended by saying she would make a valuable contribution to their project.

After this glowing tribute, the team dispersed to their desks, and Beckwith retreated to his glass cubicle where he spent the next hour hunched over his mobile phone. Then, with no explanation, he shot off on his bicycle, leaving Anne alone with a bunch of virtual strangers. She got on with most people, but she found it hard to relate to this gang of unruly layabouts.

Anne would later learn that her sneaky new boss had planted a rumour to ensure that his new recruit received a cold reception. The artful academic spun a yarn that Anne had been foisted onto their team to find reasons to 'pull the plug' on their project. Sensing their antipathy, but not knowing the reason, Anne presented a lonely figure as she settled down to study the pile of documents. Undaunted, she removed the notebook from her briefcase and tucked it into her desk drawer. *If I am to be a sacrificial lamb, I'll go down fighting,* she thought.

When team members deigned to speak to her, their attitude was that of naughty children addressing an elderly, unloved relative. "Do we salute you, Captain?" joked one wag to the suppressed giggles of his mates.

Anne felt like reminding them that her naval rank was lieutenant, but played it straight. "Please, call me Anne," she instructed them primly. After this demure response, the atmosphere became intimidating. In this corrosive atmosphere, her confidence drained away, just as Beckwith anticipated.

The stuffy open-plan office was like an oven in the August heat. In a lull, she spoke to Simon, who appeared to be the only half-decent team member. The office administrator confided that their boss 'flitted about', and 'played things close to his chest'. When the oppressive atmosphere finally became too much to bear, she sought sanctuary in the loo, where it was cooler. It was here that she recorded the morning's events in her notebook.

Although the atmosphere was unsettling, there were some consolations. Anne was fascinated by the bound documents she had been given to read. There was a wealth of information about the revolutionary new form of midget submarine they were building. The experience she had gained in Barrow provided a good grounding for the intricacies of fuel-cell propulsion. The section on control systems was intriguing. She assumed that this was where her expertise would be employed.

Office discipline improved marginally when Beckwith breezed back into the office towards the end of the afternoon. He apologised for his absence and asked Anne to 'sit in' on another informal meeting. "You don't need to contribute," he assured her in a kindly way. "You will be a spectator on our little world." Cautious of being ambushed, she made an excuse to leave the room and record his words in her notebook while taking refuge, once again, in the loo.

After noisily washing her hands, she returned to find her new boss waiting impatiently. While she had been away, the team had gathered like fawning students sitting at the feet of the sage. As the meeting got underway, the team discussed a virtual reality model that would allow the interior layout of the recovery vehicle to be visualised. With the aid of special helmets, users would be able to 'walk through' the interior of the submersible. This would enable the lay-out to be finalised; the model could also be used as a training aid.

Beckwith told his followers that he had received bids for building the computer model. "We are ready to place the contract. Are there any questions?" he asked with a sharp edge to his tone. It all seemed that this was familiar territory for other members of the team, but Anne was caught completely unprepared. One of the overgrown students kicked off the questions by asking whether the simulator codes would be compatible with the computer-aided design (CAD) package used to produce the design drawings. He wanted to ensure that any design changes would be reflected in the 'walk-through' visualisation.

The insightful nature of the questions that followed was at odds with the childish behaviour that team members had exhibited earlier. Speaking in a genial manner, Beckwith provided a fluent response to each question. In a lively discussion, team members quizzed their leader about software, fluid dynamics, control theory, stability, buoyancy and a host of technical matters. As the flow subsided, Anne felt her confidence return and decided to make her presence felt. "How much will the computer model cost?" she asked timidly.

The sage's thunderous expression showed that he did not welcome this intervention. "Young woman," he replied sternly, "could I remind you that you have only been asked to 'sit in' on this discussion." The masterful academic spoke as though reprimanding a wayward child.

This snub served to stiffen Anne's resolve. After all, she was the representative of the navy. "It's an important issue," she objected, as the team members sniggered at her embarrassment.

"Perhaps I should explain. Your role is to give us some technical advice. You are *not* here to question our commercial decisions," retorted the academic. Beckwith's red face and clenched features showed that he was having trouble controlling his anger. This was a warning of his volatile nature. "For *your* information, we have received bids from three companies. These bids had been reviewed by the navy. The navy has given their approval to sign a contract."

Anne was incensed by his patronising attitude, but she felt drained after a debilitating day, and was in no condition to challenge the team leader. To make matters worse, she was then told that documents were not to be taken from the building. "The information that I have given you is strictly confidential," declared the academic priggishly. "We don't want people leaving documents all over the place."

The hostility she experienced on the first day was unnerving for Anne, but she had survived worse. She slept badly that night, dreading another day cooped up in the stuffy office with overgrown students and their egotistical leader. Her intuitive distrust of the seedy academic seemed justified. The gaunt bearded academic reminded her of Fagin in the Charles Dickens novel *Oliver Twist*.

As she tossed and turned, she regretted relinquishing command of the patrol boat. But as she reflected, something else bothered her, and she could not quite put her finger on it. It was not until the early hours that she recognised her failure to ask about crew training. The topic had been briefly raised at the meeting and was one that was close to her heart. But she had failed to react. To ease her mind, she switched on the bedside lamp to check her notes, and found the following passage:

Beckwith told them that it was impractical to build a full-scale mock-up of the craft, and said the 'walk-through' visualisation provided by the virtual reality model would be adequate for training purposes. The use of a simple user interface for training had been discussed with the navy.

How could I miss that? she chided herself. *The oppressive heat and hostile atmosphere must have addled my brain*, she concluded with a rueful smile. It was obvious that a virtual reality system would be a useful aid for crew training. She should have taken the opportunity to raise the subject. But she noted, with some relief, that 'the navy' had been consulted on the subject. With that, she was able to sleep. When she woke, her thoughts crystallised in the bracing sea air as she took her dogs for their morning walk. It was during this walk that she decided to make it her mission to follow up the crew-training issue.

While living at home, her daily routine involved taking her pet Labradors out for exercise on the Downs overlooking Portsmouth Harbour, each morning. On that day, her attention was drawn to the mock-up of a frigate command centre that dominated the skyline. It was such a familiar feature that she took it for granted. She was well aware that full-scale mock-ups were used for training but had forgotten about it during the meeting. Chiding herself, once more, for lack of foresight, she decided to look into the matter. *Perhaps I'll get some idea from the frigate people*, she speculated to herself.

After a light breakfast with her mother, who shared her small bungalow, she set off with a revived sense of purpose. She intended to tackle her new boss about the crew-training issue as soon as she was able. But she arrived to learn that the academic was not expected in the office that day, and none of the overgrown students were expected. This took the wind out of her sails. But it was also a relief that she would not suffer their hostility.

Simon was the only other member of the team present. He greeted her in a friendly way, saying that she would have to put up with him for company because 'everyone else is out today'. This was quite normal, apparently, as most team members held other posts and only worked part-time on the project. Once she had settled at her desk, Simon came around to give her the typed minutes of the informal meeting that had taken place the previous evening. Anne was stunned by his efficiency.

The minutes were typewritten in a conversational style, which Anne found refreshing. It made a pleasant change from the large-scale military projects she had worked on, where the minutes of meetings were written in a terse, formal style, peppered with acronyms. Simon explained that their boss made a tape recording of his discussions. The recordings were handed to one of his postgraduate students, who transcribed them.

A quick scan provided assurance that the minutes were an accurate record of the informal discussion. Anne did not think it necessary to check the text in detail; after all, she had received verbal assurance that she was only 'sitting in' on the meeting. She had not taken an active part in the meeting, and much of the discussion concerned arcane technical points that had gone over her head, so she put the document aside, with the intention of reading it later.

The second day passed in a more pleasant manner than the first, and she had a long, friendly chat with Simon. It seemed that they shared an interest in dogs. Simon expressed his love for Labradors, saying he regretted that he was not a pet owner himself. They reminisced about university life, and Anne learned that Simon studied arts and had little interest in engineering.

During this amiable conversation, Anne discovered that members of the team spent most of their time doing university work, which explained their absence from the office. It was unusual for the whole team to be gathered together, said Simon. "That was why they were a bit boisterous yesterday," he added with a sympathetic smile. It also seemed that Beckwith was rarely in the office, because he travelled a great deal.

Simon spent the day quietly sorting papers. His job was to archive documents, circulate papers and organise travel and accommodation. It emerged that the main contractor was based in an office in Croydon and reported directly to Beckwith. Simon told her that copies of all specifications and drawings were sent to the Portsmouth office. Simon circulated them to the appropriate team member, with three days allowed for comments. The comments were then collated, after which Beckwith issued an official response to the contractor.

Although Simon seemed friendly, she found him strangely evasive about certain aspects of the project; he was reticent about the meeting that had taken place the previous afternoon. But rather than pursue those sensitive issues, she threw herself into the training issue. As the day passed, she became engrossed in this subject, making full use of a network of friends that she had built up while working on the nuclear submarine programme.

As commander of a patrol boat, she had spent a lot of time training members of the crew and so she could easily relate to the task. But she had no experience of building training facilities, so she sought tips from former colleagues. But there was another motivation for the phone calls. They provided an opportunity to refresh old friendships and catch up with gossip. It was a chance to regain her self-esteem, which had been undermined during the first day in this new project.

One phone call provided her with a contact at the training centre for the latest generation of frigates. When she followed this up, she spoke to the officer in charge who offered her a tour of the facility in return for information about the submarine rescue project. The promised tour would include a visit to the mock-up command centre of the advanced warship. This was just what she had been hoping for, so she asked Simon if he could arrange her travel.

At that, the amicable relationship evaporated. It seemed that Simon had been troubled about her behaviour. "You will have to ask Martin about that," he snapped back testily, when she asked about travel to the naval facility.

When Anne arrived for the third day in the dingy office, she found that her new boss was the sole occupant of the office. The academic's face was flushed purple and his expression was like thunder. This was something of a surprise, because Anne had been led to believe that the academic would be absent for the rest of the week. Beckwith summoned Anne into his glass cubicle and she felt like a schoolgirl facing a dressing-down from the headmaster.

The gaunt academic pointedly ignored her as he stabbed a phone log with his forefinger and counted out loud. When he was satisfied with the correct number, he looked up. "Who gave you permission to make *thirteen* long-distance phone calls from the office?" he demanded angrily. Anne guessed that the supposedly friendly office administrator had tipped off her boss about her activities the previous day. It was an unpleasant thought to realise that he was spying on her; but there could be no other explanation.

Anne felt a surge of anger. She was outraged that her boss should question her use of the office phone. But remembering that she was new to the job and that she did not want to antagonise her new boss unnecessarily, she controlled her temper. At first, she tried to see it from his point of view, knowing that he had to keep control of costs on a commercial project. But this did not wash. It was a false economy to impose a phone call restriction on someone who had been trusted to command a warship.

In a robust defence, Anne explained that she had phoned colleagues to find out more about naval training facilities. But this excuse cut no ice with her boss. "Who told you that crew training was your job, Lieutenant?" he demanded with a sarcastic reference to her naval rank that suggested she was getting above her station. "Another naval officer has been assigned for that duty." Anne was curious to know who the other naval officer might be, but did not think it was the right time to ask.

Then staring at her with bulging eyes, he growled through clenched teeth: "We have not set up this office to provide you with a free phone service to chat with your naval chums!" He then went on to warn her that all phone calls were logged, and that she faced dismissal if she made any unauthorised calls. He ended his diatribe with a jibe that revealed his contempt for the navy: "You are not in the navy now! We have to watch our costs on this project!"

Anne found it hard to comprehend her boss's mood swings and inconsistency. He had threatened to sack her for making unauthorised phone calls but had tolerated feckless behaviour by other members of the project team. His cutting remark about the navy awoke her fighting spirit, but if she was to prevail, she needed to bide her time.

With enormous restraint, she returned to her desk. "If he sacks me, I will make his life hell!" she muttered angrily under her breath. Beckwith's warning had the opposite effect to that intended. The warning hardened Anne's resolve to pursue the crew training issue. But she would now do it surreptitiously, without his permission. The dressing-down had also taught her to be wary of the office administrator. Although seemingly friendly, it was clear that he was a snake in the grass.

After reprimanding his new recruit, Beckwith shuffled papers on his desk in a rather aimless way. His temper tantrum left him with shaking hands. After recovering his composure, he sidled over to Anne's desk as though nothing had happened. In an affable way, he went on to describe the benefits of the fuel-cell system propulsion, as though nothing had happened. With passing time, Anne learned that these angry outbursts were as common as they were short-lived.

Beckwith seemed proud of the revolutionary nature of the project and as he spoke, Anne learned that electric power produced by the fuel cells would be fed to thrusters. The power and direction of the thrusters was to be controlled by a dynamic positioning system. This system would be fed with signals from a range of navigational equipment, including gyro-compass and sonic devices. Anne listened politely to the explanation.

With cordial relations re-established, Anne agreed to visit their main contractor to discuss the control systems. The office administrator was to organise the travel and accommodation. Just at that moment, Simon walked into the office, looking a bit sheepish. "Just the man we are looking for!" remarked Beckwith with a beaming smile.

Simon's late arrival did not fool Anne in the least. She did not believe it was an accident. He had a methodical approach to his work and was always punctual. It was a sign that the office mole knew she was to be reprimanded, and his guilty expression suggested that his cover was blown.

Having finished his lecture on fuel-cell technology, Beckwith returned briefly to his cubicle to finish some tasks. A few minutes later, he leaned down to fit his bicycle clips, donned his helmet, and strode to his beat-up old bicycle, which was chained to a lamppost on the street outside and pedalled off. This left an uncomfortable atmosphere in the office as Anne found herself alone with the office mole. The pair eyed one another in a suspicious way.

It was obvious that Simon had been told to keep an eye on her, and so Anne thought that it best to confront this head-on, rather than let the bad feelings fester. But she did not want to make an enemy of the young guy in this potentially hostile environment. So, when she challenged him, she tried to employ a little humour to smooth over the unpleasantness.

"I think you have been spying on me!" she said in a lilting voice and coquettish expression.

Simon blushed but remained silent.

Then in a more direct way, Anne laid into him. "Look, I don't want to put you on the spot, but I've just been reprimanded for phoning my colleagues, and I think you ratted on me."

Simon looked shamefaced and admitted sheepishly, "Sorry. You are right. Martin asked me to keep an eye on you," then, after a pause, he added, "he asked me what you were doing when he phoned me yesterday evening."

Anne was grateful for a straight answer and used the opportunity to raise the other matter that had been worrying her: "Am I right in thinking that another naval officer is involved in this project?" she enquired politely.

"No. Not really," stammered Simon, evasively.

"That's not what Martin told me," retorted Anne sharply. "He told me that another officer was responsible for crew training."

"Well, he was probably referring to Commander Woods," murmured Simon in a shamefaced way as he busied himself with some filing. "He's in charge of the sea trials. But I don't know anything about crew training."

Hoping to salvage something from their earlier friendship, Anne did not press him any further on that point. But neither did she want to chat to him. After the fireworks, she now suspected that Simon's professed 'love of Labradors' was a ruse to gain her confidence. But the whole episode had been a warning. She needed to be more circumspect around the office and pursue the crew training issue in her own time. The rest of the day passed pleasantly enough as she acquainted herself with the design of the submersible while Simon made arrangements for her visit to the main contractor.

The row over the unauthorised use of the office phone prompted Anne to look more closely at the minutes of Monday's meeting that Simon had given her. She sneaked out a copy as she left for home that evening, conscious of her boss's instructions that documents were not to be removed from the office. When she studied the minutes, she noticed her name was featured on the list of attendees as the 'navy representative'. This seemed to conflict with Beckwith's promise that she was to 'sit in' on the informal affair. There was no reference to her question about the cost of the contract, or Beckwith's angry response.

These might be small discrepancies, barely worthy of mention under normal circumstances, but the events that morning had shown she must be wary. Her fears receded when she read further and found that most passages accurately reflected the record in her notebook. But there was one discrepancy that seemed at odds with the otherwise accurate verbatim record of their discussion. She vividly recalled Beckwith telling them that it was not practical to build a physical mock-up of the submersible vehicle. But a couple of words did not tally with her notes, so she checked with her notebook.

Her notes read: *The use of a simple user interface for training has been discussed with the navy.*

The minutes stated: *The use of a simple user interface for training has been agreed by the navy.*

After the bruising encounter that morning, she would have to choose her battles carefully and it would be a pedantic point. But her dressing-down about the phone calls had been a salutary warning that things were not as they seemed, so she suspected some ulterior motive behind this apparently careless error.

Chapter 4

Anne Seeks Commander Woods

After her rocky start, Anne settled into the project work. After the fireworks on her second day, she was given a free hand to make design decisions. On balance, she was content, but she took care to follow the rules and handled her volatile boss as though he were a flask of nitroglycerine. Under this strict regime, she needed to confine herself to the allotted tasks; she could not use the office phone for social reasons, nor could she contact her colleagues in the navy.

During the first few months, she kept busy visiting contractors, studying design documents and configuring control systems. This was fascinating work and she had little spare time. But when the design was finalised and the frenetic pace of work slowed, she was left with time on her hands. With the breathing space, the restrictions began to rankle and she was tempted to pursue forbidden interests.

It was during this period that her interest in training was revived. To pursue this would set her at odds with her volatile boss, of course, because he had given her strict instructions that she should 'keep her nose out' of the training issue. But she believed that this was an essential duty for all naval officers, so with Simon spying on her while she worked in the office, she had to go about things in a surreptitious manner.

She compared her boss's bizarre behaviour with that of a controlling husband; a subject that was much discussed in the media at that time. Anne was puzzled by his aversion to the navy and put it down to embarrassment that he had not served in the armed forces. It did not occur to her that there might be venal motives for his behaviour. With her 'can-do' attitude, she was determined to tackle the training issue, even if it got her into hot water, so her next step was to track down the other naval officer involved in the project.

Simon had inadvertently let slip that an officer called Commander Woods was organising the sea trials of the midget submarine. When she tried to winkle further information about her fellow naval officer, she drew a blank. It was dangerous to push her luck any further with the office mole. But it was not long before she discovered that the commander was a decorated war hero of the Falklands whose exploits had become part of naval folklore.

After the unseemly row about unauthorised use of the office phone, Anne decided to use her 'old-girls' network'. If nothing else, this would also allow her to revive her moribund social life. With the responsibility of commanding the patrol boat and caring for her ageing mother, she had lost contact with friends. In earlier days, she had mixed with a lively gang of shore staff who gathered in a cavernous bar in the city centre, after work, on Friday evenings. Most of the gang worked in human resources for the navy, so they would be able to help her make contact with the commander – if anyone knew how to contact a naval officer, they would.

Anne got to know members of this gang soon after her appointment to the patrol boat, when they asked her to help them with their recruitment campaign. They wanted a female officer to feature as a 'poster girl' for their recruitment campaign. But Anne did not want to see her picture plastered over hoardings and so she refused to help them. This led a cynical male colleague to joke that she would never command a frontline warship, after refusing their offer.

But there had been no hard feelings and she remained on good terms with the recruitment team, occasionally joining them for a drink at the end of the working week. They were a fun-loving crowd, and it would be good to see them again. But to find them in the bustling bar, she needed a companion. This presented a problem, because most of the people she knew were married with young children. After retrieving a dog-eared address book from the back of a desk drawer, she found the phone number of an old school friend called Samantha, who was unattached, she believed.

After leaving school, their lives had followed different paths. They were acquaintances, who kept in touch at Christmas, rather than friends. Samantha gossiped that Anne was so obsessed with her career and would end up a lonely 'old maid'. In reality, she was jealous of Anne's success. Anne recognised this, so she sugared her invitation. "I would really appreciate your help to track down a war hero," she begged. When Samantha heard her plea, she jumped at the offer of a night on the town, curious to know who had conquered her friend's ice-cold heart. At the worst, she thought, it would also be a chance to catch up with the gossip.

Many people are put off by urban squalor, but Anne had harboured an affection for the city centre since her teenage years. The centre has a brutal concrete character, with charmless tower blocks thrown where swathes of the city had been devastated by war-time bombing. It was not to everyone's taste. Some grand Victorian buildings remained, but these impressive piles were surrounded by dereliction. But the city centre came to life on Friday evenings, with students and office workers thronging into the garish bars and nightclubs, to celebrate the end of the working week.

After pulling on some jeans and slapping on some make-up, Anne phoned for a taxi and gave the driver instructions to collect Samantha from her home. The taxi took them on to the local station where they boarded a train to the city centre. They chatted like sparrows on the way, catching up with gossip after many years. When they reached their destination, the pair were hungry, and so they headed for a cafe which served pizza. Here, they celebrated their reunion with a bottle of sparkling wine. Anne normally avoided alcohol, but she decided to let her hair down on this occasion.

With their hunger satisfied, the pair of revellers wandered to the cavernous bar where the shore staff congregated on Friday evenings. The bar was a converted bank. With the evening in full swing, the bar was heaving with customers vying to be served. Samantha dodged through the waiting throng to catch the barman's eye. She returned, triumphant, with another bottle of wine to find her friend in possession of a couple of bar stools beside a beer-stained pine shelf. While not very comfortable, this provided a convenient vantage point from which to observe the braying crowd. Anne scanned the room in search of her naval chums.

In all the excitement, Anne had failed to explain the precise nature of their evening mission. Samantha was under the impression that Anne wanted to meet the decorated war hero in this cavernous bar. "Can you spot your friend?" she asked excitedly. She had to shout to make herself heard over the hubbub. "What does he look like?"

"To tell the truth, I've never met him," admitted Anne, rather limply, regretting that she had not been more honest about her intentions. "He's a distinguished naval officer, and I need to find him." This admission created a chill between the pair. By this time, Samantha was a bit tipsy from the sparkling wine and this brought out an obstreperous streak in her character.

"I don't think you war hero exists! It's all in your imagination!" exclaimed Samantha in speech slurred by booze. Anne was unable to explain her complicated predicament in the noisy bar and was about to abandon her mission. But just in the nick of time, she spotted some familiar faces across the dingy room. Sighing with relief, she asked Samantha to look after her glass while she went over to speak to some friends. Samantha scarcely noticed her absence; she was making eyes at a young guy in working clothes.

The naval shore staff recognised Anne and greeted her like a returning hero. They gathered round to ask how she was getting on the patrol boat. Flattered by the attention, she forgot the purpose of her mission, at first. But she soon regained her sense of purpose and steered the conversation towards Commander Woods. It soon became clear that the distinguished war hero was a regular at a pub called the Admiral Bligh. This was a famous old public house which was situated near the waterfront, in the historic part of the harbour.

Having achieved her aim, Anne returned to her perch, where she found her old school friend canoodling with a burly scaffolder. Samantha greeted her returned friend coolly and showed no desire to move on from the pub. Anne did not want to visit a strange pub on her own, so, after checking that Samantha could find her own way home, she bid farewell and headed back to the station. During the return train journey, she had to fend off unwelcome advances from a couple of drunken office workers, so she heaved a sigh of relief when she was safely back in her sitting room. On the whole, it had been a reasonably successful night's work, she mused.

The discovery that Commander Woods was a regular at the Admiral Bligh pub fitted neatly with Anne's plans because her older brother Mark was due to arrive back in Portsmouth the following week on his aircraft carrier. The carrier was returning from its last tour of duty in the Persian Gulf. As a real ale enthusiast, Mark loved to visit pubs in the old part of the city where a single woman might feel uncomfortable, so he was the ideal escort.

But brother and sister had a difficult relationship; this was partly due to a five-year age gap, but Mark's drinking was another source of friction. Mark could be extremely boorish when boozing with real-ale buffs. Their sibling rivalry was inflamed because Mark had failed to live up to the family expectations, while his sister had exceeded them.

Their father had a distinguished service record and had wanted his son to follow in the family tradition. As a natural seafarer, Mark had shown great promise. But he struggled with his academic studies during officer training at Dartmouth. It seemed that he was better suited to the swashbuckling era of sailing ships than the technical wonders of the modern navy.

With hard work and the support of his wife, Mark clawed his way up to become weapons officer on board an aircraft carrier. But it seemed that this was the pinnacle of his career. There was now little prospect that Mark would match his sister's accomplishments. This rankled the capable seafarer. There were moments when Mark took pride in his sister's success, but this was overshadowed by envy, so Anne needed to approach the subject in a sensitive way.

An opportunity arose to discuss the subject when her brother phoned to speak to his mother on the carrier's return to Portsmouth. The elderly widow lived in a granny annex attached to Anne's bungalow. While mother and daughter lived independent lives, they tended to share tea in the afternoon, so Mark timed his phone call to catch them both together. During the phone call, Anne learned that her brother was acting as duty officer while the ship was in port, so he would be in Portsmouth for seven days before going home to the West Country to be with his family.

In a further stroke of luck, the duty roster allowed Mark to go ashore in the evenings, so brother and sister arranged to meet outside the dock gates at 6 pm the following Monday. Mark was puzzled by his sister's request, because they tended to move in different social circles and rarely socialised away from their homes. *I wonder whether Mother is ill*, he fretted. He recalled how their grandmother's final years had been blighted by Alzheimer's, and feared that his sister would be the bearer of bad news.

Waiting outside the dock gate at the appointed hour, Anne spotted the tall, uniformed figure march out of the dock gate. He was punctual as ever, and brother and sister headed to a small coffee bar, where they took shelter from an autumn gale. The normally calm naval officer was tense on this occasion, impatient to know the reason for their meeting. His fears were fuelled by his sister's evasive behaviour.

"Mother has been a nightmare!" grumbled Anne with a sigh, as they made themselves comfortable sitting behind glass windows dripping with condensation in the autumn chill. They were both frustrated at their mother's imperious nature, and this was one of the few things they could discuss in a dispassionate way. Mark expressed sympathy, having been on the receiving end of the old lady's sharp tongue on several occasions.

While Mark was relieved that his sister did not bring disturbing news about their mother, it left him puzzled as to the reason for the meeting, He was further perplexed when his sister asked if they could go on to the Admiral Bligh pub. This was out of character. He knew that his sister did not care for pubs or the real-ale crowd that he mixed with. But he saw no reason to object to the unusual request, so they donned their overcoats to protect them from the blustery wind and trudged round to the old historic quarter of the port.

When they entered the cosy establishment, the pair found a blazing log fire and a warm welcome. The wood-panelled bar was quiet, with only a handful of customers. Anne fumbled as she took out her purse to buy her brother a pint to welcome him home, and a glass of wine for herself. Drinks in hand, they made their way hesitantly to an alcove. Anne hoped to spot Commander Woods, without explaining her mission to her brother. Although this created an awkward atmosphere, Anne did her best to maintain the jolly façade.

Anne laughed, dutifully, at her brother's anecdotes from his tour of duty in the Persian Gulf, but resisted the temptation to respond with her own experiences on the patrol boat. She knew that her command of the patrol boat had been a cause of envy for her older brother, and that he had little interest in her submarine project activities. So, instead, she told amusing stories about her mother's foibles. Mark spoke about his wife and children. They shared other family gossip.

The time began to drag as they both walked on eggshells, trying to avoid topics that would open old wounds. Still puzzled by the purpose of their meeting, Mark noticed that his sister was sizing up each new customer. As a group gathered round the bar, Anne suggested a move to join them. Mark was only too happy to oblige with this request and it was not long before he was exchanging yarns with the regulars. While he was in full flow, Anne spoke quietly to the landlady. "Do you get many naval officers in the pub?" she asked.

"Yes. Some naval types come in on a Friday night, regular as clockwork. But that's about all," answered the landlady. "We are off the beaten track for the naval base. Our customers are mostly retired folk who live hereabouts, and the tourists, of course. We have been getting more French tourists since they spruced up the historic parts of the dock. We sell a lot of food at lunchtime. Evenings can be a bit quiet in the winter. It all depends," she added.

The landlady looked enquiringly at Mark, who was bragging in a loud voice. "My brother has just come back from the Persian Gulf on the carrier," explained Anne in a slightly apologetic way.

"We don't often see crew from the carriers," replied the landlady with a smile to show her sympathy. "They tend to head to the city centre to let off steam. We used to get a lot of trade from the navy," added the landlady as she pointed to miniature pennants from different ships pinned up behind the bar. "But this is mainly a tourist area now."

When Anne set out that night, she had hoped to run into the commander and hand over a letter of introduction. But the landlady's comments suggested that the decorated war hero would not visit the pub until Friday evening, and Anne had no desire to return, so she had to persuade Mark to act on her behalf. This was a ticklish and slightly embarrassing task. Her brother was in his element, leaning on the counter, holding forth in voluble style. She did not want to disturb the jovial banter but needed to explain her mission in private, so she tactfully steered him back to the alcove they had occupied earlier.

"Mark. The reason that I asked you to take me to this pub was that I need to send a message to a chap who comes in here," she explained with an earnest expression.

"Good to hear that you have found a man at last!" he joked in an uninhibited manner that was coarsened by pints of real ale. "Lucy was worried about you! It's about time you settled down with a bloke." Anne's single status had been a source of family concern for some years. None of the suitors lived up to her exacting expectations. Mark's wife, Lucy, had tried, in vain, to find her a partner. But with no success. As a result of all this, Anne was constantly teased about her solitary life at family gatherings. "But why don't you use the mail like everyone else?" he continued, after pausing for thought.

"I need to get in touch with Commander Woods," explained Anne as she fixed her brother with a withering stare that sent a message that she would not tolerate any more of his sexist remarks. "I expect you have heard of him. He was in the Falklands, but I can't contact him by phone. If I go through official channels, my new boss will find out, and I'll be in trouble."

She had hoped to avoid this conversation and did not know how her brother would react to her request. Despite his affable manner when sober, Mark could be an awkward cuss when he had a few pints under his belt. There was little chance that he would understand the subtleties of office life. From an early age, he had been immersed in a world of naval discipline and had little sympathy for office politics and inconsequential matters of that sort.

"Look, we're all on the same side, you know!" declared Mark, belching as some of the beer took the wrong path to his gut. His overbearing remark was the first sign of discord that evening; there was a danger that it would open old wounds.

"It's a long story," remarked Anne with a sigh. She did not relish the prospect of explaining the convoluted story to her brother, but she needed his help. "The fact is that I was hoping to run into Commander Woods this evening so I could introduce myself. But the landlady says that he does not come in every day, so I really need your help," she pleaded.

"This is something to do with your submarine rescue project, I suppose?" observed Mark disdainfully. Mark believed that naval officers should command warships, not build them. This issue had been another source of friction between brother and sister. But despite their differences, Mark felt family loyalty and wanted to know the reason behind this seemingly infantile request. "Why do you want to track down this guy?" he demanded sharply.

Anne did not want to be drawn too deeply into the convoluted story: "I need someone to hand this note to Commander Woods. That's all!" replied Anne firmly. "Some of the training staff told me that he is a regular in this pub. The note is an invitation to meet me, and provides my home address and phone number."

Mark had been puzzled by his sister's unusual behaviour all evening. The invitation to the pub was bizarre and completely out of character. Despite her denial, Mark was inclined to believe that there was a romantic angle behind her request. *Anne is reluctant to admit her attraction to a war hero*, he chuckled to himself as he took hold of the neatly addressed envelope that his sister proffered. "I think you fancy this chap," he teased, with a knowing smile.

"Perhaps I do! It's a long time since I've met a real man!" she replied to taunt him. In a way, Anne was content that her brother had misread her intentions; it saved her the trouble of explaining the complicated business. But there would be a price to pay when the news of her weird behaviour circulated around the family. It would be embarrassing.

"He always comes in on Friday evening, you said?" asked Mark, thoughtfully. Anne nodded. "That's fine, then! I'm duty officer for the rest of the week. This is a nice pub, so I'll pop in each day and hand over your note on Friday. But you will have to find yourself another delivery boy if I've not seen him by the end of the week. My leave starts this weekend and I need to spend time with the kids. They have forgotten what their father looks like!"

Although Mark was a devoted family man, his marriage was under strain due to his long absences at sea. The family's naval tradition was a source of marital discord. Mark's wife, Lucy, echoed Princess Dianna's comment about there being three in their marriage. But in her case, it was the navy that was the third partner. That was ironic, because it was the navy that brought the couple together. His wife, Lucy, was a student at the local teacher training college, who tutored him.

Mark's father commanded a cruiser in the Korean War and went on to a shore post in Hong Kong. The old sea dog had had high expectations for his first child. The young lad was sent to a private school that specialised in preparing young men for a naval career. The school had a fleet of dinghies and provided training in seamanship. The lure of sailing was a distraction for the adventurous lad, and when his father died, the schoolboy started to neglect his studies.

While Mark excelled at outdoor activities, he was not terribly bright. With poor preparation, he failed the entry exam for the officer training course. Recognising the schoolboy's potential, the naval college offered him a place, provided that he received maths tuition. After a great struggle, he mastered the maths theory needed for navigation and gunnery. His success was due to a sympathetic female tutor. During their late-night studies, the tutor took a shine to the dashing young midshipman. After a brief courtship, the pair married. Lucy was several years older than her husband.

After leaving the naval college, Lucy became a teacher at a comprehensive school. With two boys to look after, her teaching placed an enormous load on her shoulders while her husband was at sea. They had a different outlook on life and this inevitably caused marital difficulties. There were also bitter arguments around Mark's drinking habits. So, while Mark yearned to see his family, his role as duty officer did, at least, allow him to nip out to the pub without being scolded by his partner.

Though living away from home, Mark did not have unfettered freedom because crew who remained on board in port had access to a free phone line. This perk allowed them to talk to their loved ones. But this was a mixed blessing in Mark's case, because it allowed Lucy to keep tabs on his shore excursions. That was one reason why he was keen to help with his sister's mission. It was a handy excuse to slip ashore each evening.

Mark loved the convivial atmosphere of a well-run pub and saw them as a vital element of the seafaring tradition. But Lucy did not share that view. Mark's boozing sprees were a source of tension in the early days of their relationship. Lucy thought that the young lad was led astray by ne'er-do-wells in the local bars while she acted as his tutor in Dartmouth. After she admonished him about his drinking habits, he moderated his behaviour, and his results steadily improved.

With family responsibility, Mark rarely had the chance to visit the pub, and Lucy kept him on a tight rein. He was also conscious of his responsibilities as an officer while at sea on the carrier. But Wendy feared that he might slip back into his bad old ways, when left to his own devices in Portsmouth. The phone line allowed her to check what he was up to, knowing that his role as duty officer did not involve much work.

The aircraft carrier was a scene of chaos while it was moored in port, with just a skeleton crew left aboard, as shoreside workers swarmed all over the vessel. The workers clumped their mucky boots over decks that were kept spotlessly clean while the ship was at sea. The duty officer had few routine tasks to perform. An NCO and a few ratings helped Mark keep an eye on things. After a formal meeting at nine o'clock each morning, Mark had little to occupy him and spent most of his 12-hour duty watch with his feet up in the ship's office.

With his watch starting before breakfast and finishing after tea, Mark was able to slip ashore to the Admiral Bligh each evening without any trouble, but he was careful not to drink too much in case he gave the game away in his nightly phone call home. He was tempted to explain to Lucy what he was doing, knowing how thrilled his wife would be to learn that Anne was romantically involved with a war hero, but then decided that it would be better to allow this news to filter through the family grapevine. This would give him a moral high ground if Lucy decided to admonish him for going out on the razzle.

The Admiral Bligh public house was just the sort of pub that Mark appreciated and so he was only too happy to return. He made a pilgrimage each evening. Over the week, the bar staff came to accept him as one of their regulars. After the first couple of visits, a pint of real ale would be waiting on the counter ready for his arrival, at eight o'clock each evening. After paying for his beer, he would adjourn to an alcove to read the newspaper.

When he had finished the paper, he would return to chat with the locals while he downed his second pint. On his first visit, he spoke to a retired army major who propped up a corner of the bar. Mark soon learned that the old buffer was a notorious bore, and so he made an effort to avoid him. But the other customers proved to be an eclectic mix drawn from all walks of life. The bar room chatter ranged from the possibility of discovering life on one of Saturn's moons to the prospects of England winning the football World Cup. Some wag suggested the chance of the first was greater than the second.

Once the bar staff had accepted him as a regular, Mark made discreet enquiries about the elusive war hero Commander Woods. "You sometimes see him here on Friday evenings," said the barmaid with a cheerful smile. This confirmed what his sister had told him.

Friday was Mark's last night as duty officer on board the carrier before starting his leave, so he set out to the pub slightly earlier than usual. He had to travel by taxi, because the pub was some way from the gate to the naval base. The bar was more crowded than usual, with a group of people in naval uniforms huddled round one end of the bar. The sharp-eyed barmaid recognised him and poured his beer. A gaggle of office workers stepped aside to allow him to collect his glass, before reforming as a tight-knit group.

As he listened to the buzz, Mark guessed that the casually dressed naval officer sitting on a bar stool at the heart of the naval contingent was Commander Woods. The distinguished-looking man was surrounded by lively youngsters. As he read his paper, the crowd began to thin so Mark folded his paper and edged towards his target. When the last of the encircling group departed, Mark removed the neatly addressed envelope from his pocket and plonked it on the counter.

"Would you be Commander Woods, by any chance?" he asked politely.

"At your service," replied the commander smoothly.

"I've got a message for you," said Mark.

"That sounds mysterious!" replied the commander with a humorous glint in his eye as he gingerly picked up the envelope. The commander retired to the alcove so that he could read the note's contents in private. After reading the letter with a furrowed brow, the commander returned with a broad smile and greeted Mark by his name.

"Thanks for delivering the message, Mark. I see that your sister has stepped into the lion's den!" he remarked. The commander was making an oblique reference to the problems that Anne might be having with her obnoxious boss. But Mark knew nothing of these problems. After months at sea, and with little knowledge of his sister's job, he did not appreciate the implication of the remark. Mark knew nothing of the role that his sister was playing on the submarine rescue project.

Mark's blank expression showed he was baffled, so the commander steered his companion back to the alcove, to get away from the noisy barflies. As they sat together, Mark blushed with embarrassment at his role as a go-between in what he believed to be a romantic tryst between his sister and a decorated war hero. Seeing that his companion was uncomfortable, the commander lightened the mood with some small talk.

"How long were you away on the carrier?" asked the commander, as he tried to size up the situation. His reference to the carrier suggested that his sister's note included comments on his recent posting.

"Nine months," replied Mark, "mostly in the Persian Gulf."

"It's a pity that the old girl is being taken out of service!" observed the commander in a sympathetic way. The words 'old girl' threw Mark for a moment, but he soon gathered his wits. With the commander discussing the aircraft carrier, Mark was on familiar territory. He quickly regained his self-esteem. "I understand that you've had ballast problems," continued the commander. This remark suggested that the commander was well informed. Few people knew that the ageing aircraft carrier suffered ballast problems.

"We were unable to enter some Mediterranean ports because the discharged ballast water did not meet the environmental standards introduced in the past couple of years," explained Mark in a knowledgeable way. "That's why the 'old girl' is being taken out of service."

This information was classified 'confidential'; known only to a select few high-ranking officers. With the exchange of confidences, a bond was formed between the two men. This allowed Commander Woods to speak frankly about the note that he had received.

"Thanks for delivering your sister's note," remarked the commander. "It's good to know that we have got someone to stand up to that bugger Beckwith. Did your sister mention that our boys will carry out the sea trials? That's our job. We would be described as test pilots in the aircraft industry. It's the same sort of job, but not quite so glamorous!"

News that the note was work-related relieved Mark of embarrassment that he was acting as a go-between in a romantic tryst, but it was also a source of disappointment. He was as keen as his wife to see his sister settle down with a partner. "No. I've not really had a chance to talk to my sister," replied Mark evasively. The half-truth hid his embarrassment that brother and sister never discussed each other's work.

"Our team carries out sea trials of all sorts of novel craft – we tested a hovercraft recently. We suggested some modifications," remarked the commander in an enthusiastic manner. "After the modifications were carried out, the hovercraft was used to capture drug smugglers in Latin America. It was a feather in our cap. That's what the note was about. We are going to test your sister's submarine next year. But the truth is that we are not enthusiastic about the project."

The commander went on to explain his reservations about using a new form of propulsion for a submarine rescue vehicle.

He spoke in a passionate way, failing to recognise that Mark did not understand what on earth he was on about. "We think that fuel-cell propulsion is overcomplicated and unnecessary for submarine rescue operations," concluded the commander. "The money would be better spent on covert recognisance, rather than submarine rescue."

"Are you telling me that my sister's project is a waste of time?" asked Mark with a puzzled expression. He was completely out of his depth. It was all double-Dutch to the dim-witted seafarer.

"Not exactly," replied the commander as he realised that he had been carried away. "What I'm saying is that your sister has found herself in the middle of a turf war between different factions. We think that the battery-power rescue vehicles we use at the moment are perfectly adequate. But your sister's project uses a new form of fuel-cell propulsion. We think that it is a step too far. Bottom line is that it's overcomplicated, in our view."

The commander could see from his blank expression that his companion did not have a clue what he was talking about. This was understandable, he acknowledged. After all, the naval officer had just returned home from a tour of duty in the Gulf and obviously had other things on his mind, but it also gave the impression that Mark was not the sharpest knife in the box. So, abandoning his efforts to explain his thoughts, the commander stepped up to the counter to buy another round of drinks.

As Mark waited for the commander to return with their drinks, it occurred to him that the commander's trials team might provide the opportunity he was looking for. The work was just up his street. While he was not intellectually gifted, he was a natural seaman. He had learned to sail almost before he could walk. His boat handling skills were widely praised;

so performing sea trials of naval vessels would be just up his street.

During their last voyage, much of the wardroom conversation had revolved around the prospects the crew faced when the carrier was taken out of service. Their carrier was due to be scrapped before the replacement vessels entered service. This led to rumours that many of the older officers would be laid off. Mark feared that his name would be high on the redundancy list, so he was on the lookout for suitable openings ashore. The trials team was just the ticket.

When he returned with refilled glasses, the commander abandoned his attempt to explain his views about the submarine rescue project, and their conversation became humorous as they shared anecdotes of their service experience. But when they parted company, Mark took the opportunity to ask whether he could join the trials team. "Sorry, there are no vacancies at the moment," replied the commander sadly. "But we will let you know if anything comes up."

While the commander enjoyed Mark's company, he thought him a little dim. It was obvious that his fellow officer was a competent sailor, but it was also clear that he was somewhat old-fashioned and blinkered in his outlook. He wondered whether this was a family trait, but he dismissed that notion when he reflected on the note he had received. The note suggested that Mark's sister grasped the poisonous nature of the politics surrounding the submarine rescue project. He looked forward to meeting her.

Chapter 5

Anne Dexter's Tea Party

After receiving the mysterious note in the Admiral Bligh pub, Commander Woods did not have time to reply straight away. But several days later, during a lull in his busy schedule, he phoned the female officer. They agreed to meet in Anne's bungalow, the following Saturday. The commander briefly mentioned his encounter with Mark but did not go into any detail. During their phone call, Anne warned that her mother, Dorothy, would be joining them for tea.

The old lady relished the prospect of a tea party with the decorated war hero. As the widow of a senior naval officer, she knew the commander by reputation and had expectations that her unmarried daughter had finally found a suitor. "It would be a good match," she concluded with a satisfied smile. After changing into her best frock, Dorothy tutted in despair when she saw her daughter dressed in her tatty walking clothes as she laid out the cakes. "You look like an old frump," remarked the old lady tartly.

When Anne introduced the visitor as a 'work colleague', the old lady suspected that her independent-minded daughter was being coy about her relationship with the distinguished-looking gentleman. In the belief that she was interviewing a potential son-in-law, Dorothy presided over proceedings in an imperious manner. With a radiant smile, she reminisced about her late husband's war service in Korea. The commander reciprocated with stories of the Falklands War.

Anne was scarcely acknowledged during the conversation, and she felt like Cinderella as she poured the tea and handed out the cakes in a demure manner. With her mother hogging the limelight, Anne did not have a chance to discuss the submarine rescue project. So, during a rare interlude in the merry chatter, while her mother was sipping her tea, she asked whether their guest would like to join her while she walked the dogs.

The old lady would have joined them if she could, but she suffered from arthritis and was unable to walk very far. Up until that moment, the Labradors had been snoozing contentedly through the tea party, but hearing the word 'walk', they leapt enthusiastically to their feet and bounded to the front door. Mother looked bereft as she was left alone, while her daughter and her guest donned boots and coats and trudged off into the autumn drizzle for a bracing walk across the Downs.

With tails wagging, the pair of dogs snuffled at the door, impatient to gain their freedom. While Mother might rule the roost with guests, it seemed that she had little control over the well-trained dogs. They got up to all manner of mischief when her daughter was not there to keep them in check, but the dogs reacted instinctively to Anne's quiet authority. It was clear that the female naval officer was pack leader as far as the hounds were concerned.

It did not take long for the commander to pick up signals that his female companion was in a sour mood. Rather belatedly, he realised he had been so engrossed in his conversation with the old lady that he had ignored the author of the note. "Not often that I'm sent notes by a young woman," he joked in a tongue-in-cheek way. Anne did not take kindly to his clumsy attempt at humour. After the offhand way she had been treated, she felt embarrassed by the way she had approached him and did not really want to be reminded about it.

"It was an odd way to make contact," she conceded after a long pause, "but my new boss can be difficult and he did not want me to talk to you." After the fascinating conversation with the old lady, the commander had almost forgotten the reason for his visit. But Anne's comments reminded him of his feud with Beckwith and his objections to the submarine rescue project.

Anne let the dogs off their leads when they reached a patch of open grass on the brow of a hill that provided a vista of Portsmouth Harbour. The naval pair watched the dogs running free. On another day, it would have been a glorious sight, but in the drizzle, the basins of the huge harbour were hidden from view by swirling mist. As they marched over the soggy ground, the commander broke the awkward silence. "What's your role on the project?" he enquired.

"I've been reviewing the control system design," she replied, "but I want to talk to you about crew training."

"Well, I can't really help, I'm afraid," replied the commander. "It's possible that we will be involved with training after the sea trials. But nothing has been agreed. It's all up in the air at the moment. No decision has been made." The unhelpful response added to Anne's gloomy mood; she had thought that the man would be only too happy to talk about training. But she did not realise that the commander had his own axe to grind. He wanted to win Anne over as an ally against his adversary, Martin Beckwith.

"Are you familiar with the present rescue set-up?" asked the commander, after a pause.

"No, not really," replied Anne.

"Well, the submarine rescue vehicles and their support equipment are stored at a base up in Scotland," explained the commander. "We work with other NATO countries and the whole kit and caboodle can be sent to a distressed submarine anywhere in the world, in a matter of hours. Contractors look after the equipment. But we have trained people to man the rescue vehicle ready on standby. A team can be quickly assembled with medics, divers and subsea experts."

That was all very interesting but did not really help answer the question about training simulators that was vexing Anne. They walked on as Anne tried to assemble her thoughts. "How did you get involved?" asked the commander conversationally, to break the silence.

"Martin found out about my background," replied Anne absent-mindedly. "I was part of the team that oversaw construction of a nuclear submarine at Barrow. He thought that I had the right background. It was a bit of a shock really when he came to see me. I was enjoying life on a patrol boat. But the secondment allows me to look after Mother in my bungalow. So I agreed to join his team."

The commander noticed Anne's casual use of Beckwith's Christian name and wondered whether she was under the influence of her crafty boss. "What was your role on the patrol boat?" he enquired.

"I was in charge!" replied Anne in a matter-of-fact way.

That took the wind out of the commander's sails. "Wow!" he remarked unintentionally as he tried to collect his thoughts. When they arranged the meeting, the commander believed that the female officer was some lowly technocrat. The note merely stated that she was attached to the submarine rescue project and made no mention of her background in the navy. Like many of his generation, the commander found it hard to accept that a woman could take charge of a warship. Anne's comment exposed his hidden prejudice. "It must be tough accepting orders from Beckwith after running your own show," he stuttered.

"It was at first," she agreed. "The team is an odd bunch. They are like overgrown students. My boss told me to concentrate on the control system design. Martin warned me not to get involved in crew training. But I resented that! Training is an important part of an officer's duty!"

In other circumstances, the commander might have agreed with her, but he had other fish to fry. So he changed tack. He wanted to win over this female officer as an ally in his feud with Beckwith. "What do you know about the history of the submarine rescue project?" he asked.

"Not much," replied Anne.

"Beckwith dreamed up this scheme after the Russian nuclear submarine the *Kursk* blew up in the Barents Sea," explained the commander. "You probably know that the Russians dragged their heels before calling in our boys. They wanted to handle the rescue operation themselves. But they were eventually forced to ask for our help. Around thirty of the crew were huddled in the stern compartment after surviving the initial explosion. If our chaps had arrived earlier, they could have saved them. But when we got down there, they found that the escape hatch was jammed shut and it was not possible to reach them in time."

"Yes, I remember the incident," replied Anne. "It was a tragic affair."

"Well, the *Kursk* took place shortly after Beckwith set up his Marine Special Projects Agency, so your boss jumped on the bandwagon," continued the commander. "The incident suited his agenda. He was looking for funding for his agency, so he campaigned to build a new type of submarine rescue vehicle. His plan was approved. But submariners were never consulted and some of them think the new rescue vehicle is overcomplicated. My own view is that it's a vanity project to further Beckwith's career."

Although Anne had issues with her boss, she was proud of the project and thought it was worthwhile. She was starting to think that the commander's differences with her boss was more of a personal vendetta than a difference of technical issues. "Why do you think that it's overcomplicated?" asked Anne sceptically.

"We believe that the battery-propelled rescue vehicles are perfectly adequate. They have served us well in the past. The fuel-cells approach is a step too far and it will be difficult to find suitable fuel supplies in remote regions. As you know, the *Kursk* disaster took place in the Barents Sea, off the north coast of Russia. It would be difficult, if not impossible, to get hold of the special fuel in those waters."

"Have you raised this with my boss?" asked Anne doubtfully. With other things on her mind, she really did not want to get into this discussion.

"Time and time again," replied the commander with a sigh. "Each time I raise it, your boss scoffs at me. He calls me a Luddite and accuses me of blocking technical progress. But, of course, I appreciate the benefits fuel cells provide – they allow a submarine to spend more time underwater. But the fuel-supply issue needs to be addressed."

Anne could not believe that the fuel-supply issue had been overlooked. "Why didn't you raise this with your superiors?" she asked suspiciously.

"They are not interested!" replied the commander bitterly.

Anne would later learn that the commander had been hung out to dry by his superior officers, who were well aware of the fuel-supply problem. The admiral had given his support to the project while turning a Nelsonian blind eye to the fuel-supply issue. This was a cynical ploy, because they had other plans for the midget submarine. Unaware of this underhand plot, the commander continued to complain about the fuel-supply issue. But without the backing of his superior, the commander was isolated. This allowed Beckwith to brand the war hero as a Luddite, who stood in the way of progress.

When he accepted Anne's invitation to tea, the commander had hoped that he could win her over to his cause. But from the familiar way that she spoke of her boss, he was now starting to suspect that she would side against him. As they approached the road that ran along the brow of the hill, Anne called in her dogs. This was a welcome distraction. The pause gave Anne a chance to assemble her views.

"This is the first time that I've heard objections to our project," she declared, with a worried expression. "I was told that the basic concept had been approved by the navy. The outline design was finalised before I joined the project team. One day, I was commanding a patrol boat; the next day, I was a member of the team. I hardly had time to pack my bags! The work has been so hectic I have hardly had time to think. But no one else has criticised the basic design. So I'm quite surprised at your attitude!"

This subject was an unwelcome distraction as far as Anne was concerned. The reason she wanted to speak to her fellow officer was to discuss a training simulator. She felt that the commander was raking over old history and settling scores. The supposed war hero seemed unable to look at the project from a constructive point of view. Anne was proud of the innovative nature of the project and disappointed by the gripes of this 'pompous ass'.

"Look, I'm not interested in rewriting history," declared Anne earnestly. "When I joined the project team, there was a thick document that set out the design. That's the *Bible* as far as we are concerned. If there is a problem with general concept, then you will have to take it up with your superiors. But we are where we are, and I can't change what happened in the past. My only interest at the moment is crew training. I had hoped that you would help."

"Why are you so worried about training?" asked the commander.

"I think it's my duty as a naval officer," replied Anne firmly. She was disturbed that the commander could not recognise that rather obvious point. "I started to take an interest in training soon after I joined the project. On my first day, I sat in on a meeting about a virtual reality model. It was all new to me, so I didn't really understand what was going on. But it seems that the model can be used for training. The minutes of the meeting said this had been discussed with the navy, so I assumed that my boss had spoken to you about it."

"Sorry, I can't really help you," replied the commander unhelpfully. His mind was focussed on his feud with Beckwith and did not want to be deflected. The commander was, of course, aware of the virtual reality model. But the model was Beckwith's idea and not something that concerned him unduly. "We were told the virtual reality model would be used to finalise the layout of equipment inside the hull. Beckwith never said anything to me about using it as a training aid."

The pair were at cross-purposes and the conversation had reached an impasse. Anne did not want to discuss the commander's concerns about fuel supply, believing that issues of that sort needed to be addressed by those with higher authority. The commander did not want to discuss crew training. So they trudged on through the drizzle in an uncomfortable silence, each lost in their own thoughts. As Anne watched the dogs bounding through the grass, she broke the silence: "How did my boss raise the money for the project if he did not have support from the navy?" she challenged him.

"He has friends in high places," replied the commander airily.

"They must be very high places!" retorted Anne sarcastically. "I can't see him conjuring up tens of millions of pounds out of thin air!"

"Few ordinary people could raise that amount of money. But Beckwith has a lot of political clout. The rogue knows where the bodies are buried," replied the commander, as though he were privy to secret affairs.

Despite her differences with her boss, Anne was uncomfortable hearing him described as a rogue by an outsider. *Takes one to know one!* she thought uncharitably. But she kept that malicious thought to herself as they continued on. "You told me that you are involved in the sea trials?" she remarked to break the uncomfortable silence.

After all Anne's efforts to track down the illusive commander, the meeting had been a complete waste of her time. Instead of discussing training, the war hero seemed intent on discrediting the project and moaning about her boss. As part of Beckwith's team, Anne could not be openly disloyal. There were obviously faults on both sides in the commander's feud with her boss. She did not want to be caught in the middle.

"I'm surprised that your boss didn't tell you about our role," remarked the commander at length. "Seems that he doesn't want us talking together behind his back." But with that parting shot, he abandoned any further attempts to win over his female counterpart. He realised that he had adopted the wrong approach with the strong-willed young woman.

Anne called her dogs to heel and they headed back to the bungalow. When they arrived home, the pair were stony-faced and dripping wet. Mother was upset to see them looking so glum. Still harbouring the illusion that romance was in the air, she consoled herself with the notion that the couple had had a lovers' tiff. "They will get over it," she said under her breath.

While the commander had alienated the young female officer during their walk, he had enjoyed the tea party with the old lady. It had been a rare chance to reminisce with an appreciative audience. Dorothy had enjoyed meeting the distinguished war hero. The old lady was now intent on ensnaring that distinguished war hero into her family. But her daughter had no wish to see the man again; she bitterly regretted organising the affair.

After bidding farewell to Dorothy, the commander gave his business card to Anne, with the suggestion that she should keep in touch. In a fit of petulance, Anne threw the card in the bin. But after the temper tantrum, she recovered it. That was fortunate, because later that evening, she realised that her peevish mood arose from being sidelined at the tea party.

It was not just that the commander had annoyed her with his criticism of the project, but she was seething with rage at her ungrateful mother. Although she looked after the old lady, her mother never gave her credit for her successful career and treated her like a skivvy. The pain of this injustice had affected her judgement. With time, she felt guilty that she had questioned the commander's motives.

But she put these negative thoughts aside when she recalled that Mark and his family were due to visit them for Sunday lunch on the following day. This was a happy occasion – it was the first family get-together since her brother's return from the Persian Gulf. It would be a long day for the visitors; Mark had to drive his wife and two boys up from the West Country.

Everyone was in high spirits as they greeted one another, despite simmering tensions within the family. Mark was his mother's favourite and the pair adjourned to the front room where they sat chatting away happily. The old lady was keen to learn what her son had been up to in the Persian Gulf. It would give her pleasure to boast about his exploits to her circle of friends over the coming weeks. After being cooped up in the car for several hours, the boys let off steam, chasing each other noisily around Anne's garden.

Anne exchanged gossip with her sister-in-law in the kitchen as they chopped vegetables and kept an eye on a joint of pork which was roasting in the oven. In other circumstances, the pair would have been good friends, but there were tensions. The matriarch's capricious nature did not help matters. With her traditional mindset, the old lady believed that it was a daughter's duty to care for her mother. That was one reason why she deplored Anne's career. Anne saw that as grossly unfair in the modern world. She expected her brother and sister-in-law to share the burden. Lucy, meanwhile, felt that the family was overly obsessed with its naval tradition.

But all was forgiven in the heady atmosphere of the family get-together. As they chatted, Anne related the story about the artificer who mucked around with the hot water on the patrol boat. Lucy chuckled at the story. Lucy was impressed by the way that Anne had dealt with a potentially tricky situation, but this did not stop her from teasing her sister-in-law.

"Mark is a stickler for discipline. He would have thrown the book at the rascal," remarked Lucy with a twinkle in her eye. "Admit it, you were lenient because you fancy the guy!"

Anne blushed. "Well, I suppose I do, in an earthy sort of way," she admitted coyly. The pair collapsed into hoots of laughter at this.

The matriarch sat proudly at the head of the table as they sat down to eat. "Mark will carve," she pronounced imperiously. "Women don't know how to carve," she whispered in an acid aside to the two boys, who both had knives and forks in their hands as they waited impatiently for their food. Mark put on a grand show of sharpening the carving knife, serving the meat and dividing up the crackling. His mother's gushing praise for his efforts might have led an outsider to believe her son had cooked the whole meal.

With her labours in the kitchen unappreciated, Anne was teased about the war hero's visit in a merciless way. The two boys asked cheeky questions about her new 'boyfriend'. With stoic resistance, Anne refused to be drawn. The news that Mark had delivered a message to the war hero in the Admiral Bligh pub on Anne's behalf was greeted with glee by the family. This titbit of information came as a relief to Lucy, who harboured suspicions of her husband reverting to his bad old ways while acting as duty officer in Portsmouth.

While washing the crockery, Anne found herself alone with her brother, for the first time that day. They spoke briefly about her meeting with Commander Woods. They had little time to go into detail because Mark was in a hurry to return his family back to the West Country. "I thought he was an arrogant fellow," declared Anne waspishly. "He was no help with my work at all!"

Mark was not altogether surprised that the pair had not hit it off, knowing that his sister could be a little headstrong at times. "Sorry to hear that," he replied in consolatory manner. He did not wish to add fuel to the flames. "The commander seemed all right to me. As a matter of fact, I asked him if I could join his trials team. That work would suit me down to the ground."

Anne kicked herself, wondering why she had overlooked the obvious point. As a child, she was in awe of her brother's sailing skills and knew that he was looking for another posting when his tour on the carrier came to an end. *He would be an excellent candidate for the commander's trials team*, she mused, rather belatedly. But she did not have time to pursue the subject because a commotion broke out in the garden. It seemed that the over-excited boys had been teasing the normally placid Labradors and the dogs had turned on their tormentors. Anne raced out into the garden to sort out the fracas.

After waving goodbye to the visitors, Anne began to re-assess her contemptuous view of the commander. Reflecting on Mark's ambitions to join the trials team, she saw matters in a different light, so she decided to look into the commander's comments about the history of the project when she returned to work on Monday morning. With no other pressing duties, she would have plenty of time to snoop around the office, but she needed to do this behind Simon's back. She did not want her volatile boss to get wind of what she was up to.

To avoid the eagle-eyed administrator, Anne arrived early at the start of the working week. With the office to herself, she was able to search through the unfamiliar filing cabinets. Simon was meticulous, and all the project documents were stored in chronological order and marked with subject codes. Anne was familiar with the contents of the filing cabinets that surrounded her own desk – they mainly concerned her work. But she knew nothing of the contents of the other filing cabinets, tucked away in a restricted area behind Simon's desk. She wanted to take a peek, before Simon turned up.

Although the filing system was easy to navigate, she was unable to find any correspondence from the navy. This led her to believe that her boss kept all the sensitive documents locked in his office. But during the search, a file labelled *Whitebait Cove* attracted her attention. She had fond memories of the place. She had visited the small harbour with her parents when she was a child. She recalled that the harbour was situated on the estuary which extends inland from Plymouth, close to her brother's home.

Curious to learn more, she flicked through the pages, and a letter caught her attention. As she perused the document, she came across a sentence: *We have had a meeting with Commander Woods and will write about the proposed sea trials programme to your private address.* The letter was signed by *Steve Jones, Chief Executive of Offshore Submersibles*. The mention of a 'private address' was confirmation of her boss's secretive nature. It was proof that he kept a lot of information away from the rest of his team.

But she was unable to read any further because she could hear footsteps approaching. After hastily returning the file to the cabinet, she ducked back to her desk. When the office door opened, it was Simon, punctual as ever. He eyed her with suspicion and she felt a twinge of guilt as she jotted down details of the letter in her notebook. Anne was familiar with the name 'Offshore Submersibles'. The company acted as subcontractor for the fuel-cell propulsion system, but it was a surprise to learn that the sea trials were due to take place close to her brother's home.

So, later in the day, when Simon was distracted with other tasks, Anne did an online search for information about the company Offshore Submersibles. She quickly discovered that the specialist marine company occupied the site of the old boatyard which she had visited with her parents many years earlier.

As her brother lived close by, he would be able to pay the company a visit and see what was going on. That might help him get a foot in the door with the commander's trials team. So, she made a note to pass on this valuable nugget of information to her brother as soon as she could. As it happened, she was due some leave, and so she asked Simon if it would be all right if she took a couple of days off. This would allow her to phone her brother from home where the office snoop could not overhear the conversation.

This was a welcome break. With her mother to care for, she had barely had time to take a breath since joining the project team, so a couple of days at home would provide a chance to catch up with a backlog of household chores. But before starting her chores the following morning, she phoned her brother's number to pass on the news about Whitebait Cove.

The phone was answered brusquely by her sister-in-law, who was just about to leave home for work at the comprehensive. Her grumpy response made it clear that the bonhomie of the Sunday lunch had dissipated and she was in no mood to chat. When told rather bluntly that Mark was busy gardening, Anne asked her sister-in-law to take a message. Lucy grudgingly noted down the comments about the old boatyard at Whitebait Cove.

Lucy pinned the slip of paper to her 'to-do' board by the kitchen door with the intention of giving it to her husband when she returned from work that evening. She was in no rush to deliver the note, because she did not want to give her husband an excuse to shirk his family duties while he was on leave. So Mark spent the rest of the day tidying up the garden and attending to other inconsequential matters, oblivious to the valuable piece of information waiting in the kitchen.

Then to compound her sins, Lucy forgot about the phone call when she returned from a busy day at school that evening. The note was overlooked for several days. It was only by chance that Lucy noticed the scrawled message when she was cleaning up the sideboard on Friday evening. After a busy week, she could barely recall the conversation. The barely decipherable message read: *Anne phoned about a company called Offshore Submersibles. The company is based at Whitebait Cove.*

Feeling guilty, Lucy handed the note to her husband when he came into the kitchen to wash his hands after finishing his jobs in the garden. "Oh! Did I tell you about Anne's phone call?" remarked Lucy rather sheepishly. "I was getting ready for school on Monday when you sister rang, and did not really listen to what she had to say. Your sister said something about a sea trial. But we did not speak for long. You were working in the garden, and I didn't want to disturb you."

Unable to decipher the scrawl, Mark couldn't make head nor tail of the message. But he retained fond memories of Whitebait Cove and the phrase 'sea trial' acted like an electric shock, galvanising him into action. Mark's mind raced with the possibilities. If he could wangle his way into the sea trial, it might provide a stepping stone towards fulfilling his ambition to join the commander's trials team. So he was determined to visit Whitebait Cove as soon as possible. But first, he phoned his sister to see what else he could find out. But after the long delay, Mark was met with a grumpy response.

Anne had gone to a lot of trouble to let her brother know that the sea trial was at Whitebait Cove, and she could not understand why it had taken him so long to get in touch. "Lucy forgot to pass me the note," apologised Mark. Anne did not buy that story – she suspected that 'accidentally on purpose' was a more accurate way of describing what had taken place. She was only too well aware of her sister-in-law's disdain for the navy. "Are you sure that Lucy did not hide the note?" she remarked in a spiteful way.

After the bad-tempered phone call, Mark decided that it was time that he and his wife settled their differences over his naval career, even if it ended in the divorce court. This was going to be painful, because Lucy was scathing about their long separations while he was away at sea. She pleaded with him to apply for a shore job so that he could spend more time with the family. But the sea was in his blood, and he had no intention of becoming a landlubber.

Feeling guilty about the forgotten phone message, Lucy adopted a conciliatory tone at first and hid her true feelings. She expressed sympathy when her husband spoke of his sadness that his aircraft carrier was to be taken out of service. "They are recruiting young people for the new carriers, so I may be made redundant," commented Mark gloomily. But Lucy's true feelings were revealed when Mark admitted that he had put in an application to join the new carriers.

The thought of dealing with their boisterous teenage boys while her husband continued to serve at sea was unbearable. Lucy was secretly delighted that the ageing aircraft carrier was to be taken out of service. "You will lose touch with your children," she warned him. "Why don't you apply for a shore posting? You will be able to watch them grow up!" There was a danger that the argument would spin out of control. Whenever they tried to talk about Mark's naval career, they went around in circles, covering the same old ground and ending up in a slanging match.

But in a conciliatory mood, Mark spoke about the forthcoming sea trials at Whitebait Cove and his desire to join the commander's team. "If I could take part in the sea trial, it would allow me to spend more time with the kids," he pleaded. "That's what Anne phoned me about." But the words fell on stony ground. Lucy was exhausted after a busy week and could not understand the significance of some sea trials at Whitebait Cove.

When the children had gone to bed, Lucy calmed down. In a more relaxed frame of mind, her husband's words began to make sense. She recalled the dashing young sailor she had fallen in love with. The prospect of him becoming involved in sea trials while living at home seemed an attractive compromise. So she raised the white flag. "Why don't we go down to Whitebait Cove on Sunday?" she murmured affectionately as they headed to bed. "We could take my mother and the kids, and make a day of it. Perhaps have a meal in one of your pubs?"

This was a generous offer because on a previous trip to Whitebait Cove they had a blazing row which nearly ended their relationship. Lucy's suggestion of a pub lunch was another sign that she was in a forgiving mood, given her disdain for those establishments. Fearing that this harmonious mood would evaporate, Mark searched his memory for a respectable place to eat. Somewhere that served good food and had games for the children.

Their boys were aged seven and nine and had yet to reach the awkward teenage years when an outing with parents was a cause of embarrassment. So on Sunday morning, parents and excited boys loaded into the family estate car and they set off to collect Lucy's mother. The spritely old lady was waiting for them on the pavement outside her small retirement flat and she squeezed nimbly into the back seat. The two boys were delighted to see their granny and the passengers in the back seat enjoyed playing 'I-spy' during the journey to Whitebait Cove. Their route followed narrow, winding country lanes around the estuary.

Before setting off for their outing, Mark booked Sunday lunch at the Windmill public house, which had a reputation as a family-friendly establishment. The sharp-eyed boys were the first to notice the signpost to the hostelry with directions along a lane that opened into a large car park. The public house was surrounded by a garden where the children could play, so it was the ideal venue for a family outing. The pub itself was a large gabled building perched on the brow of a hill overlooking the estuary. There were various bars and dining areas.

As it was a warm autumn day, they decided to eat in the garden. They claimed possession of a stout wooden table with benches fixed on either side. The table was conveniently close to the children's playground and provided a bird's eye view of Whitebait Cove. After deciding what to eat from a menu that Mark retrieved from the bar, the boys raced off to the play area under the indulgent supervision of their grandmother. Mark returned to the bar to order the food and drinks, while his wife guarded the table.

As Lucy admired the autumn colours on the far shore of the estuary, memories began to stir in her mind of a dreadful day at Whitebait Cove. Shortly after they started going out together, Mark wanted to demonstrate his sailing prowess. So her then boyfriend hired a small yacht. It was a hot summer's day and Lucy had ignored his advice to bring warm clothes. She teased the young cadet, saying he was a sissy with all his heavy weather gear. But after sailing merrily downwind, a storm blew up, and they struggled to return to the boatyard.

Lucy was sea sick on the return trip and arrived at the landing stage soaked to the skin and chilled to the bone. This resulted in a fearful row. Lucy accused Mark of behaving like a bully, ordering her about as the dinghy jibed at the end of each tack. "It's all your fault," she declared. "You should have checked the weather forecast and you took us too far out into the estuary." Keen to placate his new girlfriend, Mark refrained from criticising her attire. The episode created a sour feeling and nearly ended their relationship.

A lot of water had flowed under the bridge since that awful day and the little harbour at Whitebait Cove had changed out of all recognition, mused Lucy as she sat nursing a glass of white wine. The old, dilapidated boatyard where they had hired the dinghy had been replaced by modern industrial buildings.

Chapter 6

A Trip to Whitebait Cove

Lucy began to relax in the warm autumn sunshine as she guarded their table in the gardens of the Windmill public house. It was a rare opportunity to get away from the demands of her teaching job and housework. She sat contentedly nursing a glass of wine as she watched her boys scramble nimbly over a climbing frame, under the supervision of her mother. A cool breeze ruffled her hair, and she felt a sense of well-being. In this mellow mood, her thoughts drifted back to the sailing incident many years earlier, while her husband ordered their food and drinks at the bar.

She recalled her irritation when Mark bossed her about on the sailing boat. "Get over to the other side," he ordered masterfully as he prepared to come around for a tack. She followed each instruction meekly as she tried to control the pangs of seasickness. The ensuing row, when they finally reached the landing stage, nearly wrecked their relationship. The memory rankled. On reflection, she could see that it was her jealousy towards her husband's adventurous seafaring life that lay behind her behaviour that day.

In her busy life, teaching unruly kids, caring for the two boys and looking after their home, she did not always appreciate her husband's passion for the sea. They were an ill-matched couple. She had deep roots in the local community. Mark, by contrast, was a gypsy at heart. He could not bear to be confined to one place. "The sea is the third partner in our marriage," she moaned, when friends tried to console her with the observation that 'opposites attract'.

Her train of thought was disturbed when Mark returned with a tray of drinks and a gleeful expression on his face. "Can you guess who I've just seen?" he asked in a rhetorical way. When his wife shook her head, he was so excited he nearly stumbled over his words. "The chap I met in Portsmouth. You know. The commander my sister wanted to meet! I delivered her note to him in a pub in Portsmouth. He runs the trials team."

Lucy did not know what to make of this. After hearing the strange story, she was starting to have doubts about her husband's role as a go-between in the Admiral Bligh pub, suspecting that it was just another excuse for him to go out boozing. *The crafty devil probably cooked up the story with his sister,* she thought maliciously. The notion that Anne was romantically involved with a war hero seemed like some romantic fiction. But with news of this sighting, Lucy was intrigued to learn more.

"Where is he?" she asked, curiously.

"Couldn't believe my eyes," replied Mark eagerly. "He's in the dining room. I'm sure it's him. You don't forget someone like that in a hurry. I'll point him out when we collect our food." They were interrupted before he could say more when a waitress arrived with the children's meals. The two boys raced over to the table and tucked into their food. Leaving the boys under the watchful eye of their grandmother, the parents headed to the restaurant, where a chef was carving large joints of roast meat.

The outing had revived something of the playful spirit that enriched the early days of their relationship. Waiting in the queue to be served, Mark surreptitiously pointed to a couple of men eating at a side table and warned his wife, 'not to stare'. With a sidelong glance, Lucy saw a middle-aged man sitting opposite a young chap, fashionably dressed in jeans and soft leather jacket. Lucy thought they looked like father and son, and immediately jumped to the conclusion that it was the younger man that her husband was referring to.

"What do you make of him?" whispered Mark in a conspiratorial way.

"He looks a real dish!" said his wife in a coquettish manner. Lucy was starting to think that there might be something in this romantic story after all.

"No. Not the young guy! I mean the grey-haired guy sitting with his back to the wall."

"You must be joking. I can't imagine your sister having an affair with that washed-up old duffer!" replied Lucy with a sour look of disdain.

"You are always trying to pair people off," joked Mark, recalling how single male teachers from her school 'just happened to drop by' when Anne paid them a visit. It was her caring nature that first attracted him to the trainee teacher. Her match-making efforts had been a constant source of amusement since they first met at a college 'hop'. Shortly after they met, Lucy organised parties where female students from her teachers' training college mingled with male students from Mark's nautical college. Several happy marriages developed as a result of those lively affairs.

"Not much luck with your sister, so far!" retorted Lucy jovially. "But I think that the young chap would suit her. I wonder who he is," she pondered inquisitively. She was slightly tipsy, by this time, after downing the large glass of house white wine. But they were then distracted as the chef served them their food. They put the subject aside as they returned to their table in the garden; plates piled high with roast meat and vegetables. The boys distracted their elders with tales of funny incidents that had taken place at school during the week.

After they'd finished their meal, Mark followed a circuitous route as he returned the plates to the counter. This allowed him to spy on the two male diners in an inconspicuous way. By that time, the pair were enjoying coffee as they sat in the main dining room. When he returned from his spying trip, he found that his wife had gone to speak to a couple of people who were sitting at another table. Assuming that they were discussing some local affairs, Mark left her to her own devices.

When Lucy rejoined the family group, she was bursting to pass on some exciting news. "I have just found out something really interesting. I'll tell you later," she whispered to her husband in a knowing way. But the two boys were becoming fractious by this time, so Granny shepherded the children towards the car, and they set off on the next stage of their journey. As they travelled along the brow of the hill, the old boatyard lay below them. Lucy feared that the sight of the old boatyard would open up old wounds. But she was relieved to see that the rickety old yard had been replaced by modern buildings.

Once they reached the village, they turned down a lane which separated a modern industrial estate from some newly built houses. A steel mesh fence surrounded the industrial site. The site appeared deserted. In search of somewhere to park the car, Mark drove to the waterfront, but there were no free parking spaces. As he reversed slowly back up the lane, they could see a stylish office building.

Lucy took pictures with her mobile phone as Mark drove past the gate. There was nothing much to see, and no convenient parking place. The two boys had become bored and fractious, and so they set off home without any further delay. Bouncing over the potholes in the country lanes, Lucy was unable to make out much detail on the small screen of her phone, and the reason for their visit was quickly forgotten. That weekend was the start of the half-term holiday, and the boys were to stay overnight with their grandmother. Mark and Lucy sighed with relief when they dropped the two boys off at Granny's flat – allowing the married couple to enjoy a rare night at home by themselves.

After his heavy lunch and a busy week of chores, Mark collapsed gratefully into his favourite armchair to read the Sunday paper in peace. Lucy hummed as she bustled around the kitchen with a smug expression on her face. She was barely able to conceal her glee at the nugget of information she had gleaned during their Sunday lunch. When she woke her husband for tea, she had a triumphant expression on her face as she prepared to drop her bombshell: "You will never guess who that young chap was at the restaurant."

"Haven't a clue," mumbled Mark in a befuddled manner. He had been snoozing and was not particularly interested in the sort of local gossip that fascinated his wife. As he came to life from his snooze, he picked up the remote control to switch on the TV.

"His name's Steve Jones," said his wife.

"So what?" replied Mark with a puzzled expression on his face.

"That's the name in Anne's note!" announced Lucy triumphantly as she thrust the note down on the table in front of him, with the flourish of a magician pulling a rabbit from a hat. "He's the boss of the marine business at Whitebait Cove!"

That revelation roused Mark from his post-lunch torpor. He blinked as he sat up in his armchair, wondering what other titbits of news she had gleaned from her grapevine of informants. The retired naval officer was aware that his wife had built up an impressive network of informants through her teaching and community activities. Few local affairs passed beneath her radar. This was a great blessing for her husband, who was blind to activities taking place right under his nose.

Lucy could hardly wait to tell her husband about the conversation which had taken place while he was returning the plates from their Sunday lunch. It emerged that she had spoken to a teaching assistant from her school, called Doris. During their conversation, it emerged that Doris's husband, Stan, acted as harbour master at the boatyard at Whitebait Cove. So, the young guy talking to the commander was Stan's boss. Stan was the only employee to retain his job when the yard was sold to its Dutch owners. In his new role as harbour master, Stan maintained records of all the boats that berthed at the quay. He was also responsible for keeping the premises clean and tidy.

Mark was impressed with his wife's sleuthing ability. The valuable nugget of information might help him wheedle his way into the trials team. After all, the harbour master was bound to know all about the sea trials of his sister's midget submarine, so the guy would be a useful contact. It was just the foot in the door he had been looking for. In his excitement, he phoned his sister to celebrate the news.

Lucy purred with pride and hoped this would help heal their marital rift. She knew that, deep down, her husband resented her teaching career. He wanted her to devote more of her time to looking after the boys, though he did not say it openly. Mark felt that his wife took too much on her shoulders, and expressed hidden feelings by finding niggling little faults with the way she brought up their children.

Although Mark's naval career was the main source of marital discord, Lucy believed that her husband could be more supportive of her various interests when he was on leave. She fretted that as he settled into middle age, her husband was becoming reclusive and snobbish. When she first met the dashing young cadet, she was impressed by his vigour. But as he aged, he had lost his zest for life.

Lucy wanted her husband to become involved in community activities. Away from her teaching duties, Lucy belonged to all sorts of clubs and associations. It made her angry that her partner did not give her any support. She thought that Mark's long periods of service on board the aircraft carrier gave him an excuse to put his feet up when he came ashore.

This was another reason that she was pleased with her encounter with Doris and Stan during their Sunday lunch. The couple were both down-to-earth characters, rooted into the local community. Stan had an allotment and was treasurer of the local bowling club. He would be the ideal person to encourage her husband to take an interest in local affairs. These thoughts occupied her scheming mind as the evening passed.

Looking up from his newspaper from time to time, Mark watched his wife's mind whirring away. He suspected that she was hatching some Machiavellian plot, but despite the warning signs, he was caught unawares when she looked at him. "Is there anything else that I can do to help you join the commander's trial team?" she asked with a beguiling smile. Reacting to this seemingly generous offer, Mark fell straight into the carefully laid trap.

"It would be really helpful if you could introduce me to Stan," replied Mark, oblivious to the scheme that his wife was plotting.

When Lucy bumped into Doris in the school canteen the following day, they chuckled like a pair of evil witches as Lucy put her plan into action. The idea was to put Mark's name forward to join the bowling club, without his knowledge. Lucy knew that this would make her husband steaming mad, because he had a snobbish prejudice against bowling. Mark had once made a disparaging remark about the activity, describing bowling as a sport for the 'flat cap brigade'.

But the pair of conspirators calculated that the prospect of meeting Stan, and learning more about the goings-on at the boatyard at Whitebait Cove, would be sufficient incentive for the conceited naval officer to join the club that he so despised.

When Mark mentioned his wish to meet the harbour master, that evening, Lucy assured him that arrangements were already in hand. "I'll drive you over to meet him later this evening," replied Lucy brightly. As he climbed into the family car, Mark had no idea that he was to be the victim of a prank. He naturally assumed they were both going to visit Stan at his home. But when Lucy stopped outside the bowling club, he was slightly uneasy. "Stan is waiting for you inside," remarked Lucy with a cunning smile.

Lucy departed in a cloud of gravel, leaving her husband standing bewildered outside the nondescript clapboard building. Collecting his faculties, Mark followed the instructions on the wall and pressed the call button to gain admittance. The entry system buzzed, allowing him to push the door open. Once inside, he was told that Stan was in the middle of a bowls match, but that someone else would be along to see him. As he stood forlornly in the entrance foyer, he was met by the club secretary in a navy blue blazer. The man handed Mark an application form to complete. "We've been expecting you," remarked the club official.

Mark thought that there had been a mix-up, but he did not wish to insult his host, so he completed the application form as he surveyed the dimly lit foyer. After completing the formalities, the club secretary took the puzzled naval officer on a quick tour of the clubhouse and introduced him to members socialising in the bar. The arrival of a naval officer was met with some ribald remarks – a hard core of club members were army veterans. A former sergeant major announced in his parade ground voice: "Stand by your beds, the navy's here!' The club secretary told the old fellow to 'mind his manners' and took Mark to a bowling green to learn the ropes.

This was the first time that the naval officer had played bowls, but he soon got the hang of the sport and showed sufficient promise for his name to be added to the list of 'reserve members' for the club's team. After his initial reservations, Mark began to enjoy himself. After buying a round of drinks, the naval officer was accepted by the club members, and it turned out to be an amusing session. Stan came to join the party sometime later, after finishing his game. But carried away by the cheerful banter, Mark had by that time forgotten the reason for his visit.

Lucy could not get much sense out of her husband when he meandered home later that night, much the worse for drink. Not wishing to share a bed with the drunken sot, she ordered him to sleep in the spare room. But as her husband was victim of her dastardly plot, she forgave his boozing on that occasion. It gave her quiet satisfaction that her husband was engaged with the local community. Lucy waited to quiz her husband about the bowls club when he was *compos mentis* in the morning.

Breakfast was traditionally a time of reconciliation after one of Mark's boozing sprees. On that day, Mark woke ashen-faced and sheepish. But as he gradually came to life, he admitted that he had enjoyed himself at the club and regaled his wife with some amusing anecdotes about the characters he had met. After his first visit, Mark visited the club several more times during his leave. It was an excuse to have a drink and get out of the house. But he did not learn much about the sea trials at Whitebait Cove, during these visits.

As treasurer of the bowls club, Stan was an important figure within the bowling fraternity, and he bustled around organising club affairs, so Mark rarely got a chance to talk to the old fellow about the boatyard at Whitebait Cove. But during one exchange, Stan let slip that Sam Wheeler's old boatyard had been transformed into a modern marine business headed by a go-getter guy called Steve Jones. The rickety old buildings had apparently been demolished and the site divided up for industrial and residential purposes. The quay had been renovated, and new industrial buildings had been built in place of the old wooden boatsheds. But Mark's leave came to an end before he could learn more.

Mark harboured fond memories of his evenings at the bowls club when he returned from his leave. A sad mood prevailed on the condemned warship. Mark felt jealous when colleagues were transferred to the shipyard at Rosyth, where the first of the new aircraft carriers was due to be commissioned. Mark was left as part of a team to decommission the old ship. Their first task was to oversee the transfer of live ammunition to an arsenal on the rocky Scottish coast. The carrier then returned to the naval base at Portsmouth where other weapons were stripped away.

The tedious work involved frequent arguments with officials over disparities between the ship's records and those held by the defence ministry. Each round of ammunition needed to be accounted for. After removal of the munitions, the hull was systematically stripped of its weapons, military electronics and fittings. The hangar, which had once buzzed with activity, had an increasingly forlorn appearance. The grey steel walls were marked with dark patches where pieces of sophisticated electronic equipment had once been fixed.

Some weeks after the carrier returned to the Portsmouth naval base, Mark was placed in charge of the decommissioning team. "This will be my only command," he joked ruefully. To raise the morale of his team, Mark managed to lay his hands on some smart furnishings and fittings, and he used them to create a comfortable base for his team in what had been the captain's dayroom. His squad consisted of two lieutenants and some seasoned NCOs. The friendly gang dubbed themselves the 'skeleton team' as they supervised the dockworkers. Black humour tended to pervade their conversation.

One benefit of staying on the old ship was that Mark was able to spend time over Christmas with his family. Shortly after arriving home, it so happened that Mark ran into the bowls club treasurer, while out buying a Christmas tree. Stan asked why he had not visited the bowls club in the past few weeks. "We have been decommissioning the old aircraft carrier," replied Mark. This was the first time the pair had spoken to one another outside the bowls club, and Stan was more forthcoming than usual.

"Looks like my time's up with the navy," said Mark with a sad expression. "I'm looking for an opportunity ashore. Don't suppose that there are any vacancies at the boatyard?"

"We are looking for someone to handle the work boat in the spring," replied Stan helpfully. "It would only be a part-time job, but it might suit you while you look around for something more permanent." With Christmas shopping to collect, Mark had no time to discuss this further, but the idea was an attractive prospect.

Much of the banter of the 'skeleton team' reflected their sadness that they all faced the end of their naval careers. As the day approached for the enormous steel hulk to be towed away to a Turkish breakers' yard, team members received their discharge papers. To keep up morale, the team marked each departure with a 'wake' at the local boozer. Mark's turn came in due course. Mark opened the thick envelope with a sense of foreboding.

He was taken aback to receive an offer to serve as naval attaché in Rome, as an alternative to early retirement. The Italian posting was a plum job and it would provide a stopgap while the second new carrier was brought into service. But he did not want a desk job, and there was no way that Lucy would move to Italy. Lucy was committed to her teaching position and had made it clear that she would be livid if her husband joined one of the new carriers.

While he pondered his options, he also gave some thought to Stan's offer at the boatyard, and that was a factor that eventually swayed his decision. It would be fun to muck about on boats during the spring, he thought. Stan had made the offer in a light-hearted moment, and it might not amount to anything, but there was a slim chance that the temporary job might allow him to wheedle his way into Commander Woods's trials team.

So after talking it over with his wife, Mark reluctantly accepted early retirement. This was a bitter pill for the once-ambitious naval officer to swallow. While his naval career had been successful by most standards, his achievements were a pale shadow of his forbears and scarcely matched those of his younger sister. He bitterly regretted that he would not take command of a warship.

Lucy was overjoyed with Mark's decision, but husband and wife realised they would have to economise. With a small navy pension and Lucy's modest teaching salary, the couple would be just able to make ends meet – but they would have to forgo luxuries. So, having made the wrenching decision, Mark got in touch with Commander Woods to ask whether there were any vacancies in his team.

The approach was no surprise to the commander, because he had been following Mark's progress with interest. This was not difficult, because the dying hulk of the aircraft carrier dominated the skyline from his office window. The commander was impressed with Mark's leadership skills but doubted that he had the intellectual capacity for his trials team.

In a modern world, the performance of a new craft needed to be assessed in an analytical manner. This called for an understanding of fluids mechanics and other scientific subjects. Most members of the trials team held postgraduate degrees. While the commander did not feel that Mark had the academic ability to join this elite group, he thought that Mark would be a useful man to have about the place. When the commander discussed this with the admiral, the old fox shared his opinion.

So the commander did not want to frighten Mark away with an outright rejection. "We do not have any vacancies at the moment. There might be another job better suited to your talents," remarked the commander when Mark phoned him. In the friendly conversation that followed, Mark mentioned that he might take a holiday job at the boatyard at Whitebait Cove. The commander was intrigued and asked Mark to keep in touch. This information was relayed to the admiral.

Mark was attracted by the prospect of pottering around on boats in springtime. It was like a romantic dream after a depressing winter watching the old carrier being stripped apart. In any event, the job would provide a useful stopgap as he found his feet ashore and searched for a permanent job. But Stan's offer had only been made in casual and light-hearted manner, and might not amount to anything. Furthermore, Lucy warned him that Stan might not take kindly to Mark's presence at the boatyard. He might view the naval officer as a threat to his position.

So, rather than approach the club treasurer direct, Mark put out feelers. He asked Lucy to have a quiet word with Stan's wife, to gauge the temperature. The result of her enquiries was intriguing. "Stan exaggerated his importance at the yard and he is not in a position to offer you a job," remarked Lucy, with a downcast expression. "But the old boy is retiring, and the yard is looking for someone to replace him!" she added after a pause for dramatic effect. "You need to send in your application in writing," she added encouragingly.

The somewhat slap-dash approach to recruiting adopted by Sam Wheeler had been replaced by a formal process taking account of equal opportunity rules. So Lucy helped her husband to draw up a curriculum vitae that would give him a fighting chance of winning the job. But they faced an enormous challenge because most other applicants had a track record in that type of work. It was only as the result of a chance conversation between Commander Woods and the chief executive at the yard, Steve Jones, that Mark reached the final round.

"I understand that you are looking for a new harbour master," remarked the commander as he chatted to Steve on the phone one day. "Bit of a coincidence that, because one of our chaps has put in an application. Good chap, called Mark Dexter. He decided to take early retirement from the service so he could stay close to his family. The fellow deserves a break." After the phone call, Steve was curious to know how the newly retired officer's application had fared. The first phase of the recruitment process to weed out unsuitable candidates was delegated to one of his administrative staff.

So Steve stopped by the administrative office on his way home. He found two stacks of applications with Mark's application in the 'reject' stack. It soon became obvious that all those in the 'call for interview' stack had experience of managing ports for coastal shipping, in accordance with the job description. The reference to coastal shipping on the job description was a hangover from the days of Sam Wheeler when the quay had been used to load and discharge small cargo ships. The job description needed to be updated, thought Steve.

The harbour at Whitebait Cove was no longer used for cargo movements, but it was shortly to be used for naval trials, so the following morning he spoke to his recruiting assistant and explained that the job description needed to be revised to take account of the forthcoming naval trial. The job now called for experience of naval operations. So the weeding-out process was repeated. When Steve next checked the applications the following day, he was satisfied to see that Mark's particulars had now been transferred to the top of the 'call for interview' pile.

The retired naval officer was now the favoured candidate for the simple reason that none of the other candidates had experience of naval procedures. Steve felt slightly uneasy that he had interfered with the interview process, but he managed to persuade himself that he had done so in an ethical way. When Mark was interviewed, he had little trouble impressing the selection panel with his knowledge and experience.

He was offered the job and arrangements were made for him to start work at the yard as soon as he was released from the navy. It was decided that he would work alongside Stan while he 'learned the ropes'. Mark was slightly apprehensive about this transition period, in the belief that the older man would resent his presence at the yard.

While the commander was gratified to hear of Mark's appointment, this benign sentiment was not felt by the incumbent harbour master. Stan suspected that the navy had ganged up to oust him from his position, so he greeted his replacement in a cold and offhand way. Stan had enjoyed unchallenged authority on the waterfront since Sam Wheeler's days, and he did not take kindly to the interloper. The proud club treasurer thought that Mark had taken advantage of his friendship and gave the new posh bloke short shrift.

Experiencing a growing sense of animosity at the yard, Mark breathed a sigh of relief when Stan was finally shown the door. But this left the newly retired naval officer with massive headaches, because his predecessor had not taken the trouble to impart his knowledge or experience. But Mark was at least free to do things in his own way, whether he made mistakes or not. Little did the poor fellow know that he had become embroiled in an undercover plot that was being orchestrated by the admiral from his home in leafy Hampshire.

Chapter 7

The Admiral Pulls Strings

Rear-Admiral Sir Richard Walters took special interest in the submarine rescue project, after crossing paths with the young Martin Beckwith at his boarding school. After rising through the ranks, Walters was Commander-in-Chief (C-in-C) of the Special Ships Group. This was a motley flotilla of unorthodox and downright weird naval craft based near Gosport. The C-in-C's formal title was a bit of a mouthful, so his staff referred to Walters as the 'Admiral'.

The wily old fox spent most of his time pottering around his garden in a leafy Hampshire village. He would venture out from time to time to advise the government on defence policy. His group also acted in a liaison role with commercial shipping and performed a range of other functions, such as testing unusual naval craft. One of their most challenging roles had been to prepare merchant ships for the Falkland War.

At first sight, the Admiral appeared like a bumbling school teacher. His *laissez faire* attitude allowed disciplinary standards to slip on the base. Critics remarked that the C-in-C could 'not run a bath' without the support of his formidable secretary, Caroline Haywood. The 'Dragon', as she was known, was a tall, upright woman who ran the base with ruthless efficiency.

But behind the Admiral's bumbling image lay a sharp mind. Victims of his cunning schemes warned the unwary to count their fingers when they shook hands with the crafty devil. He was well informed, thanks to friendships forged during his boarding school days. The sly old fox cultivated an obtuse manner so that his adversaries let their guard down. If Beckwith had heeded this warning, he would have acted in a more circumspect manner, not least because the midget submarine would make a handy addition to the Admiral's small fleet.

Walters encountered Beckwith as a new boy at his boarding school. As a prefect, Walters formed the view that young Beckwith lacked moral fibre and mixed in bad company. After leaving school, Walters followed the young lad's progress with a mixture of incredulity, distaste and faint amusement. He watched the awkward, gangling youth morph into a left-wing rabble-rouser. But amusement turned to rage when Walters saw an inflammatory polemic penned by his fellow pupil. The article blamed the ills of the nation on the malign influence of the 'old-school network'.

Beckwith's bizarre antics became a topic of conversation at old boys' reunions. It was at one of those events that Walters was shown another polemic entitled: *Kursk disaster highlights needs for improved submarine rescue capabilities*. The article was written by a well-known journalist, but the article had Beckwith's fingerprints all over it. It expressed the view that the navy was run by a bunch of 'technical dinosaurs'. It was shortly after this article was published that Beckwith put forward his proposal for a submarine rescue vehicle employing fuel-cell propulsion.

If approved, this would be the first construction project for the newly established Marine Special Projects Agency (MSPA). To gain support, Beckwith embarked on a high-profile media campaign portraying him as a hero in a 'David and Goliath' struggle with the navy top brass. The campaign won support from left-wing politicians, but to achieve his aim, the academic also needed to persuade the naval procurement committee of the benefits.

The submariners were lukewarm about Beckwith's scheme, so the procurement committee consulted the Admiral, in his role as government adviser. This played right into the Admiral's hands because he had other purposes in mind for the midget submarine. He could not show his hand at the outset, but with the casting vote, the crafty old fox held the whip hand.

So, playing things by the book, the Admiral asked his subordinate, Commander Woods, to carry out a technical assessment of the project. He did so without telling the commander that he had another purpose in mind for the midget submarine. But the crafty old fox told the commander to address two separate issues in two ways. The first issue was whether fuel-cell propulsion was viable. The second was whether there was a need for a new rescue craft. The final report came in two parts.

The first part of the commander's report described fuel-cell propulsion as a 'promising technology' for the next generation of midget submarines. The second part questioned the need for a new rescue vehicle and raised concerns about the need for special fuel when performing rescue missions. When the Admiral received the report, he forwarded the first (positive) section to the procurement committee but 'lost' the second (negative) section. This part of the report was never seen again. The Admiral refrained from confiding his motive for this devious move to the commander.

In his covering letter to the committee, the Admiral echoed the commander's praise for fuel-cell propulsion but he then added that it was not his place to comment on the need for a new submarine rescue vehicle. *This is a matter for the submarine service*, he wrote. Oblivious to the fuel supply concerns contained in the second (lost) section of the report, the committee approved Beckwith's scheme. The press release announcing their decision emphasised the rescue role, saying that it would benefit all maritime nations.

The commander wrongly assumed that both sections of his report had been passed to the procurement committee, so he was astounded to learn that the project had been given the go-ahead. It was at that point that he described his superior officer as a 'dithering old fool'. Oblivious to what was taking place behind his back, the commander was set up as a dupe.

When the commander aired his concerns in public, he was branded a 'technical dinosaur' by Beckwith. The Admiral failed to ease the commander's discomfort. Quite the reverse. When the Admiral heard the caustic comments describing him as a 'dithering old fool', it amused him. The remark suited his strategy. The old fox had some tricks up his sleeve and did not want to show his cards just yet.

Some of the Admiral's inner circle suggested that the midget submarine should be acquired through official channels. But this was not possible because the government had authorised the project on the understanding that it would be used for submarine rescue operations. To further complicate matters, Beckwith wanted to retain ownership of 'his' midget submarine to justify the continued life of his newly established agency. The academic would fight tooth and nail to retain 'his' creation. To add another layer of complication, there were other branches of the navy that coveted the revolutionary craft.

This was just the sort of puzzle that the old fox enjoyed and he decided to play a waiting game. He knew the ambitious academic would overplay his hand at some stage. When he did, the Admiral would pounce. While he waited, the Admiral pulled strings from the sidelines. His first move was to prevent Beckwith from obtaining the military-grade equipment needed for the submarine rescue role. This was fairly simple to achieve, because the Admiral was on friendly terms with the firms that supplied these fittings. So all he had to do was hint that future orders might be jeopardised if they supplied Beckwith's project.

The Admiral's shrewdest move, however, was to ensure the commander took charge of the sea trials of the midget submarine. This allowed the wily old fox to keep an eye on things. Achieving this called for some guile because the sea trials would normally be carried out by the submarine service. But the Admiral concocted a story that his trial team would be better able to cope with the revolutionary fuel-cell propulsion system.

While all this was going on, the Admiral was studying emerging maritime threats. His brief was to find unorthodox, cost-effective solutions. With budget constraints, the navy's fleet was contracting. The government was struggling to fund the new aircraft carriers and other construction programmes. There was much talk of 'asymmetric threats'. This led some cynics to question the value of the 'vanity projects'.

Naval strategists were concerned with refugee problems in the Mediterranean, rising tensions in the Persian Gulf and Russian activity in the Baltic. It was thought that the Russians were using midget submarines for covert surveillance along the Baltic coast. While some of these reports were alarmist and fell into the 'false news' category, the drip-drip of news raised fears over the vulnerability of pipelines and cables on the seabed.

When the navy top brass raised these concerns with the government, ministers pointed to the huge construction programmes and refused to release additional funds. So, in his advisory role, the Admiral set out to find an alternative source of finance. His liaison role with merchant shipping companies was particularly valuable in this respect. The navy had a long history of cooperation with the shipping industry.

The Admiral had been inspired by a book describing 'Q-ships' during the war. This involved fitting battered old cargo ships with concealed weapons. With a limited stock of torpedoes, a submarine commander would not want to waste a torpedo on an old rust bucket. So, rather than fire a torpedo, the submarine would surface to attack the innocent-looking ship with its deck gun. Having lured the submarine to the surface, the 'decoy ship' would then uncover its weapons and return fire.

After reading this, the Admiral toyed with the idea of using a somewhat similar arrangement for covert surveillance in hijack-infested waters off the Horn of Africa. Commercial vessels could be adapted in some way to assist the naval forces. An arrangement of that sort might help plug the gap when warships were withdrawn from the region. But the details of the scheme needed to be hammered out in cooperation with the shipping industry.

Over the years, the Admiral had developed close relationships with influential figures in the shipping world. So he wrote suggesting that a brain-storming session should be held in the heart of the City of London. Soon afterwards, a small band of maritime experts gathered in a dingy office in Fenchurch Street. The focus of their first session was to discuss the recovery of ships that had been captured – this remained an intractable problem even for naval forces present on the scene. Once ships were captured, it had proved almost impossible to recover them without ransom payment. At that time, a couple of ships remained under pirate control anchored off the coast of Somalia.

The shipping experts approached the talks with reluctance because the question of ransom was a delicate subject. Shipowners tended to approach this in a pragmatic manner, believing that the safety of a ship's crew outweighed ethical questions. This set them at odds with the government, whose policy was to refuse payment under any circumstances, so the mariners expected to receive a dressing-down from officials.

The group of maritime experts comprised a shipping executive, an insurance underwriter, a master mariner, a chief engineer and a naval officer. The gathering was overseen by some youthful civil servants who made little contribution to the discussion. The first session was chaired by Lieutenant Robert Bracknell, who represented the navy.

The naval officer opened the meeting with a presentation of anti-piracy operations. The civil servants took notes in a studious manner throughout the session. After providing an overview of the situation, Bracknell explained the practical problems. He explained that modern frigates were unsuitable for the sort of close-quarters operations that were needed to recover captured ships. A boarding party on a helicopter or rigid inflatable boat would be vulnerable to gunfire.

After explaining the practical difficulties of recovering a captured ship, Bracknell reminded the mariners of ways in which shipping companies had cooperated with the navy over the years. During his presentation, he outlined the role of Q-ships to illustrate his point. The mariners listened politely to the presentation but had little to contribute. The press-ganged group felt they had spent the morning in a schoolroom.

The mood lightened, a touch, when the meeting adjourned for lunch. Released from the dingy room, the mariners engaged in banter on their way to a City pub. With common background, they quickly bonded outside of earshot of the youthful civil servants. "My guess is that those guys were spooks," suggested the master mariner. This was met with guffaws from his companions. But this led on to a running joke in which the callow civil servants were compared with film stars from the Bond movies.

After their liquid lunch, they returned in a mischievous mood, and the running joke kept them entertained for the rest of the afternoon. During this session, they exchanged notes with rude remarks. In this subversive atmosphere, they began to explore outlandish ideas, some serious, and others humorous. When these ideas were aired, most were dismissed out of hand, but one held promise. This involved approaching a captured ship from underwater.

"We could use some subsea equipment that has been made available by the slump in the offshore industry," suggested the insurance underwriter in a tentative way. The mariners were aware that the offshore contractors used all manner of sophisticated equipment to work on the seabed, but none of them were expert in the subject, so the meeting was adjourned while the civil servants looked for expert help.

The Admiral was delighted with the outcome of the meeting, because it paralleled his own thinking on the subject. The wily old fox knew that people resented having plans thrust upon them. He believed that it was better if they came up with their own solutions. But there was no harm in nudging them towards the midget submarine concept that he was keen to employ, so Commander Woods was despatched to speed things along. The Admiral was confident that he would steer the team in the right direction, even though he did not appreciate what the Admiral had in mind.

The Admiral had high regard for the commander's ability as a naval officer but thought that the 'war hero' tag had gone to his head. "The commander can be a bit of a prig," he remarked to his secretary in a peevish moment. "He needs bringing down a peg or two." This was the reason why the old fox accidentally 'lost' the second section of the commander's assessment of the submarine rescue project.

The old fox knew that the loss of a key section of the report would cause the commander grief, and took impish delight in watching the tussle between the vainglorious subordinate and the subversive academic that it generated. The vicarious pleasure he gained from watching their feud was somewhat akin to that which his ancestors derived from watching a cockfight. While gently steering his subordinate in the right direction, the Admiral had no intention of confiding his plans to the commander just yet.

To help the process along, the Admiral invited the commander to his home for a 'glass of sherry'. The old fox wanted to plant a few ideas that might set him off on the right track. The commander welcomed the invitation, believing that the social evening would be a chance to clear the air. Their relationship was, understandably, frosty, by this time, given the Admiral's underhand dealings. But the commander had not had a chance to argue his corner.

Most of their dealings took place on the naval base under the Dragon's unnerving scrutiny. The commander did not have a chance to speak openly on those formal occasions, because the Admiral's secretary, Caroline Haywood, ruled the roost in his office. Staff on the naval base lived in fear of her vicious tongue.

The Admiral was a widower, and he lived alone in a Victorian rectory set in a large garden in the heart of a village in the Hampshire countryside. A plump, jolly woman came in each day from the village, to cook for him and clean his home. When the commander arrived, the old boy was pottering around in his greenhouse dressed in corduroy trousers and a jacket with worn sleeves. The sight confirmed the commander's view that his superior officer was a 'dithering old fool'. The old boy was busy removing side shoots from his beloved tomato plants when the commander arrived.

When finally satisfied with his pruning, the old boy put down his tools and sauntered into the drawing room with the commander trailing behind. The genial old boy showed his guest to an armchair and left him to wash his hands. On his return, the Admiral poured two small glasses of sherry. He tried to set his guest at ease with small talk about the garden.

"It's been a good year for the tomatoes," he said proudly. The commander tried to show an interest for the sake of politeness but had little to contribute. "Do you garden?" asked his host at length.

"No, never had the chance," replied the commander brusquely.

"Every man should have a hobby," remarked the old boy as he sat quietly watching the setting sun. Then, as if a fleeting thought occurred to him, the Admiral turned to business.

"Before I forget," said the Admiral, "I had a call from a salesman chappy yesterday. He asked me about your submarine rescue project. It seems that his company is worried about the propulsion system that you are using. He wanted my assurance that the newfangled propulsion system will work. The company don't want to end up with egg on their face if the project turns out to be a fiasco. What are your thoughts?"

The commander had been getting steadily more frustrated by the old boy's lackadaisical manner and could hardly contain his rage at that foolish observation. It was not 'his' project and he had warned about the risks of using fuel-cell propulsion for rescue operations in the second part of his report. The second part of that document laid out his objections in great detail, but it seemed that these warnings had fallen on deaf ears. What really infuriated the decorated war hero was that it was only after the prompting of some 'salesman chappy' that his superior officer had taken the matter seriously. If it had been anyone else, the commander would have given him a piece of his mind.

The commander did not normally mince his words, whether he was speaking to the First Sea Lord or lowest rating on board the ship. But he was disarmed by the congenial atmosphere and the Admiral's whimsical behaviour, so he tried to frame his response in a diplomatic way. Taking a deep breath, he explained, once again, why he believed fuel-cell propulsion was unsuitable for the submarine rescue operations. "I've been worried about this project from the very start," he concluded after setting out his arguments. "I think that Beckwith is using this project to advance his career, and not for the benefit of the navy."

The Admiral listened thoughtfully as he toyed with his glass of sherry. "It's not really my business," commented the old boy airily. "We know Beckwith's a scoundrel. But he is a clever so-and-so and has political support in Westminster, so we have to live with him for the time being. But I just wanted to warn you that there are storm clouds on the horizon. There is a risk that the suppliers will withhold vital equipment if they are not satisfied that the submarine's propulsion system is sound. Beckwith won't be able to complete his project."

"What exactly does the company supply?" asked the commander with a puzzled expression. "Beckwith can probably get the parts from someone else."

"The company supplies the hatches and docking systems for rescue operations," replied the old fox with a knowing expression. "From what I understand, you can't carry out a submarine rescue without those bits. Beckwith won't be able to get the equipment anywhere else." The Admiral's sudden interest in this subject puzzled the commander, given the scant interest in the report he had written, so he probed to see if there was a deeper motive for his remark.

"I'm sure that Beckwith has thought of that," observed the commander. "A single supplier can't stop someone building a submarine."

"Well, that's *not* quite true," replied the Admiral. "The midget submarine will not be able to dock with a disabled naval submarine without the special equipment that they manufacture. As you know, the hatch and docking system need to be built to military standards to ensure they mate properly." This took the wind out of the commander's sails. He wondered how the Admiral had acquired such detailed knowledge of an arcane technical issue.

Realising that the whimsical old fox was not quite as daft as he appeared, the commander put aside his grievances for the moment and settled back to enjoy his glass of sherry. "Of course, the midget submarine could be used for another purpose," he speculated, at length. "Then you would not need the special hatches." As he made the remark, he was watching the sunlight reflected though the auburn leaves of the trees in a nearby copse. It was a glorious spectacle.

"Yes. That thought has just occurred to me," replied the Admiral obtusely, with the barest hint of a smile. The light from the setting sun reflected from the angular features of his face.

"Has the "salesman chappy" put his view in writing?" asked the commander as he tried to figure out precisely what the crafty old devil was up to. As he made that remark, he watched the old boy closely, trying to read his thoughts.

"Not yet. The company is trying to decide its position," replied the Admiral. "It would be a great pity if Beckwith's project hit the buffers, but we need to prepare for the worst," he added sardonically with all the assumed sympathy of an undertaker. Then after savouring that bitter-sweet thought, he continued. "Perhaps we could find another use for Beckwith's midget submarine?" he suggested with a wicked grin.

"Yes, perhaps we could!" concurred the commander as he tried to guess what the old fox was up to. A vista of possibilities suddenly opened up. The undertones of their discussion had forced the commander to reassess his opinion of the 'dithering old fool'. But before he had a chance to probe the old fox's motives any further, his host changed tack. "Anyway, that's enough about your rescue project. That is not really my affair!" declared the old boy brightly.

"The real reason that I asked you over is that I've got a job for you. I'd like you to go to a meeting with some shipping folk next week. They are discussing the hijack situation in the Indian Ocean. As you know, the government wants shipping companies to contribute to the protection force. That will allow us to move our warships to the Med. It's just an exploratory meeting, you know. A chance to kick some ideas around. I'd appreciate it if you would sit in and report back."

"Be my pleasure," replied the commander. "Are there any points you want me to make?"

"No, not really," said the Admiral casually. "Just be my eyes and ears and report back what they are talking about." As the commander got up to leave, the old fox looked him squarely in the eye. "Please don't tell anyone else about the salesman's comments. We don't want 'our friend' to get the wrong end of the stick!" he instructed in a quiet but forceful way.

The commander was left puzzled by the strange meeting. The Admiral was protective of his privacy, and few staff were invited to his home. The meeting was an unusual honour, so the commander was in a conciliatory and pensive mood as he returned home. It was obvious that he was an unwitting player in some elaborate game. But he had no idea what was going on.

The commander was disappointed when he arrived for the meeting in Fenchurch Street. He was expecting to hobnob with the high and mighty of the shipping world in a plush boardroom. Instead, he entered a dingy room occupied by a grizzled gang of mariners under the watchful eye of a couple of callow young civil servants. The only person he recognised was Lieutenant Robert Bracknell. The pair had both been involved in a naval exercise a few months earlier. As they waited for the second session to start, the lieutenant explained the situation to his senior colleague, but he did not get very far before they were asked to take their seats.

"We have been joined today by James McCredie, a subsea engineer; by Phillip King, a naval historian; and by Commander Woods from the navy," explained the bumptious civil servant who was acting as chairman of the meeting. The civil servant then went on to summarise the deliberations of the previous session. It emerged that Phillip King had written the book about Q-ships which had inspired the Admiral's plans. The session opened with a description of some subsea achievements in the North Sea and Gulf of Mexico.

James McCredie explained that most operations were now carried out on the seabed with submersible vehicles. The vehicles were normally controlled via an umbilical cable and were able to hover or 'fly' in any direction under control from the surface. He outlined the wide range of tools that could be used by these remote operated vehicles. Once they had absorbed this information, the old sea dogs started to speculate whether these subsea tools could help them to recover a captured ship.

McCredie was asked if it would be feasible to cut a hole below the waterline of a captured ship and attach some form of entry hatch. This was not considered feasible. The subsea expert pointed out that restrictions in the length of an umbilical cable meant that a support ship would need to be stationed within sight of the captured ship.

"The umbilical cable delivers electric power and control signals from the host vessel to the ROV," he explained patiently. "Of course, the industry has developed autonomous vehicles that can submerge and follow a programmed path without an umbilical cable. They are only used to survey the seabed at the moment, but there is a huge research and development effort to extend their capabilities."

They went on to discuss diving, with McCredie describing suits that allowed divers to operate in 'one-atmosphere' conditions and eliminated the need for decompression. As a newcomer, the commander had little to contribute to the discussion. But as he sat twiddling his thumbs, he recalled the Admiral's throw-away remark about using Beckwith's midget submarine for another role, so he asked the subsea expert what he knew about midget submarines. "That's a bit outside my field, I'm afraid," replied McCredie. "We don't use manned submarines in our business. They tend to be used for deep ocean research or tourist trips."

At that point, the chairman asked Phillip King to pick up the discussion. King proceeded with a presentation about the role of midget submarines during World War II. In his presentation, the naval historian outlined how a fleet of midget submarines attacked a German battleship while it was moored in a sheltered anchorage.

"Each of the X-craft was fitted with an airlock to allow divers to enter the water," explained King with an authoritative air. "This allowed the divers to cut through the steel mesh barrage that guarded the entrance to the harbour. The divers also released mines that were attached on each side of the X-craft. The mines were dropped on the seabed beside the battleship and were set to detonate after the X-craft had made its escape."

King was an engaging speaker, and it was for this reason that he appeared on TV from time to time. The old sea dogs were fascinated by his stories. This led to a lively discussion during the coffee break about the possible role of midget submarines for recovering hijacked ships.

But the commander was unsure how much he could reveal to outsiders about the submarine rescue project. This placed him in an invidious position. So, recalling the old maxim 'to use his initiative,' when the meeting reconvened, the commander raised his hand to make his first contribution. "It's *just* possible that a midget submarine might become available," he speculated to the astonishment of those present. He had no authority to make this offer, but his words dovetailed neatly with King's presentation about X-craft.

This led to excited discussion of some outlandish ideas. In this feverish atmosphere, the commander realised he had overstepped the mark. He had no idea whether he could trust this group of strangers, so when the mariners pressed him for more details he chose his words with great care. "Please don't take this as a firm offer," he urged. "All I'm saying is that it *might be possible* to lay our hands on a midget submarine. It's an outside chance. I'll raise the subject with my superiors."

The commander's vague suggestion put the cat among the pigeons – it raised more questions than answers. The mariners did not know whether a midget submarine would be available or not. When pressed for clarification, the commander was forced to retreat from the room. He needed to speak to the Admiral to get his views. But when he phoned the naval base, he was told that his superior was away, and he should call again the following morning. The absence confirmed his suspicion that the crafty old fox had set him up.

With the commander's departure, the meeting adjourned for lunch, and the assembly split into different factions. The subsea engineer made his apologies, saying that he had to return to his office. Lieutenant Robert Bracknell remained in the conference room, as he wanted to speak to the commander when he returned. With nothing to hold them back, the mariners asked the naval historian to join them for a session at a City pub. In the cheerful banter on their way to the pub, the commander was dubbed 'Q' for his role in supplying exotic gadgets.

After making his phone call, the commander returned to the dingy room, where he found the lieutenant sitting alone. All the others had departed for lunch. The pair of naval officers were both hungry and so they headed outside to buy sandwiches. The streets were thronged with office workers and it was impossible for them to speak. But when they returned to the dingy room, the lieutenant could see the commander was wrestling with a dilemma.

In the belief that it would be safe to confide in a fellow officer, the commander explained his predicament. After briefly outlining the submarine rescue project, he continued. "The project has run into a problem. It seems that they may not be able to obtain the military-grade hatches and docking systems needed for rescue operations."

"I can't see that would be too much of a problem," observed the lieutenant.

"Neither do I," admitted the commander. "But the Admiral thinks it's important. I suspect that the old devil is up to something. He made a remark about looking for alternative roles for the midget submarine." Then after a pause, he added, "I'm beginning to think that is why he asked me to attend this meeting."

"How on earth can we get our hands on the midget submarine?" asked the lieutenant doubtfully. "You know what the Whitehall pen-pushers are like. The Admiral will have to go through channels. There must be other branches of the navy who want to use the craft."

"He's a devious old so-and-so. I haven't a clue what he is planning!" replied the commander dejectedly. They sat in companionable silence as they chomped their food and pondered the issue.

"It reminds me of an incident in the desert a couple of years back," observed the lieutenant with a humorous expression. "I was acting as liaison officer to a squad of marines. They wanted a drum of cable for one of their operations. They put in an official request at the army base, but it was turned down by the quartermaster. There was a big row. Seemed unlikely that they would succeed.

"But the squad would not accept no for an answer, so a couple of lads simply drove to the base, cut through the wire fence and nicked a drum of cable. The paperwork was in such a mess and the stores did not miss the cable for a week. There was a bit of a stink, of course, but in the end, they blamed the Arabs. The local tribes would nick anything that was not bolted down. They are always after cable because of the value of scrap copper."

The tale amused the commander. He admired the

lieutenant's 'can-do' spirit, contrasting it with that of the modern generation, who refuse to take risks and insist on doing everything by the book. It was at that moment that the idea of stealing the midget submarine took root in the commander's mind. It seemed a preposterous idea. But the crazy notion brightened his mood during the afternoon session.

The mariners' liquid lunch was a lot less raucous than their previous outing. The notion that they might acquire a midget submarine gave them a sense of purpose, and the naval historian had a calming influence on the unruly gang. The mariners appreciated the historian's seafaring tales and treated him like an honoured guest. The gang had little trouble finding a table in the once bustling bar. The bars and restaurants were almost deserted as a result of alcohol restrictions imposed by City institutions.

On their way to the pub, the mariners contributed to a pool and the insurance broker was 'volunteered' to place their food and drink orders at the counter. As the rest of the party waited at a table, they revived the running joke about the civil servants. "Commander Woods could be 'Q,'" remarked one wag. "You know. The boffin who supplies the spying kit."

When the historian heard this remark, he asked whether any of the party had heard of Q-ships. "It's my pet subject," he declared eagerly, "but I was asked to give a talk about midget submarines."

Keen to learn more, the mariners egged him on. With that, the marine historian explained how old cargo ships were fitted with concealed armament during the war. "The guns were camouflaged so the vessels appeared like run-down tramp steamers or trawlers. These Q-ships were manned by naval personnel, but they were disguised to look like a rabble of scruffy seamen. They lured submarines to the surface, where they could be destroyed."

The insurance broker who was ordering drinks at the bar caught part of the discussion. When he returned to their table, he put in his two pennies' worth. "I expect the Germans knew what we were up to!" he commented cynically.

"No. You are wrong!" retorted the celebrated author. "The government went to a lot of trouble to keep the role of those ships secret!" Then to emphasise his point, he asked, "Have you heard the story of the 'secret VC'?" He then regaled the party with a story about the Victoria Cross awarded to Lieutenant-Commander Gordon Campbell, who was commander of the decoy ship *Farnborough*.

"As skipper of the decoy ship, Campbell deliberately provoked an attack from a submarine that was lurking in the area. When the decoy ship was struck by a torpedo, the engines were shut down, the boiler vented and some of the crew took to the lifeboats as though they were abandoning ship. Reacting to this carefully staged ruse, the submarine commander surfaced to finish off the disabled ship, but some of the crew remained on board the decoy ship. They opened fire on the submarine. The engines were then restarted, and the decoy ship rammed the submarine and sank her. Campbell was awarded a Victoria Cross for his heroism."

"All very interesting but what has that got to do with us?" commented the insurance broker. The marine historian was unfazed by this cynical observation.

"Well, the decoy ship operations were surrounded by strict secrecy at the time, and so the reason for the VC was never made public," continued the marine historian smoothly. "The medal was described as the 'mystery VC' in the press of the day. The navy did not want the enemy to learn the purpose of these decoy ships. It was only after the war ended that the public learned the truth about the incident."

As the food arrived, they began to speculate about whether a decoy ship could be used in some way to protect other merchant vessels from hijackers. That idea was met with scepticism. One problem was that pirates would be suspicious of an apparently innocent-looking cargo ship loitering in pirate-infested waters. Shipping movements are well known to the pirate gangs off the Horn of Africa, so any unusual behaviour of a ship would soon become common knowledge in the pirate hideouts. With that, they reluctantly set off to the dingy conference room.

On the way, a taciturn master mariner, who been listening carefully to the conversation, broke his silence. "A suction dredger might be the answer you are looking for," he suggested quietly. "A ship like that would not look out of place loitering in pirate-infested waters. It would be only natural to have security guards onboard.

"A trailing-arm dredger is designed to suck up spoil from the seabed," he explained in an authoritative manner. "The spoil is fed into hoppers, where it is stored until it is dumped onto the seabed somewhere else. You could easily conceal a midget submersible among the tangle of pumps, pipes and hoppers below decks."

Picking up on the commander's remark that a midget submarine might be made available, the mariners put together a plan. In this scheme, the submarine would be concealed at the base of a hopper. The midget submarine could be launched through the hinged cargo doors, similar to those used to dump spoil onto the seabed.

While this appeared an outlandish scheme, the mariners agreed that it deserved further study. It all depended on whether the commander could provide the midget submarine, and whether they could raise the funding. The funding would have to be raised from private sources, given the government cut-backs. After kicking some ideas around, the outline began to emerge.

The operation would be run by a tight-knit team working on a commercial basis at arm's length from the defence ministry. This would avoid unnecessary bureaucracy. To keep costs down, they would recruit retired seafarers. There was a huge pool of suitable people. It was thought the older seafarers would be less likely to spread news of their activity by social media. This would help ensure that news of their operation did not leak to the pirates.

On their return to the dingy conference room, the mariners were bursting to explain their outlandish plan to the naval officers who had remained behind. As the feasibility of the scheme hinged on whether the commander could provide a midget submarine, they pressed him, once again, to clarify his position. But the war hero refused to give them an answer. This put a damper on things, the discussion petered out, and the meeting was adjourned.

As the mariners drifted away, the commander stayed behind to talk to the civil servants who had organised the affair. Like the mariners, he harboured suspicions that the callow youths belonged to the secret service. They would not give him a straight answer on that point, but he did learn that they were attached to the Cabinet Office and prepared briefings on matters of national security. The commander was surprised that their deliberations should interest the inner circle of government.

In the course of the conversation, the commander learned that there was great concern about the capability of the naval fleet as a result of a House of Commons committee inquiry. The report by the Defence Committee noted that with just nineteen frigates and destroyers, the size of the naval fleet 'was at a dangerous and a historic low'. The shortage of warships was made worse by problems with the all-electric propulsion system fitted to the most modern frigates. The media had started to ask awkward questions, so senior government figures hoped that the shipping industry would help plug the gap.

The commander was summoned to the Admiral's home to brief him on the meeting. As he waited to see the wily old fox, he began to develop cold feet over his rash suggestion that a midget submarine might be made available to the shipping people. The remark was made on the spur of the moment, but in the cold light of day he realised that he had greatly exceeded his authority and had misled the shipping people.

Feeling a bit sheepish, the commander provided a slightly watered-down version of events when he finally met up with his superior officer. "We explored some ideas based on naval experience with decoy ships during the war," explained the commander disingenuously. But this sanitised account of the meeting did not tally with what the Admiral had heard through the grapevine.

"You haven't told me the full story, young man!" barked the wily old fox, with a knowing gleam in his eye. "I heard that you offered them a midget submarine."

The commander wondered just how much more his superior knew. To clear his throat, he swallowed some lager. The Admiral was serving canned lager on that hot, humid evening, rather than his usual sherry. He did not care too much for its taste, but it would be rude to refuse the proffered drink. After bracing himself, he delivered a more accurate account of what had taken place. But in his desperate effort to escape censure, he became tongue-tied.

"The mariners discussed what they might be able to achieve *if* a midget submarine could be made available," he explained in a pedantic manner. "I did *not promise them anything,* nor did I reveal any details of the submarine rescue project." He then went on to speak in general terms about the meeting, noting the presence of young civil servants from the Cabinet Office.

The commander was braced for a tongue-lashing but, instead, the old fox congratulated him with a smile. "Well done!" remarked the old fox briskly. Then, after refilling their glasses, the Admiral added: "We need to keep this between ourselves for the time being." With that, the Admiral changed the subject, moving on to matters of little consequence. The cunning old fox was still reluctant to confide his ambition to acquire the midget submarine.

The commander was in a mischievous mood when he returned home from the meeting that night. As he lay in bed, he dreamed about stealing the submarine from under the nose of the obnoxious academic. But how to get away with it? *We could always say that the submarine sank during the trials*, he speculated. But he dismissed that idea because it would be easy to search the seabed for the wreck. It was at that point that he recalled the lieutenant's amusing tale about the theft of copper cable in the desert.

That might have been the end of the story if the commander had not learned that a parcel of property at the abandoned Portland naval base was to be sold. The parcel consisted of a small wharf and a large warehouse. It would be the ideal place to conceal the purloined submarine.

Chapter 8

A Texan Takes Charge

While the commander was dreaming of ways of purloining the midget submarine, the creator of this revolutionary craft was having problems of his own. When the project was launched, Beckwith had unfettered control, thanks to the supine nature of the supervisory board. When he established the Marine Special Projects Agency (MSPA), the crafty academic ensured that a majority of the board members would do his bidding. Several events conspired to upset this agreeable scenario.

The first setback was a change of government, with the new administration intent on reducing the budget deficit. In an era of austerity, the friendly government appointee was replaced by a hard-nosed accountant who took a red pen to the agency's spending plans. There followed a second blow when a cooperative board member suffered a heart attack. So, with the loss of these two allies, Beckwith was subject to scrutiny.

Matters came to a head when the board learned that the project was running behind schedule and that it would not be possible to purchase the equipment needed to dock the rescue vehicle onto a disabled submarine. The supplier gave the impression it would supply the specialised docking equipment but then declined to provide a quotation. The reluctance to quote was a mystery. But it later emerged that the company was wary of fuel-cell propulsion and did not want to damage its reputation by becoming involved in a risky project.

After receiving the bad news, there was a stormy board meeting. During the discussion, the hard-nosed accountant made a scathing attack on the management of the project. When a vote was called, the board voted to replace Beckwith as project manager. The artful academic was seething with rage at his unceremonious dismissal.

But the vote did not affect Beckwith's position as head of the Marine Special Project Agency (MSPA). So the academic retained that figurehead role for the time being, and this allowed him to rebuild his political support from the headquarters in Whitehall. From this small cubbyhole, Beckwith was able to assess which way the wind was blowing in the corridors of power.

With many of his moderate left-wing MPs losing influence at Westminster, he started to cultivate friendships with those of the hard left. Relegated to the wilderness, he spent his time wining and dining potential political allies. But with the loss of many of his contacts, his future looked increasingly bleak. The funding for the submarine rescue project was at risk, and there was little prospect of expanding his empire.

The funds for the submarine rescue project had been advanced by a number of financial institutions on the understanding that their money would be repaid when a lease was signed with the navy. The loan was underwritten by the government. But there was a clause which stipulated that the lenders could repossess the vehicle if the MSPA failed to achieve certain performance targets. The delayed completion thus placed the project in jeopardy.

The breach of the loan terms did not worry Beckwith too much because he saw it as part of the 'project game'. The academic might have been more wary if he had known the identity of the lenders. It later emerged that the debts had been snaffled up by wealthy individuals who were in league with the Admiral. Beckwith was oblivious to this worrying development, and he was happy to leave the project's finances to the project manager who succeeded him.

After removing Beckwith as project manager, the board sought a replacement. The person they were looking for needed a proven track record to drive the project forward. They finally settled on a pugnacious Texan character called Sam McCarthy. The new project manager had completed some large North Sea projects on time and budget. Though he appeared an amiable fellow, he was a formidable character with a fiery temper.

Within days of arriving, the Texan had shaken up the project team in the Portsmouth office. In a purge, the overgrown students favoured by Beckwith were replaced with seasoned engineers. Anne Dexter and Simon, the office administrator, were the only two members of the original team to survive this cull. The Texan appointed Anne his deputy.

With a reinvigorated team, the Texan's next task was to investigate why they had been unable to purchase the military standard docking system. There was a need for airlocks and hatches to allow the rescue vehicle to dock with a disabled submarine. This equipment was vital for the success of the project. The Texan spoke to the manufacturer: "We are only prepared to supply the specialised military equipment when we are satisfied with the performance of the fuel-cell propulsion," came the blunt reply.

This created a chicken-and-egg situation because it would not be possible to demonstrate the diving performance of the midget submarine without some form of seal for the hull openings. To resolve this conundrum, the Texan issued orders for blanking plates to be fitted over the lower hull opening where the airlock and docking equipment would normally be fitted. The trials crew would still be able to gain access to the interior by means of a standard hatch fitted on the top of the hull. This would allow the sceptics to witness the diving performance of a stripped-down submersible vehicle.

Having solved that problem, the next task was to expedite the production of detailed drawings showing the layout of the equipment within the hull. The Texan's predecessor had tried to use a virtual reality model to fix the position of equipment within the cigar-shaped hull. But this had been a fiasco. The virtual reality model had failed to show small items, such as cable runs and switchgear, so the shipyard had been unable to finalise the detailed drawings.

The failure of the virtual reality model was a serious setback. So, after consulting Anne Dexter, his deputy, the Texan decided to revert to a traditional approach. So, they decided to build a full-scale mock-up of three sections where most equipment was concentrated. Anne was to supervise this work. The midget submarine was to be built in five sections, welded together to form a watertight hull. Each section would be fitted out with equipment before it was joined to its neighbour. This would reduce the amount of work within the cramped confines of the closed hull.

The hemispherical bow section housed the pilot's control console behind a transparent acrylic dome; another operator station was located in the tubular mid-section; another hemispherical section housed fuel and oxygen tanks, batteries and power generation equipment at the stern. Plywood mock-ups were to be built of those three sections of the vehicle. But there was no intention to build a replica of the two simpler tubular sections located fore and aft of the mid-section.

The team found an old warehouse in the naval dockyard where they were able to assemble the plywood mock-up sections. It later emerged that Commander Woods had pulled strings to make the warehouse available. The bow, stern and mid-ship sections were laid out in their relative positions on a warehouse floor. Once the plywood structure had been built, it was possible to move the smaller items around to evaluate the layout.

Real components were used for the most part, but dummies were substituted in a few cases where this was not possible. Once the project team were satisfied with the layout, drawings were produced by the main contractor and sent to the shipyard. The mock-up allowed the various elements of the control system to be connected for an integrated test. This ensured that all elements of the control system worked together and bugs were resolved before the equipment was installed in the pressure hull.

A small team of tradesmen was recruited to build the plywood replicas, and it was Anne's task to oversee their work. The tradesmen were a cheery gang, but they were skilled at their trade. They showed genuine interest in the project, and respect for their boss. Anne enjoyed her role and found that it made a pleasant change from shuffling papers about in the stuffy project office. The atmosphere on the project was greatly improved with the appointment of the new project manager and departure of the overgrown students.

Commander Woods was delighted when he heard that the obnoxious academic had been replaced as project manager. He was also pleased to hear that a full-scale mock-up was going to be built of congested parts of the submersible. To show his gratitude, he arranged for a disused warehouse to be made available for the mock-up. This warehouse happened to be close to his office on the naval base. Few people were aware that he had pulled strings to achieve this aim.

After giving the Texan time to settle in, the commander wandered round to the project office to size the fellow up. After the feud with Beckwith, he was prepared for a confrontation with his replacement. The commander was *persona non grata* under the previous regime, but he received a polite welcome from Simon on this occasion.

After a few words with the office administrator, the commander was ushered in to meet the project manager. Entering the inner sanctum, the commander found the incumbent flicking through a pile of documents with a stony expression. The commander stood waiting as the bear-like fellow finished his task. With a sigh of satisfaction at reaching the final page, the giant rose ponderously to his feet and extended his hand with a welcoming smile.

"Glad to meet you, Commander. Understand that you are the navy man who is going to test our baby. Always pleased to cooperate with the navy!" he declared in his Texan drawl that was strong enough to curdle the coffee.

The commander reflected his folksy style: "Sounds like you hail from across the pond!"

"Yes, sir! Came over twenty years ago and been working in the North Sea ever since. But things are slow up there in Aberdeen, so I thought I'd try my hand at some navy work."

After his rancorous dealings with Beckwith, the commander was relieved by his successor's seemingly cooperative and friendly attitude. He felt an immediate rapport with the burly fellow and was confident that they could establish a good working relationship. When he asked how the project was progressing, the Texan explained that designers were having difficulty squeezing all the equipment into the tight confines of the submersible's pressure hull.

"We have the same problem on the rigs," he added. "Some rigs you can't hardly move for all the gear piled on. But this baby is full to bursting, so we decided to lay all the kit out in the workshop, see how it fits together, before we start building her."

The Texan went on to explain that small-scale models were sometimes used to finalise the position of equipment on offshore platforms, but that this was the first time he had used a full-scale model for optimising the layout. "One of your people came up with the idea. We can check how all the gear can fit inside the hull. Seemed like a good idea, so I gave the scheme the go-ahead."

The commander resisted the urge to note that he had proposed building a full-scale mock-up six months earlier, but that this idea had been dismissed by the arrogant academic. He simply nodded and allowed the Texan to continue with his diatribe.

"Beckwith wasn't happy," commented McCarthy bluntly, "but I soon put the boy straight!"

The throw-away comment made the commander smile. It seemed that Beckwith had finally met his match with this tough fellow. But he had no time to reflect. The phone rang, and the fast-talking Texan made a sign that their meeting was at an end. Although it had been a brief encounter, it left the commander greatly encouraged.

But he also felt a twinge of unease as he walked past Anne Dexter as he made his way out of the shabby office. Anne was sitting at her desk, minding her own business. He acknowledged his fellow officer with a wave of the hand, but she responded in a perfunctory way. He did not linger to speak to her. There was a frostiness in their relationship, and the commander felt ashamed of his boorish behaviour at the tea party with her mother.

The atmosphere in the shabby open-plan office had greatly improved with the arrival of Sam McCarthy. Anne felt far more comfortable working with seasoned engineers rather than the overgrown students of the previous regime. But while the Texan controlled the project team, his predecessor continued to exert a malign influence from Whitehall. Beckwith did this with the aid of Simon, his loyal sidekick. The office sneak passed on malicious gossip to his master. The commander's visit would inevitably feature in the day's report.

The office sneak hovered outside the project manager's cubicle while the commander was talking to his boss. With the commander's departure, Simon dashed back to his desk and jabbed furiously at his computer keyboard. After reporting back to his master by email, the office sneak slipped outside, pretending that he wanted to smoke a cigarette. It was a clumsy effort. He really wanted to speak with former members of the team who 'just happened to stop by'. Anne watched from the corner of her eye as the unwholesome gang conspired like a witches' coven. She could not resist a smile, recalling that the non-smoking Simon was a health fanatic.

The commander skipped along the pavement on his way back to the naval base, impressed by the way the forceful Texan had established control over the project. The meeting suggested that the pugnacious project manager had the full confidence of the supervisory board of the Marine Special Projects Agency (MSPA). He appeared to be the sort of man who would stand up to the artful academic, who was no doubt scheming his revenge in his London lair.

The Texan did indeed have the backing of the board of the MSPA. The reshaped board was dismayed at the way the project was going. They wanted an individual with a proven track record. There was a limited pool of suitable candidates for this demanding role, and the tough-talking Texan was one of the few to meet their requirements. But in accepting the job, the Texan demanded 'full authority' to make decisions. The board had conceded to this and promised to back him to the hilt.

The project made swift progress under the new management. The design was finalised and construction got underway within a matter of weeks. The submersible rapidly took shape at the shipyard, and basin trials were scheduled to take place early in the New Year. The purpose of the basin trials was to ensure that the midget submarine was stable and seaworthy.

After the basin trials, the submersible was to be transported to the boatyard at Whitebait Cove. The commander's team would then perform diving trials of the 'stripped-down' version of the submarine rescue vehicle in the open sea. On successful completion of the diving trials, a demonstration would be laid on for senior naval figures. A decision would then be made about fitting the special docking gear needed for its submarine rescue role. So much hung on the success of the diving trials.

If the senior naval figures were satisfied with the underwater performance, the submersible would be fitted with the special hatches and airlocks that would allow the rescue vehicle to dock onto a disabled submarine and evacuate survivors. The company that supplied the specialised docking equipment wanted to assure itself that the fuel-cell propulsion was up to the job, and did not want to risk their reputation by association with a doomed project.

Beckwith fumed in his Whitehall cubbyhole, green with envy, as he watched the Texan steering his pet project to success. Although excluded from the project work, the academic was responsible for negotiating a lease arrangement with the navy. In doing so, the academic focussed his energy on the demonstration that would follow the diving trials. This fixture was the one bright light on the otherwise gloomy horizon. He wanted to ensure that the demonstration received plenty of media coverage. Media coverage would allow him to promote both himself and his newly established agency.

When he had a moment to spare, Beckwith dreamed up wheezes to undermine the 'hillbilly pig farmer' who had usurped his position as project manager. By discrediting his successor, he hoped to be reinstated as project manager. In that way, he could take full credit for the craft when it was unveiled to the public. But his plans were thrown into disarray when Simon phoned with the news that an Argentinian submarine had gone missing in the South Atlantic.

The German-built submarine was, apparently, on routine patrol when it ran into difficulties near the Falkland Islands. This was an opportunity for Beckwith to remind his political allies of the potential value of his project, so as soon as the government departments opened for business the following morning, he hit the phones in order to persuade his political allies to offer assistance with the rescue effort. But his voice was lost in the cacophony of similar suggestions. In the days that followed, ships from many nations joined a massive maritime search. The incident attracted media attention from around the world.

Sadly, the marine search effort for the Argentinian submarine was in vain and the operation was scaled back when naval experts concluded that there was insufficient air to support life onboard a sunken vessel. The submarine was 'presumed lost' with its crew of forty-four. The wreck of the submarine was eventually discovered in around 800 metres of water around a year later. This was a cause of enormous distress among the families of the crew, but it was also a blow to the artful academic who had hoped to capitalise on the disaster for his media campaign.

With little else to keep him occupied, Beckwith's thoughts reverted to the forthcoming press launch. Under his plan, the media coverage would be kept low-key during the construction and sea trials of the midget submarine. But the successful completion of the sea trials would be celebrated by a flamboyant press launch and media blitz. While the academic hoped that the media launch would enhance his reputation, he also saw it as an opportunity to take revenge on the commander and other detractors.

After the purge of staff that he had recruited, Simon was the last person that Beckwith trusted in the Portsmouth office. The office administrator demonstrated loyalty to his former boss by passing on details of any mishaps but, to their dismay, there were few of these. It was really galling for the academic that the man he described as a 'hillbilly pig farmer' proved a capable manager. But he managed to make mischief nonetheless.

A chance arose to embarrass his detractors when Beckwith was invited to give evidence to a parliamentary committee on naval procurement. Although the academic was only due to play a small part in this affair, the hearing would provide him with a stage to stir up trouble. To prepare the ground, the academic met with a friendly tabloid hack for a meal. The purpose of the meeting was, supposedly, to brief the journalist about the power problems with the latest generation of frigates. This issue was widely discussed within the marine community at the time but was not widely known to the public.

The 'off-the-record briefing' took place in an upmarket West End restaurant. Wine flowed freely and Beckwith pretended to speak in an indiscreet way as they dined. In his diatribe, Beckwith skilfully distorted the facts to give the appearance that senior naval officers were responsible for the frigate fiasco. He then embellished his narrative with anecdotes from the submarine rescue project that showed the navy in a poor light. In doing this, his guns were aimed squarely at Commander Woods.

"That clapped-out old warhorse is a technical dinosaur!" declared the artful academic, as though under the effect of alcohol. "He hasn't got a clue about modern technology. It's the old-school types, like him, who block progress!" Although the meeting was supposedly 'off-the-record', Beckwith knew that his unscrupulous hack would ignore the protocol and print his comments verbatim.

The words duly appeared in a feature article in a popular Sunday paper, just as Beckwith had planned. The grossly slanted article criticised the 'old buffers' who dominated the Admiralty with quotes attributed to a 'well-informed source with close links to the defence ministry'. The article caused a storm in Whitehall, just at the time when naval procurement issues were being investigated by the parliamentary committee. The article had thus served its purpose to set the agenda for the committee session.

Beckwith made sure that each member of the committee received a copy of the inflammatory article on the day that he was to appear. The committee deliberated for most of the session on questions relating to the power problems experienced by the latest frigates and delays to the frigate replacement programme. This hearing attracted a great deal of media interest because one of the modern frigates had been towed ignominiously into port, after suffering a power failure.

It was only towards the end of a long and gruelling session that the scheming academic was called to appear before the committee. In his introduction, Beckwith outlined the role and benefits of his newly formed Marine Special Projects

Agency (MSPA) in a well-rehearsed and polished manner. He was then questioned by the committee chairman, who suspected that the witness was the source of quotes in the 'old buffers' article. In his reply, the artful academic pretended to distance himself from the critical article.

"We have a fantastic working relationship with naval personnel, and I have the greatest respect for them," he claimed in the oily tones of the insincere. His real views became evident when he responded to planted questions from one of his political allies. The friendly MP, called Robert Hodges, asked in a hesitant and quizzical way, "Can you explain the reason for the delay to your submarine rescue project?" This slow ball was a gift to the artful academic.

"Well, that's a tricky question," replied the academic with feigned sorrow. When pressed for an answer, Beckwith sighed. "Well, the navy wanted us to change the position of electrical equipment. That created a lot of problems," he explained slowly. Then warming to his theme, he continued in a more animated way: "The navy wanted to check the layout inside the hull and so we created a virtual reality model, but they were not happy with that. So we had to build a full-scale wooden mock-up for them."

"What was wrong with the virtual reality model?" asked Hodges.

"The navy couldn't understand it!" replied Beckwith disingenuously, with a sarcastic sneer.

"Is that why the project is running over budget and behind schedule?" asked Hodges, tossing his friend an easy ball.

"Yes," replied Beckwith as he smashed the ball into the grandstand. "I'm afraid so!"

That was a hideous distortion, but the words were unchallenged. It was the end of a busy day and Beckwith's contribution was a matter of limited significance in comparison to the power problems on the frigates, so none of the committee members felt it worth pursuing that line of questioning, and the session was wound up, although the exchange was recorded verbatim in the transcript, but it was a peripheral issue and did not feature in the committee's report.

The project team in Portsmouth was unaware of the lies that the academic had been spreading at the committee meeting. The episode might have been consigned to history, had it not been for a sharp-eyed bureaucrat beavering away in the defence ministry. After reading the twisted account in the transcript, the pen-pusher sent a message to the C-in-C of the Portsmouth base demanding to know why the 'navy' had obstructed Beckwith's project. On another occasion, the Admiral would have brushed this away, but the mention of Beckwith's name was like a red rag to a bull.

Recalling the obnoxious pupil at his boarding school, the Admiral regarded the criticism as a taunt. The old boy recognised that it was all part of Beckwith's campaign to vilify the old-boy network. Much to the surprise of his staff, the old fox challenged the allegation. In an unusually testy mood, the Admiral summoned Commander Woods to a formal meeting to account for his actions. The meeting took place under the steely gaze of Caroline Haywood, who was taking notes.

The old boy intended to give his subordinate a severe dressing-down. The secretary savoured the moment, believing that the commander was receiving his dues. The decorated war hero had a frosty relationship with the formidable woman. The Dragon smiled thinly, watching the commander standing meekly to attention in front of the Admiral's desk as he was passed a copy of the letter from the ministry official.

"We have received this allegation that the navy was responsible for the project running over budget and behind schedule," barked the old fox in an accusing manner. The commander was caught off-guard and was completely flummoxed. The decorated war hero had no direct role in the project. Having gathered his wits, he expressed outrage at the implied criticism, but when pressed by his superior officer he was unable to provide a convincing defence.

"Beckwith sent me a mountain of documents. You can't expect me to keep track of them all," pleaded the commander lamely. "I did suggest that the switchgear should be moved closer to the pilot seat. But that's all. A small change like that would not delay the whole project!"

As he spoke, the Dragon scribbled furiously in her notebook with the sadistic expression of a hanging judge. The formidable woman could not wait to see the vainglorious 'war hero' cut down to size. But her thin smile evaporated when the old fox asked his subordinate about the virtual reality model. "I had nothing to do with that!" declared the commander with relief. "You will have to speak to Lieutenant Anne Dexter. She was seconded to the project."

That comment defused the confrontation and also muddied the waters, because it was not clear whether Anne Dexter represented the navy or not. Although the commander had got himself off the hook, he came to regret his words, feeling guilty that he had passed the buck to the female officer. This would further complicate their already difficult relationship.

Realising that the situation was more complex than he first thought, the Admiral demanded to see 'all the records'. This placed the commander in an invidious position because he needed Anne's help to assemble the relevant documents. His relationship with Anne was fragile and he knew that she would be incensed by the implication that she had impeded the project, so he felt distinctly queasy about approaching the female officer.

The commander had the benefit of a staff car and normally went about his duties in a brisk manner. But steeling himself for what was likely to be a bruising encounter, he dawdled on his way to the warehouse, where Anne was supervising the wooden mock-up. To collect his thoughts, he first stopped off at the canteen. While he toyed with the coffee cup, he recalled how he had been blinded by flattery when drinking tea with the matriarch.

The flattery had marred his judgement and led him to assume that the apparently docile daughter would share his critical views about the submarine rescue project. This had been a serious error of judgement. He had failed to recognise that the strong-willed young woman had views of her own. A rift had been created when Anne dismissed his views as they walked the dogs. It had been foolish to underestimate her, and he did not want to make the same mistake again.

Their relationship had thawed somewhat since that first awkward encounter. But there were now well-defined boundaries between them. Anne made it clear that she did not wish to hear any more of his conspiracy theories. Neither did she welcome the commander's criticisms of fuel-cell propulsion. The commander feared that by buck-passing, he would open old wounds.

Summoning up his courage, the commander ordered his driver to take him to the warehouse where the wooden mock-up was being assembled. He arrived to find Anne chatting in a friendly way with a tradesman. Anne was in a sunny mood and acknowledged her visitor in an offhand way. The commander interrupted, to pass his female counterpart a copy of the complaint. Anne's first reaction was to laugh it off and dismiss it as rubbish. "Some bureaucrat has got the wrong end of the stick. 'The navy' is not running this project!" she commented in a light-hearted manner, before resuming her conversation with the tradesman.

"The Admiral is taking this very seriously," insisted the commander firmly. "Perhaps you should take a closer look."

Anne's features clenched in rage when she read the transcript of the committee hearing that was attached to the official's note. After reading Beckwith's derogatory comments about the virtual reality model, Anne exploded. She grabbed her mobile to demand an explanation from the man who had recruited her. When she reached the Whitehall office, she was told that the scheming academic was absent and was not due back for several days.

The commander was relieved that he was not the target of her anger on that occasion, but his sense of well-being was short-lived. "We need to set the record straight," demanded Anne, who was in high dudgeon, as she stomped out of the warehouse. "We'll have to sort this out with the project manager. Can you give me a lift?" The commander was only too happy to oblige and it did not take long to reach the Portsmouth project office in his staff car. Anne's cheeks were burning red when they burst into the Texan's cubicle.

"Have you seen this!" demanded Anne angrily as she thumped the note down onto the Texan's desk. "Beckwith is trying to blame 'the navy' for obstructing the project!" The burly project manager was taken aback by the fury; he was in the middle of an important telephone conversation.

By this time, the Texan was accustomed to his deputy's temper tantrums. His first reaction was to pour oil on troubled waters. When he scanned the transcript, he saw a reference to the virtual reality contract fiasco and quickly surmised that Beckwith was trying to shift blame for his incompetent contractor. It was a messy situation and the wily Texan had no desire to be drawn into a political dispute. "You don't want to get caught up in politics," he warned. "It will suck you down!"

"We need to set the record straight!" demanded Anne self-righteously.

The Texan had other things on his mind and wanted to sidestep this awkward affair. "This is a naval matter!" he told her firmly. "The Admiral needs to give evidence to the committee to defend the service." But then relenting, he adopted a more conciliatory tone. "Perhaps we can help a bit. I'll ask Simon to go through the files and collect all the material about the virtual reality contract. We'll send the documents over to the Admiral and the old boy can defend the navy."

Anne was alarmed by the Texan's half-baked plan, as she knew that Simon was the office mole reporting back to Beckwith. There were obviously some murky goings-on and she did not want to be caught up in the thick of it. *Asking Simon for help is like asking a fox to guard the henhouse*, she thought. The commander had his own qualms about the Texan's plan. He felt guilty about the stack of unread documents that were gathering dust in his office. He wondered what embarrassing evidence Simon might find in that great heap of paper.

But neither Anne nor the commander thought it prudent to air their fears about the Texan's proposal, so Simon was given the go-ahead to assemble the documents. Beckwith's sidekick showed his administrative efficiency as he ploughed rapidly through the records and collected all the relevant papers. But he did so with his master's interests at heart. When Anne peeked at the chosen documents, she could see that they portrayed a distorted version of events. Some crucial documents that pointed to Beckwith's failings had been omitted. But it was a tricky point to prove and she could only do so by revealing her diary record; and she did not wish to do that unless absolutely necessary.

The Admiral looked balefully at the stack of paper that was sent by Simon to his office at the navy base. "I haven't got time to read that lot!" he told the Dragon. "Could you go through them for me and give me a summary?" Fired by hatred for the subversive academic, the old fox kept badgering his secretary to finish the job. "What have you found, Miss Haywood?" he asked testily the following morning.

"It's all a bit of a mess," replied Miss Haywood as she handed the Admiral a copy of the email in which the commander asked for the electrical circuit breaker to be moved.

The Admiral read the offending document. "Why does that silly idiot always want to stick his nose into other people's business?" murmured the Admiral acerbically. "This is going to make things awkward."

After careful study, Miss Haywood failed to find any solid evidence to refute Beckwith's allegations. The documents showed the commander in a poor light. It was clear that he had asked for the circuit breaker to be moved. But he had also suggested that the navy should be given a chance to review the internal layout of the midget submarine. He had received copies of all the correspondence concerning the unsuccessful virtual reality contract. But there was no evidence that he had questioned any of this material. To muddy the waters, the documents failed to show whether Anne Dexter was a representative of the navy or not. It was, in short, a right royal mess.

A few days later, Anne Dexter and the commander were both summoned to the Admiral's office to formulate the navy's response. Once they had gathered around the conference table, Miss Haywood outlined her findings. She tabled the email in which the commander asked for the switchgear to be moved closer to the pilot's seat along with Beckwith's objections. These documents seemed to confirm Beckwith's allegations to the defence committee that the navy had obstructed the project.

Then Miss Haywood presented a document in which the commander recommended that experienced submariners should review the internal layout, and Beckwith's response suggesting that they use a virtual reality model. "All correspondence relating to the virtual reality contract was sent to the commander," stated Miss Haywood accusingly. "I could not find evidence that he objected to the contract being awarded to a newly formed company."

Then, to the dismay of the naval officers, she presented minutes of a meeting, attended by Anne Dexter, which stated that the 'navy approved' the virtual reality contract award. Anne erupted in anger at this allegation. She was outraged that her 'watching-brief' presence at an informal meeting had been interpreted as the navy's approval of the award of a controversial contract. Up until that point, she had maintained her notebook as a personal record, but now she used it to set out her defence.

"Here," she announced defiantly, when she had thumbed through to the correct page, "that meeting was held on the day that I joined the project." She then paused to read what was written in the diary. "Yes. It's all here!" she crowed, with the satisfaction of a person who has been vindicated. "Beckwith asked me to *'sit in'* on an *informal* meeting. I did *not* take an active part in the discussion. So, *he is lying!*"

To support her story, Anne handed the Admiral her diary. "You can see my notes here. I had only just joined the team on that day, so I assumed that Martin Beckwith had discussed the virtual reality contract award with another naval officer."

With emotions running high, the Admiral chipped in with his conclusion: "It seems that the finger of blame is pointing straight at you, Commander!"

The commander knew he had been skewered. It would be almost impossible to defend his position because of the sloppy way he dealt with paperwork. It was a convoluted story. Yes, it was his idea that submariners should review the internal layout. But it was not his idea to use a virtual reality model, nor had he approved the contract award. But he was on a tricky wicket, and trying to defend his position might do more harm than good.

There was a glimmer of good news, however. The documents showed that the decision to terminate the virtual reality contract was made by the Texan project manager, and not by anyone directly connected to the navy. The documents also showed that the Texan was responsible for the decision to build the wooden mock-up. But taken overall, the documents did seem to support the allegation that 'the navy' had delayed the project, to a small extent.

The pair of naval officers listened with increasing frustration to this clinical analysis of their actions. The submarine rescue project was controversial, and the circumstances surrounding it were complex. It was easy to make wild accusations, and hard to disprove them. The Admiral had listened without comment. It was obvious to the old fox that the commander had been set up by Beckwith. But there were other issues at stake. The Admiral's aim was to acquire the midget submarine, and if the commander had to be sacrificed in the process, so be it. So he raised his hand to ask for quiet.

"We all know that Martin Beckwith is a cunning devil, but on this occasion he has got the better of you both," concluded the Admiral. "We might be able to challenge some points, as Caroline pointed out, but your sloppy paperwork has let you down, Commander. You will have to take this on the chin." Then he continued in an enigmatic way: "Beckwith may have won this round, but he has not won the war."

As they retired wounded from the meeting, Anne felt resentment towards her companion, thinking that the war hero's cavalier attitude had got them into this mess. The commander's failure to deal with paperwork had allowed the artful academic to outmanoeuvre the pair of them. Of course, Beckwith was a devious so-and-so, but you cannot expect people like that to play by the Queensberry rules. It can be a dog-eat-dog world on big projects and you need to cover your backside, she thought.

The commander felt guilty about his failure to keep his paperwork in order. Until that time, he tended to scoff at 'desk jockeys', but this was a painful wake-up call. He promised to pay more attention to his in-tray in future. There was another reason for his sense of unease. He was unsure whether he could confide in the female officer about the meeting in Fenchurch Street. This presented a quandary because he did not know where her loyalties lay. She had shown herself as a loyal member of Beckwith's project team during their early discussions.

Beckwith kept clear of his Whitehall cubbyhole after the defence committee hearing on the pretext that he was on sick leave. This 'strategic absence' allowed him to avoid the inevitable furious response to his criticism of the navy. But there was another motive for his absence – he wanted to lure senior naval figures into a trap, by provoking them into attending the next session of the defence committee inquiry, to defend themselves.

The attendance of a naval officer at the committee would provide him with an opportunity to expose their ignorance of fuel-cell technology. His left-wing friend, Robert Hodges, would help him achieve this aim by asking some planted questions. But the Admiral sensed a trap and declined an invitation to appear at the next session of the committee hearing. Instead, he sent a mild note to the committee chairman, which read as follows:

We have been made aware of the allegation that 'the navy' obstructed the submarine rescue project, which is misleading. We wish to remind the committee that the project is undertaken by the Marine Special Projects Agency (MSPA). 'The navy' has no role in project execution. A naval officer has been seconded to the project team, but the officer does not represent 'the navy'. The views expressed by serving naval officers are intended to assist, not to hinder, the project team.

When the commander read this note, he was disappointed that the Admiral had not defended him more robustly, but in his heart, he knew that he had let the side down by not maintaining better records. He was still suffering these mixed emotions when he visited the Admiral at his home, for the third time, a couple of weeks later.

Although absent from his office, Beckwith was able to keep abreast of unfolding events with the aid of his office mole, Simon. The stream of tittle-tattle amused the artful academic and revealed disarray in the naval camp. "The old warhorse is running around as though his tail's on fire," reported the office mole gleefully on one occasion. "Lady Muck has been given a dressing-down by her navy pals!" on another. The derogatory language showed the contempt the pair felt towards servicemen.

Shortly after the defence committee stunt, the artful academic received a boost when he learned that his friend had recovered from a heart attack and was able to resume his position on the supervisory board. The friend's return gave him greater power, although it would not provide him with an absolute majority on the board. There was another sign that the tide of fortune was turning in Beckwith's favour with the news that the Texan was to relinquish his role as project manager.

After receiving these glad tidings, Beckwith lobbied the board members for his reinstatement as project manager. After a fractious meeting, the artful academic achieved his aim. This was a great victory because it meant that he would take charge of the project during the sea trials and media launch. This provided the academic with an opportunity to advance his career and promote his agency.

Beckwith's return would also allow him to reap revenge on those who had stood in his way. The 'old warhorse' was firmly in his sights. It was unsurprising that the commander viewed this prospect with dismay. He had established a good working relationship with the Texan, and the prospect of working with the artful academic during the forthcoming sea trials filled him with gloom. This was an added burden on top of the guilt he felt for his shoddy paperwork.

Chapter 9

The Admiral has a Score to Settle

Beckwith's reappointment as project manager had many benefits; not least that it allowed him to line his pockets. The academic understood the difficulty of controlling costs in the final commissioning stage of a construction project, so he planned to exploit that loophole to enrich himself. He was confident that he could milk the system. Sadly, in his reckless action, he failed to take account of one of the fellow pupils from his boarding school days.

Watching patiently from a leafy village in Hampshire, Rear-Admiral Sir Richard Walters was keeping a close eye on Beckwith's antics. The old fox was supported in that endeavour by Felix, his accountant; and by his subordinate, Commander Woods. Felix briefed the Admiral on the artful academic's financial wheezes. The commander was organising the sea trials, which placed him in a grandstand seat to observe what the academic was up to.

Still feeling guilty over the sloppy paperwork that led to the defence committee fiasco, the commander feared a severe dressing-down when he approached the Admiral's home for their third informal meeting, so he was relieved to discover that the old fox wanted to discuss the sea trials of the midget submarine instead. This was a break with routine. Operational matters, such as this, were normally discussed at the naval base, under the scrutiny of the Dragon.

Freed of worries over paperwork, the commander settled down for a convivial evening with his superior. The pair chatted amicably as they lounged in comfy armchairs watching the setting sun. After some chit-chat, the Admiral steered the discussion to business. Though supposedly discussing the trials, the old fox showed an unusual interest in the coastal village in the West Country where the trials were due to take place the following spring.

Distracted by the pastel shades as the sunlight reflected from the base of an unusual nimbus cloud formation, the commander at first failed to notice anything strange about this. "The ministry has chartered a small offshore supply ship called the *Normandy* to act as a base for the sea trials," commented the commander as he swirled his glass of lager in a languid way. "The ship will be berthed at a quay. The quay is owned by a marine business that has been established on the site of an old boatyard."

"Who runs the marine business?" asked the Admiral sharply. The old boy knew the answer to that question, but he wanted to squeeze more details from his subordinate.

"Steve Jones is the chief executive," replied the commander.

"What's his background?" asked the Admiral tersely.

The commander was shaken from his torpor by the incisive nature of the question. He turned abruptly to look at his host as he tried to fathom what the old fox was up to. "He's a go-ahead young guy – full of energy," observed the commander. "He joined a shipping company as a graduate trainee. But the company went bust, so he was transferred to a tanker fleet. He was regarded as a high-flyer in the shipping world, one of the first of the new generation of graduate marine engineers. Worked his way up the ranks and then came ashore to their head office."

"Sounds like a pretty impressive character!" remarked the Admiral.

"Yes, he is! We go fishing together, so I know him quite well," replied the war hero. The commander was mystified by the significance of this subject, but he could not find a clue in the Admiral's poker face. "Steve gets things done. But he can be pig-headed at times," continued the decorated war hero in a more considered way. "He has upset some local people. He can be a bit impetuous and rubs people up the wrong way."

The Admiral was pleased with the commander's reply. It confirmed what he had learned from other sources. It seemed that Steve Jones was just the sort of chap he needed to help with the undercover operation he was planning. "Can we trust him?" he asked obliquely.

"Depends on what you have got in mind," replied the commander cautiously. "Steve cares about his boatyard. He has no family commitments and so he might be up for a challenge of some sort." Satisfied with the answer, the old fox settled back to enjoy the view of the sunset.

As the sun dipped, it created an auburn glow among the leaves of the lime trees on the far side of a neighbouring meadow. The pair were sitting side by side, relaxing with their drinks, in a mellow mood. As the commander took a sip of his lager, he suddenly recalled that Mark Dexter had just been appointed as harbour master at Whitebait Cove. This seemed to chime with the Admiral's train of thought.

"Did you know that one of our chaps is harbour master at Whitebait Cove?" observed the commander casually. "It's a real coincidence. He's Anne Dexter's brother. You know, the female officer who has been seconded to the submarine rescue project, so two members of the family have connections with the same project." The Admiral pretended to know nothing of this, despite having pulled strings to achieve this beneficial outcome.

"What do we know about the new harbour master?" asked the old boy innocently.

"Mark served as weapons officer on the old carrier," replied the commander. "From what I've heard, he's a competent fellow. He did a good job overseeing decommissioning." The commander went on to tell the amusing anecdote about how Mark had delivered his sister's note in the Admiral Bligh pub. "Mark seems like a decent enough chap. He wants to join our trials team. But he didn't have the right technical qualifications. He's not as bright as his sister. She was a controls expert on the nuclear submarine programme."

"Sounds like an interesting family," observed the old fox in a conversational way. He wanted to conceal the fact that he had gone to considerable lengths to bring about this advantageous state of affairs. The Admiral felt a sense of satisfaction that pieces of the jigsaw were falling neatly into place.

The pair sat contentedly with their drinks in the warm evening air as they watched the sun dip below the horizon. The Admiral broke the silence after a short time. "Have you got any plans to visit Whitebait Cove?" asked the old boy casually.

"I need to discuss the sea trials with Steve Jones," replied the commander. "But there's no rush. The sea trials are not due to start until next spring so there is plenty of time. If it's all right with you, I would like to take a couple of days off to go fishing after visiting the yard. But I'll leave my trip until after the bank holiday to avoid the holiday traffic."

They went on to discuss other matters and the Admiral asked what progress had been made with the plans to protect merchant ships from pirates. The commander said he had nothing further to report. "It's all up in the air at the moment," explained the commander. "We have some ideas, but we don't have any funding. We are not planning to hold any more meetings until that is sorted out."

"You could tell Steve Jones about your ideas," suggested the Admiral with a crafty look in his eyes. "Combine business with pleasure. Kill two birds with one stone!" added the old fox ambiguously "While you are there, you could ask the young fellow whether his yard has any financial problems. We might be able to help." The commander was puzzled by the obscure remark, but the old boy was not inclined to elaborate. To change the subject, the cunning old fox spoke about some inconsequential matters concerning the naval base.

The old fox touched on the subject once more as the commander was preparing to depart. "Let me know how you get on with Steve Jones," remarked the Admiral as he escorted his guest to the door. "You could have a word with the new harbour master while you are down there."

The commander felt a sense of exasperation on his way home. He knew the old fox was up to something, but what? The old boy had a habit of speaking in a vague way and it was difficult to pin him down. *Why the sudden interest in the boatyard's finances?* he mused. But he was not one to reflect, so in the best traditions of the services he would 'use his initiative'. The commander was slowly becoming accustomed to the Admiral's whimsical ways. At times, he felt like one of those clockwork toys that can be set off to bounce off any obstruction that it encounters. The Admiral was obviously using him to some end, but what was it?

It later emerged that the Admiral had learned of the boatyard's financial plight from his accountant friend, Felix, and they hoped to use this knowledge to their advantage. The pair were cooking up a plan in which shipping companies would provide financial assistance in return for Steve's cooperation in acquiring the midget submarine. The Admiral wanted to use his subordinate as a *conduit* in the delicate negotiations. But in his obtuse way, he had failed to prepare the war hero for his mission.

Had the commander been aware of these facts, he might have approached his meeting with the yard's chief executive in a more circumspect manner. But the Admiral was playing his cards close to his chest, as ever.

Commander Woods wanted to combine business with pleasure when he visited Whitebait Cove to discuss the sea trial. After a short meeting with Steve, he planned to take a few days' leave. To avoid the busy holiday season, he delayed his visit until after the bank holiday. He had visited the yard several times before while searching for a suitable site for the sea trials. During the visits, he had become friendly with Steve Jones and introduced him to fly fishing. So he hoped to finalise arrangements quickly, so they could enjoy time on the river.

The shallow water trials of the midget submarine were due to start the following spring and these would be followed by deep-water diving trials in the open sea, most likely after the Easter holiday. The arrangements had been agreed in principle but there were some details to tie up. After driving down to the West Country, the commander was ushered into Steve's stylish office, where he found Mark Dexter sitting silently alongside the chief executive.

When the commander entered the office, he barely recognised Mark in his civilian clothes. The once distinguished-looking officer looked a shadow of his former self. It was clear that the newly retired naval officer was still feeling his way in his new role as harbour master. As the meeting got under way, Mark behaved diffidently, deferring to his boss on most matters. Neither Mark nor the commander mentioned their meeting at the Admiral Bligh pub.

Before settling down to their business, the commander stepped out onto the balcony for a moment to appreciate the view. But as he surveyed the stunning panorama, he noticed the desolate state of the yard. There were few signs of activity. When he stepped back inside, Steve tried to put a brave face on things: "Yes, business is a little bit slack at the moment. There's a slump in the offshore oil and gas world, but it's only a temporary blip. We should be back to normal soon."

After welcoming his visitor, Steve warned he 'had a lot on his plate' and could not spare much time. This suited the commander just fine; the war hero's thoughts were focussed on his fishing trip. So they went about their discussion in a brisk, business-like way. "The midget submarine will be housed on an offshore supply ship called the *Normandy*," explained the commander as he handed over details of the ship. "We need to moor the *Normandy* at your quay, down there. It is slightly larger than the ships you usually handle, so you may need to check the depth of the channel.

"The trials will take place in the estuary or in open sea, so they won't have a great impact on your day-to-day activities," continued the commander. "But we need some temporary office space for support staff, and some additional security."

As they sipped coffee sitting round the conference table, they agreed that two portable cabins would be needed. One cabin would house the navy trials team and the other would be used by the project staff. "The Texan will organise the portable cabins before he relinquishes his role as project manager," explained the commander. "Martin Beckwith will resume his role as project manager later this year, so you will need to deal with him during the sea trials." Then the trio descended to the car park to decide where the cabins should be located. There was plenty of free space, and they were spoiled for choice.

After following his master in silence, Mark felt the need to make a contribution to the discussion. He wanted to make his presence felt. "I can sort out the power, water and drainage for the portable cabins if you like," he offered in a bumptious way. The remark attracted scant comment as they went on to discuss the yard security during the trials. This presented real problems. The yard was surrounded by a high chain-link security fence with a single entrance. While the entrance gate was open to visitors during the day, it was locked at night. This would prevent the crew of the *Normandy* from being able to access the vessel at night.

The trio returned to Steve's office to consider this matter. "Security is *my* responsibility," declared Mark in a more forceful manner. He felt sidelined in the discussion so far and wanted to show he was not the young executive's lapdog. "It's my job to move all loose equipment into the buildings at night, and lock the buildings. I have to make sure that no one is left behind when I lock the gate on my way home. The yard is protected by alarms and spotlights at night. A security firm sends a patrol car round at regular intervals during the night and they receive a signal if an intruder alarm is activated."

"Have you had any problems?" inquired the commander courteously as he switched his attention from Steve to the newly retired officer.

This question floored Mark, and he immediately regretted his assertive remark. The truth was that Stan had not briefed

Mark about security breaches and had left the records in a mess. The proud bowls club treasurer had taken umbrage at the way he was treated. These small acts of revenge were intended to sabotage his successor. This left Mark shuffling his feet under the table in embarrassment. The newly retired naval officer looked pleadingly at his boss, hoping he would extract him from the mire.

"We suffer from vandalism from time to time, like everyone else, but we have only had one really serious incident," explained the young executive smoothly. "There was a major break-in around nine months ago, before Mark joined us. A gang of scrap metal thieves cut through the fence and broke into the main workshop. Somebody must have tipped them off that we were storing a large amount of titanium alloy at the time. A patrol car spotted them and gave chase. But the villains escaped with a large haul of valuable material. The police know who they are, but they did not have enough evidence to prosecute them."

"Well, you will need to change your security when we start the trials. I suggest that you provide a security hut and barrier," proposed the commander in a grandiose manner. "The security hut will need to be manned twenty-four hours a day, because the *Normandy*'s crew will remain onboard overnight."

Steve was aghast at this outrageous demand. This called for massive changes to the yard and it was not clear who would foot the bill. "That's all very well," he stuttered with a reddening face, "but who is going to pay for all that?"

The commander did not usually trouble himself with trivial commercial matters. "You will have to take it up with the ministry," he replied airily. But Steve was determined to resolve this crucial issue straight away, so he retrieved the contract file and thumbed rapidly through the pages to check the terms of their agreement. After reading some pages, he summarised the position. "It's all here in black and white. It's clear as day!

"There is a clause in the contract that states that the navy is responsible for any additional security arrangements needed for the sea trial. So we will have to pass the buck on that one, I'm afraid," he declared with a relieved expression. "The project team can probably organise the changes. They will also have to arrange their insurance, so we'll have to put the ball back in their court, thank you very much."

Steve was relieved that the boatyard would not be faced with the cost of security changes; he already had enough financial problems without that additional expense. But then adopting a more conciliatory attitude, he turned towards his subordinate. "Perhaps you could speak to the project team about this, Mark?" he suggested helpfully. "You'd better speak to Beckwith. He will be in charge of the project when the trials start next spring."

After making that closing remark, Steve started rustling papers in an impatient way as a sign that their meeting was at an end and it was time for his visitor to leave. The commander took the hint, but he would not be rushed. He was curious to learn more about the break-in at the boatyard. Steve's comment chimed with some thoughts stirring in his brain.

"It's a strange coincidence. We were talking about scrap metal theft the other day," remarked the commander in a jovial fashion as he retrieved his serge overcoat from the coat rack. "A colleague told me a story about a quartermaster who refused to hand over a drum of cable that a squad of special forces needed for an undercover operation in the desert, so the squad broke into the store and pinched the drum of cable. They blamed the loss on thieving Arabs."

Steve did not find the story amusing – the theft of scrap metal was a subject that made him hopping mad. "We have a major problem with scrap metal thieves down here," observed Steve with a sour expression as he looked up reluctantly from his papers. "They will pinch anything. One gang had the cheek to pinch the brass plaque from our village war memorial. Another gang removed manhole covers from the streets, would you believe! It was amazing luck that no one fell down one of them! They have even pinched live power cables from the railway! I'm surprised they were not electrocuted!

"The police think that an insider was involved in our break-in because the villains knew where to find the expensive material," continued the young executive as he warmed to the subject. "Someone must have tipped them off. The police know who was responsible, but the villains are always one step in front. After the break-in, we take great care. We keep all the valuable stuff under lock and key."

"Well. we'll need to keep an eye out during the sea trials then," remarked the commander, in a half-hearted effort at humour. "The hull of the midget submarine is made of an expensive titanium alloy. That metal is worth a small fortune."

"That's no joke!" replied Steve with a stormy expression, showing his annoyance at being distracted from his papers yet again. "The gang have large transport vehicles. They made away with a couple of tons of copper from the railway. With vehicles like that, they could cart away your midget submarine with no trouble at all, so I'm glad it's not our job to guard it!"

Before departing, the commander reminded Steve that he was staying for a few days and asked whether the young executive would like to go fishing. He spoke in a tentative way, fearing a testy rebuke, but the busy executive let down his guard for a moment, and they arranged to meet on Sunday morning. But with that, Steve shooed the visitors from his office and resumed his paperwork, signalling that he did not want any further distractions.

On his way to the car park, the commander asked Mark if he wanted to join their fishing trip on Sunday. "Thanks for the offer, but my wife keeps me busy at weekends!" replied Mark in a hangdog way. The commander gained the impression that the newly retired naval officer had not yet come to terms with retirement from the career he loved. But he had only made the offer out of a sense of politeness.

The presence of his retired colleague would prevent him raising some delicate matters to which the Admiral had alluded. *Perhaps Steve will understand what the Admiral was on about, because I don't understand any of it,* mused the commander, in anticipation of their fishing trip on Sunday. The commander did not have a clue why he had been asked to broach the subject of boatyard finance and felt uncomfortable doing so.

But the war hero was looking forward to a day on the river and hoped he could encourage his young friend to relax. *It will do the young fellow good,* mused the commander. *He was in a tetchy mood today. I can see why he upsets people.* This was an accurate diagnosis. Since taking the helm at the boatyard, Steve had angered the local people in many ways, not least by restricting access to the waterside.

The previous owner, Sam Wheeler, allowed the public to wander freely on the quay, so there was outrage in the local community when a chain-link fence was erected to prevent them reaching that part of the waterfront. Steve's brusque manner did not help when he sacked most of the long-standing employees. As a result of his inconsiderate behaviour, he faced hostility in this picturesque backwater.

Steve might have won goodwill if he had bothered to listen to Stan, who was the sole staff member retained when he took charge from Sam Wheeler. The harbour master wanted to introduce his new boss to the quaint local customs. But his efforts were spurned and the once-loyal harbour master turned against his employers. Steve's brash approach created hostility towards the new owners of the boatyard. As a result, the young executive found it prudent to rent a flat in Plymouth to escape the poisonous atmosphere and malicious local gossip. The commander recognised the problem during his first visit to the boatyard and hoped to help ease the situation by introducing the boatyard boss to a local sport.

The commander was a keen angler with friends in the area. That was one of the reasons why he had chosen the boatyard at Whitebait Cove for sea trials. Sensing the hostility between the new owner and the locals, he wanted to introduce the work-obsessed young chief executive to his favourite hobby. The commander hoped to provide fatherly advice during these relaxed outings. The plan was reasonably successful. As Steve developed an interest in angling, his relationship with the local community began to thaw.

By good fortune, the commander was friends with a farmer with fishing rights to a trout stream close to the yard. Steve had joined the commander on trips to the angling pitch on two previous occasions. As he set off for his third outing, the young executive drove over to collect the commander from his guesthouse. The pair travelled on to the stream, arriving when the sun was still low on the horizon. After parking the car, the pair assembled their rods, donned their waders and stepped out into the ice-cold stream.

On that particular morning, the tendrils of mist twined around the low hanging branches creating an ethereal atmosphere. They spent the morning in silent concentration as they cast their lines back and forth to tempt the sleek fish with colourful lures among the rocks, whirlpool and eddies. When the sun rose in the sky, they gathered their meagre catch, packed up their gear and set off to enjoy a hearty Sunday roast at the Windmill public house.

Mark and his wife had spotted the pair of anglers at this public house some weeks before. This was their regular venue after a morning fly fishing on the river. As they settled down to lunch, Steve spoke about his personal problems. The young executive admitted to mistakes and welcomed advice about dealing with the truculent locals. He found it easy to speak to the commander about these delicate matters because he was an outsider. There was no risk that his remarks would surface to fuel the gossip mill.

They avoided talking about the submarine rescue project during these discussions because this was a source of discord between the two strongly opinionated men. Steve was a strong advocate of fuel-cell propulsion and would brook no criticism of the novel technology. This had led to a heated argument on one occasion, when the commander expressed reservations about the project. Steve took this as a slight and did not give the older man a fair hearing.

If he had been more patient, Steve would have learned the commander had gone to great lengths to assess the benefits of its fuel cells. While the older man was impressed with the potential of this innovative technology, he foresaw practical problems with refuelling in remote locations where submarine disasters occur. So he reluctantly came to the conclusion that fuel cells were not well suited to submarine rescue work. Steve was unable to understand the commander's nuanced point of view.

This misunderstanding was caused by Steve's sometimes brash and impetuous nature. It was for this reason that the commander was uneasy about raising the question of the boatyard's finances. The commander did not want to blunder into the subject and start another row, so he allowed the conversation to flow along its natural course, prepared to ignore the Admiral's request to raise the subject. But in the course of the conversation, Steve made a comment that provided an opening to this sensitive issue.

"Things are quiet at the boatyard at the moment," admitted Steve, with a worried look on his face as he fiddled with some crispy crackling on a plate piled high with roast meat from the carvery. This was an unusual admission from the cocksure young businessman. "We've had to lay off six staff, and we may let more people go," continued Steve ruefully. "Things are unlikely to improve. The crude price has recovered a little, thanks to the OPEC deal, but it will take a long, long time for confidence to return to the North Sea."

"Yes. It did seem quiet," sympathised the commander. This was an understatement – the war hero was shocked at the lack of activity and had a mental picture of tumbleweed blowing through a Wild West town. "You must be getting some military work?" he added encouragingly.

"That's our bread and butter at the moment," replied Steve. "I would like to build up that side of the business, but we are also looking at opportunities in merchant shipping. A lot of new business will be created by the strict new exhaust gas rules. But that will need investment and the board is not keen. They want to close the yard and build more houses."

"They will never get planning permission for that!" replied the commander forcefully.

"It will be an uphill struggle," admitted Steve. "We promised to maintain a marine business when we applied for the planning permission to redevelop Sam Wheeler's ramshackle old boatyard. The planning permission allowed homes to be built on half the site, but it requires us to retain a marine business on the other half."

"How could they get around that?" asked the commander solicitously.

"The Dutch owners have got some slick lawyers," said Steve. "The lawyers will argue that the marine business is not viable, and threaten to close it down. The council does not want to have a derelict site on its doorstep, so the Dutch owners think the council will back down."

This was the first time that Steve had mentioned the Dutch corporation who owned his company to the commander. The boatyard now formed a small part of a huge shipping and property conglomerate with headquarters in Amsterdam. "Are you saying that the Dutch board wants your business to fail?" asked the commander with an outraged expression.

"It sometimes seems that way! But they will never admit it," replied Steve with a desolate air. "Our main problem is that we have not been paid for your submarine project. That would ease our cash flow situation. Things are dire. We can scarcely afford to pay our staff."

This was the first time that the young executive had revealed problem with the boatyard business during their fishing outings. The remark presented the ideal opportunity to mention the Admiral's suggestion that they might help with Steve's financial woes. Unfortunately, the commander knew little about those matters and was not entirely clear what the Admiral had in mind. But he ploughed on nonetheless, using his initiative.

"How much are you owed for the midget submarine?" asked the commander as he struggled to view matters from a business perspective.

"Around five million pounds," replied Steve. "That's a good part of our annual turnover."

"We might be able to help," said the commander somewhat vaguely.

Steve froze as he was about to place a tasty morsel of pork in his mouth. He was startled by the commander's comment. He felt like a man standing on the gallows who had just received a note that there might be a reprieve, or not. Returning his fork to his plate, he attempted to clarify what he had just heard: "Are you telling me that you can persuade Martin Beckwith to pay our bill?" he demanded sharply.

"I doubt that he could influence that guy," replied the commander, back-pedalling madly as he realised that he was getting out of his depth. In a flash, the commander recalled his feud with the academic and his acute embarrassment over the defence committee debacle.

There was no way that they could influence Martin Beckwith to pay his dues. "I thought that the Texan was in charge," he blurted out. "Can't you talk to him about your payment problems?"

"The Texan can sign off small invoices, but Beckwith is still head of the Marine Special Projects Agency," explained Steve with a sigh. "All large payments need to be cleared by him. When our invoices are sent to the head office of the MSPA in Whitehall, they just sit on them!" That was the bugbear. Steve felt deflated, realising that the commander's offer amounted to little more than hot air. This was not the reprieve he had hoped for.

"Beckwith changed the rules. He has to countersign all cash payments over six-figure sums, so he is able to use his power to hold back payment from contractors that he does not like."

"That's crazy!" remarked the commander.

"You're telling me!" declared Steve bitterly. "Our accounts department can never get hold of the blighter. When they do speak to him, he has all sorts of excuses. He told us the paperwork was not in order. Then he argued that components did not have fire safety certificates. He is a crafty so-and-so. He never uses the same excuse twice. The shipyard has the same problem. They were told that their welding was not up to the code. We know that he pays some of the contractors but holds back money from the rest. We suspect that he is running out of cash. That's why the payment rules were changed. His sources of finance must have dried up."

"If Beckwith cannot raise the money, perhaps the Admiral could," suggested the commander with jaunty optimism. Steve laughed dismissively at this far-fetched idea. As he leaned back in his seat, he tried to work out what the commander was up to. He was becoming suspicious of his friend's motives and wondered where the conversation was leading. There had been rumours that another branch of the navy wanted to get its hands on the midget submarine. *So what is the commander up to?* he wondered. After collecting his thoughts, he looked the commander square in the eyes and asked: "Are you telling me that the Admiral wants to buy the midget submarine?"

"Yes, and no," replied the commander as he squirmed with embarrassment. He recalled the Admiral's vague comment about confiding in Steve about the meetings in Fenchurch Street. "We could do with a midget submarine for covert coastal surveillance work."

"Well, don't expect my help!" growled Steve, who felt that the commander had pushed his luck too far, taking advantage of their friendship. He had enough on his plate trying to persuade Martin Beckwith to pay his bills. His efforts to chase up these payments would be put in jeopardy if he became embroiled in a dispute between different branches of the navy.

"Look. It's best if you speak direct to the Admiral," said the commander, who now regretted venturing into this dangerous minefield. "I'm just passing on a message. The Admiral hinted that he might be able to help with your financial problems. He did not explain what he had in mind, so it's best you speak to him. I'm just the messenger."

They sat in silence as they finished their coffee. The commander realised he had overstepped the mark and upset his young friend. In an effort to make amends, the commander paid the bill. Steve responded by offering his erstwhile friend a lift back to his guesthouse. But his grudging manner persuaded the commander that it would be wise to refuse the offer, so they shook hands in a perfunctory way and the commander made his way back to the guesthouse in a taxi, feeling rather shamefaced.

Chapter 10

Steve Lured into a Team

When the Admiral found out what had taken place at Whitebait Cove, he concluded that he had chosen the wrong person to act as a go-between. His subordinate's ham-fisted approach had created a rift with the young fellow who ran the boatyard, but the mission had not been a complete wash-out. The old fox was intrigued to learn that the yard was being deliberately starved of cash by its Dutch owners. That piece of intelligence confirmed what he had been told by other sources.

The motivation of the Dutch corporation was obvious. Closure of the marine business would allow the industrial side of the site to be developed for residential property. The Admiral did not care too much about the boatyard; he simply wanted to recruit the young executive to join the undercover operation that he was planning. The young executive's background was ideal for this assignment. All the signs suggested that the young guy was a capable manager with a technical knowledge of ships.

When the Admiral made a vague suggestion that he would help with the boatyard finances, it was intended as a lure to snare the young executive into his camp. In the original plan, the commander was to act as a go-between during these negotiations. But after the war hero's *faux pas*, the Admiral needed to find another intermediary. This was a major setback.

To solve the problem, the Admiral was forced to call on Sam McCarthy, the Texan project manager. Few people knew of their friendship – they seemed an unlikely pair. The old fox was reluctant to adopt this solution because the Texan was involved with the project, so he would be an obvious suspect if something untoward were to happen. But he had no choice.

The Admiral need not have worried because McCarthy was only too happy to help. The mission fitted in well with the Texan's plans because he was due to visit the boatyard to discuss the portable cabins needed for the trials of the midget submarine. It was to be the Texan's last visit to the yard before he relinquished his role as project manager. He planned to use this as an opportunity to mend fences created by his aggressive approach.

Unlike the commander, the pugnacious Texan had an adversarial relationship with the yard boss, and the meetings would often descend into an exchange of insults. McCarthy would descend like the wrath of God, accompanied by his technical specialists. He would berate the staff and reel off complaints about delivery, equipment defects and sloppy paperwork.

The bear-like McCarthy would resort to colourful language. "We might as well wait for a hog to clean out its sty!" was his folksy way of expressing displeasure that a deadline was missed. His frequent reference to 'hogs' earned him the sobriquet 'the Texan pig farmer' among those who were the object of his opprobrium. This was all a familiar part of the 'contract game', of course, and there was no real malice intended.

But the boot was on the other foot at this final meeting because all the equipment had been delivered and all the snags had been ironed out. So, on this occasion, it was Steve who was calling the shots. The Texan was in the naughty seat, over unpaid bills. Having endured tirades, Steve relished the opportunity to hit back at his feisty opponent. After all their efforts, Steve was incensed that they had not been paid for their work.

Although Steve spoke in a quiet, calm manner, he laid out his grievances in a stinging style that deflated the larger-than-life Texan. McCarthy took the criticisms on the chin. But he did so in the knowledge that the payments were being deliberately withheld by Martin Beckwith from his Whitehall bunker. After the harangue, Steve expected the Texan to slink away with his tail between his legs. But the tongue-lashing was like water off a duck's back. The thick-skinned Texan soon bounced back, asking Steve to join him for lunch. This was a bit strange, given their rancorous relationship.

Steve initially declined the Texan's offer. Unlike other businessmen, Steve disliked entertaining clients. He led a busy life and had better things to do than talk to dull-witted businessmen about golf and their most recent foreign holiday. These bores reminded him of the first-class passengers on the *Sea Ranger*. The privileged people would eat, drink and sun themselves, oblivious to dramatic events taking place on the decks below.

Life below decks on the decrepit old ship was enlivened by scavenge fires in the engine room. The clapped-out engines broke down every other day and there were frequent problems with drunken and mutinous crew. But none of these troubling matters disturbed the tranquil life of the pampered folk in the first-class lounge. Their superior attitude reflected that of many in the business world.

In any event, the Texan's invitation did not fit with the young executive's busy schedule. It would also be uncomfortable as the adversaries tiptoed around the inflammatory issue of the unpaid bills. But the pugnacious Texan would not take no for an answer. So, recalling the old adage that the customer is always right, Steve reluctantly accepted the invitation. The pair then made their way to the Windmill, which was the only half-decent restaurant in the area.

After being ushered to their seats in the yawningly empty dining room, they sat in awkward silence at a square table that was too small to accommodate the Texan's corpulent body. The Texan surveyed the menu with baleful eyes. He yearned for barbecues of sizzling steak that were the norm in his home state, but such feasts were a distant memory. Despite living many years on this side of the Atlantic, he was not acclimatised to stingy English fare.

"Sorry to drag you from your desk," drawled the Texan as he squirmed on his under-sized chair. The bear-like fellow spoke in an unusually amiable manner as he tried to thaw the frosty atmosphere with his prickly guest. "I know you are a busy guy, but this is my last visit to your yard. I want to thank you for your hard work." Steve knew the Texan was moving on, but his departure hardly warranted a celebration, given their fractious adversarial arrangement.

Steve respected the Texan as a tough adversary but they had little in common except their business dealings. It still rankled that he had to spend his lunch hour with this boorish yank. "Who is taking over?" asked Steve, in an effort to make polite conversation. There was no need to ask the question; he already knew the answer – Beckwith was to resume his role as project manager. But the question filled the silence.

"Martin Beckwith," replied the Texan with a frown as he studied the menu. Steve was not sure whether the sour expression was caused by his disdain for the food or contempt for his predecessor. These doubts were soon dispelled. "Glad I'm not in your shoes. That low-life is sitting on your bills!" declared the Texan in an outburst of honesty. Steve was taken aback by the unexpected admission.

There had been suspicions that Beckwith was blocking payment of his bills, but this was the first time that the Texan had admitted it. It was also a credit to the straight-talking guy that he had refused to pass the buck on this inflammatory issue. It showed he was a stalwart character.

Having scanned the menu, the Texan settled reluctantly for a quarter-pound steak, chips and peas. Steve followed suit and tried to attract a waitress, but the young guy forgot about the order when his dining companion dropped a bombshell. "I understand Commander Woods spoke to you about your financial problems," growled the Texan in a casual way. Steve was dumbfounded and wondered how the Texan knew about their private conversation.

"Who gave you that idea?" he replied in a non-committal way.

"Rear-Admiral Sir Richard Walters. He told me that he has offered to help you," replied the Texan nonchalantly. "The Admiral is a good friend." The waitress was hovering over their table, waiting in vain for the dining order. Steve ignored the waitress as he tried to make sense of what he had heard. Seeing that his companion was distracted, the Texan assumed the role of host. "Two steaks, burned on the outside, rare in the middle, with all the trimmings," he barked in his folksy drawl.

The Admiral's name had come up from time to time during Steve's conversations with the commander and had also been mentioned by various people. But Steve had never met this elusive character. "Commander Woods reports to the Admiral, I believe," observed Steve tentatively as he tried to adjust to the fast-changing scene. "I understand that he has a lot of influence, but I have never met him. How do you come to know him?"

"We met at an antiques auction when I first came to your country, back in the 1970s," replied the Texan in a matter-of-fact sort of way. "We share an interest in naval history. I only accepted the job as project manager as a favour to the old boy." Steve wanted to know more about this unlikely relationship, but the Texan showed no interest in discussing the matter further.

By this time, Steve was warming to his dining companion, thinking that he was of a different calibre to the run-of-the-mill pen-pushers he normally dealt with. He was curious to learn more about the 'Texan pig farmer'. It was fascinating to discover that the bear-like fellow shared an interest in naval history with one of the country's most senior naval officers. He was impressed.

"I didn't want to speak at your yard – walls have ears, you know!" confided the Texan, "but there are things you need to know before Beckwith comes back to the helm. What I'm about to tell you is strictly off the record and might change your view of the project. Did you know that submariners don't want the rescue vehicle?" he added with a conspiratorial wink. "They don't believe fuel-cell propulsion is suitable for rescue work."

Whenever the commander had expressed that view, Steve had jumped down his throat, even though they were friends. But hearing the comments from the Texan shone a different light on the subject. This was a worrying revelation for the young executive. Steve nodded wearily. "Yes, the commander said as much!"

The young executive was angered by the direction of the conversation. It had been a huge challenge to build the fuel-cell propulsion system and he was proud of their achievement. Completion of the project should be a reason for celebration, but he was met instead with questions about the suitability of the rescue vehicle and aggravation over unpaid bills. The navy's inter-departmental politics was none of his concern.

The Texan ignored the red flush of anger in his dining companion's face and ploughed on with all the sensitivity of a Sherman tank ploughing through a minefield. "The Admiral understands the drawbacks but he okayed the project nonetheless," declared the Texan in a matter-of-fact way. "The old boy wants to use the midget submarine for something else."

Steve felt a surge of anger, but he checked himself, realising that the Texan did not have an axe to grind and the comments echoed the commander's views. In other circumstances, it might be an intriguing story, but the naval shenanigans were making his life difficult. Steve was starting to feel like the meat in a sandwich between warring factions of the navy. "Are you telling me that my cash flow problems are being caused by an inter-departmental dispute in the navy?" he demanded indignantly.

"I'm afraid so," said the Texan bluntly, showing little sympathy for the young executive's plight. "You need to understand that some powerful people are gunning for Beckwith. His agency has run out of money. The bottom line is that you are unlikely to receive the cash you are owed. Admiral Walters may be able to find a way through the financial morass. That's what the commander was trying to tell you last week."

"But where will the Admiral find the cash?" asked Steve, with a puzzled expression, as he tried to make sense of what he had heard. "We are owed millions of pounds."

"He's working with people in the shipping industry," explained the Texan calmly. "It's all part of a grand plan to deal with hijackers in the Indian Ocean. He is assembling a team and he would like your help. The shipping people will provide all the cash the Admiral needs."

The Texan went on to explain that if Steve 'played ball' then the Admiral would pull strings to settle the outstanding bills and provide fresh capital for his boatyard. The Texan would not be drawn on what sort of *quid pro quo* the Admiral would require in return. But there was an implied threat that if he did not accept the Admiral's terms then his yard would face ruin.

Although spoken in a calm, straightforward manner, the words were chilling. Steve did not take kindly to threats, and in any other situation he would have told his diner companion to take a hike. But his yard faced dire problems and it would be foolish to ignore this potential life line. Not wishing to commit himself, he asked the Texan how he became involved, in the hope that the question would throw some light on this confusing situation.

"My son served as a second mate on a tanker in the Merchant Marine," said the Texan. "One of the Indian crew told him a chilling story about a hijacking off the coast of Yemen. He told me about it when he came home on leave, so I want to do something about it. The subject came up when I was invited round to dinner with the Admiral one evening. We started to kick some ideas around. After that, the old boy arranged for some shipping people to flesh out plans. They have had several meetings in Fenchurch Street."

Their conversation was interrupted when the waitress served their meals. The Texan did not utter a word as he chomped his way through the food. After clearing his plate, the bear-like fellow stretched, burped and took up where he had left off. "The Admiral would be happy to talk to you at his home. He's an interesting old boy, you should learn something!" The Texan then declined 'something from the sweet trolley' with a disdainful sweep of his hand. "Must get going," he added. "It's a long way back to Portsmouth."

After settling the bill from a bulging wallet, the Texan struggled to squeeze his large frame into Steve's low-slung sports car, but they soon arrived back at the boatyard. The meal left Steve shell-shocked and it took him time to digest what he had learned. His first reaction was to rail at the injustice. After years of hard slog, his company was denied payment because of a dispute between different branches of the armed services. A lesser man might have been crushed by this blow. But the young guy was made of sterner stuff. He was like an intrepid mountaineer who had conquered one daunting ridge only to find that an even higher peak lay ahead. But how should he proceed?

Steve was in two minds whether to accept an invitation to the Admiral's home. On the one hand, he was wary of being dragged into an inter-departmental dispute within the navy, but at the same time he felt that it was his duty to explore every avenue to prevent collapse of the boatyard. In the end, he decided that there would be no harm in exploring an offer of financial help, so he made arrangements to visit the elusive 'Admiral' to find out what he had to say.

This lukewarm approach was mistaken – the young executive was stepping into a lion's den without taking steps to prepare. Steve's complacency arose because he believed that naval officers were brave and honourable but naïve about business matters. 'All spit and polish and no brains', was the disdainful view expressed by some of his pals. This was an apt description of the commander, who had little understanding of business affairs, but it did not apply to the Admiral, who had many close friends in the financial world.

Steve felt quietly confident as he arrived at the Admiral's home to find his host dressed in his tatty old gardening clothes, clipping the hedge of his large rectory garden. The eccentric old buffer apologised for his scruffy appearance and asked Steve to wait in the sitting room while he washed his hands. "I'm waiting for a colleague to join us," explained the genial old fellow. A plump, jolly woman lumbered into the sitting room bearing a cup of tea, spilling some in the saucer as she stumbled over a rug.

"Thought you might like a cuppa after your long journey, dearie," she declared with a thick country accent. "Don't know whether you take sugar, but I've put three spoons in anyway. You young people need your energy!" This remark caused Steve to wonder whether he had wandered unwittingly into a comedy show, or a home for the mentally deranged.

After washing his hands, the Admiral padded back into the sitting room and began to fumble about with an old-fashioned television set that was hidden inside a polished walnut cabinet. Steve assumed that the batty old man was trying to keep him amused. This notion did not sit well with him. The go-getting young guy thought that daytime television was an opiate for the lazy and indolent.

Steve grimaced at the foul, stewed taste of the tea as the picture finally flickered onto the curved cathode ray screen. There was no sound to accompany the picture. It took some time for the young executive to realise that the programme was not a daytime chat show, but a real-life horror movie. The television displayed an image of half-starved seamen, held in a barbaric prison, begging for help. It made harrowing viewing. The young executive turned away in horror when masked desperados appeared with knives, fearing that he was about to watch an execution.

When his genial host had completed his chores, he ambled back into the sitting room and smiled in a kindly way at Steve's squeamish reaction. "Hope that did not upset you too much," remarked the mischievous old fox, with a twinkle in his eye. "You may be interested to know that the video was accompanied by a ransom demand for ten million dollars. I hope that it did not shock you, but I need to get your attention. You can see the problem we are dealing with. I showed you the film because I need your help. I believe that Sam told you something about our plans."

"S ...S ...Sam didn't say much," stuttered Steve as he struggled to gain his orientation. "He did mention some plans to protect merchant shipping from pirates." After a long drive from Plymouth, the film had knocked him completely off balance and he was having trouble making sense of what was taking place. "But the reason that I came today is that Sam told me that you might be able to help with our yard's financial problems."

"Well, one thing at a time," replied the Admiral doubtfully. Then after pondering the question for a short time, he continued. "How important is the yard to you?"

"It's very important," replied Steve boldly as he started to regain his mental balance. "I feel responsible for my workforce. That's just a start."

"Do you get support from the Dutch owners?" enquired the old fox.

"Yes, they are supportive," replied Steve cautiously.

"But are they prepared to provide all the capital you need?" asked the Admiral, fixing the young executive with his piercing blue eyes.

That perceptive question led Steve to realise, too late, that he had badly misread the situation. His host might look like a scruffy old codger, but it was clear that the old boy was sharp as a razor. Only a handful of people knew that the Dutch owners had denied Steve's request for a capital injection. It was obvious that the old fellow had done his homework.

The failure of the Dutch owners to support the boatyard kept Steve awake at night. He was infuriated by the lack of support as his business struggled to weather a slump in the offshore industry. Almost all offshore businesses were in trouble. But his cash flow problems were exacerbated because he had not been paid for the submarine rescue project. As a result, the yard was on the brink of collapse. The young executive had trouble paying staff. He was at his wits' end, so he was cautious about framing his reply.

"Can you persuade Martin Beckwith to pay his bills?" Steve asked hopefully.

"We might be able to provide some help," replied his host in an oblique manner. "It depends on what you can do for us. But you need to speak to my accountant. He will be here in a few ticks."

There followed an uncomfortable silence as they waited for the accountant to arrive. It was a relief when they heard a car crunching over the gravel drive. The modest saloon car ground to a halt next to Steve's sleek sports car. The Admiral shuffled off to admit the visitor. The new arrival was a slightly built man called Felix Sikorski. He was sharply dressed in a three-piece suit and carried a smart leather briefcase. His leather brogues were polished to a sheen that would pass military inspection. They wasted no time as they settled down to business.

"Felix. What can you tell us about Mr Jones's company?" asked the Admiral smoothly.

Felix withdrew some papers from his briefcase and spoke in the staccato manner of a Polish intellectual. He proceeded to reel off a string of figures: "Year 2013; turnover £31 million; profit £0.5 million; bank deposits £2.1 million. Year 2014; turnover £29 million; losses of £600,000; bank deposits £1.7 million. Year 2015; turnover £19 million; losses £1 million; bank deposits £30,000."

He returned the papers to his briefcase. "Those are *not* the figures of a healthy business, are they, Mr Jones?" he observed in a clinical manner. "Your boatyard is haemorrhaging cash! It won't be long before the administrators are called in, so what are you going to do about it?"

In other circumstances, Steve would have told them that his financial affairs were none of their business. But he was cornered and disorientated in the deceptively benign surroundings. The young executive had experienced an emotional roller coaster since arriving at this mad hatter's tea party. After watching the harrowing film, he was left reeling by a savage clinical analysis of the yard's dire financial situation. It was as though these people were able to read his inner thoughts and divine his most lurid fears.

"I ... I ... don't know where you got those figures, but they are misleading," he stuttered. "They don't show the true situation. You know there has been a slump in the oil and gas industry. Most businesses like ours are experiencing problems, but we have a recovery plan."

"Please tell us about your plan. We are most interested," challenged Felix with the sinister smile of a cat toying with a mouse. As Steve started to speak, the accountant deftly removed papers from his briefcase. The young executive was rattled, and his throat was dry as a result of the tannin in the ghastly stewed tea. "Our priority is to secure payment for the submarine rescue project," he croaked. "That should sort out our immediate problems.

"We will lay off some staff to reduce costs. In the long term, we hope to win some new business from the shipping industry. Opportunities should arise from the tighter exhaust emission rules that are due to come in over the next couple of years. We hope to sell exhaust gas scrubbing systems. We are also developing an insulated tank for storing liquefied natural gas. I have put all these plans to our Dutch owners."

As he spoke, Steve began to recover his confidence. This was familiar ground for the young executive. He had made numerous business presentations about the emission regulations and believed his well-honed arguments would impress these people, but his hopes were dashed when the Polish accountant held up his hand to stop him. His dour expression suggested that the accountant was unimpressed with what he had heard so far.

"We are developing a 'Type B' self-supporting storage tank for liquefied natural gas," read Felix from a paper that he was holding. "Do you recognise those words?" he asked acidly. Steve's face reddened and he felt a further tightness in his throat. Those were the exact words he had used in a letter to the Dutch owners. It suggested that the accountant had access to confidential information. This was deeply disturbing and led the young executive to wonder what else this magician knew about his business dealings.

"Don't be embarrassed. It's a good plan," commented Felix, whose dour expression gradually transformed into a sickly smile. "We support the plan," he added before plunging in the knife, "but, sadly, your Dutch owners do not!"

"Where did you get that document?" demanded Steve angrily.

The accountant frowned at this and the Admiral stepped in to pour oil on troubled waters. "Felix is well informed about these matters," explained the genial old buffer in an emollient way. "It's probably best that you do not ask him where he gets his information. He has his sources."

If this was a game of poker, Steve would be holding a poor hand. These people knew his financial predicament and there was little point in trying to pull the wool over their eyes. But he was not done yet. As he composed himself, he recalled how the Russian army allowed Napoleon to occupy Moscow before they drove the marauding invaders out of their country, so he decided that it would be wise to give some ground before going on the offensive.

"I know that our finances are in a mess," admitted Steve as he retreated to a defensible position, "but it's been a long journey from the West Country and I was told that you might be able to help. So what can you do? Can you persuade Martin Beckwith to pay his bills?"

Now on the defensive, Felix was forced to admit that he did not have any influence over the artful academic. The smartly attired man went on to repeat much of what the Texan project manager said over lunch in the Windmill public house. "Sorry, we can't help you there," he admitted. "Beckwith's agency is short of funds and can't pay its bills. They have to persuade the navy to sign a lease for the new submarine rescue vehicle. Until they do so, they have no money to pay you.

"The agency has a real fight on its hands. The submariners don't believe that fuel-cell propulsion is suitable for rescue work," continued Felix. "The ministry is dragging its heels over the lease. That is why the agency is unable to pay its bills. Beckwith expects that the navy will change its view after the demonstration. His political friends could help force the navy to accept the submersible."

These comments confirmed Steve's suspicions. After his lunch with the Texan, Steve formed the view that elements within the navy were trying to use underhand methods to lay their hands on the midget submarine. It now seemed that he was in the presence of the architect of that dastardly plot. "So what do you recommend I do?" asked Steve to test his theory.

"One way that you might be able to escape your financial mess is to look for another role for the midget submarine," replied the Admiral with a friendly smile, to give the impression that he was doing his visitor a favour. "It might be difficult, though. Martin Beckwith will not be happy with that idea, and he might try to sabotage your efforts."

Steve discerned a cunning look in his host's eyes. The exchange confirmed his suspicions that his apparently genial host was up to mischief, but he did not want to reveal his hand just yet. "What role were you thinking of?" he asked innocently. He intended to keep some cards up his sleeve until he had figured out another game plan.

"Good question!" replied the cunning old fox as though the thought had not occurred to him. "Perhaps surveillance, or something like that," he suggested airily. "The fuel cells would be ideal for covert surveillance. They would allow the submarine to spend a long time on the seabed."

Steve took some satisfaction from that remark because it showed that his host appreciated the benefits of the innovative fuel-cell propulsion system they had taken so much trouble to develop, but he could also see that he was being distracted from the original purpose of his visit. He had driven for several hours from the West Country to visit the Admiral in the faint hope that he might provide a solution to his financial woes. But he had not, so far, heard the slightest hint as to how his problems might be resolved. He needed to force his hand.

"This is all very interesting," said Steve, "but you are talking about internal squabbles in the naval high command. Those arguments do not really interest me. My problem is simple. I want my bills paid! If you are unable to help me, then it's been a wasted trip, and I shall make my way home." With that, he collected his belongings and rose from his chair to depart.

"Well, we *might be able to* help you there," replied the Admiral in a tantalising fashion, "but not in the way that you expect."

"Well, I'm listening," replied Steve. The young executive turned and returned hesitantly to his seat.

"We could persuade your Dutch owners to support your recovery plan," replied the Admiral, as though laying out a full house in a poker game.

This was an attractive offer. It went to the heart of his difficulties. Steve was enraged that senior executives from the Dutch conglomerate had rejected his recovery plan. They were willing his business to fail so they could pursue their building development project, but these people seemed to know what was going on. So perhaps they were his saviours after all. But Steve needed assurance that they could deliver on their offer. "What guarantee can you give that the Dutch owners will support my plan?" he demanded.

"None, I'm afraid," said the Admiral wearily. "It's too early to say how things will all play out. But you can see from Felix's investigation that we have gone to a great deal of trouble. We understand your predicament and sympathise, but we want your help in return. A *quid pro quo*, you might say."

"What do you want from me?" demanded Steve guardedly.

"We want you to run a dredging business," said the Admiral in a matter-of-fact way. "We need you to set it up and get the business going. We will pay the going rate."

"Did you say *dredging business?*" exclaimed Steve incredulously. This was all becoming stranger by the minute. He was not sure that he had heard the old boy correctly and had no idea why a naval officer wanted to make such a bizarre request.

"Yes. *Dredging business*," confirmed the Admiral, placing careful emphasis on the words. "It's not quite as straightforward as it sounds. The dredger will provide a base for special forces in trouble spots, like the Horn of Africa. We need someone to run the ship and look after the operational side of things. If you can help us with our plan, then we will try to persuade the Dutch owners to support the recovery plan for your boatyard."

Steve could not believe what he was hearing. This was the last thing that he had anticipated on his long drive to Hampshire. He was dumbfounded and unsure how to react. The Admiral saw his confusion but continued to outline his proposal.

"We've looked into your background and think you are the right person for the job. It will be a challenge, but worthwhile. You have seen the problems that the victims of hijacking face on the video, so it's a worthwhile task and we don't want you to accept the job in a half-hearted way. You won't be directly involved in military activities – that will be handled by specially trained people, but this is your chance to save the boatyard. I doubt that anyone else can help. So if you are unsure about our proposal, then I suggest you return to your yard and wait for the bailiffs to knock on the door!"

Steve could not take in everything that had taken place since arriving in this bucolic setting less than an hour earlier, so he declared "That was the last thing that I expected! If you don't mind, I need to think about what you have said and talk things over with the commander. It seems that we got off on the wrong foot on this."

"Good idea," replied the Admiral reassuringly. "Have a word with the commander. We'll let him know that he can confide in you. The commander understands the lay of the land – he is part of the team. Let me know what you decide in a couple of weeks. I hope you decide to join us, but please do not repeat what we have said to anyone else."

The short meeting had been an emotional assault on the young executive, but he would later learn that it was a carefully choreographed affair. The Admiral did not normally bother with garden chores – he employed a gardener from the village to cut his hedge. The cunning old fox had adopted an absent-minded persona to wrong-foot his guest. The Admiral had learned of Steve's reputation when talking to people that he met at maritime conferences. He wanted to entice the successful young executive into his team, but on the right terms.

The old fox was able to offer Steve a rescue package because he was friendly with the head of the conglomerate that owned the boatyard. The conglomerate had grown from a small family-owned shipping company. In the post-war years, the business expanded and diversified into other areas. The founder of the enlarged company remained the major shareholder, but in the past few years, he had handed over control to the younger generation of the family. Watching from the sidelines, the family patriarch was dismayed, as his successors had turned their backs on their shipping heritage to concentrate on the property side.

In their desire to build a property empire, the younger generation of the family refused to inject cash into the ailing marine business at Whitebait Cove. The patriarch was reluctant to use his voting rights to overrule their plans, fearing that it would create a family rift. Neither did the octogenarian wish to take back control of the business. When the Dutchman confided his dilemma to the Admiral, the old fox suggested that his shipping interests should be split off and run as a stand-alone business.

The Admiral had ulterior motives for this advice. The old fox hoped that the stand-alone shipping business would fund a scheme that he had been planning to protect merchant shipping from hijackers. The patriarch shared the Admiral's concerns about this subject and his associates were represented at the meetings in Fenchurch Street. In fact, it was the patriarch who suggested that Steve should become involved in the scheme.

The family patriarch admired the way that Steve had transformed Sam Wheeler's rickety old boatyard into a modern go-getting business, but his admiration for the young guy was a cause of resentment within his family. The young generation feared that Steve was being groomed to take control of the whole business. In a sly move to promote Steve's interests, the patriarch had leaked embarrassing details of the boatyard's financial plight to Felix.

Felix quoted those figures during his discussion with Steve at the Admiral's home. The Dutch patriarch had also provided tips that would enable the old fox to recruit Steve into their covert operation. "The young guy is always up for a challenge," confided the Dutchman to the Admiral during a quiet conversation, "but he has a bit of a big head and is susceptible to flattery." These observations showed keen insight. Steve was extremely ambitious, and his discontent stemmed from frustration at being held back by things outside his control.

Steve's thoughts were in turmoil as he drove home from the Admiral's pleasant country retreat. It seemed as though he had lived through an episode of *Alice in Wonderland*. The crazy meeting had been an assault on his emotions. His crafty host had played on his fears for the survival of the boatyard and his sympathy for captured seamen. But as the young guy cruised down the normally busy motorway, in his sports car, he began to regain his bearings. The motorway was unusually quiet as he purred through some roadworks at a steady 50 mph.

As he reflected, he realised he had become obsessed with a few intractable problems, such as the unpaid bills, and had failed to view life in a creative way. *It was pointless to swim against the tide*, he mused. The meeting had persuaded him to look to new horizons. Two ideas dominated his thoughts.

The first was that he and the commander were mere pawns in a bigger game. The second, that followed on from the first, was that he had treated the commander in a shabby way by questioning his motives for criticising Beckwith's project.

The meeting, and the preceding lunch with the Texan, had forced Steve to reconsider his attitude towards the submarine rescue project. It was clear that he would have to make peace with the commander. Prior to his meeting with the Texan, Steve believed that the project was backed by the navy and that the commander was a lone critic. But it now seemed clear that the commander's critical views were shared widely within the service and that his friend had been set up as a fall guy in some convoluted plot.

It was clear both from what he had learned that day and from what the Texan had told him, that the commander's reservations about the use of fuel-cell propulsion for rescue operations were quite legitimate and that they were widely held within the submarine service. Steve was also embarrassed that his overly suspicious nature had led him to believe that the commander inviting him on fishing trips had some base motive. That suspicion was unfounded.

It was also apparent that the embarrassing details of the yard's financial plight quoted by Felix had been supplied by a mole inside the Dutch conglomerate. Steve felt contrite. It was clear that he had been blinded by his yard's technical achievements and had not taken the trouble to listen carefully to what the commander actually said. He had bridges to mend, so he phoned the commander as soon as he reached Plymouth. It was not an easy call. Apologies did not come easily to the ambitious young guy.

"I'm sorry if I was rude during our fishing trip," mumbled Steve in a sheepish way. "It seems that we have got our wires crossed."

The commander thought it a feeble apology. Steve had questioned his honour, which was hard to forgive. All he had done was speak the truth as he saw it. "Glad you have finally seen things from my point of view," replied the war hero acidly. "What made you change your mind?"

"I spoke to Admiral Walters this morning. He wants me to run a dredging business. They said something about an undercover operation and suggested that I should talk to you about it."

The commander was cagy in his reply, not knowing whether Steve could be trusted with the full story. "Our plans are still at an early stage," he explained. "We do need someone to run a dredging company. The company will be quite legitimate. But the dredger will provide a base for undercover operations."

The commander was still smarting from their quarrel and could not resist the temptation to have fun at his friend's expense. "Glad to hear that you are thinking of joining us," he added amiably. Then after a pause, he continued. "Did the old boy tell you that the dredger will act as a base for Beckwith's midget submarine?" *That should put the cat among the pigeons*, he thought mischievously.

This left Steve spluttering with confusion. It was all too much to take in. "How *on earth* do you plan to get hold of the midget submarine?" asked the young executive at length, with an incredulous air.

"Don't know yet," replied the commander airily. "We haven't worked that out yet! But we will come up with something!"

This infuriated the young executive. The commander had kicked him in the teeth because any funny business by the navy would imperil his efforts to recover the cash he was owed. But as the absurdity of his situation dawned on him, Steve's sense of humour returned. If he was involved in a game, he might as well play ball, he thought.

"I'm surprised you want to use the submarine. After all, it's propelled by fuel cells!" quipped the young guy. The self-deprecating nature of this remark helped to dispel the animosity that had grown between the two men since the Sunday lunch. It was as though a dam had burst to release the growing tension. The commander responded to the olive branch.

"Well, perhaps you can explain the benefits of your new-fangled propulsion to our gang in Fenchurch Street," suggested the commander with a chuckle. He was relieved that they had managed to settle their differences in an amicable way. In the conversation that followed, Steve agreed to visit Fenchurch Street to learn more about the undercover operation.

Steve arrived in Fenchurch Street to find mariners assembled in the same dingy conference room that they had occupied on previous occasions. The motley crew were chatting in one corner of the room, poking fun at the young civil servants who were trying in vain to supervise them. A rostrum and easel had been set up at one end of the room. The mariners had been told that Steve was involved in the construction of a new midget submarine, and so they gave him a warm welcome. His presence gave substance to the commander's vague suggestion that a midget submarine might be provided for their mission.

Before the mariners had a chance to question Steve, the commander strolled briskly into the room and called the gathering to order. Steve felt uneasy when he noticed the sharply dressed accountant he had encountered at the Admiral's home sitting by himself at the table, with a sour expression. Felix nodded towards Steve in a perfunctory greeting. But the accountant's body language suggested that he had differences with the commander.

Lieutenant Bracknell had, by this time, returned to his warship in the Persian Gulf, so the commander was the only naval officer present. The commander asked if anyone objected to him chairing the discussion. There were no objections. So, after introducing the newcomers, he signalled that Felix should address the gathering.

The accountant's solemn manner was at odds with the boisterous behaviour of the mariners. "Gentlemen," he declared as he stood stony faced before the rostrum, "you will be pleased to know that after *considerable* effort, I've raised the funds for your mission. I can only hope that you use the money wisely." After that brief statement, he returned to his seat, where he sat in a sphinx-like silence, like a spectre at the feast.

The glad tidings would have been greeted with applause had the accountant's presence not dampened the atmosphere. The accountant's beady eyes flicked from person to person as he watched the proceedings with the sour expression of a vicar who had wandered by accident into an orgy. He muttered disdainfully as the commander summarised the deliberations of the previous meetings, showing little enthusiasm for their mission.

"Over the past sessions we have looked at some unorthodox ideas for protecting ships from hijackers in the Indian Ocean," declared the commander in an upbeat manner as he scanned his prepared notes. He went on to explain how the risk of hijacking had been reduced thanks to the fleet of warships sent to the Indian Ocean. He illustrated this with figures. "There have only been two incidents in the last six months," he announced proudly. "One ship was recovered by negotiation. A Chinese commando team stormed the second ship and managed to free all of the crew.

"But we can't maintain our task force in the Indian Ocean for much longer," he told them. "Our warships are needed to tackle the refugee crisis in the Mediterranean." He went on to explain that frontline warships were not particularly well suited to policing pirates. "The effectiveness of conventional warships is also being eroded as local fishermen use social media to track the movements of the fleets," he warned. Then he went on to describe the problem of recovering captured ships and their crew.

Having explained the difficulties, he went on to point to reasons for optimism. "Law and order are being restored under a semblance of democratic government in some provinces around the Horn of Africa," he explained in the uplifting tone of an evangelist. Then he went on to describe the embryonic plans agreed at previous sessions, with the aid of graphics.

"Our scheme should help keep tabs on the villains," he observed. "We plan to hide a midget submarine in the hopper of a suction dredger. The dredger will act as the mother ship. The ship will dredge channels to new ports that are being built along the coast. It will provide a base for covert surveillance of the local pirate gangs, and it will house security personnel. Well, that's the theory. Now we need to work out how we can achieve that in practice."

As he listened, Steve was intrigued by the boldness of this plan. It was the first time that he had considered the benefits of fuel-cell propulsion for this role. The fuel cells would allow the midget submarine to remain submerged far longer than a conventional battery-powered craft, so it would be able to venture much further from the mother ship. But there was an elephant in the room. As things stood, the midget submarine did not belong to this motley crew and he had failed to explain how it would be acquired. The commander had studiously avoided that crucial issue.

As the commander wound up his presentation, he turned to Steve. "I'd like to introduce Steve Jones, who is the genius responsible for designing a revolutionary new form of propulsion for submarines," he announced flatteringly. "Steve, could you please describe the benefits of this technology for our guests?"

Steve did not know how to approach his presentation. His brief was to explain the benefits of fuel-cell propulsion, which was simple enough, but the commander had given the impression that the submarine would become available to this operation. He had no idea whether this was the case, so as he approached the rostrum the young executive's mind was racing. He decided to start by explaining the background to the submarine rescue project.

"A couple of years ago, the Marine Special Projects Agency embarked on a project to build a revolutionary new form of submarine rescue vehicle," explained Steve. The words were a major digression from his prepared notes. "This will be the first British-built submarine to use fuel-cell propulsion. Our company was contracted to assemble the system. The sea trials of the prototype will be carried out from our boatyard.

"The trials will take place in two stages," he continued. "In the first stage, the focus will be on the diving performance. This technology was first used in German submarines, but we have no experience in this country as yet, so the trials may reveal teething problems. Once the navy is satisfied with the diving performance, the prototype will be returned to the shipyard, where hatches and airlocks will be fitted. These will enable the submersible to perform rescue operations. Further trials will take place to test the rescue functions."

He then proceeded to deliver the presentation in accordance with his prepared notes. After briefly describing the principles of fuel-cell propulsion, he unfurled some illustrations with facts and figures to show how fuel cells would increase the submerged range of a midget submarine. The group listened with interest to the presentation, but most were too polite to ask the obvious question. A master mariner eventually expressed what others were thinking.

"That's all fine and dandy!" barked a ruddy-faced master mariner. "Fuel cells might be the dog's bollocks for submarine propulsion, but from what you say, the rinky-dink craft has been built for submarine rescue. We are not interested in rescuing sailors from the seabed! We want to carry out covert surveillance work along the coast."

"I'm afraid that I shall have to defer to the commander on that point," said Steve diplomatically as he blushed red with embarrassment. Steve wished the ground would open beneath his feet. But he had done his bit. The commander had got himself into this predicament, and he would have to extract himself from the mire. Steve was curious to see how he would do it.

"Thanks, Steve, for explaining the benefits of fuel-cell propulsion," said the commander in an unusually emollient way. He then sidestepped the awkward question as he bluffed it out. "To fully understand the overall situation, you will also need to look at it from the navy's point of view," he continued airily. "I hope that you now see the benefits of fuel-cell propulsion.

"This technology has great potential. I have seen it for myself. A few months ago, I visited a German submarine that employed the technology. It was most impressive. But, sadly, our colleagues in the submarine branch do not really feel it appropriate for a rescue vehicle. It's important to recognise that the German submarines are not wholly dependent on fuel cells. They use fuel cells in a hybrid arrangement, so there are back-up systems."

The mariners became restive at this waffle. They could also see a simmering tension between the commander, the young executive and the sour-faced accountant. The ruddy-faced master mariner, once again, summed up the rancorous mood in a succinct manner. "Before you get carried away with all this, you need to sort out who owns this fantastic midget submarine," he growled. "When we know who it belongs to, we can talk about our plans!"

The commander's authority drained away with this acerbic comment. Some wags began to josh around, ignoring the purpose of the meeting. As he watched discipline break down, Felix began to discuss the nature of 'ownership' with his neighbour. The pair bandied terms such as *theft, repossess, lease* and *impound* as the debate became more heated.

In an attempt to reimpose authority, the commander asked them to explain what they were talking about. "Look at it this way," said Felix to the now silent assembly. "Let's imagine that a person buys a house with the aid of a loan from a building society. You would describe him as the owner, would you not?" He then embarked on a long diatribe to question whether this was the case, given that the building society could repossess the property under certain circumstances.

Although the commander did not quite follow the argument, he gained the impression that there was a legal mechanism that would allow them to acquire the midget submarine without Beckwith's approval, so he phoned the Admiral to pass on this good news. Expecting to win praise, he received a stern dressing-down instead. The Admiral was infuriated that his subordinate had strayed into areas where he lacked expertise.

"I think it's best if you leave the financial side to me, young man!" growled the old boy in a sharp rebuke. "My family raised money to build the navy fleet for King Henry the Eighth. When I was a child, my father would talk about his City dealings at the breakfast table. I can tell you more about finance than you will ever want to know. Your friends have got the wrong end of the stick. What you are talking about is akin to a hostile takeover bid. That happens from time to time in the City."

"Sorry. I don't see what is wrong in discussing it," spluttered the commander, who was taken aback by his boss's venomous reaction.

"Don't you read the financial pages?" demanded the old fox with an exasperated sigh. "The papers are full of stories about hostile takeover bids. Yes. We might be able to acquire the midget submarine in that way, but a move like that would put us in the media spotlight. The whole world would know what we are up to. We would be playing right into Beckwith's hands. He knows how to use the media to pursue his own ends, and would run rings around us, so we need to play our cards carefully! Please remember that this is a *secret operation*."

After reprimanding the commander, the Admiral phoned his accountant, Felix, to admonish him for making mischief. So, with matters at an impasse, it was decided to call a halt to the series of meetings at Fenchurch Street until it was known whether the midget submarine would be made available to them.

The mariners were pleased that the meeting was adjourned early because it provided a rare opportunity to enjoy a liquid lunch. In the previous months, City institutions had issued edicts banning employees from drinking alcohol during the working day. The old-timers were up in arms about the draconian rules, but the early finish provided an excuse for them to indulge.

With the Fenchurch Street meetings postponed, the commander felt free to join the mariners on their pub outing. They set off in a jovial mood, recounting anecdotes. When it came to his turn, the commander repeated the story about the squad of marines who stole a drum of cable in the desert. In this anarchic atmosphere, a bizarre plan began to take shape.

Back in leafy Hampshire, the Admiral was satisfied with the way that things were going, although annoyed that his financially illiterate subordinate had strayed beyond his remit. In the previous weeks, the old fox had learned about Beckwith's dodgy dealings through his old-boys' network. The Admiral knew that the academic was on a sticky wicket and only had a limited period to sign a lease agreement with the navy. Failure to meet this deadline would allow the lenders to repossess his submarine. This placed the Admiral in a strong position to acquire the craft.

With that knowledge, the Admiral held Beckwith's future in his hands. It amused the old fox to watch the egotistical academic strutting about, completely oblivious to the fate that awaited him. Beckwith's career was built on a foundation of sand. One push would bring the whole rotten empire crashing to the ground. But the success of their hijack prevention venture depended on secrecy, so the Admiral needed to play his cards close to his chest. This was why he was angered by his accountant's loose remarks at the meeting.

Chapter 11

Steve collects debts and fishes with Mark

Steve was unable to join the mariners on their pub outing because he had another task. The young executive had to visit Whitehall to chase up unpaid bills. But before setting off on that unpalatable duty, he dallied, wandering the streets, to soak up the atmosphere. For him, the City of London had an intoxicating atmosphere evoking wealth, sophistication and power. He came across a small park shaded by London limes. Here he stretched out on a park bench to watch the smartly attired office workers swarming the streets like a colony of worker ants.

As he relaxed in the shade, the young guy recalled the exhilaration he felt on his way to an interview with the Boston Line. The now defunct shipping company occupied plush offices in nearby Leadenhall Street. Finely crafted models of the company's fleet were housed in glass cases in the foyer of the imposing stone-clad building. The well-groomed staff welcomed the sixth-former like a princeling. As a naïve schoolboy, who had never travelled abroad, the prospect of sailing to the Orient was alluring.

But he put these pleasant memories aside as he steeled himself to challenge Beckwith about the unpaid bills. This problem had been weighing on his mind, but the young executive approached it with renewed vigour thanks to the stimulating environment. The morning meeting had helped to brighten his mood. The enthusiasm of the mariners signalled a fresh start, with new horizons, although there remained awkward questions about the ownership of the midget submarine.

The meeting in Fenchurch Street had done nothing to solve his boatyard's acute cash flow problem, and that was his immediate concern. The unpaid bills for the submarine rescue project placed the yard's survival in jeopardy. From his conversation with the Texan, the young executive knew that it was Beckwith who was blocking payment so Steve steeled himself to 'tackle the blighter' as he trundled around the rickety old Circle Line to Charing Cross.

When he alighted at Charing Cross, it was pleasant to mingle with the foreign tourists as they wandered carefree into the bars and restaurants. So, rather than take the direct route, he took a detour, heading down Villiers Street to the Thames Embankment. The young executive wandered along the riverbank before heading reluctantly towards his Whitehall destination.

Some weeks earlier, the commander had given Steve the name of a friend who worked in the Whitehall building that housed the Marine Special Projects Agency. On his arrival, the friend vouched for Steve at the security desk and this allowed the young executive to roam the building. So, when Steve burst into the MSPA reception area, he caught his adversary off guard.

"I can only spare a couple of minutes. I have to see the defence minister," lied the quick-witted academic as he rapidly recovered his poise.

With that, Steve vented his pent-up rage. "Why haven't you paid our bills?" he demanded, slamming his fist down on the table.

"The project office is responsible for authorising payments," retorted the academic with a look of injured innocence. "You must know, our policy is to pay all our accounts on time."

The academic was lying through his teeth. Steve knew that approval for payment of large bills was being overruled by Beckwith from his London office. But the young executive could not nail that lie without revealing what the Texan had told him during their farewell lunch, so Steve's assault was halted in its tracks. As Beckwith assumed the upper hand, he made a conciliatory gesture.

With that, the academic called Simon on the internal phone. "We have a payment problem. Could you bring me the Whitebait Cove file? I need to investigate an unpaid bill," instructed the academic, with the pretence of being cooperative. After studying the file, he looked at Steve with a mournful expression: "It seems that your invoices have been rejected. There were anomalies with the shipping documents. You will have to sort that out with the Portsmouth office and submit the correct paperwork."

Steve could barely contain his wrath. Beckwith had resurrected a problem that had already been sorted out with the Portsmouth office. Now, Beckwith wanted to reopen the dispute to use it as an excuse to withhold payment. "The problem arose because one of our engineers took some vital component to the shipyard in the boot of his car while he was commissioning the fuel-cell system at the shipyard," explained Steve angrily. "We were doing you a favour. He wanted to save time – it would have taken several days to deliver the component in the normal way."

"There was a hiccup in the paperwork because our engineer failed to follow the correct procedures for the delivered goods," explained Steve through clenched teeth as he fought to control his anger. "We discussed all this with your office in Portsmouth and they were happy to sign off the invoices. In any case, your engineers signed an acceptance form for the fuel-cell propulsion system. The system has been fully tested. We quoted you for a system, not a kit of parts, so we are entitled to payment for the whole contract value."

Beckwith dismissed these arguments in an airy fashion and claimed that he was only following standard commercial practice. "We follow procedures! We cannot hand out money on a whim!"

Steve was not a violent man by nature, but he was tempted to reach across and throttle the academic by his scrawny neck. Recognising the warning signs, Beckwith made preparations for a hasty departure. "You're a crook," shouted Steve as the artful academic dashed towards the door. This kerfuffle caused amusement among the boys and girls in the reception area.

"Get your paperwork sorted out and we will pay you!" retorted Beckwith as he scuttled out of his sanctuary. "And could I suggest that you make an appointment the next time you come around with your begging bowl. This is not a charity for hard-up businessmen!" added the fast-retreating figure, when safely out of range of physical attack. Steve later learned that meeting a minister was yet another of Beckwith's fabricated stories.

Steve was left fuming with the injustice. His staff had gone to great lengths to design and supply the revolutionary fuel-cell propulsion system, but they had received no reward for their efforts. Steve loathed the task of chasing up unpaid bills

– it was an unpleasant task at the best of times, but he had never faced such a slippery customer. On the train journey home, he calmed down, recalling the meeting in Fenchurch Street. *Beckwith might have got the better of me this time, but the game is not over!* he mused.

When he returned to the boatyard the following morning, he called in his clerical staff and told them to sort out the paperwork. He was not going to make the same mistake twice. When his engineer took a key component to the shipyard in the boot of his car, he was doing the customer a favour. It normally took a couple of weeks to deliver a piece of equipment, and this would have delayed commissioning. But this 'favour' was now being used as an excuse to avoid paying what was due to the boatyard.

The Texan approved payment of the bill, but the approval was then overruled by Beckwith in his role as head of the Marine Special Projects Agency. The young executive realised that it was naive to expect goodwill to be reciprocated by the two-faced academic. Steve did not make the same mistake twice.

After speaking to clerical staff, Steve consulted his lawyer, Mike Vince, to see whether he could help recover the outstanding debt. The lawyer's natural hangdog expression became anguished as Steve explained the paperwork discrepancies. The lawyer's cynical attitude was the result of many fruitless years of chasing debts. He held his head in his hands in dismay as Steve explained the various snags with the paperwork.

The cost of a project tends to escalate as client requirements change. In this case, the cost variations had been agreed with the Portsmouth project office as work progressed. A dossier of paperwork recorded the changes, but Steve's staff had failed to obtain a contract variation from the Portsmouth office to summarise all the agreements. These paperwork snags would greatly complicate court proceedings.

"We have a good working relationship with the Portsmouth office, so I wasn't too worried about the discrepancies," explained Steve. "The project office in Portsmouth was happy to sign off our invoices, but Portsmouth was apparently overruled by the London headquarters of the Marine Special Projects Agency. It seems the agency is short of cash. The boss of the agency is a dodgy character. He had tried every trick to avoid paying what is due!"

The lawyer sighed as he sucked the well-chewed tip of his pen. "A court case won't help you much with the state that your paperwork is in – a good barrister could run circles round you. Your people should have got a contract variation," he concluded acidly, as though he was ticking off a naughty schoolboy. Steve turned red in the face, almost incoherent with anger.

"Whose side are you on?" shouted Steve at the hapless lawyer.

The lawyer was used to these outbursts and calmly responded: "I'm sorry but you cannot expect to win a legal case unless all the paperwork is in order." Steve threw his hands up in disgust and slammed the door as he made his exit.

Some hours later, the lawyer relented and phoned with a suggestion. But the lawyer warned that his ideas might not be welcome, because the original contract had been badly drafted. "It would have been a lot easier if you had signed a 'turnkey' contract," observed the lawyer as he twisted the knife in the wound.

"That's fine for you to say," retorted Steve angrily, "but it was a tough fight to win the contract. We got the best terms we could."

"Bear with me," replied the lawyer in a more optimistic tone. "I know that you had a tough time winning the contract, but there might be a way out of this quagmire. You told me that you have a good relationship with the Portsmouth office, so perhaps they can help you square things up. The problem seems to lie in London."

"Yes, we have a pretty good relationship with the Portsmouth office at the moment. The project manager is tough, but fair. So he might be able to help us," replied Steve in the hope that the lawyer might be able to help. "But he is moving on shortly, so we have to sort all this out before Martin Beckwith resumes his role as project manager. He is the dodgy fellow in London who is creating problems that I told you about."

"Well, I've got an idea, but it's a bit risky," said the lawyer.

"What have you in mind?" asked Steve hopefully.

"At the moment, the contract itemises all the bits and pieces that you are supplying," said the lawyer. "There is a discrepancy between the deliveries made, the contract paperwork and delivery notes. That would prove a nightmare if we took your client to court."

"Yes, that's the problem," replied Steve, impatient because they were repeating themselves and going around in circles. "I know it's all a bit of a mess, but we need a solution."

"Well, what I suggest is that you ask the Portsmouth office to issue a contract variation that is drawn up as though it was a 'turnkey' project," explained the lawyer.

"I don't quite understand," replied Steve, as he started to show interest in the plan.

"Well, perhaps you could persuade your friendly project manager in Portsmouth to issue a contract variation so that it simply reads, *Supply a fuel-cell propulsion system for the overall contract value of so-and-so*. This would replace all the previous paperwork," explained the lawyer. "Once you have the contract variation, you should cancel your previous invoices and issue a fresh invoice to cover the whole contract value."

Steve thought this sounded too easy to be true. "What's the catch?" he enquired suspiciously.

"Well, there are drawbacks," admitted the lawyer. "First, you will need the cooperation of the Texan project manager in Portsmouth. That might be difficult because it's not in your client's interest. Another drawback is that it will delay payment in the short term. When you cancel your invoices, you set the clock back to zero on your payment terms, but if the client refuses to pay then that may not be too worrying." Then after a moment he added, "What are your payment terms?"

"Our terms call for cash thirty days after delivery of equipment," said Steve, "but that's a bit of a joke. You know what it's like – most customers drag their heels. We have to chase them up, and most of the big customers take three months to cough up! But Beckwith's invoices are now six months overdue."

"If Beckwith's agency is short of cash, it could become insolvent. That's a risk you should consider. If that happened, you might only receive a small proportion of what you are owed," declared the lawyer. Then upon reflection, he added. "If you follow my advice, you stand a better chance of receiving some cash if your client goes into liquidation."

The thought that Beckwith's agency might go into liquidation was too painful for the young executive to contemplate so Steve put that out of his mind for the time being. "Do you think we should go to court?" asked Steve.

"We will have to wait a few months. My plan makes things more difficult for you in the short term – your client will have a reason to delay payment yet again if you cancel the invoices," explained the lawyer in a thoughtful tone. "But my plan will put us on safer ground if we decided to go to court next year. For the plan to work, you will need to straighten out the paperwork, so you will need cooperation from the Portsmouth office."

The Portsmouth project office proved unusually cooperative and provided the contract variation by return of post. This surprised the boatyard staff, who expected a pitched battle with the pugnacious project manager. In previous contract disputes, they would slug it out for many weeks before their client granted the slightest concession. The staff attributed the Texan's helpful attitude to the notion that he was 'de-mob happy', as he was to relinquish his post as project manager. Steve was the only one who knew that the Texan's cooperation was a reward for his visit to Fenchurch Street to discuss the Admiral's plans.

The new contract variation placed the boatyard on a sounder legal footing in the long term, but it also forced the boatyard to cancel the previous invoices. They also needed to wait for a certificate from a classification society before submitting fresh invoices. The certificate provided evidence that the propulsion was built to specification. This delay set the clock back on recovering the money they were owed. This resulted in the company breaching its lending covenants with the bank, but the bank proved remarkably understanding after the Admiral pulled a few strings.

Steve dreaded Beckwith's return as project manager. He wanted nothing to do with the two-faced swindler. When they first met, the young executive thought the academic was doing a good job promoting innovative technology. But as time passed, it became increasingly clear that the academic was a shyster motivated by greed and self-interest. The obnoxious man took pleasure in provoking his adversaries.

Beckwith resumed control of the project on a bleak mid-winter's day when construction of the submarine was approaching completion at the shipyard in Barrow. Once complete, the craft would be subject to basin trials to test buoyancy and stability. The craft was then to be transported to Whitebait Cove for diving trials. During these trials, the midget submarine would be housed on the *Normandy*.

Commander Woods was in charge of the navy team that was to carry out the sea trials. The team had been allocated a portable cabin in the car park of the boatyard. Another portable cabin was provided for Beckwith's project team. The Texan had made arrangements for installing the two portable cabins before relinquishing his post. The portable cabins were positioned side by side, facing towards the quay where the *Normandy* was to be moored. Mark had arranged for the cabins to be hooked up with electricity, water and phone lines in his role as harbour master.

When Beckwith moved into his cabin, his first major task was to modify the yard's security arrangements to allow access to the quay during the night. Night access was not possible under the pre-existing arrangements because the gate to the compound was locked at the end of the working day. There were plans to install a guard house at the entrance to the yard to overcome this problem.

The security changes irritated the yard staff, and Beckwith's malign presence was a thorn in his side to their chief executive. The gangling figure wandered around the boatyard as though he owned it, smugly satisfied that he had got one over on the young executive in their dispute over late payment. In his terms, cancellation of the invoices was a victory because it set the clock back on his debts. On the rare occasion when they crossed paths, the academic would rub salt into the wound, with jibes about 'getting the paperwork right'.

Steve could barely contain his rage and feared that he would be provoked into intemperate action, so he went out of his way to ignore the obnoxious man. To allow communication, Steve delegated Mark to deputise for him over the security changes. The newly retired naval officer was better able to deal with the academic in a calm, dispassionate way.

This arrangement suited Mark. Having settled into the role of harbour master, the newly retired naval officer welcomed the opportunity to exert his authority. The security changes provided an opportunity to demonstrate the leadership skills he had acquired in his years in the navy. But the negotiations proved trickier than he expected. Beckwith proved to be a slippery customer to deal with.

Under the contract terms, the security changes were to be funded by the government, with Beckwith acting as agent. It later emerged that Beckwith had duped officials into accepting these generous terms in order to feather his own nest. The academic planned to employ a dodgy security firm in return for a backhander. He was confident that he could get away with this, believing that the newly retired naval officer was naïve about the commercial world.

The artful academic was contemptuous of Mark, believing he had led a cloistered life during his public school education and naval service. He thought that the 'stuffed shirt' lacked the street wisdom he had acquired at the comprehensive. If he had the chance, Beckwith intended to implicate the former naval officer in his dodgy deals. There were plenty of opportunities to do that, because there were to be major changes to the yard's security arrangements.

Beckwith's plan involved rerouting the chain-link fence, allowing an electric sliding gate, security barrier and security hut to be erected at the entrance to the car park. The security hut would be manned twenty-four hours a day. Visitor access would be controlled by the security barrier during the day. The sliding gate would provide additional protection for the quay during the night. This plan caused consternation among the yard staff.

Once the fence was rerouted, it provided a forecourt where vehicles would stop while security checks were made, before they entered the car park. The prospect of security checks on arrival at work enraged the yard staff, and there was further anger at the potential loss of parking spaces. The academic hoped that squabbles over those matters would distract Mark's attention from his choice of security firm. The former naval officer behaved just as Beckwith predicted.

"This is outrageous!" declared Mark when Beckwith tabled the plan. But when he raised the issue with Steve, his boss gave him lukewarm support. At first, Mark appreciated being given a free hand, but as time passed he became exasperated by the young executive's *laissez faire* attitude. After all, the security changes were undermining staff morale, and Mark was bearing the brunt of their grievances.

"You will have to take a tough line with that twister," was Steve's sanguine response on one occasion. "Don't forget that we expect to be reimbursed for all this disruption."

After that, there were monumental rows over the allocation of costs between the different parties. Compromise was reached after days of wrangling. The agreed changes to the boatyard security were finally set out in a bound document. The study was sent to the bureaucrats in Whitehall, who sanctioned the expenditure. The boatyard management were sent another copy for approval.

The study described how the yard entrance was to be remodelled, and provided details of the barriers, guard house and identity cards to be issued to all employees. The study described operational matters, such as shift patterns, and laid out the financial compensation for the changes. The name of the chosen security firm was buried deep within this thick tome. Beckwith hoped that this small detail would be overlooked by the bureaucrats and by the naive harbour master.

The artful academic was accurate in his assessment. Mark did not recognise the name of the company in question and had little knowledge of the security business. He was happy to defer to the academic on this matter; after all, the security firm would be guarding his property, so it made sense for the academic to choose a reliable firm. That might have been the end of the matter had Mark not mentioned the firm to his wife while they were chatting one evening.

Lucy had little interest in the boatyard, but she was keen for her husband to make peace with his predecessor, Stan. The rift had become a source of concern for Stan's wife who was a teaching assistant at her comprehensive. The two women knew that Stan resented Mark's appointment as harbour master. The older man's pride was hurt, and this led him to behave in a churlish way, but times move on. As bowls club treasurer, Stan had found a new lease of life. He spent each afternoon at the bowls club – his daily itinerary was regular as clockwork.

The wives felt that the embers of the friendship could be rekindled, with encouragement, so Lucy set out to persuade her husband to revisit the bowls club. "You haven't been to the bowls club for a long time," she murmured in an endearing way as they headed to bed one evening. "Why don't you visit tomorrow? It would do you good to get out. While you are there, you could ask Stan about the firm you mentioned. Stan knows what's going on in the area."

Mark was apprehensive about the reception he would receive at the club. He feared that Stan might stir up resentment towards him. This would not be difficult, because there had been an undercurrent among the former squaddies, who had a jaundiced view of the officer class in general, and the navy in particular, so Mark made his way to the clapboard building with some trepidation. But he need not have worried; when he entered the bar, he was welcomed like a long-lost friend. "Well, look who's here," growled a grizzled character sitting at the end of the bar. "It's Nelson's grandson."

"Hi, Bert," replied Mark with a smile of relief. "How are you doing?"

"Haven't seen you for a while. Where have you been then?" inquired the old wag in jocular vein. "Cruising round the Persian Gulf in your daddy's yacht, no doubt!"

"No, I'm a landlubber now," replied Mark. "Is Stan about, by any chance?"

After learning that Stan was playing on an outside green, Mark joined the rowdy gang who were clustered around the bar. Mark related some anecdotes. Stan viewed this scene with baleful eyes when he returned to the bar, after finishing his match. He thought that Mark was making jokes at his expense. *It was bad enough when the naval officer pushed me out of the boatyard. Now he wants to take over the bowls club*, he thought malevolently.

"Would you like a drink?" asked Mark in a friendly way, failing to recognise the ruffled feathers.

"No, thanks," replied Stan in a fit of pique. Not wishing to join the rowdy gang, the club treasurer moved to the other end of the bar where he pretended to discuss urgent club business with one of the staff, but the conversation soon dried up. So Stan swallowed his pride and returned to join the club members gathered around Mark. Relieved to find that he was not the butt of their jokes, the club treasurer invited the former naval officer to join him at a table where they could 'catch up' with events at the boatyard.

"The yard has been quiet since you left. We're just waiting for the sea trials in the spring," observed the newly retired naval officer, who was, by this time, mildly intoxicated. "You've probably heard that there are plans to install a guard house."

This news surprised Stan. It seemed that there had been some major changes at the yard since he had left. As they talked, the club treasurer was won over by Mark's breezy confidence and charm, despite himself.

The club treasurer was flattered when Mark asked his opinion about the security company they planned to use at the yard. Stan prided himself on being the fount of all knowledge when it came to local matters, so it pained him to admit that he could not help. "I've never heard of the firm," he admitted with the downcast look of a quiz contestant who could not answer the jackpot question. "They sound like a pretty rum outfit to me. But I'll ask around, if you like."

"Thanks, Stan," replied Mark airily, with no real intention of following this up. Stan went on to reminisce about his days at the boatyard in a boastful way to remind listeners that he was a man of stature in the local community. Many of the stories were part of folklore, dating back to the war, which was a golden era for the yard. While Mark knew that the events had taken place before the club treasurer's time, he did not want to wound the older man's pride by saying so. But while it had been an amiable conversation, the club treasurer still harboured a grudge against the 'posh naval officer'.

It irked the club treasurer that he did not know the security firm. He feared that he had lost face. So, with nothing much else to do, he toured some of his old haunts over the following days, to see what he could discover. What he learned was fascinating. It seemed the security firm was owned by some dodgy characters with underworld links. This knowledge gave the self-righteous club treasurer malicious pleasure. As the feelings of resentment welled up, he decided to keep the information to himself.

Mark would have remained ignorant of the firm's dodgy owners had Stan's wife not got wind of what her husband was up to. Stan let slip what he had learned when he returned home in a slightly tipsy condition from the bowls club late one night. Doris was aware of her husband's grudge against the 'posh naval officer' who had replaced him at the boatyard, but she did not think it right to withhold vital information. So she badgered her husband to tell Mark what he knew. This made Stan feel guilty and he became sheepish each time he admitted that he had not spoken to his successor.

This developed into a full-blown row one evening. In a furious rage, Doris told her husband to 'grow up' and 'act like a man'. Doris understood her husband was brooding about the loss of status, but she would not accept that excuse for withholding vital information. She also felt a sense of loyalty towards Lucy. The two wives, who worked at the same school, were fed up with the squabbling between their husbands. "It's high time that you found some purpose in life beyond your blessed bowls club," declared Doris in the heat of the moment.

Chastened by his wife's vitriolic words, Stan made a detour to Mark's house on his next outing to the bowls club. He felt ill at ease as he approached the middle-class enclave on the edge of the town. The stooping elderly figure made his way hesitantly to the front door with his flat cap clasped in his tightly bunched fists. When Lucy answered the door, she reacted with irritation. Caught in the middle of her household chores, the hard-working teacher looked dishevelled. "Visitors normally call at the side door," she declared tartly. "I'm afraid my husband is out at the moment, but I'm expecting him home soon. Would you like a cup of tea while you wait?"

After stepping gingerly through the door, Stan clumped over the pristine cream carpet with his muddy boots, causing further annoyance. Embarrassed by the footprints on the carpet, Stan perched awkwardly on a kitchen stool, trying to make up his mind whether to remove the offending footwear. Lucy did her best to make light conversation as she made tea and prepared the evening meal, but it was a huge relief to both of them when Mark's car scrunched up the gravel driveway. Lucy popped her head out of the side door and made a vigorous hand signal to show that she had an unwelcome visitor.

After a stressful day dealing with staff gripes at the boatyard, Mark had forgotten about his trip to the bowls club, so he was puzzled to find Stan in the kitchen. The pair adjourned to Mark's den, to allow Lucy to get on with her household chores. Since retiring from the navy, Mark had adopted a closet under the stairs to act as his office. After shoehorning themselves into the cramped space, the two men settled down to business. "I'm afraid that I've got some bad news for you," declared the club treasurer in a gloomy tone. "The security firm you told me about is run by a load of crooks!" Mark was too shocked to reply.

"At first sight, the outfit looks okay," continued the club treasurer. "They have all the licences they need and they provide bouncers for night clubs, but there is a seamy side to the firm. A chap I know told me it is owned by gangsters from Romania. They employ thugs to recover gambling debts as a sideline. When the police investigated an incident, the witnesses were threatened. The firm has not been charged with anything, but it's a dodgy outfit!"

Having done his duty, the club treasurer sidled off, leaving Mark looking bemused. As Stan padded through the kitchen in his socks, he acknowledged Lucy with a bashful smile and made his way to the side entrance, taking care not to leave any more footprints. Alone in his office, Mark's first reaction was to phone his boss to pass on this worrying news, but there was no reply. It later emerged that Steve was travelling back from a meeting in Fenchurch Street at the time.

When Mark caught up with his boss the following morning, he passed on the comments about the security firm's underworld links, but the young executive took it in his stride.

"Typical!" sighed Steve cynically. "That is just what you would expect from that idiot!"

Mark was astonished at his boss's easy-going attitude. "Well, if you are not going to do anything about it, then I will!" he declared self-righteously.

"It's not our business, Mark," retorted Steve calmly. "Beckwith chose the firm. It's not our job to tell him what to do." Steve's *laissez faire* attitude left the newly retired naval officer feeling impotent, and wondering whether he was being set up as a fall guy.

"What happens if they let thieves into the boatyard to steal our property?" demanded Mark angrily.

"You will just have to make sure that they don't!" replied Steve airily. "Beef up the locks on the workshop doors!" Then with an imperious wave, Steve signalled that their meeting was at an end. After dismissing his subordinate, the young executive reached for his mobile phone and began to ruffle through some papers. The newly retired naval officer felt belittled by his boss's cavalier attitude as he retired to the sanctuary of his tiny cubicle. He might have been more sympathetic to his boss if he had known what was taking place behind the scenes.

With no hint of events percolating in the background, Mark was seething with rage about the off-hand way he had been treated. His grievances had been steadily brewing since starting his new job. *The title harbour master was grossly misleading,* he mused. In the final weeks with the navy, he had dreamed of spending the summer mucking around on boats. The yard did, indeed, have a workboat. He was responsible for operating it, but he rarely had the opportunity to take it out.

After Stan's departure, Mark learned that as 'harbour master', his duty was to organise the office cleaners, window cleaners, sort out parking problems, building repairs and dustbins. The term 'caretaker' would have been a more apt description for this thankless role. He felt that Steve had misrepresented the job during his interview. The only reason that he stayed on was the opportunity to work with the commander's trials team, which he hoped to join.

But there were limits to what he would put up with. There was no way that he would turn a blind eye to the criminal links of Beckwith's security firm. So, after collecting his thoughts, he stomped back to challenge his young boss. When he burst into the plush executive office, Steve was engaged in an animated conversation on his phone, as usual. But this did not deter the newly retired naval officer. Ignoring an imperious signal to wait his turn, Mark grabbed the telephone and pressed the call termination button. "I've had enough!" he declared.

Steve was outraged by the intrusion. He was in the middle of negotiating an extension to a crucial bank loan. Mark's intemperate outburst had jeopardised his efforts to keep the yard afloat. In a fit of rage, Steve was tempted to accept Mark's resignation; after all, the former naval officer had scarcely distinguished himself. There were better qualified candidates for the role of harbour master. But, with iron resolve, he managed to control himself, recalling that Mark's naval connections might assist with the plans being hatched in Fenchurch Street.

The two men squared up and glared at each other. It could have easily ended in a brawl, but calm prevailed, and they agreed to settle their differences away from the office. The cooling-off period ensured that the chief executive was free of the distractions that occupied every minute of his working day.

"Why don't you join me fishing on Saturday?" he suggested in a conciliatory gesture. Mark was not sure how Lucy would react to this offer and did not relish a day out on the river with this cocksure guy but, regretting his rash behaviour, he accepted the invitation.

Lucy had mixed feelings about the fishing trip. In some ways, she was pleased – she thought that it would do her husband good. Mark was becoming an old grump, weighed down with family worries, and it needed someone to shake him up. His young boss might be just the right person to do that. She was impressed by the young guy she had seen in the Windmill public house. Mark moaned about his boss, of course. But she knew that the old grump disliked anything that created waves in his stodgy, middle-class life.

But she was annoyed that her husband had accepted the invitation without asking her permission and that it would be another excuse to avoid his family duties. So, in revenge, she refused to let Mark use the family car. This was yet another battleground in their marital wars. While Mark was at sea, Lucy used the car every day. It was handy for shopping and ferrying the boys to their various clubs, but that was no longer possible, because Mark needed the car to travel to work. The rest of the family were forced to walk, cycle or use public transport during the week. This created animosity.

"I don't object to you going fishing on Saturday," announced Lucy decisively, "but you can't use the car!"

"But how will I get to the river?" moaned Mark plaintively.

"Tell your boss to pick you up!" replied Lucy unsympathetically.

"Steve won't like that! It's miles out of his way," argued Mark. The thought of begging his boss for a lift was humiliating.

"Well, we could invite him in for a cup of coffee – it's nice to meet people that you work with."

"So that's what you are up to. You fancy my boss!" retorted Mark, who was experiencing a pang of jealousy as he recalled Lucy's admiration for the young guy when they first set eyes on him in the Windmill public house.

Lucy was not attracted to Steve – he was not her type – but she did think he would make a good partner for her sister-in-law. But she kept that thought to herself as she fuelled her husband's jealousy. "That's outrageous!" she replied with feigned indignation. "The thought had never crossed my mind. It's just that I need the car for shopping – I assume that you want to eat next week?"

Mark knew he had lost the argument, and that he would have to go cap in hand to ask for a lift. That placed him in an ignominious position, but it turned out that the young executive was only too happy to oblige. When Steve arrived on Saturday morning, he was relaxed and in good spirits. The sleek sports car caused a stir when it pulled up in the cul-de-sac leading to Mark's home. It attracted admiring looks from the neighbours.

As Lucy prepared to greet the boss of the boatyard, she changed into tight-fitting jeans and a low-cut top. The provocative clothes fuelled Mark's suspicions that his wife fancied the flash young executive. Lucy welcomed the young guy with a friendly peck on the cheek, insisting that he stay for a cup of coffee. As they sat in the kitchen, she behaved in a flirtatious manner, laughing at his jokes. Her coquettish behaviour was intended to tease her husband.

After coping with Mark's long absence at sea, Lucy was now struggling to come to terms with his presence in the family home. The old grump hung around the house moaning and disrupting her well-oiled routine. He was reluctant to help with chores. There were times when his selfish ways drove her to distraction. Steve helped to lighten the atmosphere.

His presence created a playful air of mischief that had been missing since the early days of her marriage.

The family environment brought out a warm side of Steve's character. The young guy found it easy to relate to her teenage sons. Before leaving, he spent a few minutes kicking a football about with the two boys in their tiny garden. While speaking to the family, Steve adopted a self-deprecating attitude. The easy rapport with the boys further fuelled Mark's jealousy. But Mark received his visitor in a courteous manner, despite his angry feelings towards his boss. He did not want workplace arguments to intrude into his family life.

To add to Mark's discomfort, he was ill-prepared for the fishing trip. Earlier that morning, he had collected together some old fishing tackle from the loft, but it was not fit for the job. He felt embarrassed as he loaded the tatty gear into the sleek sports car. No one seemed to notice his discomfort as Lucy and the boys gathered to wave the anglers off in a cheerful way. Lucy challenged the pair of anglers to bring them back a fresh fish for supper. Mark was like a spectre at the feast. The newly retired naval officer was subdued, braced for a row over his problems at work as soon as they departed.

In preparing for the day on the river with his subordinate, Steve was forced to acknowledge that he had treated Mark in a shabby way. He needed to make amends. So, before setting off that morning, he had drafted letters to defuse the situation. Before Mark had a chance to open his mouth, Steve pulled into a lay-by, switched off the engine and handed Mark a couple of sealed envelopes.

Mark was psyched up for a blazing row, but Steve's conciliatory gesture took the wind out of his sails. "I'm sorry if I was unsympathetic the other day," said Steve apologetically. "You were right to warn me about the security firm. I should have listened to you, but I have other worries. I hope that this will put your mind at rest."

The first envelope contained a copy of a letter to remind Beckwith that his Marine Special Projects Agency was responsible for security at the boatyard, once the agreed changes were carried out.

The second envelope was addressed to Mark personally. The enclosed letter outlined how his role would evolve as the sea trials of the midget submarine got underway. Under his new job description, he would no longer be responsible for yard security and caretaker duties. Instead, he would have a full-time role liaising with Commander Woods and his trials team. Mark was disarmed by this unexpected olive branch. The news that he was to work closely with the navy trials team was particularly welcome.

But while the letters absolved him of responsibility for security, it failed to address the ethical question of employing a dodgy security firm with underworld links. Steve had ducked that particular point. "I still think that we should tackle Beckwith about the security firm," he commented as he digested the content of the letters. But it was a mild rebuke. Mark did not want to push his luck too far after such a fulsome apology.

"That might be the correct thing to do in the navy," replied Steve disingenuously, "but we work to different rules in the commercial world. It's dog eat dog. If we tell Beckwith how to organise his security, he will blame us if something goes wrong. Anyway, you have no real proof that the security firm has underworld links. It is only scuttlebutt and rumour."

In other circumstances, Mark would have pressed his argument more forcefully. But he was grateful that his new role would allow him to work with Commander Woods. It might be a stepping stone to joining his team, so he decided to let the matter of underworld links drop for the moment. For the first time that day, Mark started to look forward to a day on the river.

The pair headed to the trout stream where Steve had fished with Commander Woods on three previous Sundays. The commander had made the arrangements. The stream was popular with fly fishermen and was unusually busy for a Saturday morning. Without the commander's guidance, the novices made fools of themselves. Mark's rudimentary fishing kit attracted scornful looks from seasoned anglers along the riverbank. His gear was designed for sea angling and was ill-suited for the fast-moving trout stream.

Mark watched glumly as the trout swam up to his bait, and then swam away with a disdainful flick of the tail. Steve was no expert and did little better. As the hours passed, their amateur efforts attracted ridicule from the seasoned anglers, so they decided to call it a day.

As they slunk away shamefaced, they made jokes about the 'blind leading the blind'. The embarrassment helped the pair to bond together. It so happened that the stretch of river was close to a pub that Mark frequented before he was married, so Mark suggested they adjourn for a pie and a pint. This would be an opportunity to get to know one another, away from the irritating problems of the yard.

The old thatched inn lay concealed at the end of a lane. Steve was grateful for a guide to the countryside, which he still found faintly alien. It was a scorching August day and the sun beat down on the fields of stubble; the rhythmic sound of combine harvesters could be heard in the distance. The pub provided a refreshingly cool refuge from the summer heat.

A couple of old-timers were leaning against the bar and they seemed to recognise Mark. They nodded as the former naval officer stooped to clear the low entrance porch, but did not speak to him. The novice anglers were served grudgingly by the landlady, who spoke with the gruff, down-to-earth tone of a heavy smoker. In the tranquil atmosphere and bucolic scenery, Steve began to speak freely about his personal life.

Up until that day, Mark had thought his boss was a 'city slicker' and so he was surprised to learn that he had trained as a ship's engineer after graduating from university. Steve spoke about his sea-going experiences and became nostalgic about this period of his life. Mark found it difficult to picture the slightly built young guy wearing a boiler suit in a ship's engine room. Somehow, he doubted that his boss had the physique for tough work, like flogging bolts.

Steve was wary of drinking too much while driving his sports car and monitored his alcohol intake. "I'll just have the one," he told Mark firmly.

"Yes, that's fine with me," replied Mark with a hint of disappointment. But their resolve was put to the test when one of Mark's drinking buddies bowled into the bar. The roguish character insisted on buying a round.

At first, Steve refused the offer. Mark, on his best behaviour, followed his boss's example. But the newcomer was in an ebullient mood and took umbrage at this slight. The novice anglers, who were thirsty on this blazingly hot summer's day, succumbed to the temptation. After that, things slipped out of control. It became a rowdy session and the trio were reluctant to leave the cool interior when the landlady tossed them out at two o'clock in the afternoon.

When Steve totted up the drinks, he realised that he was well over the limit, so they had to delay their departure while he sobered up. To kill time, they set off on a leisurely walk. Their route took them along a bridal path that zigzagged between harvest fields where huge wheel-like bales of straw were lying in the stubble. The path led to a rise with a view of the junction between two lobes of the Plymouth estuary. The long walk gave them a chance to talk things over. The conversation turned to the trials of the midget submarine.

"Did you know that my sister works on the project?" remarked Mark at length.

"Well, I never!" replied Steve, who was intrigued to learn of the family connection. "I thought you said your sister was a naval officer. What is her role on the project?"

"Yes, she *is* a naval officer," replied Mark with a touch of family pride. "She commanded a patrol boat! But she was transferred to Beckwith's project team in Portsmouth. Don't ask me what she does – I haven't a clue." The disdainful tone of the final comment hinted at Mark's disapproval of his sister's involvement in the project.

"It's a pity that you didn't mention this before," replied Steve. "You know that we are owed a lot of money for the equipment we supplied. She might be able to help us get our money."

"Probably some bureaucratic snarl-up," replied Mark casually. This complacent attitude left Steve dumbfounded. *Service people think that money grows on trees*, thought the young executive uncharitably. But he was, nevertheless, intrigued to learn that Mark's sister worked on Beckwith's project. *The family link is a weird coincidence. Maybe we can use it to our advantage*, he thought to himself.

Since attending the meeting in Fenchurch Street, Steve had spent some time discussing cunning ways of acquiring the midget submarine with Commander Woods. At one point, the commander suggested that, with his naval background, Mark might be able to help them. But Steve dismissed this proposal. He thought Mark was a bit slow on the uptake. It would take too long to explain the convoluted story to the dunderhead, but the news that Mark's sister was involved with the project opened new possibilities.

While Steve reflected on this, in the burning hot sun, their conversation turned to other topics, and it was not long before they reached the top of a rise that provided a stunning view of the two arms of the estuary. Looking at his watch, Steve did some mental arithmetic and decided that it would be safe for him to drive by the time they got back to his car. The journey back was uneventful. When they arrived, Lucy demanded to see their catch, and the teenage boys joined in the chorus.

The family teased them unmercifully when the pair of novice anglers admitted they had not caught a single fish. Lucy invited Steve in for tea, but the young executive declined, saying he was due to meet a female friend in Plymouth. Lucy was mildly disappointed to learn that the young guy was dating. Her embryonic match-making plans had hit a rock. She wondered what the girlfriend was like and made a mental note to persuade her husband to investigate.

The family gathered around the front door to wave goodbye to their visitor. In reality, the young guy faced a lonely evening waiting for Jackie. He was never quite sure whether she would call round to his flat after she had called last orders at the pub. *But it has been an enjoyable day, and Mark is an amiable fellow,* he mused. He felt a pang of envy. His bachelor life seemed sad and empty after the warmth of his welcome in Mark's home.

While Steve derived pleasure from his relationship with Jackie, the landlady of the Feathers, it was a transitory affair and was unlikely to lead anywhere. Jackie was stunningly attractive, but she was dedicated to her pub and had an army of admirers. Steve knew that he was just the latest of her conquests, and it was only a matter of time before he was given the elbow. He really needed to look for a less exotic partner.

Steve's mind drifted on his way back home to his flat, and he wondered what Mark's sister was like and whether she could play a role in their undercover operation. He was curious to meet her. *She must be an exceptional person to command a patrol boat,* he mused. Lucy's mind was occupied in a similar way. She had been impressed with the dashing young guy and was busy dreaming up a way to introduce him to her sister-in-law.

Chapter 12

Mark Hosts a Fishing Trip

After returning from his fishing trip, Mark collapsed into his armchair for a nap. After finishing her chores, his wife joined him in the sitting room. Settling down to knit a jumper in front of the television set, Lucy contrasted the two men. *It's like comparing a carthorse with a thoroughbred,* she mused. *My husband is going through a difficult time. He misses the comradeship and prestige of being a naval officer and is a bit jealous of his new boss.*

As she surveyed her husband's handsome features, she felt affection, recalling the best aspects of his character. *They both have good points,* she thought with an air of satisfaction. Steve's brief visit had breathed new life into their married life. While many people thought that the young guy was driven by ambition, she had seen a warmer side to his nature that day. She was impressed by the way he related to her teenage sons.

It is those qualities that would make him a good match for my sister-in-law, she mused as she knitted away contentedly. Lucy recalled her carefree college days when she brought couples together. The visit had revived those dormant matchmaking skills. As the jumper took shape, she plotted her next move. *The first step is to encourage Mark to go fishing with his boss. Then we will invite the young guy for a meal when Anne is visiting*, she concluded.

The matchmaking plans may come to nothing, of course, but Steve would be a good friend for my husband. The fishing trip showed that the young guy had a moderating influence on her husband's sometimes wayward character. Mark sometimes acted in a boorish manner after drinking with his real-ale cronies. While he had not been violent, this was a flashpoint in their marriage. Her husband's drunken antics unsettled the boys. But it seemed that on the fishing trip, the young guy kept her husband well in check.

"You seemed to enjoy your day out on the river," remarked Lucy as her partner roused himself from his slumber. Then after a pause, she continued. "You went straight to the pub, didn't you?" she teased. "That's why you didn't catch any fish!"

In response, Mark chuckled and threw a cushion at his partner. But beneath the light-hearted banter, there was a painful sting in Lucy's remarks. It was a sharp dig at his drinking habits and his sporting prowess.

"You can't catch fish if you haven't got the right gear," retorted Mark, to defend himself.

"Well, why don't you buy some fishing gear then?" replied Lucy. "You could take up fishing as a hobby. It would do you good."

"Do you really mean that?" replied Mark suspiciously.

The turnaround in attitude took Mark by surprise, not least because Lucy had been nagging him about shirking his family duties. There was also the question of cost. They had both agreed to rein in their spending after his early retirement from the navy. And fly fishing gear did not come cheap.

"It would give you a chance to get to know your boss better," said Lucy coyly. This put a different slant on things.

Mark could see cogs whirring in his partner's cunning brain. *Lucy is up to something,* he thought to himself. But he played along in a wary fashion.

"*You* should take up a sport," responded Mark, tongue in cheek. "Why don't you join the tennis club? We could play together." Lucy knew he was taking the mickey – they both knew that she loathed outdoor sports, and was a poor tennis player.

"I don't really care for the tennis crowd," she replied defensively. "Those snobs are a stuck-up clique." But her husband's salvo did not distract her, and she continued doggedly with her matchmaking mission: "I was serious about the fishing gear. You need a hobby, and fishing would suit you. It's an ideal sport for a retired old codger like you!"

Mark ignored the 'codger' barb as he started to consider the proposal. He needed an interest and it would make sense to become an angler. It would have been a pleasant outing on the river if he had the right gear. The retired naval officer had been a keen rugby player in his youth, but he was really too old to play. He would love to sail, but he could not afford a yacht. The bowls club was all right, but he had not really formed a rapport with the members.

Fly fishing might be the answer. But it would be expensive, so why was Lucy so keen for him to take it up? He knew his wife had an ulterior motive, but he could not quite figure out what she was up to.

"What did you make of my boss?" he asked as he tried to smoke out the motive for her unexpected generosity.

"Quite dishy!" she teased, echoing the comment that she made when they saw the young guy in the Windmill public house. But then in a more thoughtful way, she continued: "He seemed like quite a nice chap." Lucy's intuition told her that beneath the ambitious outer shell, Steve was a decent fellow. This contradicted the view that her husband had expressed since starting work at the boatyard, Mark describing his boss as arrogant and devious. The fishing trip had softened his view somewhat, but he remained suspicious of his cocksure boss.

"He told me that he trained as a ship's engineer," observed Mark to concede a point. "That changed my view of him. It's the first time he'd mentioned that he worked at sea. He didn't seem the type, somehow." Their discussion was cut short when Lucy got up to answer the phone. It proved to be a long call from one of her colleagues at the comprehensive.

Left on his own to brood, Mark's charitable view for his boss, developed during the fishing trip, started to evaporate and jealousy started to rear its ugly head. Mark had an uneasy sense that his family had been taken in by a smooth-talking conman that day. He was overcome by a sense of foreboding as he recalled Steve's complacent attitude towards the dodgy security firm. He kicked himself for his cowardly failure to duck that issue. He had failed to stand firm on principles that he held dear.

Mark felt ashamed as he came to appreciate that he had been bought off with insubstantial promises. So, while it had been a pleasant day, nothing had fundamentally changed to relieve the antagonism that he felt towards his boss. He still distrusted the smooth-talking young guy. It reminded him of the Christmas Day when British soldiers played football against the Germans in no man's land, during the First World War. After that truce, they returned to shooting at one another, as though nothing had happened.

After a late-night tryst with Jackie on Saturday night, Steve had a lazy day on Sunday. He spent the morning pottering about in his flat then wandered down to the Feathers for a pint at lunch time. It was an opportunity to plan for the week ahead. As he mulled over the fishing trip, he formed the view that the retired naval officer was good company. He was an honest and dependable fellow. The trouble was that he was not the sharpest pencil in the box and, to make matters worse, he was a stickler for the rules. It was hard to see how the newly retired naval officer would help with the caper he was planning with the commander.

His thoughts then turned to the coincidence that Mark's sister was involved in Beckwith's midget submarine project. She sounded like an extremely capable young woman. So perhaps she could help them. Preoccupied with that thought when he arrived at work on Monday morning, Steve sidled round to his subordinate's office for a chat. He leaned casually on the doorpost of the tiny glass cubicle that Mark occupied. This was out of character for the workaholic young executive, who rarely strayed out of his office at this time of the week.

Mark found this overture unsettling, not least because he had been brooding over the dodgy security firm all night and was in two minds as to whether he should raise the issue once more. "Is there something that I can do for you?" asked the newly retired naval officer testily.

Steve was taken aback by the chilly welcome and replied awkwardly, "Just taking a breather. I enjoyed meeting your family on Saturday. How do you fancy another fishing trip?"

Mark thought that Steve was laying it on a little thick. As it happened, he was thinking of taking up fishing, but he had no intention of sharing this new hobby with his slippery boss. Their Saturday outing had been a one-off to settle differences at work. Moreover, the pair had made complete fools of themselves on the riverbank. The former naval officer had no intention of allowing the young guy to join his circle of friends.

But he did not want to alienate his boss unnecessarily. "Lucy and the kids were glad to meet you," he remarked in a neutral tone, "but I need new gear before I go fishing again." Steve's smirk suggested this was a gross understatement, but the young executive could tell that his subordinate was not in the mood to chat. The sound of a mobile phone ringing disrupted the conversation. Steve ducked away to answer the call. When the call ended, Steve came back to speak to his subordinate in a normal businesslike way.

"The firm may be able to help with the fishing gear," declared the young executive with a mischievous smile as he regained his poise. "If you read the letter that I gave you, you will see you are responsible for 'hospitality' under your new job description. I didn't mention it on Saturday – but you will have to entertain VIPs from time to time. Some of our clients are keen anglers, so I would like you to organise fishing parties. We'll pay for your gear. But you will also need to polish up your fly-fishing skills! I've also arranged for you to attend a training course."

After dropping that bombshell, Steve wandered back to his plush office, leaving Mark embarrassed that he had misread the situation. *That's odd*, he mused, *what's Steve up to now?* But the newly retired naval officer was not inclined to dwell on the imponderables of life. He gave the matter little thought as he got on with his normal routine. Later that morning, he received a phone call about the fishing gear. It was not until later that he discovered that the call was from a long-established field-sports emporium.

"We've been asked to meet you so you can choose some fishing gear," said the caller with a snooty, cut-glass accent. Mark could not believe what he was hearing. He was not too busy, because the yard was quiet, so he arranged to visit the store later that afternoon. With a sense of curiosity, he slipped off from work earlier than usual and made a detour to visit the quaint old store, nestling in a cobbled alley close to Plymouth's fish market.

The emporium had the gentile run-down air that is euphemistically described as 'patina' in the antiques trade. The sales assistant greeted him in an obsequious manner and injected the word 'sir' into every sentence. In other circumstances, this would be pretentious, but the newly retired naval officer was seduced by the aura of quality of the merchandise on display. It was like an Aladdin's cave. Racks of shotguns, polished saddles and riding gear stretched into the dark recesses of the store, where an impressive display of fishing tackle was hidden.

Mark was only too glad of advice from the white-haired sales assistant because he lacked knowledge of fly fishing. He felt like a child in a sweetshop and left the store with a long wooden box containing a split cane rod, a famous-named fishing reel, a net for his catch and a stiff paper bag bursting with small boxes holding fish hooks, lures and accessories. The booty was all charged to the boatyard.

When he arrived home with his haul in time for tea, he was unloading the family car when Lucy returned on her bicycle from a frustrating day teaching at the local school. Not knowing the fishing gear was a free gift from the boatyard, she exploded. "How dare you buy all that expensive stuff without asking me!" she barked as she wheeled her bicycle crossly into the garage. Mark did not have a chance to explain.

Lucy was under the impression that her husband had taken her tentative offer to purchase some fishing gear as the green light to splash out a large sum of the family cash on top-of-the-range sporting equipment. "But the boatyard is paying!" shouted Mark in desperation as his wife stomped into the garage to park her pushbike. His words fell on deaf ears. Lucy was, by that time, out of earshot, hidden behind a garage wall.

"I don't want to hear any more about it!" she yelled as she re-emerged from the dark recesses of the garage. "You can return all that stuff first thing tomorrow morning! We can't possible afford those playthings on our budget." With that parting salvo, she slammed the side door behind her on her way to the kitchen to make their family tea. The subject was closed as far as Lucy was concerned, and there would be no further discussion.

Mark spent an evening in the doghouse and an even more uncomfortable night sleeping on the sofa in the living room. When he set off for work early the following morning, he left a handwritten note with a copy of the bill showing that the fishing gear had been paid for by the boatyard. After reading the note, Lucy felt ashamed of her angry outburst. They made up the following evening and laughed at the misunderstanding.

Later in the week, Mark found a note lying on his desk. *I've made arrangements for you to receive private tuition from the water bailiff who looks after the stream where we fished last Saturday*, it read. It went on to outline the training course and was signed by Steve. For the following weeks, Mark spent a couple of hours each Wednesday afternoon learning the art of fly fishing. On completion of the tuition, he was expected to organise a fishing trip for a party of businessmen.

It later emerged that the fishing party was crucial to the future of the boatyard. This explained Steve's generosity. If the visit was a success, the Dutch owners would bail out the yard and invest in new facilities. After their pleasant outing on the riverbank, the young executive was confident that the newly retired naval officer was the right person to entertain the important visitors. With his amiable personality, he was well suited for the task.

The investor's visit marked a change in the strategy of the Dutch conglomerate that owned the boatyard. This came about when the patriarch learned about the plans to build houses on the commercial part of the original boatyard site. As major shareholder, the patriarch was determined to retain the marine side of the business. He felt a duty to his ancestors, who had deep roots in the shipping world.

But the patriarch had a tough battle on his hands, since he needed to raise capital to support the ailing boatyard. The purpose of the visit was thus to persuade some wealthy individuals to invest in new facilities that would be run as a fifty-fifty partnership with the boatyard. The plans called for facilities to manufacture exhaust gas scrubbing equipment. This equipment would enable shipping companies to comply with newly introduced emission rules.

There was great demand for equipment of this sort following the introduction of strict new rules to reduce the emissions of toxic exhaust gas from ships. The new investment would also fund some research work. But before committing their cash, the investors wanted to visit the yard and assess the situation for themselves, knowing that the future of the yard depended on the success of the visit. Steve was making meticulous preparations for their visit. The young executive thought that Mark was the right person to entertain the important guests.

It later emerged that these investors were also bankrolling the Admiral's embryonic scheme to protect merchant shipping from hijackers. Few people at the boatyard were aware of the link between the two schemes. Some of the potential investors had been present at the brain-storming sessions in Fenchurch Street.

When briefing his subordinate about the impending visit, the young executive nominated Mark as his deputy. Steve also promised that the former naval officer would lead the exhaust gas scrubbing venture, if it went ahead. In the meantime, there was already plenty of work to keep Mark busy while he organised the fishing party. He had to keep an eye on work to remodel the yard entrance, which was organised by Martin Beckwith, and make preparations for the trials of the midget submarine.

Contractors came on-site towards the end of the year. After rerouting the chain-link fence, they installed mechanised barriers on the entrance to the car park. The next big job was to install the guard post. This was a rather fanciful name for the cheap wooden shack that was provided for the purpose. The hut was to be manned twenty-four hours a day to allow access to the *Normandy* while it was berthed at the quay for the sea trials. Some wags in the boatyard dubbed these arrangements 'Checkpoint Charlie' after the notorious passage through the Berlin Wall.

The construction work was organised by Martin Beckwith, but Mark had to ensure that the building work did not interfere with day-to-day operations in the yard. While a thankless task, the work did allow him to regain a sense of purpose that had been missing since retiring from the navy. The once-proud naval officer was having difficulty adjusting to his new life on dry land, but these humdrum tasks allowed him to channel his energy into a productive direction.

The party of investors arrived while the contractors were busy remodelling the entrance to the boatyard. Mark was responsible for organising the transport, accommodation and catering for their visit. The former naval officer hired a minivan to collect the party from Plymouth railway station on Monday afternoon and transport them to a guesthouse. The van was barely large enough to accommodate all their luggage and fishing tackle. After meetings at the yard, the fly-fishing expedition was due to take place on Wednesday, the final day of their visit.

Mark collected the party from the guesthouse after breakfast on Tuesday, and they spent the rest of the morning closeted in Steve's office. Here, they reviewed plans for the proposed new manufacturing facilities. Mark then led a guided tour of the existing workshops and quay. The party showed unusual interest in security changes. If the former naval officer had been more perceptive, he might have asked why that was. After all, the sea trials had nothing to do with the exhaust gas scrubbing venture, and the temporary guard hut was to be removed when the sea trials were completed.

After the tour of the yard, the meeting resumed in Steve's office and continued until the end of the afternoon. Mark was preparing to drive the investors back to their guesthouse, when he was waylaid by his boss. Steve led him to a quiet corner of the car park where they could speak without being overheard. "We are expecting another guest tomorrow," whispered the young executive in hushed tones, but he would not elaborate. "Don't worry, he will make himself known to you," remarked the young executive in a mysterious way.

Mark mentioned this episode to Lucy when he got home that evening. This added to Lucy's suspicions that her husband was being drawn into some murky business. Prior to Steve's visit, Lucy had taken little interest in the boatyard. But the more she learned, the stranger it sounded. She could scarcely believe that her husband had been provided with free fly-fishing gear and angling lessons. Then there was the weird story about the dodgy security firm. This did not make any sense.

Why doesn't my husband realise he is being drawn into some skulduggery? she wondered with a sense of exasperation. *Is he blind to what is going on?* So when she learned that an unnamed guest was to join the fishing party, her sleuthing instincts moved into top gear.

Oblivious to mysterious events taking place around him, Mark set off in the rented minivan to collect the investors on Wednesday morning. This was the third and final day of their visit. When he arrived at the guesthouse, he found that Commander Woods was to join the party of anglers. This was a welcome sight because it would allow Mark to find out more about the trials team. It did not occur to the former naval officer to ask what business the commander had with the investors. After all, the new manufacturing venture had no connection with the sea trials.

Once the party reached the riverbank, the water bailiff directed the guests to their fishing pitches. The pitches had been marked with flags at around 20-yard intervals along the bank of the fast-flowing stream. Mark patrolled the riverbank to see that all his guests' needs were satisfied. The former naval officer spoke to the guests in turn and it was some time before he was able to speak to the commander.

"Steve tells me that you need some angling tips," said the commander teasingly as he cast his line skilfully towards a silvery shadow lurking behind a rock.

"Yes. I would value your advice!" admitted Mark modestly. "I'm still a beginner."

The commander reeled in his line and offered the rod to Mark with the challenge: "Well, let's see what you can do!"

Mark took the fishing rod and whipped it back and forth to assess its stiffness. When he had a feel for the gear, he cast towards the same rock. The fly landed close to its target, but the trout was not fooled by the garish lure and dived into a deep pool.

"Not bad," said the commander, who was quite impressed with Mark's angling technique.

"Beginner's luck," said Mark modestly. Then after a pause he admitted that the water bailiff had given him some tuition. The commander chuckled and encouraged him to 'have another go'. Mark cast upstream to allow the lure to drift down with the current.

"Steve tells me that we'll be working together," said the commander in a comradely way as Mark watched the fly drifting swiftly downstream. Mark did not reply immediately because his attention was concentrated on a wily prey lurking under the swirling water. When he reeled in the line, Mark took the opportunity to ask whether there were any vacancies in the trials team. The tense moment might prove a turning point for the rest of his career.

"Don't suppose that there are any vacancies?" asked the former naval officer with bated breath as he returned the fishing rod.

"Sorry. No," replied the commander curtly as he cast towards another silver shadow hiding behind some river weeds. "Truth is that we are running down the trials team. Sorry to disappoint you." The commander actually had another mission in mind for Mark, but it was a delicate matter.

Feeling dejected at the prompt rejection, Mark was about to leave to attend to the other guests, when the commander wound in his line and turned to look at him. "There are no vacancies in the trials team, but we might be able to offer you some form of employment. It might suit you," remarked the commander in a quiet voice. This stopped the former naval officer in his tracks.

"What sort of job?" asked Mark curiously. He was yearning to return to sea.

"Can't tell you too much. It's all at an early stage," replied the commander mysteriously. The war hero was playing his cards close to his chest for the time being.

The former naval officer was left slightly perplexed by this comment. It had not occurred to him to ask why the commander had joined a group of investors who were supposedly funding new manufacturing facilities at the yard. The answer, of course, was that the investors were bankrolling the Admiral's venture to protect merchant ships from hijackers. They needed Beckwith's midget submarine. To acquire it, they needed Mark's help. That also explained why the investors showed such an interest in security measures at the boatyard.

In their secretive discussions with Steve, the investors had been debating how Mark would fit into the picture. They arrived at the consensus view that the former retired naval officer was a potential obstacle to their plan. There was no doubt that Mark was an honourable man, which was all fine and well, but his strict moral values were incompatible with the underhand dealings needed to achieve their planned objective, so the commander was asked to sound him out.

"How much do you know about the midget submarine?" asked the commander as he cast the fishing line onto the turbulent water once again.

"Not much," replied Mark, now regretting that he had taken so little interest in his sister's work. The apathetic remark persuaded the commander that he would have to provoke a reaction from the dull-witted fellow.

"Did Steve tell you that we are going to steal the midget submarine?" declared the commander. The remark was intended to shake the former naval officer out of his complacency. It had the desired effect.

"You must be joking!" blurted out Mark as he peered suspiciously at his companion. Noting the humorous, almost challenging glint in the commander's eye, the former naval officer came to the conclusion that he was the butt of a practical joke. But he dismissed that notion when the commander continued in a chilling tone. "I'm not joking! We need to talk about this when your guests have gone."

While the exchange had a sobering effect, Mark had little time to consider the implications because he had other things to worry about. For the rest of the morning, he went about his duties as host in his normal, stolid, reliable manner. A catering van turned up at one o'clock and the guests gathered round a trestle table that had been set up in the shade of a weeping willow. Mark passed sandwiches and cans of beer to the hungry and thirsty anglers.

After their lunch, the contented anglers returned to their pitches for the final session. When Mark's watch finally read three o'clock, he rounded up his guests and loaded them into the minivan, along with their tackle and the fish they had caught. After collecting their luggage from the guesthouse, he drove to the railway station and saw the visitors off on the Waterloo train. The guests were effusive in their thanks, and Mark was left with a sense of satisfaction for a job well done.

As they set off from the station, the commander was the only passenger remaining in the minivan. So this was a chance for Mark to challenge the war hero about his extraordinary remark about stealing the midget submarine, but his approach was rebuffed. "We can talk about it at the guesthouse," promised the commander. When they reached the guesthouse, Mark found Steve waiting in the sitting room. He felt as though he had been cornered, and his instinct was correct.

"I can see that the commander has told you our little secret," remarked Steve with a teasing smile. "He thinks that we are going to steal the Crown Jewels!" added the young executive, giving the commander a sly wink.

Steve knew these words would act like a goad to his subordinate, but he wanted to test the former naval officer's reaction. They needed to know where they stood. Their plans were gathering momentum and it was important for them to know whether Mark would play ball. As things stood, Mark was head of security and thus a threat to the caper they were planning. If the former naval officer reacted in a self-righteous way, there was a risk that he would scupper their entire scheme.

So it was a showdown, with Steve playing the nasty cop, while the commander played the good cop. Steve believed that the former naval officer would be more inclined to listen to the commander. After all, they both shared the same service ethos. This was make-or-break time.

With his head in a spin, Mark could not make sense of what was taking place; it was all too clever for him. "I don't think this is funny," remarked the former naval officer censoriously, in response to Steve's joke about the Crown Jewels. "The commander told me that you plan to steal the midget submarine. You could end up in jail for that! If that was intended to be a joke, then it's not a very funny one. I am getting fed up with your games!"

"It's good to see we have one law-abiding citizen among us," retorted Steve in a mocking tone to raise the tension still further. This touched a nerve because Mark was often teased about his 'by-the-book' attitude by fellow officers on the aircraft carrier, but mockery did not deter him from doing the *right* thing.

"Well, what are you really up to?" demanded the former naval officer angrily. The words were uttered with the strident tone that he used to reprimand miscreants on the warship.

The commander watched the exchange with a suppressed smile, but he eventually stepped in to put an end to Mark's misery. "Don't rise to the bait," advised the war hero. "Steve is just winding you up! Do we really look like a pair of hardened criminals?"

While Mark was more inclined to listen to the decorated war hero than his slippery boss, he remained baffled by the bizarre remark about stealing the midget submarine. For a moment, he wondered whether he had misheard or got the wrong end of the stick.

"Okay," replied the former naval officer reluctantly. "I'm listening."

"We are planning an undercover mission that will affect the boatyard," explained the commander in a down-to-earth way. "Steve only found out about this a few weeks ago. He has kindly agreed to help us. We hoped that you would do the same, but you got on your high horse about the underworld links of the security firm. That upset the applecart. That's when Steve asked for my help to square things with you!"

Mark felt cornered. "Are you with the Secret Service?" he enquired, eyeing the commander suspiciously. Mark believed in the traditions of the navy and had a jaundiced view of the Secret Service. While serving in the Gulf, there was an episode when a scruffy individual arrived by helicopter on the aircraft carrier. The bumptious guy was greeted like visiting royalty and was ushered into the captain's quarters. Mark was outraged that seasoned naval officers were forced to follow orders from an upstart like that.

"We're *not* members of the Secret Service," confirmed the commander in a reassuring tone. The commander happened to share Mark's disdainful view of the Secret Service. "But we are involved in some clandestine work. We want to protect merchant ships from pirates. To do that, we need the midget submarine that is being tested in your boatyard."

"If you need the midget submarine so much, why don't you go through official channels and ask the defence ministry to hand it over?" asked Mark with a look of outrage. The innocuous remark revealed just how naïve he was about the internal politics of the armed forces.

"Martin Beckwith won't accept that," replied the commander with an air of exasperation. As he spoke, he glanced at Steve, sending the message, *here we go again!*

"But you can surely argue your case?" insisted Mark. The commander did not want to pursue this train of argument. It was a long and convoluted tale, far too complicated to explain to this bonehead in a few minutes. Either the former naval officer trusted them, or he did not.

At the time of their conversation, plans to purloin the submarine were at an embryonic stage, and success depended on whether Mark would collaborate. In his role as harbour master, the former naval officer was in a position to scupper their plans. That was one reason why Steve had made organisational changes to relieve him of that responsibility for security, but they knew that the self-righteous fellow could still cause them trouble. They had to find a way to explain the dilemma to the dull-witted man. "Sometimes you simply have to put your faith in people without knowing all the facts," declared the commander with a sigh.

There was silence for a few minutes as the protagonists weighed up their positions. If his boss had asked him to collaborate with some dodgy dealings, Mark would have dismissed the notion out of hand, but hearing the same request from the commander threw a different light on things. After all, he was a decorated war hero with an excellent reputation in the service. "Can you give me a guarantee that you will not break the law?" asked Mark cautiously.

"Good question!" replied the commander. "We will try to keep things legal, but we can't give you a guarantee. All we can say at this stage is that we are pursuing a worthwhile cause. If you want to understand our motives, you had better speak to your sister. She's not part of our team, but she is aware of some unsavoury aspects of the submarine rescue project."

This muddied the waters. Sibling rivalries created turbulent emotions for the former naval officer. Mark had no desire to discuss his troubled family relationships with these two men, nor did he want to speak to his sister about the project that she was working on. "Well, what do you want from me?" asked Mark with a defeated expression.

"Nothing much really," replied the commander with a look of relief. "The less you know, the better. We'll make sure that you are not implicated in any wrongdoing, but you will have to refrain from reporting anything suspicious at the yard *until you have spoken to us*. You stirred up a hornet's nest when you asked Stan about the security firm. Stan is a gossip. Now the whole village knows what's going on. We are worried that he might let the cat out of the bag. So, if you are worried about anything, *speak to us first*. Don't talk to outsiders, *talk to us!*"

Faced with a tricky moral dilemma, Mark set out his terms. "I'm not happy with what you have told me, but I *will* speak to my sister. If things are as bad as you suggest, then I'll do my best to help," he pledged, but he continued with a warning. "Please don't assume that I will turn *a blind eye* to law-breaking."

"Fair enough," replied the commander, "but to repeat, please *speak to us* before you report anything suspicious to anyone else."

Having set out his position, Mark returned to the boatyard, leaving the commander to mull over the situation with Steve. Before going their separate ways, they acknowledged that it would be foolish to take Mark's cooperation for granted. After all, the skittish fellow might prove to be a loose cannon who would derail their plans, so the planning was put on hold while they waited to hear how the former naval officer reacted to what he had learned.

When he arrived home, Mark kept quiet about the troubling conversation with Steve and the commander. But he found it increasingly difficult, not least because he needed to consult his sister about her project. Up until that point, Mark had assumed that the submarine rescue project was a huge success, like the rest of his sister's glittering naval career. It now seemed this was not the case, but it would be painful to discuss this issue because they avoided talking about their work. So Mark kept putting off the unpalatable task.

By fortunate coincidence, Mark's sister phoned some days later to say she was travelling to Cornwall for a short break. "I'm having problems at work," explained Anne. "Is it all right if I stay with you for the night?" This remark chimed with suggestions that the project was in trouble. The overnight stay would provide an opportunity for Mark to broach the subject. Lucy was also looking forward to her sister-in-law's visit because it would give her a chance to catch up with family gossip and pursue her matchmaking plans.

It became apparent in the following days that Anne's problems had arisen when Beckwith returned as project manager. Up until that point, there had been a cheerful atmosphere in the Portsmouth office while the Texan project manager was in charge. Thanks to their hard work, the submarine was approaching completion, but when Beckwith resumed his role he poured scorn on their achievements. He scoffed at the wooden mock-up, describing it as 'Dexter's folly'. The slur was aimed squarely at the female naval officer. Anne was only too glad to escape the poisonous atmosphere.

After a difficult week and a frustrating journey through heavy traffic, Anne arrived to stay with her brother in a foul mood. She raged about 'the roadworks on the blessed A303' and her 'boss's obnoxious behaviour'. Lucy had never seen her sister-in-law so distressed, but Anne's normal good humour was revived in the warm but chaotic family atmosphere. When the boys returned from school, they made cheeky jibes at their aunt, much to their mother's annoyance. But Anne took it in good part.

Later in the evening, when the boys had gone to bed, the adults sat around chatting. In this jovial atmosphere, Mark recalled the episode when he delivered her note to the commander in the Admiral Bligh pub. The women giggled at the silly story as they shared a bottle of wine. As they relaxed, Lucy teased her sister-in-law, suggesting that she fancied the war hero. This revived the running joke from the previous family gathering.

Still stressed after her frustrating week in Portsmouth, Anne was drinking more heavily than usual. "The commander behaved like a pompous ass when he came to tea with Mother in the bungalow," she declared sanctimoniously. The strident tone suggested that she was becoming tipsy. "*Of course*, mother thought the war hero was the *bee's knees*. They got on like a house on fire, but the chauvinist treated me like a *skivvy*. He had the *cheek* to say that our project was a waste of time."

Then, swilling wine around her glass, she continued. "My view has changed since then. The commander seems like a decent-enough chap. He comes around to our workshop from time to time." She delivered that sage-like observation with a hiccup. "A bit pompous perhaps, but he's not a bad chap. Beckwith loathes the guy. The two men can't stand one another." After that, she stared vacantly into her glass. It was clear that she had drunk too much. This was out of character for the self-possessed young woman.

Lucy was alarmed at her sister-in-law's uninhibited behaviour and looked sharply at her husband as if to ask whether they should carry their inebriated visitor to her bed. But before she could do so, Anne revived and started to speak passionately about her work. "The truth is that it was a dreadful mistake to join Beckwith's project," declared Anne in a self-pitying way.

"The commander says the project is a waste of time. I resented that at first, but I was wrong. Submariners have told me that they do not want a new rescue vehicle. They are satisfied with the gear they have already. The project was foisted on to the submariners by some politicians in Whitehall. They call it a 'vanity project' to boost Martin Beckwith's career."

Mark's ears pricked up at these telling remarks. This was the first time that his sister had opened up to him about her naval career, but he knew that it was the alcohol talking and he did not want to take advantage of her frazzled condition. So, before his sister could make any more embarrassing revelations, Mark bid them good night and headed up to bed. Left on their own, the two women chatted until the early hours of the morning.

When Anne set off on Saturday morning, she was sheepish about her uninhibited behaviour the previous evening. To make amends, she offered to drop the teenage boys off for their soccer training on the way to meet her friends in Cornwall. The offer was gratefully accepted because it allowed Mark and Lucy to share a leisurely breakfast in their kitchen. A rare treat. As they lounged around in their dressing gowns, Lucy reflected on her sister-in-law's visit. "I've never seen Anne so upset," remarked Lucy.

They both knew that Anne was a robust character who could take care of herself and kept her problems to herself. But from her wine-fuelled ramblings the previous night, it became clear that her boss was an obnoxious swine who was up to no good. "Your sister told me that her boss is a real terror," observed Lucy as she munched contentedly on her breakfast cereal.

"Well, she's had it easy, up to now!" replied Mark unsympathetically as he rubbed his chin, deciding whether he needed to shave.

Lucy knew that her husband was envious of his sister's successful career and this had been a source of marital discord. "That's not fair!" replied his wife tartly as she put bread in the toaster. "Your sister works hard and deserves her success!"

"You might be right" conceded Mark grudgingly as he yawned.

Lucy retrieved the toast and plonked one slice on her husband's plate. Mark slapped a thick dollop of butter on the toast as he tried to stifle the feeling of envy that he felt for his sister's glittering career. The affectionate atmosphere encouraged Mark to open up about the strange events at the boatyard. "There's no doubt that Anne's boss is a rogue – he is a pain in the backside at the boatyard."

"Why is that?" enquired Lucy innocently. Mark embarked on a plodding explanation of the security changes at the boatyard. He spoke in general terms, as he did not wish to reveal confidential information about the commander's plot. But Lucy knew that he was holding something back, from the stilted way he expressed himself. He was unusually reticent, and this roused Lucy's sleuthing instincts, yet again.

"Don't you think that it is odd that both you and your sister are involved with the same project?" asked Lucy, gazing enquiringly into her partner's eyes.

"No, not really," replied her husband disingenuously as he turned to avoid her gimlet stare. "Never crossed my mind!" Lucy raised her eyebrows in disbelief as she poured herself another cup of coffee from the percolator on the sideboard.

Lucy could tell that her husband was lying. *He can't be that dumb!* she thought to herself, *so what is really going on?* Using all her feminine wiles, she was determined to winkle out the truth. "So, your sister's boss is running the trials of the submarine?" she remarked with the air of an innocent abroad. She knew this was incorrect. It was a ploy to prise more information from her secretive partner.

"Well, yes and no," explained Mark in the plodding way of a 'man in charge'. "Beckwith's team built the midget submarine but the sea trials will be organised by Commander Woods – that's the chap that we saw having lunch with Steve at the Windmill. Anne is a member of Beckwith's team. The sub will be housed on a North Sea supply ship called the *Normandy* during the trials. It's Beckwith's responsibility to guard the ship. He is installing barriers at the yard entrance and organising security guards."

This chimed with what Lucy had gleaned from her sister-in-law the previous evening. After reflection, Lucy took another stab in the dark. "Commander Woods – was that the chap you met in the pub in Portsmouth?" she remarked with a pensive expression, as though she was trying to get to grips with a complicated scenario.

"Yes, that's him," replied Mark, rather testily. He was becoming impatient about running over old ground. "I've met him several times now. He joined the fishing party that I organised last week. It was a bit of a surprise. He turned up out of the blue!"

As they chatted, Lucy began to assemble the jigsaw. As they spoke, Mark let slip that the guests who attended the fishing party were wealthy individuals who planned to invest in new facilities at the boatyard. *That made sense*, she thought, but it raised many questions. Why had the commander joined the party? What was he up to? It all confirmed her belief that her husband had been caught up in some sort of conspiracy.

As she pondered this mystery, she recalled an indiscreet remark that her sister-in-law made while under the influence of alcohol the previous evening. Anne let slip that her boss spied on her phone calls and was determined to prevent her meeting the commander. Lucy wanted to get to the bottom of the mystery, so she decided to tackle her husband head-on. "Why did the commander join the fishing party?" she asked with a determined look in her eye.

That was the key question. After all, it was unlikely that a serving naval officer would be an investor in a manufacturing business. "I don't know," replied Mark with a guilty look as he tried to avoid mentioning the undercover plot to commandeer the submarine. He did not want to let the cat out of the bag. "The commander is a keen angler and seemed to know some of the businessmen," was his lame response. "Steve told me there would be another guest, but it was a real surprise when the commander turned up."

Then, after a pause for thought, Mark realised he could not deceive his wife any longer. He was no good at keeping secrets and knew from experience that she would eventually wheedle out the truth, so he decided to confide in her.

"Look. Strange things have happened at work recently," admitted Mark with a worried expression. "It all started when Steve told me to oversee the security changes. It's a big job. Then, Stan told me that Beckwith had chosen a security firm with underworld links. Steve didn't show any interest when I told him about that. Then, to cap it all, the commander said they plan to steal the submarine."

"You're joking!" retorted Lucy gleefully.

This was more exciting than she anticipated. She urged her husband to continue and chuckled appreciatively at each revelation. "Steve and the commander are in league," explained Mark with a solemn expression. "They cornered me in the guesthouse after the businessmen left on the train to London. They told me that they were involved in some sort of operation to protect merchant ships from hijackers. Steve wanted to know how I would react. They would not tell me any more about it. They want me to turn a blind eye to criminal activity."

Lucy was delighted by what she heard but was disappointed that her partner was so half-hearted about it. She recalled the outrageous pranks and practical jokes from his college days, but he had aged prematurely. The dashing cadet had morphed into a disillusioned middle-aged grump who feared breaking the rules and upsetting the status quo. So Lucy made it her goal in life to reawaken her husband's buccaneering spirit.

Lucy's campaign got underway when the family gathered for Sunday lunch. To liven the mood, Lucy recalled her husband's famous pranks during his school days. "Your father sneaked out of his boarding school and spent the evening in the pub," she revealed. "He got into bad trouble when the teachers found out!" The boys hooted with laughter at the story. They had always seen their father as an unbending disciplinarian, and they were amused to learn that he broke the rules in his youth.

Mark glowered at the head of the table, embarrassed by the memory. But all was forgiven when the couple made up that evening, after the boys had gone to bed. Lucy reassured her husband. "You take life too seriously," she soothed him. "You seem to think that the world will come to an end if you make a mistake. It's time that you learned to trust people." Mark dwelt on those words as he lay in bed that night, and woke up with a new perspective on life.

Chapter 13

Mark Joins the Gang

After his Damascene conversion, Mark had little time to brood, because he was busy preparing for the sea trials of the midget submarine. One urgent task was to clear a channel to the boatyard. The *Normandy* was to act as the base for the trials and it was the largest ship to sail that far up the estuary, so the former naval officer needed to ensure that it had a clear passage to the berth. This involved taking soundings and laying buoys along a channel. Some small boats were moored along the route, and these needed to be moved.

The yard staff were looking forward to the sea trials because it would give them a chance to see the revolutionary midget submarine in action. The workforce was proud of the novel fuel-cell propulsion system they had created, but there were also rumblings of discontent about the trials. The unsightly portable cabins in the car park were one source of grievance, as were the disruptions caused by the security changes. Beckwith did not help matters, because he refused to listen to the staff complaints.

As the trials approached, contractors rerouted the security fence and installed a barrier and guard house at the yard entrance. This work caused no end of aggravation. Things came to a head when the yard foreman was unable to get into the car park because an open ditch had been dug across the entrance. He stormed into Beckwith's portable cabin but was sent packing. "If you have a beef, speak to your management," was the academic's dismissive response.

After being appointed as Steve's deputy, Mark needed to resolve these petty grievances and so he bore the brunt of the hostility from the yard staff. This placed him in an invidious position. Mark was greeted with snide remarks when he visited Beckwith's portable cabin to complain. Beckwith called the former naval officer 'Captain Fish Finger' in a cynical reference to the seafood commercial. These confrontations confirmed his sister's view that Beckwith was a scoundrel who could not be trusted.

Despite the grievances, there was an air of excitement as the workforce gathered on the quay to watch the arrival of the *Normandy*. The yard staff had been looking forward to their first view of the revolutionary midget submarine. As the ship approached, Beckwith was closeted in his portable cabin. But before the ship could berth, a minivan slew into the car park, followed closely by a truck laden with security barriers.

Half a dozen burly security guards were disgorged from the minivan and headed straight for Beckwith's portable cabin. A few minutes later, Beckwith emerged, followed by a retinue of security guards, and they proceeded to hustle people back from the quayside. In the scrum, the staff were unable to watch the ship docking in the quay. The *Normandy* was an imposing sight as it slid through the flotilla of small fishing boats and yachts that were moored in the shallow water of the harbour.

With its brightly painted bridge and living quarters stacked above the bow, the ship had a large unobstructed deck for the transport of cargo on the open stern deck. The thrusters stirred up the mud as it turned and moved crabwise towards the quay. A seaman threw a mooring line and Mark caught it. The former naval officer had somehow freed himself from the main body of the workforce who were being herded back to the office building. But one of the security guards grabbed the rope and wrenched it from his hand, gruffly ordering the former naval officer to join the rest of the yard staff who were huddled by the office building.

The guards made the lines fast to bollards. Then they positioned portable barriers to prevent yard staff from reaching the quayside. *No Entry* signs were fitted prominently above the barrier. All these measures reinforced the message that visitors were *not welcome*. Beckwith was the first person to board the *Normandy* once the gangway had been made fast. After bounding onboard, the lanky academic clambered up to the wheelhouse, emerging a few minutes later with the skipper trailing behind. The old sea dog bore a sour expression as the pair came ashore and disappeared into Beckwith's cabin.

The disgruntled yard staff returned grudgingly to work, grumbling at the way they had been treated. They were disgusted at the surly behaviour of the guards and were disappointed that they could not see the midget submarine. The craft was hidden under a tarpaulin on the stern deck. This sour atmosphere pervaded the boatyard for the remainder of the sea trials.

Commander Woods drove into the car park shortly after the arrival of the *Normandy*. He marched straight to the portable office that was allocated for his trials team. As he passed the adjacent cabin, he overheard a commotion. The decorated war hero only caught the end of this conversation, but it caused him to smile nonetheless. "I want you back at this quay by four o'clock, sharp, *every day!*" barked the academic. "That's not a request. *That's an order!*"

"But we have to take account of the tides ..." replied the weather-beaten skipper in a diffident hangdog tone. The old sea dog was unable to finish before he was rudely interrupted.

"Don't tell me your problems! I've got enough of my *own,"* shouted the bumptious academic. *"Get back here by four o'clock each afternoon* and that's an end of it."

The old seafarer shook his head in disbelief; there was no way that he could win a battle with this overbearing client. He had to obey his paymaster's orders. "Anything you want. You are the boss!" conceded the old sea dog with a cowed expression. When the skipper stepped out of the portable cabin, he raised a bushy eyebrow as he made eye contact with the commander, who was loitering outside. The commander winked in response. *That idiot has a screw loose!* was the unspoken message.

After dropping off his briefcase in his own cabin, the commander went to see Beckwith in his lair. Beckwith greeted the commander with a sycophantic smile. *That is a change of tune,* thought the commander.

The academic addressed the commander in an ingratiating way as they discussed the trials. "It's not often that you get to work with a decorated war hero," remarked the academic. The reason for the flattery was that his visitor was in a position to pass judgement on the performance of the midget submarine for the navy. So the balance of power had shifted, dramatically.

After suffering months of slurs from the academic, the tables had turned, and the commander was able to reap revenge, if he so wished. It would be easy to extract his retribution, because the sea trials were to take place far from the coast, beyond the academic's control. This gave the commander an opportunity to exaggerate faults. A critical report would sink Beckwith's agency, and that was something the academic needed to avoid at all costs.

The commander had no intention of using such deceitful tactics, but it was an unspoken threat, nevertheless. To counter this threat, Beckwith felt that he should exert influence over the sea trials, as the backseat driver. To allow him influence over the trials, he took care to ensure that the crew of the *Normandy* and the security guards were all loyal to him. Another wheeze was to insist that the *Normandy* return to Whitebait Cove at the end of each day.

This was wasteful because of the time lost transporting the submarine back and forth to the deep-water trials area. This waste was exacerbated by the tidal movement that restricted the docking of the *Normandy* to certain times of the day. The skipper tried to raise this point. "It will allow the boatyard to rectify problems overnight," he declared.

The real reason for adopting this wasteful procedure was that it would allow Beckwith to dispute any adverse findings at the end of each day. In this way, he would have a measure of control over what appeared in the final report to the navy. The commander knew what he was up to but decided that it might suit their purposes to go along with Beckwith's plan.

After meeting with Beckwith, the commander had to speak to Mark. On the face of it, this was part of his normal routine. But on this occasion, the commander needed to address the former naval officer's qualms about their clandestine plan to purloin the midget submarine. This would be a difficult conversation, so they needed to meet away from prying eyes.

Commander Woods spotted his newly retired colleague embroiled in an argument with the security guards. When the altercation ended, the commander caught his eye and signalled that they sneak round behind the workshops to a space where waste bins were housed. This was one of the few places in the yard where they could speak out of earshot of others. They made their way separately to this secluded spot.

Mark arrived, fuming with rage when they met. "Beckwith's guards won't allow our staff to eat their sandwiches on the quayside," he moaned. This was a huge blow because the yard staff normally sat on the quay during their lunch break. Failure to win this concession showed that Mark had little influence without the support of his boss. Steve's absence in these turbulent times was another source of his ill temper. Mark was left to face the wrath of the workforce, as usual.

The commander expressed sympathy, but it was only a token gesture. He was in a cheerful mood after a satisfying meeting with his adversary. "What did you think of the show?" asked the commander with a grin, as he scanned round to make sure they could not be overheard.

"Not much!" replied Mark angrily. "Our people wanted to see the new submarine. But instead they were set on by thugs. They can't get near to the ship, and even if they could, the submarine is hidden under a tarpaulin." This made him spitting mad because the yard staff saw the former naval officer as complicit with the security changes imposed on them.

As an outsider, the commander was untroubled by these internal yard matters. He tried to lighten the mood. "We have to protect the submarine from snoopers," he mimicked, in the phony North London accent that Beckwith adopted to burnish his working-class credentials. Then, turning to serious matters, he explained why Beckwith wanted to impose these over-the-top security arrangements.

"It's all about public relations. Beckwith wants to control the media coverage. He wants to hide the midget submarine from the press until the trials have been successfully completed," explained the commander patiently. "When he's ready, he will organise a big jamboree and unveil his creation to public acclaim. It's a publicity stunt."

Mark could not care less about publicity, but the surly behaviour of the guards was driving him balmy. The former naval officer could understand why people loathed the egotistical academic who was the architect of this mess. He had yet to meet anyone who had a good word to say about the scoundrel. With a look of disgust, he surveyed the new guard house, the entrance barriers, the portable barriers along the quay and the surly security guards.

"So we have to accept all those changes just to help Beckwith get good media coverage for his project!" remarked the former naval officer with an air of disbelief.

"All paid for by HM government!" confirmed the commander. "That tells you a lot about our friend's character, does it not?"

"My sister really loathes the guy," exclaimed Mark, before checking himself. As soon as the words slipped out, the former naval officer regretted them. He did not want to be drawn into a discussion about his sister, given their difficult relationship.

"I was going to ask whether you had spoken to your sister," remarked the commander with an air of satisfaction. This was an easy entrée to the delicate subject of the caper they had planned.

"My sister stayed overnight last Friday, but we did not really have a chance to speak, with the kids and all that," mumbled the former naval officer as he shuffled his feet in a sign of his discomfort. "She was owed some leave and was on her way to join some friends who are surfing in Cornwall."

"What's her next assignment?" asked the commander conversationally.

"We didn't talk about it. We are not that close and rarely discuss our careers," admitted Mark ruefully. Uncomfortable with the direction of the conversation, the former naval officer tried to change the subject: "You still haven't really told me what you and Steve are up to."

"Look. It's best that you don't know too much," said the commander, who feared that the former naval officer was a loose cannon who could threaten their clandestine mission.

"I might be able to help," suggested Mark hesitantly, to signal his willingness to support the conspirators. A number of factors had combined to change his view – his sister's disdain for her boss and his dislike for the loathsome academic. But his change of attitude could also be attributed to a bolder, more rebellious outlook on life, fostered by his wife.

"Well, there is one thing you could do," replied the commander cautiously. In the pause that followed, Mark's brain conjured up all manner of heroic deeds, so he was slightly deflated by the commander's tame response. "We would like you to go on a fishing trip with Steve in the Highlands," continued the commander.

"Fishing?" echoed Mark, with a bewildered look.

As he spoke, Martin Beckwith stepped out of his portable cabin and started to head in their direction. The commander noticed him coming and covered his mouth as a warning. Before they parted, he made one final remark: "Perhaps you could have a word with Steve about the fishing trip." With that, they walked off in different directions, careful to avert any suspicion that they were conspiring together.

The conversation left Mark no wiser about what was being planned. The fishing trip made little sense and would need Lucy's permission. His wife would not allow him to swan off to the Highlands without a sound reason. To further complicate matters, he had to talk it over with Steve, but his boss was nowhere to be found, as usual, so he relegated the commander's comment to the back of his mind as he returned to his normal duties.

In the days that followed, the *Normandy* became a familiar sight at Whitebait Cove, but the submarine remained hidden from view under a tarpaulin on the stern deck. The yard workers and local residents had little idea what the revolutionary craft looked like. The submarine had already been classed as seaworthy at the shipyard. After a naming ceremony, a series of tests were carried out in a dry dock at the shipyard to check the watertight integrity, buoyancy and stability. This was followed by a thorough technical survey by a classification society.

After an official handover to the Marine Special Projects Agency, the midget submarine was loaded onto the *Normandy* and transported to Whitebait Cove, where the sea trials were to take place. The first series of tests was then carried out in the shallow water of the estuary to set up the system that controlled the flooding of the ballast tanks. These trials ensured that the craft would submerge smoothly and safely.

Mark had already identified a site where these shallow-water tests could be carried out without interfering with shipping movements. After choosing the trials site, the former naval officer informed the port authorities and marked the area with buoys. These initial trials got off to a slow start because the crew of the mother ship fumbled with the launching system. Once launched, the midget submarine was manned by three members of the navy trials team.

With the lengthy launch procedure and daily return to Whitebait Cove, it took the trials team more than a week to commission the ballast system. With this task completed, the diving trials could commence in deeper water. This called for a longer voyage to the open sea. The stresses in the titanium hull were monitored as the craft was submerged to ever-increasing depths. The methodically collected data was transmitted back to the shipyard designers. The trials team carried electronic test equipment to log all this information.

As the work progressed, there was a need to make adjustments and rectify faults. This work could not be carried out on the mother ship because the *Normandy* was only able to carry nine people, due to the limitations of life raft capacity. So, with the ship's crew of six and the three members of the trials team, the ship could not carry technicians, so modifications had to be carried out back at the boatyard.

Another problem arose because the old-fashioned radios on the mother ship were unable to transmit the test data files to the shore base. Beckwith was aware of all these shortcomings when he selected the old tub. This was used as an excuse for the ship's return to the boatyard at Whitebait Cove by four o'clock each afternoon. A great deal of time was thus wasted travelling back and forth to the trials site each day.

As a result, the trials progressed slowly and the comings and goings of the mother ship became a familiar part of daily life for the residents of Whitebait Cove. There was little incentive to speed up the trials because the government was paying whatever it cost and the navy had no real interest in taking on a new submarine rescue vehicle, so it suited everyone that the trials should be spun out for as long as possible. In an ironic twist, Beckwith actually benefitted from extended trials because it boosted his agency fees.

The slow progress of the trials suited the crew of the *Normandy* down to the ground. It was like a summer holiday. The motley gang regarded their assignment as an 'easy number' in a benign part of the world. They knew that once this job was completed, they would once again have to grapple with cumbersome drilling gear in the storm-tossed North Sea. It was also a pleasure to spend each night in harbour. This was an unusual luxury in their line of work.

When the skipper accepted that his ship was to be moored in harbour each night, he arranged for his wife to stay in a guesthouse where he could join her. In the days that followed, he drew up a roster to allow other crew members to bunk ashore. One unfortunate soul was designated to remain on board as watchkeeper, but the rest were able to escape to comfortable lodgings on the shore. A couple of young deckhands found friendly local girls who could put them up. The others booked into guesthouses so the ship was left deserted at night, with the exception of the watchkeeper.

After they had settled into this routine, the skipper began to wonder whether it was necessary to maintain a watch through the night. The watchkeeper's only task was to keep an eye on the generator and life support systems. There was little point in running the generator if there no one on board, so the skipper asked Mark to rig an electric supply from the quay to power the freezer in the galley, and other essential services. With a security guard at the gate to protect the vessel, the entire crew could spend the night ashore.

In his new role, Mark was responsible for liaising with the sea trials team, and this allowed him to watch the comedy show from the sidelines. The commander introduced Mark to the three-man team on the morning after the *Normandy* berthed at the yard. The trials team consisted of a naval submariner and a couple of technical experts. They gathered in the portable office in the car park for the introductory meeting. With his service background, Mark quickly established a rapport with the submariner.

The commander did not take an active part in the trials. After briefing his men, he returned to the Portsmouth naval base, leaving the team to get on with their work. The team boarded the mother ship before it headed into the estuary to the trials site. After the day's trials were completed, the crew of the mother ship had strict orders to hide the midget submarine under a tarpaulin. After docking, the navy trials team reported to Beckwith in his portable cabin and downloaded trials data from their portable computers.

Mark watched this farce with a mixture of amusement and annoyance. The trials were a source of grievance to the yard staff. The staff were angry that they needed to show a security pass at the security hut, where the guards acted in a surly manner. There were also rumblings of discontent that they could not see the new submarine. Mark had to deal with their gripes. It was an unpalatable job, and his boss was little help. Steve was rarely seen in the yard during that period. The reasons for his absence were the subject of gossip.

With little work to keep them occupied, the disgruntled staff had time on their hands. In the poisonous atmosphere, rumours circulated. One particularly malicious rumour suggested that Steve was avoiding the yard because he was frightened of Martin Beckwith. Another nasty rumour suggested that the yard was going to close and that Steve was looking for another job. But among all the doom and gloom, it seemed that the midget submarine performed better than expected. Diving trials provided evidence that the new craft could stay submerged for far longer than its battery-powered equivalent.

Two innocuous events combined to bring this incendiary atmosphere to a climax. The first incident occurred one morning when Beckwith marched into a workshop. "I need you to drop everything to modify this piece of pipework," he barked. The work needed to be done quickly to allow the day's trials to get underway. The tradesmen were normally a helpful bunch but in the febrile atmosphere, the academic's domineering attitude was a step too far, and they took umbrage.

The tradesmen then learned that they had been excluded from the grand inauguration of the revolutionary craft. Many politicians, ministry officials, naval officers and journalists had been invited to the event, but none of the craftsmen appeared on the invitation list. The ceremony was due to take place on a ferry that had been specially chartered for the occasion. They took this as an outrageous snub. There was talk of revenge against the intruders in the car park.

The following morning, Mark arrived to find graffiti scrawled on one of the portable cabins that had been planted in the car park. The words *What about the workers?* had been daubed in garish spray paint. The newly retired naval officer was outraged at this and could not believe that his fellow employees would indulge in that sort of childish prank, but his efforts to find the culprit were met with a wall of silence. Sniggering remarks behind his back showed the depth of hostility towards the outsiders encamped in the car park.

Mark wanted to raise this matter with Steve, but his boss was nowhere to be seen. This added to his contempt for the slippery young guy. While the graffiti reflected badly on the boatyard, it was not, technically, Mark's responsibility. Under the new regime, Beckwith was in charge of security. Mark was determined to tackle the academic about it. A chance arose when Mark spotted the lanky figure striding across the car park. The former naval officer stepped into the academic's path.

"Have you seen that?" demanded Mark indignantly, pointing to the disfigured wall.

The lanky academic swerved past Mark without breaking step. "Yes. I thought it was quite imaginative," replied Beckwith dismissively, with a sickly smirk.

"Do you know who did it?" demanded Mark as he set off in pursuit.

"Local kids, most likely. It's just a childish prank!" replied the academic in a throw-away manner over his shoulder.

"Have you called the police?" shouted Mark as he struggled to catch up with the fast-striding academic.

"No need to trouble the boys in blue. My chaps can handle it," replied Beckwith casually. With that, the lanky academic ducked into his office, slamming the door behind him.

Mark could not believe Beckwith's complacent attitude. The graffiti might not be important in itself, but it was a sign of lax security. *Some vandals could have crept past the security guard without being seen*, he speculated. *The night guard was probably sleeping on the job. The incident provides evidence that the security firm is not up to the job.*

When Mark arrived home, he was fuming about the graffiti business. This amused Lucy at first, but when her husband kept ranting on about guards sleeping on the job and the dodgy security firm, his wife got fed up. Lucy told her husband to speak to the bowls club treasurer. "Stan knows what is going on at Whitebait Cove," observed Lucy wisely. "He will be able to identify the culprit." Mark was wary of taking that course of action, recalling the warning that Stan was a gossip, but he decided to wander round to the bowls club nonetheless. He received a cool reception.

Stan had not seen Mark since visiting his home to warn of the dodgy security firm. He took umbrage that Mark had failed to heed his warning. To complicate matters, Mark needed to keep certain matters secret, so it was an awkward and disjoined conversation when they finally met together. "There is a lot of bad feeling towards the navy trials team," observed Mark in a casual way. "Someone daubed graffiti on the portable cabins."

"It's probably an outsider!" asserted Stan with the benefit of local knowledge. "All the locals know that the guard skips off during the night shift." This shocked Mark. The former naval officer knew things were bad, but had no idea that security had become so lax. It explained how vandals were able to enter the yard undetected. "I can't understand why you put up with it," observed Stan with an air of incredulity. After mumbling something unintelligible, Mark said he had to get home. He did not want to be drawn into that delicate subject.

When Mark arrived at the boatyard the following morning, he found the guards scrubbing furiously to remove the graffiti from the wall of the portable cabin. This was a surprise, given Beckwith's complacent attitude the previous day. The guards must have started early because they had nearly finished the task when Mark arrived at 8 am. It was obvious that they wanted to remove the paint before the staff arrived for work.

The frantic efforts of the guards did not square with the academic's complacent attitude in the car park the previous afternoon. It later emerged that Beckwith was incandescent with rage and had given the guards a furious dressing-down about the incident, but he had concealed his fury to prevent the police becoming involved. This was his greatest fear; that an investigation would throw light on his illicit activities.

Chapter 14

The Heist is Planned

With little else to keep him busy during the sea trials, Martin Beckwith devoted his time to organising a press launch for the midget submarine he had created. Invitations to the grand affair were sent out to important figures in government and the military. A famous chef was hired to cater for these VIPs on a chartered ferry. After unveiling the midget submarine with a fanfare, the craft would be put through its paces, to demonstrate its diving performance.

The purpose of this lavish event was to 'sell' the submarine rescue vehicle to the navy.

The academic was confident the navy would sign a lease for the submersible vehicle after witnessing its remarkable diving performance. The government lease would solve his financial problems. The guest list included a select band of journalists and TV crews. The carefully choreographed affair was intended to silence critics and showcase the achievements of his Marine Special Projects Agency.

Beckwith had courted the media throughout his career. The academic was confident that the diving demonstration would produce impressive TV footage for the evening news. As an added benefit, the glitzy affair would allow him to exact revenge upon his critics. To this end, he primed journalists with awkward questions. His target was Commander Woods. The press would interview the technical dinosaur as the person responsible for the sea trials.

When the Admiral learned of Beckwith's ambitious plans, he realised he only had a short window of opportunity before the midget submarine was to be snatched from his grasp. The midget submarine had performed extremely well during its sea trials, so other branches of the navy would fight tooth and nail to acquire the craft. It was unlikely that it would be assigned to his rag-tag fleet.

So the Admiral invited his two most trusted henchmen to a meeting at his home to discuss how they could acquire the submarine. Felix advocated caution. "We need to negotiate in good faith," advised the Polish accountant.

Commander Woods poured scorn on what he regarded as a gutless approach. "That guy will never hand over his baby!" asserted the decorated war hero testily. "Not in a million years!"

The Admiral knew that the commander bore a grudge against Beckwith, and thought it might cloud his judgement. "Let's forget about your feud for a moment," declared the old fox. He wanted his two henchmen to work together in a friendly fashion to find a solution. "We need to look at this in a sensible way." Then turning to Felix, he asked: "What makes you believe Beckwith will do a deal with us?"

"My City friends have purchased most of the debt for the submarine rescue project – *thanks to my efforts*," explained Felix smugly. "If the covenants are breached, which seems likely, we can repossess the midget submarine, so he has no choice."

"He has a point!" commented the Admiral solicitously. This provoked a wrathful response from the decorated war hero. "How many times do we have to tell you!" thundered the old warhorse as he tried to nail the argument. "Dealing with that slippery bugger is like trying to nail jelly to the ceiling. Yes, you can find some legal loophole, but Beckwith will turn to his friends in the media, and the whole world will know what we are up to, so bang goes our undercover operation!"

The commander's statement echoed the Admiral's own opinion on the matter. But the wily old fox was hiding his cards for the time being; he wanted his two henchmen to resolve their differences without his involvement, if possible. "Okay," responded Felix disparagingly. "So what is *your* plan?"

"We will pinch it!" replied the decorated war hero with an unnecessary show of bravado.

"Brilliant!" retorted Felix sarcastically, as the muscles around his mouth clenched tightly. "Your trials team will be chief suspects. The police will be round to arrest you in *five minutes*. The whole team will end up in jail."

"Not if we are cunning," argued the commander in a more conciliatory way as he retrenched in the face of the acerbic onslaught. This was not the first time that his gung-ho attitude had got him into trouble. "We find someone else to steal the craft and ensure that all our people have alibis when the midget submarine goes missing."

"Well, don't ask me to help with your stupid plan," retorted Felix dismissively. "You might be happy to spend Christmas in jail, but don't ask me to join you!"

The Admiral watched as the pair fought like ferrets in a bag. It was an amusing diversion, but if a solution was to be found, he needed to deal with them separately. "Thanks for your views, Felix," he said in a firm tone to end the debate. "I'll think about what you said." Then he made a signal to show that he wanted to talk to the commander alone: "Could you stay for a few minutes, Commander, and explain more clearly what you have in mind?"

The Polish accountant resented being given his marching orders. He rose up from his chair with a pinch-faced expression that showed he had taken umbrage. As he collected his thoughts, the Admiral watched the aggrieved money man depart in silence.

"Congratulations, Commander!" barked the old fox with a look of irritation. "You have managed to upset the only sensible member of my team."

"What did I do?" replied the commander with a look of injured innocence. In truth, the war hero took great pleasure in winding up the stuffy accountant. This was not difficult because the Pole had a short fuse and reacted volcanically to the slightest impropriety.

"You could have sugared the pill a bit!" chided the Admiral. "What possessed you to say 'we will pinch it'? You must have known how Felix would react!"

"Well, your accountant really irritates me!" replied the commander. "Everything has to be 'just so' in his oh-so-perfect world. He's not prepared to take any risks!" This remark infuriated the old fox, who knew the perils that the Polish man had faced escaping from the grip of the Soviet Union, but he also had great respect for the commander's courage, knowing that he had proved himself during the Falklands War.

"You know your trouble, Commander, you underestimate your fellow man," observed the Admiral with the wisdom of old age. "Okay, you proved yourself in the Falklands, but Felix is as brave as you are. He just looks at life in a different way. Felix calculates the odds before he jumps in, but you just dash in without considering the consequences."

Having got that beef off his chest, the Admiral asked how his subordinate proposed to 'pinch the submarine'. In reply, the commander outlined an outlandish plot that had been dreamed up by the gang in Fenchurch Street. The plan was to commandeer the *Normandy* with the help of outsiders. "That sounds fanciful," observed the Admiral with a quizzical expression. "The boatyard staff will know what you are up to."

The commander acknowledged this with a nod. He went on to describe a fishing trip charade that would remove Mark from the scene of the crime and provide Steve with an alibi. The Admiral was impressed with that idea. "Beckwith has made enemies in the boatyard," argued the commander. "Few tears will be shed if the submarine is pinched from under his nose."

"Steve Jones understands the situation and is prepared to help," argued the commander. "He has sea-going experience, so he can help to commandeer the *Normandy*."

"But who will take charge of the operation?" enquired the Admiral sceptically. "You can't lead it, nor can any of your team. You will be prime suspects." The commander could not answer that. It was clear that his plans had not been fully thought through. It might have been the end of the matter, had it not been for Lucy, who acted as the catalyst to solve the riddle.

As the mother of two energetic boys and a teacher at the local school, Lucy led a hectic life, so she did not normally pay much attention to her husband's work. But her sleuthing instincts were awoken when Mark told her about the fishing trip to Scotland. She would not give her partner permission for that under normal circumstances, but when she learned that the fishing trip might be part of a caper to target Anne's obnoxious boss, she was intrigued.

The Heist is Planned

Lucy recalled her sister-in-law's alcohol-fuelled remarks about her loathsome boss, so her imaginative mind went into overdrive. *This would be a chance for Anne to get her own back*, she mused with a mischievous smile. This would also fit neatly with her matchmaking plans because it would throw her sister-in-law together with the dashing young executive. But they needed to be careful how they raised the subject because Anne still worked for the project team and she might take offence and betray their plans.

So Lucy approached the matter in a roundabout way while chatting to her sister-in-law on the phone. "You wouldn't like to keep me company while Mark goes fishing in Scotland?" she enquired casually. "It's not much fun being left here on my own." Anne was puzzled by this remark because Lucy had spent long periods coping on her own while Mark was at sea. So why was Lucy so keen for company? Fearing that something was amiss, Anne wanted to find out more.

"Everything all right between you and Mark?" she asked inquisitively.

"Yes, fine," replied Lucy. After several other probing questions, Lucy (accidentally) let slip that Mark's fishing trip to Scotland 'had something to do with Commander Woods'. Anne thought that was a decidedly odd comment, but on reflection, she decided to have a quiet word with the war hero, to try to make some sense of it. Although their relationship had got off to a stormy start, Anne was now on cordial terms with her distinguished colleague, but she had not seen him for some time because she no longer worked at the naval base.

After completing the wooden mock-up, Anne was confined to the dreary project office in an industrial area of Portsmouth, where she was assembling instruction manuals for the midget submarine before returning to the navy. This was a tedious business, so she invented an excuse to return to the warehouse where the mock-up was built. This allowed her to visit the commander in his office. "What's all this about a fishing trip?" she asked with a teasing smile after some general chit-chat.

"What do you mean?" replied the commander innocently.

"Why have you sent my brother on a fishing trip to Scotland?" demanded Anne in a more direct manner. With that challenge, the commander knew that he would have to level with his bright female colleague. If he could not win her over, she would winkle information from her brother and let the cat out of the bag.

"You may not like this," he warned with a grave expression, "but we plan to commandeer your submarine and we would like you to help us." This stopped Anne in her tracks and she did not know how to react. But after giving Anne time to take in the significance of his words, the commander went on to explain the motives. As he proceeded with his long diatribe, the war hero watched her reaction tensely. It was a relief for the commander when Anne's expression softened to show her support for the crazy scheme.

Anne was stimulated by the prospect of real action after months shuffling papers behind a desk. It would be a chance to regain her sea legs before returning to full-time navy service. The caper would fit in with her plans because she was due to take some leave. So, that evening, she phoned Lucy to say that she would love to stay while Mark was 'fishing in Scotland', leaving the full implication of the statement unsaid.

After the plans were approved by the Admiral, Anne was appointed leader of a boarding party that was to commandeer the *Normandy*, with Steve's support as deckhand. But there remained the need for a mechanic as a third member of the crew. This would be a tricky post to fill because the vessel was in a 'dead-ship condition' when boarded, so the mechanic would need to start unfamiliar machinery. It was Lucy who once again helped to solve this riddle.

Lucy recalled the hot-water shower incident that took place shortly before her sister-in-law relinquished her command of the patrol boat. She recalled her sister-in-law describing the prankster as an 'extremely capable mechanic' and knew that the guy was in debt to Anne. It was thanks to Anne that the prankster was transferred to a modern frigate, rather than being drummed out of the navy. "The artificer sounds just the sort of guy you need," she suggested when they were chatting together, but Anne had doubts.

"It's unlikely that the guy will remember me," replied Anne. "He will be in his element on the new frigate because he loves dealing with complicated machinery. I doubt if he will be interested in our sideshow. In any case, the frigate was stationed in the Med the last I heard."

"You are a defeatist," retorted Lucy. "There's no harm having a word with him. After all, he owes you a favour – he could have been thrown out of the service." This prompted Anne to phone an acquaintance at the Portsmouth naval base, who provided some surprising news. It seemed that the artificer had been dishonourably discharged from the navy after punching an officer in the face. It seemed that he was now employed as a craft lecturer at a training college.

The war hero was alarmed at the prospect of working with the reprobate when he heard the idea, but Anne promised to take responsibility for the mechanic's behaviour. "He has a quick temper," asserted Anne in the mechanic's defence, "but he is a decent chap at heart and knows his job."

The commander had grave misgivings, but after Anne's reassurances, he gave way. After all, she was in charge of the mission, so it was only sensible that she chose her team.

"You can approach the guy," he agreed, "but I want to speak to the scallywag to set him straight!"

After making enquiries, Anne learned that the mechanic had moved out of his family home. It seemed that his wife had petitioned for divorce. After being chucked out on his ear, the mechanic was staying in a seedy bedsit on the outskirts of Portsmouth. This information should have set off warning signals but, sadly, it did not. It was typical of Anne's impetuous nature that once embarked upon an action, she would not deviate from her intended path.

"Hello, is that Andrew Blackwell?" asked Anne confidently, when the phone call was answered.

"Speaking," came the wary reply. The artificer did not recognise the voice and feared that it might be some busybody chasing up his late alimony payments.

"You may remember me. I was your commander on the patrol boat," declared Anne, rather pompously.

The mechanic sighed with relief but did not know how to respond. After an eventful posting on the frigate, he only retained a hazy recollection of the patrol boat, but the shower incident stayed fresh in his mind. "Do you need help with your plumbing, ma'am?" he quipped.

As a civilian, Anne no longer had authority over him. "No. You're the one who needs help with plumbing, if your antics on the patrol boat were anything to go by," she replied.

It was a poor attempt at humour, but the discharged artificer chuckled nonetheless. Anne wanted to keep the conversation light-hearted and inject a little humour.

"Good to hear from you, ma'am. I miss the old tub sometimes," replied the mechanic in the familiar way that he adopted with mess room pals. "How did you get my number?"

"Yes, I miss the patrol boat as well," replied Anne with

genuine feeling. "An old colleague in personnel gave me your number."

"How are you getting on in Civvy Street?" asked the mechanic.

"Not so well, really," replied Anne with a sigh. "How are you getting on? I hear that you have had a spot of bother."

"Got slung out of the service for punching one of your pals. I'm training lads at the college now," replied the artificer with a despondent sigh. "It's not a bad job, pays my wages. But how can I help you?"

"We need a mechanic for an offshore supply ship berthed in the West Country, one weekend, later this month," explained Anne in a businesslike manner, being careful not to mention the undercover nature of the work. "The ship is carrying a midget submarine. We need to move it a couple of miles down the estuary. I'm standing in as skipper. We need someone else to take care of the machinery. Your name came up."

"Sounds like my sort of thing," replied the discharged artificer enthusiastically. "But why can't you use the regular crew?"

"They are all on leave over the weekend," replied Anne enigmatically. "You know. Spanish practices and all that." This comment was met with a worried silence. The term had acquired a particular meaning in the mess room of the patrol boat. Subterfuge was sometimes needed to keep things running because it could take weeks to get hold of a spare part through official channels. On one occasion, an old hand on the patrol boat got hold of the head gasket for an air compressor in a barter deal with his opposite number on a frigate moored alongside.

While this sort of illicit activity was frowned upon by authority, seasoned officers found it wise to turn a Nelsonian blind eye, so the artificer was naturally wary of being lured into a trap. "How do I know that I can trust you?" he asked suspiciously.

"You can ask Commander Woods," replied Anne reassuringly. "He will call round to your training school to sort out the details." Those words were met with silence at the other end, but they had the desired effect. The commander had a reputation for bravery on the lower decks after defusing an unexploded bomb in the bowels of a warship.

"Can't ask for better than that," replied the mechanic in due course.

When not boasting about his sexual exploits on the patrol boat, the mechanic had a more wholesome reputation as a storyteller. He had collected a fund of anecdotes during his years of service. Young ratings would sit entranced by his tales of heroism, mishap and mayhem. The unexploded bomb story was one of his favourite yarns.

The following day, the commander called round to see the mechanic at the training school. The pair had lunch together in a cafe, where the commander issued his instructions. The mechanic was to take the train to Plymouth on the appointed day. Someone would collect him from the station and brief him about the operation. "But don't tell anyone about the mission," warned the commander. In return, he was paid cash in hand. This arrangement suited him fine because he could hide the money from the taxman and from his wife's divorce lawyer.

Jackie was recruited as the fourth member of the gang, almost by accident, during a late-night tryst with Steve, in his flat. The young executive was moaning about a surly security guard, called Squires, who was employed at his boatyard.

"The man is upsetting our staff and making life a misery," complained Steve.

"Do you mean Brian Squires?" asked Jackie with a look of distaste.

It turned out that this reprobate had done something to upset the landlady some years earlier. The petite landlady was unwilling to reveal precisely what had taken place, but it was some unforgivable deed. So when Steve let slip that he needed to trick the guy, he had little trouble persuading the petite landlady to help him. This would allow Jackie to exact revenge against the scumbag.

Jackie agreed to play two parts in the caper. Her principal role was to lure Squires from his guard post to allow Steve and his confederates to slip into the boatyard. Her second task was to arrange a late-night party at the Feathers. The 'lock-in party' was intended to ensure that those involved in the sea trial could explain their whereabouts during the heist. After all, the crew of the *Normandy* and the trials team would be chief suspects if anything untoward were to happen to the midget submarine.

The party was ostensibly arranged to celebrate the completion of the sea trials of the midget submarine. All those involved in the trial were invited to the late-night party, along with their female partners. Care was taken to ensure that images of all members of the trial team were recorded on the bar's CCTV video system. This was to be done in a way that would confuse investigators. With video cameras pointing in different directions, it would take investigators considerable time to assemble the evidence. This delay would throw the investigators off the trail of the real culprits.

For Jackie, organising the lock-in party was routine, but luring Squires from his post was a much less palatable task. To succeed, she needed to cultivate a close relationship with the odious fellow. This part of the operation caused Steve great anguish. His relationship with the landlady was important to him because he had few friends in Plymouth. But for Jackie, friendship with Steve was a casual affair with no commitment on either side, so Steve did not relish the prospect of his female friend dallying with the odious security guard.

Jackie sometimes reminded Steve of a stray alley cat. Every few days, she would knock on his door in the early hours of the morning after chucking out the regulars from her pub. The pair would share coffee then snuggle up before spending the night in bed together. It was on one of those nights that they had discussed the boatyard plot. But Jackie had many admirers and Steve knew their frail relationship would be ruined if he were to become possessive. In many ways, they were two lost souls, seeking solace with one another.

Jackie had a racy history. She had become pregnant as a teenager while working as a barmaid in a South London pub. The feckless father deserted her, and she had been forced to bring up her daughter on a shoestring, in an era where single mothers were stigmatised. Her daughter grew up to become a well-respected nurse, who worked in a teaching hospital in London. It had been a tough life for parent and child, leaving Jackie with a deep distrust of braggarts.

Steve later discovered that Squires had molested the daughter while she was an underage teenager. It was a murky and unpleasant affair, and the young executive did not want to probe the matter too deeply. Jackie was consumed with hatred for Squires, and was only too keen to take part in the escapade. It would allow her to reap her revenge.

While the commander was content for Jackie to help with their mission, the news was not so well received elsewhere. Lucy feared that her involvement with the mission would upset her carefully constructed matchmaking plans. From their brief conversation before the fishing trip, Lucy had gained the impression that Steve was besotted with the racy landlady. *It's all going to end in tears,* she fretted. But always looking on the bright side, Lucy dismissed these fears in time.

If the hussy dumps him, at least Anne will be there to pick up the pieces, she thought uncharitably. Lucy believed that the pair were made for one another. To smooth the path of romance, she proposed that her home should be used as a base for the escapade. This would allow her to resolve any hiccups between her prickly sister-in-law and the driven young executive. This made sense because Anne was going to stay in her home while husband Mark travelled to Scotland on his fishing trip charade.

With a team finally assembled, it was possible to move forward with the mission. The plans to commandeer the midget submarine had been master-minded by the mariners in the dreary conference room in Fenchurch Street, with Steve's assistance. This had left Steve with little time to 'mind the shop' at Whitebait Cove. The young executive's absence had caused unrest in the boatyard, leading one wag to liken him to 'a rat abandoning a sinking ship'. The young executive's long absence also caused Mark grief.

With no restraint from the yard boss, Beckwith behaved in an autocratic manner, stirring up resentment among the staff. With feelings running high, there would be no sympathy if anything untoward happened to his midget submarine. While this made life uncomfortable for everyone concerned, it was a benefit to the caper. "Give a man enough rope and he will hang himself," observed the Admiral enigmatically when he heard of discontent in the yard.

The staff griped about the surly security guards and the lack of access to the quay. Beckwith was blind to the animosity and strutted round the yard like a proud peacock.

"All he needs is a chariot and slave to whisper in his ear, and he could be Caesar returning from conquering his foes," quipped the wag.

One reason for Beckwith's pride was that 'his' midget submarine had performed better than predicted. In his dreams, he savoured the adulation that he would receive when his creation was unveiled to the public. In these dreams, he would be vindicated against the naysayers of the navy. It also gave Beckwith malign pleasure to know that the boatyard was on the verge of bankruptcy, and that the chief executive was barely able to keep the enterprise afloat.

As the sea trials approached completion, Beckwith instructed his sidekick, Simon, to prepare invitations to the grand inauguration ceremony. A world-class chef had been hired to cater for these luminaries on a chartered ferry. The guest list included political friends, together with a select band of journalists and several TV crews. The carefully choreographed shindig would silence critics and showcase the achievements of his agency. Beckwith had courted the media throughout his career. To ensure maximum impact, the academic imposed a media blackout until the grand inauguration.

While Beckwith was polishing his plans for the press launch, Steve paid an unexpected visit to the yard. By this time, speculation about his absence had reach fever pitch, and rumblings of discontent were starting to get out of hand. The young executive dashed towards the office building. By the time he reached the foyer, he was besieged by employees with queries. He brushed them aside and bolted up the stairs to take refuge in his office. He did not emerge from his sanctum until the end of the working day when the yard would normally be deserted.

Several staff members lingered in the open-plan office, trying to look busy, after knocking-off time. They wanted to know what the yard boss was up to. Mark was, by this time, the de facto second-in-command in the yard, though he had none of the status symbols for this position. The former naval officer occupied a glass cubicle set apart from the open-plan area, with thin panel walls providing little privacy. This led yard staff to contrast Mark's spartan office with the palatial accommodation of the young executive.

With Steve's absence, the tiny cubicle had become the beating heart of the business. It was the administrative hub where employees brought their complaints and contractors received their instructions. During the working day, there would often be a queue of people waiting to consult the newly retired naval officer. When they spoke to the second-in-command, they were forced to stand in his doorway because the cramped space was barely large enough to contain a desk and filing cabinet, let alone a visitor's seat.

A hushed silence settled over the adjoining offices as Steve emerged from his cloister and headed towards Mark's cubicle. There was an expectant air as Steve shoehorned himself into the tiny cubicle and tried to pull the door closed behind him, without success. The hinges creaked to show they needed oiling. The stay-behinds watched expectantly. A couple of brave souls sauntered past on spurious errands. They could tell that Mark was in high dudgeon, ready to give his boss a piece of his mind.

"Am I glad to see you!" growled Mark. "We've got a mutiny on our hands and you are nowhere to be seen!" The former naval officer's cheeks glowed red with anger as he glared fixedly at his young boss.

"I'm sorry, Mark. I've let you down," replied Steve in an unusually contrite tone.

"Did you see the graffiti?" demanded Mark angrily.

"Yes. Dreadful business!" replied Steve sympathetically. "I'm sorry that you've been left to hold the fort."

"Where have you been?" demanded the former naval officer angrily.

"I've had medical problems," replied Steve disarmingly. "A heart attack. But, please, keep it to yourself – if word gets out, it will scupper our expansion plans for the new manufacturing facility. My doctor has told me to take things easy." This was absolute nonsense, of course. But Steve knew that employees were listening to their conversation, and wanted to broadcast a false message.

The news that Steve had suffered a heart attack knocked Mark off balance, for a moment, and he felt a wave of sympathy. After all, it seemed plausible. It was common knowledge that Steve was a workaholic who was unable to relax. Just the recipe for a heart attack. The news also reflected the views of some sympathetic members of staff who believed Steve might be suffering from overwork. "I'm sorry to hear that," replied Mark apologetically. His guns spiked.

"The specialist told me to take a break," said Steve, feigning self-pity. "So I plan to spend a few days on a fishing trip up in Scotland." This left Mark confused. Nothing more had been said about a 'fishing trip' since his conversation with the commander, in their secretive discussion behind the workshops. Mark had been planning to raise the subject with his boss but had not had the chance because the guy was never there.

"Commander Woods told me the Scottish trip—" blurted out Mark. But before the gullible fellow could finish his sentence, Steve grimaced and made a hand to signal to suggest that 'walls have ears'. Though slow on the uptake, the penny dropped and the former naval officer did his best to enter into the spirit of the game. But Mark was not a natural liar and his words were uttered in a stilted fashion. As they chatted, Steve waxed lyrical about the attractions of salmon fishing in Scotland, with Mark injecting the odd comment and nodding from time to time. "It sounds fun! Where are you planning to go?" asked the former naval officer in a friendly way.

"Nothing planned as yet," replied Steve. "I'm looking for someone to join me. It's lonely travelling alone." Then after a pause, he continued: "I don't suppose that you would be interested in a trip up north?"

By this time, the former naval officer had got into the swing of things. He took the cue.

"I'd love to. It would be a chance to use my new fishing gear. I haven't had a break since I retired from the navy, but I need to check with Lucy. She might not let me go." Then after some idle chit-chat, Steve collected his briefcase as he prepared to depart.

Fearing that the yard boss would discover them spying on him, the stay-behinds shuffled hurriedly back to their desks. When Steve spotted the guilty-looking employees as they pretended to work, he was confident that news of his heart attack, and the Scotland fishing trip, would sweep the boatyard in the coming days.

Having deceived his staff into believing he had suffered a heart attack, Steve was free to devote all his time to planning the embryonic pirate protection mission. At daily meetings in Fenchurch Street, he briefed the mariners on the unfolding events at the boatyard. This information helped them to formulate a plan to acquire the midget submarine by stealth. While they did so, the team were also working on plans to acquire a dredger.

Felix Sikorski was in the process of finding a suitable vessel after securing funding from some City institutions. Steve was asked to establish a dredging business to support the undercover surveillance operation. One of Steve's first jobs was to rent an office to act as headquarters for the dredging business. This was fairly straightforward, but recruiting staff to manage the dredging operation proved to be a more difficult challenge.

Recruiting seafarers is normally straightforward. There are agencies that specialise in that task, but the undercover nature of the business prevented him from following that traditional route. As he pondered the issue, Steve recalled a Scottish engineer, called Alex McKay, who had the uncanny knack of dealing with troublesome machinery. The Scotsman would be just the person to run a dredger.

When sailing as a cadet, Steve served alongside the cantankerous Scotsman on a ship called the *Sea Ranger*, but they had a troubled relationship. So he needed a go-between. Another shipmate, called Bill Prior, was the obvious candidate for that delicate role. *Bill is the sort of solid and reliable type you could trust*, thought the young executive. It would do no harm to sound them both out, so he invited the pair to a reunion.

Neither engineer showed any enthusiasm for a reunion, but Steve won them over when he told them that he ran the boatyard at Whitebait Cove. The pair were curious to revisit the boatyard. It so happened that they had both worked under its previous owner, Sam Wheeler, so the trio agreed to meet on a Friday afternoon at the *Nautical Inn* in Plymouth. Their meeting proved an awkward affair. But a tour of the boatyard the following day was more successful.

Towards the end of the boatyard tour, Steve showed his guests the revolutionary midget submarine hidden on the rear deck of the *Normandy*. This was risky because Beckwith had issued strict instructions to prevent people from boarding the ship without his permission. To outwit him, Steve hoped to sneak aboard when the yard was deserted. But the security guard spotted the trio boarding the ship and tipped off the academic. The security guard were more alert than usual, as a result of the graffiti incident.

This led to an embarrassing confrontation. The academic turned up unexpectedly and caught the intruders red-handed.

The Heist is Planned

Heeding the old adage, 'discretion is the best part of valour', Steve beat a hasty retreat from the *Normandy*. He was forced to swallow his pride and accept loss of face in front of his guests. In order to continue their conversation, Steve arranged to meet the pair at the Feathers pub for lunch. The choice of venue was a source of surprise to the two older men.

Chapter 15

Steve Sounds Out his Old Shipmates

Bill Prior and Alex McKay had no idea what they were getting themselves into when they accepted Steve's invitation to the reunion. They had no idea that they had wandered into a hornet's nest. The meeting with their young shipmate Steve in the Nautical Inn was a disaster, but the tour of the boatyard at Whitebait Cove proved to be more entertaining. Towards the end of the tour there was an angry confrontation on the *Normandy*. With that, the pair scuttled down the gangplank, sniggering like naughty schoolboys. They left their embarrassed host to deal with the angry bearded guy.

As they made their ignominious departure from the yard, there was another incident at the gate. As the security guard raised the barrier, he raised two fingers at the small hatchback. Bill was shocked by the rude gesture. He was suffering from a mild hangover and could not understand the reason for this threatening behaviour. Alex made a mental note to 'find out what that was all about'.

Then, with a start, Bill recalled that the guard had been dancing with Jackie when he sidled into a nightclub in the early hours of the morning. When the petite landlady saw him enter the club, she breezed over to chat. Jackie looked stunning in a short, slinky dress. She had no wish to snub her dancing partner; she wanted to express sympathy over the loss of Bill's wife, but the jealous security guard interpreted her actions as a slight. The rude gesture was a small act of revenge.

"I've just remembered where I've seen that fellow before. He was dancing with Jackie when I arrived at the Ritzy," remarked Bill as he pulled out onto the main road. Alex's antennae started to twitch at this juicy revelation. Despite his grumpy appearance, he had a mischievous nature and was determined to winkle out the rest of the story. He planned to tease his pal about it later in the weekend, but for the time being he had another target for his mischief.

"Steve's met his match with that bearded guy!" remarked the Scotsman mirthfully, as he recalled the confrontation at the boatyard. The *faux pas* was a source of jolly banter as they drove back to the guesthouse, and they were in high spirits as Bill parked his car. After a quick wash and brush-up, they set off for lunch at the Feathers. Jackie greeted them in a friendly way and gave Alex a knowing wink. "Have you recovered from your night out?" she enquired teasingly as Bill approached the bar. They each ordered steak pie and real ale, and sat down at a table, waiting for their young friend to arrive.

"Well, well. What's going on between you and Jackie then?" asked Alex provocatively.

"I told you. I bumped into her in a nightclub last night. She was dancing with that rude security guard. That's all," replied Bill as he tried to conceal his attraction towards the svelte landlady, even to himself. But Alex knew that he had hit a sensitive spot, and continued to probe. After a few minutes, Bill got fed up and decided to put an end to the innuendo.

"Just drop it, will you!" he barked.

Alex made a sign to show his lips were sealed, and they ate in stony silence when the food arrived. The silence was broken when Steve walked into the bar, dressed casually in jeans and a soft, black leather jacket. Bill and Alex expected their former shipmate to walk straight to their table, but to their surprise the young guy stopped to chat to Jackie. They whispered together like a pair of conspirators as they stood by the 'lift-up' section of the bar. When Jackie was called away, Steve picked up three pints of real ale waiting on the counter and carried them over to the table where his former shipmates were eating. It was something of a juggling act because he was clasping a newspaper under his arm. The pair of old-timers were puzzled by their young friend's familiarity with the landlady.

Steve greeted the pair of diners with a smile: "Had a nice meal, chaps?" he remarked as he planted the drinks down on the table and withdrew two envelopes from his jacket pocket. He placed the envelopes on the seat, alongside his financial paper.

"Yes, thanks. The meat pies are great," replied Bill with a slightly rueful expression. He had felt a pang of jealousy as he watched Steve's intimate conversation with the landlady and was curious to find out about their relationship: "Are you a regular here?"

"It's my local, but I only drop in at the weekend. They get a good crowd and I like the local beer, but I have to be careful about drink driving. I use the car a lot and don't want to risk my licence," explained Steve. "The landlady used to live close to my home in South London. Neither of us has roots in Plymouth, so we have something in common."

Bill thought there was more to it than that. The intimate nature of Steve's discussion with the landlady made him feel like a clapped-out old codger, but then he cheered up when he recalled the rumpus at the boatyard. Their cocksure young friend looked like a naughty schoolboy caught stealing apples when he was scolded by the tall bearded guy. In truth, the incident helped to break the ice of their frosty weekend reunion, and helped to rebuild their camaraderie.

Steve was sitting with his back to the door and asked the others to keep a lookout for a colleague who was due to join them. "I think your pal has just arrived!" announced the Scotsman with a mischievous look in his eye, a few seconds later. "Yes. A tall bearded guy has just walked in. He looks *really* angry and is heading right towards us!" Steve looked startled, fearing that Beckwith had tracked them down. But he turned to find the doorway was empty. It was a silly practical joke, but it helped lighten the mood.

After some friendly banter, Steve steered the conversation in a serious direction. He planned to approach the undercover operation in a roundabout way, firstly by telling his guests about the dredging company that he was setting up, but he did not intend to tell them anything about the undercover side of the operation until he knew he could trust them. His first task was to find out whether his former shipmates would be interested in working for him.

When he broached this, the old-timers looked shocked. After the rocky start to their so-called reunion, they were wary of dealing with the slippery young guy. Neither of them felt they had the right experience for the high-tech business they had visited that morning. Seeing their concerns, Steve tried to put them at ease. "We are looking for experienced people, like yourselves, to manage a small dredger. This will be an entirely new venture. It has no connection to the business you have just seen."

Bill was irritated by this, thinking he was being given the runaround. *What is the real purpose of the reunion and why have we been given a VIP tour of the boatyard?* he mused. Nothing made any sense. It would have been perfectly simple to ask if they were interested in working for a dredging company without all that rigmarole. "If you wanted to offer me a job on a dredger, why didn't you ask me?" he replied brusquely. His response chilled the earlier jovial atmosphere.

"Look. I don't want people at the yard to find out about the dredging plans. That's why I didn't mention it earlier," explained Steve disingenuously. "Only one other person at the yard knows the plan, and he's coming here to meet us. We need people with different skills for the dredging business. I wanted you to see what we have achieved at the yard before asking you about the dredging business, but you don't need to make up your minds straight away." Bill thought he was talking nonsense, but this time, he did not interrupt.

"It's a complicated story," continued Steve, "but here is my proposal. I'm prepared to offer you a week's consultancy work. Your time and expenses will be paid, and you are under no obligation. When the week is over, you can then make up your minds whether you want to join the dredging business." Steve then passed them the envelopes that he had tucked away beside the table. "These letters set out the terms for the consultancy work," he explained.

As he passed them their envelopes, a young man stepped into the bar and looked around rather nervously for a few seconds before spotting them. When he came over to join them, Steve introduced Tim Wesley as one of the designers of the fuel-cell propulsion system. As Tim sat down in a spare seat, Bill asked if he wanted a drink. Tim refused, saying he was meeting his girlfriend later, and only had a few minutes to speak to them. Alex's scowling expression was an indication that he did not welcome the intrusion.

"Steve told me that you saw the submarine this morning," commented Tim brightly. This was quite an accolade, given that few other people at Whitebait Cove had been privileged to look beneath the tarpaulin. "It's a fantastic piece of kit. I can explain the background of the submarine rescue project, if you like," continued the young designer enthusiastically.

"We don't know anything about submarines, but if that's what you are here for, then you had better get on with it," replied Alex sourly. Tim was tempted to tell the Scotsman to 'get lost', and walk out of the pub. He had better things to do than explain innovative technology to this ignorant dunderhead. But he was wary of using intemperate language in front of his boss, so he took a subtle dig at the old curmudgeon. Looking the Scottish engineer straight in the eye, he asked: "Perhaps you could tell us about the *Kursk* disaster."

Alex was proud of his encyclopedic knowledge of maritime affairs, but he knew little about the navy. It was his blind spot. The question completely flummoxed him. "All I know is that a Soviet nuclear submarine blew up in the Arctic," blustered the Scotsman. "What does that have to do with me?"

"Did you know that the explosions registered as earthquakes on seismographs around the world?" explained Tim authoritatively. With that, he went on to describe the rescue efforts and the involvement of Western marine contractors. Tim then explained how this incident inspired the development of the submarine rescue vehicle that they had seen on the deck of the *Normandy*. He described the fuel-cell system and other innovations, such as the advanced computer guidance system. "The submersible vehicle is really versatile. It will be used to rescue crew from disabled submarines anywhere in the world, but it could be used for other purposes," he added as he concluded his monologue.

"Wouldn't it be simpler to install fuel-cell propulsion in an existing submarine, to see how it performs?" asked Bill, who sensed the animosity between Alex and the over-enthusiastic young designer, and wanted to lighten the atmosphere.

"Possibly," said Tim, "but the new vehicle has other features, such as a titanium alloy hull, that allows it to dive to greater depths."

Alex took umbrage at being lectured by 'a young lad who was barely out of diapers'. He showed his irritation by picking up a tabloid newspaper that was lying on a nearby table and starting to read it in an ostentatious manner. "You must be living on a different planet," he grunted. "What has any of that got to do with me?"

Steve had been listening to the presentation with the look of a proud father. The young designer had expressed his yard's achievements in a clear and articulate way. Saddened by Alex's negative reaction, he interceded to calm the growing confrontation. "Bear with us, Alex," he begged. "We'll join up all the dots for you soon."

Then Bill joined in the fray. "Shut up, Alex. I find this interesting, even if you do not!"

Alex was riled that they had ganged up against him and could see no point in continuing the conversation. "If ye all want to talk about submarines, that's well and fine. But I got some shopping to dee. So I will leave ye all to it!" The exaggerated Scottish brogue was a sign of his annoyance.

With that, the truculent Scotsman flounced out, for the second time that weekend. "I'll see you back at the guesthouse, my old pal." He slammed the door on his way out, leaving the trio sitting in bemused silence. "Alex can be a bit pig-headed at times," remarked Bill with exasperation as he watched the fast-retreating figure. Then in a valiant effort to defend his pal: "He's cleverer than he looks, and is a damn good mechanic," he pleaded, as the party broke up in disarray.

The weekend reunion had been a wash-out. It had failed to rekindle the friendship of the former shipmates. After flouncing out of the Feathers, Alex spent the afternoon ferreting around bric-a-brac shops in the lanes surrounding the fish docks in the historic part of the town. The Scotsman became so engrossed in his hobby of collecting shipping memorabilia that he completely forgot about his obnoxious behaviour in the Feathers.

Bill berated his friend when they met in the hotel bar later that evening and there followed a bad-tempered spat. "Don't get yourself in a lather," retorted Alex as he brushed off the criticism.

It's like water off a duck's back, thought Bill malevolently. He knew that he could not win an argument with the headstrong Scotsman, so he changed the subject to a less contentious issue. They discussed Steve's job offer and agreed that the offer of paid consultancy work was 'a bit odd, but too good to turn down'.

Steve had given each of them a pack of documents that set out the terms for a week's consultancy work with details of pay, travel and living expenses. The documents placed unusual emphasis on confidentiality but failed to explain what the work entailed. There was only a brief mention of the dredging business. It was all a bit of a mystery.

The two old shipmates had little inclination to continue their conversation, so while Bill stayed up for another drink in the small bar, Alex headed to his room for an early night. They would have a few days to consider the job offer. Steve told them that he was planning a break in Scotland over the following week. The consultancy work was due to start the following Monday, if they were willing. Bill welcomed the interval because he needed to sort things out at home and collect his belongings.

But Alex moaned about the need to travel back and forth to his home in Glasgow, 'just so the lad can go fishing!' He was nevertheless glad to receive an offer of well-paid work: "If the young fool is happy to pay us, I'm only too happy to take his money!" he remarked as they parted company that evening. The Scotsman seemed oblivious to the offence he had caused during the weekend.

The Scotsman was munching contentedly on his plate of bacon and eggs at breakfast on Sunday morning, when Bill called into the dining room to say cheerio to his old pal. Bill had eaten earlier. The 'bean counter' (as Alex sometimes called him) started to see the funny side to things on his way back to London and felt affection for his cantankerous pal, forgiving his annoying ways, for the moment.

Chapter 16

The Conspirators Gather

As the sea trials of the midget submarine were approaching completion, plans for the heist were gathering momentum. It was early spring, and as the trees and bushes were coming out into bud after a long, bitter winter, thoughts were turning to holidays. So there was little surprise when word circulated the boatyard that the chief executive was travelling to Scotland for a week's fishing, with his deputy, Mark. This news seemed to justify earlier rumours that the chief executive was recovering from a heart attack.

Steve was rarely seen in the boatyard during the sea trials, leaving the day-to-day yard administration to his deputy, Mark. But he put in an appearance on the final day of the sea trials. The young executive said farewell to the trials team on a Friday afternoon, in mid-April, as they were clearing their gear from their portable cabin in the car park. "We will be back in a couple of weeks," they remarked. "Beckwith wants us to lay on a demonstration of the submarine as part of the inauguration ceremony."

After seeing off the naval team, the young chief executive set off from the boatyard in his sports car, with his deputy in the passenger seat, ostensibly on their way to a fishing trip in the Highlands. Mark told yard employees that his wife was staying behind to look after their two children, and that his sister, Anne, was to keep his wife company. Anyway, that was the official story. The real story was somewhat different.

With Mark on his way to Scotland, the two teenage boys were packed off to stay with their grandmother. With the children out of harm's way, the semi-detached house became a rendezvous point for the conspirators. With the decks cleared, Anne took charge of the mission as though she was leading the D-Day Landings.

Once settled in, she established a command post in Mark's study, with a chart of the estuary pinned to the wall. In addition to the chart, Anne had been given some technical manuals describing the machinery onboard the *Normandy*. These had been supplied by one of the Admiral's friends, who worked as a class surveyor.

As D-Day dawned, Anne felt the familiar rush of adrenalin she experienced at the start of every daring mission. She waited impatiently for other members of the boarding party to report. A taxi finally drew up outside the semi-detached house at around three o'clock in the afternoon. Andy, the mechanic, alighted and shared a joke with the cab driver as he searched the pocket of his grimy jeans to find a twenty-pound note to pay the fare.

The mechanic swaggered towards the front door with the bearing of a football hooligan setting off for an away game. "Where are the rest of the gang?" he demanded in a voice braying with bravado as he was admitted to the small semi-detached house.

Lucy surveyed the new arrival with distaste. "Could you remove your trainers," she asked politely as she surveyed the messy footprints on her pristine carpet. The disgraced petty officer was travelling light, with all his possessions contained in a well-worn knapsack. "Anne is in the study," Lucy informed him tetchily. "Steve should be here shortly."

"Is that it?" remarked the artificer contemptuously as he barged rudely past his kindly hostess. The disgraced artificer had gained from Commander Woods that he was to play a part in a risky mission, not some milk-sop family excursion. The scruffy fellow hiked up his grimy jeans as he approached the inner sanctum. With ingrained naval training, he was about to announce his arrival with the words, *Reporting for duty, ma'am.*

But he checked himself, recalling that Anne was now in Civvy Street. So, in a half-hearted attempt at humour, he corrupted the naval formalities: "Plumber reporting for duty." The joke fell flat. This subject was wearing thin. Anne did not take kindly to being reminded of the scalding water incident. Watching events from the corner of her eye, Lucy was astounded at the guy's impudent behaviour, but Anne seemed to take it in her stride.

"Brought your tools?" she demanded sternly.

"S … S…Sorry, left them at home," he stammered. The beginner's error embarrassed him and, for once, he was unable to fire back a humorous repost.

"Well, you are no good for man or beast without your tools," replied Anne tartly. "Sit down and I'll be with you as soon as I've finished checking this chart." This took the wind out of his sails and he sank down onto a chair with the appearance of a deflated balloon. Sitting meekly, he watched as Anne charted a course for their late-night mission. The route would take them from the quay at Whitebait Cove to a jetty in a military training ground near an uninhabited village called Leighton Hollow.

This was quite a tricky route, with conservation areas, shallow water and sand banks to negotiate. It was also necessary to take account of the tides. Anne was unable to finish her task because she lacked the fine details of the shallow water leading to the boatyard. Mark had prepared the channel in preparation for the sea trials, but these soundings were not shown on her chart.

Watching from the kitchen, Lucy was impressed that her sister-in-law was able to assert her authority without the need for gold rings on her uniform. The chastened artificer sat meekly, as though he were waiting to see the dentist. When Anne had finally finished studying the chart, she turned to the scruffy mechanic and beckoned him to her desk.

"I take it that Commander Woods told you about our plans," she remarked in an officious way.

"Yes. He told me we were to break into a boatyard and commandeer a small ship, and sail it down the estuary," replied the artificer respectfully. There was no trace of the insolence with which he had bowled into the house.

"It should be fairly straightforward then," remarked Anne in a businesslike way. "The ship is unmanned at night and it is only protected by a single security guard. The security guard will be lured away, and we will have keys for the gate to the wharf."

"Sounds like a doddle!" observed the mechanic as he started to recover his cocky self-confidence. "I take it that you want me to look after the engines."

While pretending to go about her daily chores, Lucy watched the unfolding drama in Mark's study with eagle eyes. She had placed her ironing board near the kitchen door to provide a vantage point to observe her visitors. This was the most thrilling thing to happen in her busy but humdrum life for some time. She watched her sister-in-law as she became engaged in an increasingly animated discussion with the scruffy mechanic.

As the conspirators got down to business, they began to study some technical manuals. "We need to look through this lot," declared Anne pompously. The manuals provided details of all the ship's machinery. Anne was in her element as they worked smoothly, using naval jargon, to assemble their plans. Lucy was impressed by what she saw.

Lucy sometimes found the authoritarian side of Anne's character strident and intimidating. It was for that reason that they had not really gelled as friends. When roused, her sister-in-law resembled her domineering mother. Before joining the navy, Anne acquired the nickname 'bossy boots' among sniggering school friends. Men tended to find the assertive side of her character difficult to cope with. As Lucy ironed the clothes, she wondered how her sister-in-law would get on with Steve.

As she set about another pile of ironing, Lucy spotted Steve arriving in a second cab. The once-dashing young executive looked tired and wan – a pale shadow of the young guy who visited their home on the day of the fishing outing. Steve had travelled from Torquay that morning; he was taking refuge there while supposedly fishing in Scotland. The journey from Torquay had been tiresome because Mark had taken his beloved sports car on the fishing trip charade. So the young executive was forced to use public transport.

Lucy later learned that the young guy had been press-ganged into joining the caper, much against his will. The future of the boatyard hung on the success of the late-night mission, and this naturally made him nervous. Steve's unease was augmented by the knowledge that the female naval officer did not want civilians on her team.

In persuading Anne to accept the civilian, the commander had argued that Steve had 'served at sea' and had 'knowledge of the estuary'. This was disingenuous. It was many years since Steve had served on a merchant ship, and he did not know much about the estuary – it was Mark who had taken the soundings.

Anne had never met Steve in person, despite them both being involved in the submarine rescue project. In any other situation, Anne would have enjoyed meeting the young guy. But as leader of the boarding party, the female naval officer needed a capable seaman. Steve did not measure up to that task.

As Steve fumbled in his pockets for change to pay the cab driver, Lucy threw open the front door in a welcoming gesture. After pleasantries, Lucy directed her visitor to the study, where the naval pair were closeted. The young executive hovered hesitantly in the door, waiting to be acknowledged. The burly mechanic glanced at the slightly built figure and turned away with a scornful expression, pointedly ignoring him. Anne greeted the new arrival with a lukewarm smile. "Commander Woods told me that you are in charge of the boatyard at Whitebait Cove," she remarked in an acid tone.

"That's right," confirmed Steve, nodding in agreement.

"Well, you have arrived just in time," continued Anne in a strident tone. "I need the soundings that you took in the estuary. Do you have them with you? I will need them to chart our course."

"I'm afraid that I can't help you with that," replied Steve, with a hangdog expression. "Our harbour master surveyed the channel. You probably know that this is his house, but he is up in Scotland at the moment." With all his other problems, the last thing Steve expected was this thankless reception. Over the past week, the young executive had chased up unpaid bills, sacked staff, dealt with hard-nosed bankers and set up an office for a dredging business, and now he had been asked to participate in this ridiculous escapade.

To add to his woes, the exhausted executive had forgotten to bring details of the navigation buoys and soundings in the channel. In this punch-drunk state, Steve had also forgotten that this formidable naval officer he faced was, in fact, Mark's sister. The commander had failed to mention that point when he had conscripted Steve as a member of her team.

"Yes. I know that this is his house!" replied Anne tartly. "Mark is my brother! I have been here many times!" She turned her back disdainfully on the new arrival as she continued to talk in a conspiratorial way with the artificer.

The pair viewed the escapade as a routine operation. After many years of naval training, they quickly settled into the routine of the operation. Of course, they were keen to achieve their objective, but failure would not be the end of the world for them. If the mission was aborted, they would justify their actions by saying they were merely following orders.

Anne did not suffer fools gladly. After the gaffs, she dismissed the new arrival as a liability. *He might be a good businessman,* she thought uncharitably, *but the fellow will be damn all use to us tonight.* But in making this censorious judgement, she failed to appreciate the huge weight of responsibility that rested on the young executive's shoulders. He had far more at stake than anyone else in the room.

Lucy watched the unfolding events with a sinking feeling. The camaraderie between her sister-in-law and the scruffy mechanic was troubling. There was a natural bond between the service people from the patrol boat, and she feared that her matchmaking plans were going awry.

After a frustrating journey, Steve was hungry and thirsty, and he could no longer stand the poisonous atmosphere. Anne and her accomplice were so absorbed in their deliberations that they failed to notice as Steve slipped out of the claustrophobic study. The young executive sighed with relief as he took refuge in the cosy kitchen, where Lucy was ironing.

"Could I have a glass of water?" he croaked with a parched throat. Steve felt as though he had stumbled into an oasis after trekking in the blazing desert sun. The homely atmosphere was balm to his troubled soul.

"Looks like you have been through the wringer!" observed Lucy with a sympathetic smile. "Would you prefer a cup of tea?"

"Love one if you don't mind," replied Steve gratefully. Then after a pause he pointed to the study and continued with a pained expression: "They gave me a hard time!" For once, he let his guard slip. The ambitious young executive looked like a frightened little boy.

"Anne can be a bit of a tartar at times!" commented Lucy compassionately. "It runs in the family. They are all naval types. Anne takes after her mother."

Chapter 17

The Heist Gets Underway

The frustrations of a gruelling week began to slip away as Steve settled into the kitchen, sniffing the aroma of garlic and newly baked bread. Setting aside her ironing, Lucy stretched her arms and wandered over to the sink to fill the kettle. She took pity on her careworn visitor. *The young guy looks a pale shadow of his former self*, she mused. Lucy was happy to chat; it was a chance to give her flagging matchmaking efforts a boost.

From her vantage point, Lucy could tell that Steve had created a poor impression on her hard-boiled sister-in-law, and vice versa. Anne had not shown the slightest flicker of interest in the eligible young guy. While first impressions are often misleading, Lucy was troubled that the slovenly mechanic seemed to be attracting Anne's affections, but Lucy refused to hand in the towel. The first round had not gone well, but she wanted to build up the young executive's confidence for the rounds ahead.

As Steve perched idly on a stool, Lucy busied herself

making the tea. Steve contrasted the messy, lived-in kitchen with the pristine carpet leading from the front door to the living room. The kids were obviously excluded from that respectable part of the house. This added to a picture of contented domesticity. For a moment, the young executive felt a tinge of jealousy for Mark's happy family life, but his thoughts turned to the late-night mission.

The young executive had been stung by Anne's withering words. He wondered why he had failed to recognise that the leader of the boarding party was Mark's sister. That was foolish! In his fragile mental state, he blamed the commander. *He could have warned me*, he thought bitterly. But he dismissed that notion, acknowledging that there had been plenty of clues. The young executive kicked himself for his absent-minded behaviour. With all his other cares, he had sleepwalked into this situation.

As Lucy waited for the kettle to boil, Steve voiced his thoughts and they began to discuss the family connection. "Mark and his sister come from a distinguished naval family," explained Lucy as she warmed the teapot with the boiling water. "Mark is *always* reminding me that his illustrious ancestors sailed with Nelson at Trafalgar. Don't *get him going* on that subject! His grandfather served at the Battle of Jutland and his father was in the Korean War.

"Mark's parents expected their son to follow in the family tradition, but he failed to live up to their high expectations. He finds it hard to accept that his sister has outshone him in the service that he cares for. Did you know that Anne commanded a naval patrol boat before joining the project team in Portsmouth? She is a real high-flyer."

This did not surprise Steve in the least. He was still smarting from his bruising encounter with the formidable naval officer. "That might explain why she is treating our escapade as though she were leading the Normandy Invasion!" observed Steve sarcastically. In a whisper, Lucy conceded that her sister-in-law could be a 'bit of a battleaxe'.

"Strange that brother and sister are so different," remarked Steve in a quiet voice so that he could not be overheard. "Your husband is not like that. He's a placid type."

"Yes. He's a pussy cat really," agreed Lucy, with the trace of a smile, as she poured the tea. "He's been a good father to our two boys, on the whole, but I worry sometimes that he lacks drive and that he drinks too much. It's the female side of the family that rules the roost, you know. Mark's mother is a bit of a tartar. She can be frightening at times."

While they chatted, Lucy's sleuthing instincts returned. Her husband had told her something about the reasons for his trip to the Highlands, but there were some big holes in the story. She hoped to fill in the blanks with nuggets of information from her visitor.

With a few probing questions, she pieced together the information and soon understood why they wanted to commandeer the submarine that night. But that was neither here nor there as far as she was concerned. Lucy was more interested in the human side of the drama. She was curious to learn about Jackie's role in the plot, and her relationship with Steve.

But their conversation was curtailed when Anne poked her head round the kitchen door to summon Steve to the study. Steve gulped the last dregs of tea and reluctantly relinquished his comfy perch. "Back to the salt mine," he sighed. But as he prepared to leave, Lucy nudged along her matchmaking plans.

"You know, you have much more in common with my sister-in-law than you realise," she observed in a kindly way. "You are both dedicated to your work. You are both prepared to upset people to get your own way. At heart, you are both decent people, so don't judge her too harshly. Anne can be abrasive, but she is only trying to make sure everything goes well tonight."

Any goodwill that Lucy's remark might have generated was quickly dispelled when Steve stepped into the dragon's den. The reason they wanted to speak to him was to ask what he knew about the lifting gear for the midget submarine. They might need the gear to offload the midget submarine onto a rickety jetty at Leighton Hollow.

"Sorry, I can't help you," admitted Steve ruefully. "We did manage to sneak on board the *Normandy*, but the submarine was hidden under a tarpaulin on the stern deck. We were thrown off before we had time to study it. I'm not familiar with the lifting gear. It was not part of our contract."

"Just thought I would ask," remarked Anne dismissively before resuming her discussion with the mechanic. "You'd better explain the plan to the new member of our team," she suggested as their conversation came to an end. She made the remark in a derogatory manner to suggest that the newcomer had little to contribute to the mission. Teacher's favourite puffed out his chest with pride as he proceeded to explain the plan.

"We don't know how the crew left things, but we will have to start the emergency generator when we climb on board. That should be pretty easy," he declared with a self-satisfied sneer. "The plans show that the emergency generator is located on the deck below the bridge. We'll be able to start it with a hand crank. Once it's running, we will have lights and power, so we should be able to start up the main machinery without too much trouble. So it should be a doddle."

"Well done! Sounds like you have covered all the important points!" said Anne, with greater appreciation than was warranted. The smug pair were indignant when the newcomer had the temerity to interrupt them.

"Jackie will bring the keys for the yard gate to my flat later this evening," remarked Steve with a slightly croaky voice.

"Whatever!" retorted Anne in a blasé way. Anne saw nothing unusual in this. After all, it was reasonable to expect the yard boss to have keys to the yard. That was why he had been invited to join their mission. The female naval officer had no idea of the trouble that Steve had gone to. The commander had failed to tell her about the security changes or the role that Beckwith played in guarding the ship.

Steve felt bile rising in his throat. He had risked his fragile relationship with Jackie, the pub landlady, to obtain a set of keys, and this pair of ingrates did not show the slightest sign of appreciation. By this time, Steve had formed an uncharitable (and unspeakable) view of their female team leader and thought the mechanic was a braggart.

The atmosphere in the cramped, airless room was oppressive and there was little good will among the three members of the boarding party. Steve's remark about the delivery of the keys to his flat caused them to reconsider their assembly point for the late-night escapade. After a short debate, Steve agreed that his flat could be used as a base. The plan was to assemble in his flat at 11 o'clock that night while they waited for Jackie to deliver the keys. This was a great relief for Lucy because she could not stomach the presence of the slovenly mechanic in her home. Steve was less than happy about the arrangement.

But transport remained a problem. The use of taxis during their late-night mission was out of the question. That form of transport would leave a trail of evidence pointing towards their guilt. "Why don't I drive you?" suggested Lucy enthusiastically. She was now infected by excitement for the caper. With her two boys staying with their grandmother, she was free to ferry the gang around in the family car. The other members of the boarding party were only too happy to accept her offer.

The choice of Steve's flat complicated the situation because the young executive's alibi depended on people believing that he was fishing in Scotland, so it was important that he was not seen on his home turf. To achieve that, he was staying in a guesthouse in Torquay. The guesthouse was convenient because it was close to an office that he planned to use for the dredging business. Returning to his flat would call for stealth, not least because he needed to evade the nosy neighbour who lived on the ground floor and watched his comings and goings with eagle eyes.

The old lady liked to spread malicious rumours. Steve reacted by winding her up. When Jackie stayed overnight, the old lady made oblique references to falling moral standards. So when Steve left for his 'fishing trip', he let it be known that she would be using the flat while he was away. In a mischievous mood one evening, he embellished the story. "Jackie might hold a party, so I hope she won't make too much noise!" he remarked, knowing that it would annoy the old busybody.

This proved fortunate because a party would help explain why people were gathering in his flat while he was supposedly in Scotland. Under the pretext of the party, the gang would be free to come and go at will. But Steve still needed to slip in unobserved if his fishing story was to hold water. This called for careful stealth and subterfuge. There was only one brief window of opportunity in which to enter the building. Steve had to sneak into his flat when the old lady was playing bingo at a social club on Saturday evening.

Steve was proud of his stylish flat, and he did not relish the prospect of accommodating the gang. After his first encounter, he had developed an antipathy towards the mechanic and the feeling was mutual. They exchanged few words in the taxi as they travelled to his flat in Plymouth. When Steve tried to start a conversation about the late-night mission, to break the silence, the mechanic dismissed his query in a condescending manner: "Stick with me, son, and you will be okay."

The mechanic whistled casually as he clumped into the two-bedroom flat. It did not occur to the slovenly fellow to remove his filthy trainers. Steve grimaced at the muddy trail as he guided his unwanted guest to his spare bedroom. The mechanic dumped his knapsack on the newly cleaned duvet. "You might like to take a shower," suggested Steve tactfully. The ingrate ignored the offer, impervious to the implied criticism of his personal hygiene.

Showing no inclination to even wash his hands, the artificer sauntered back into the sitting room, where he demanded to see the football results on television. Steve acquiesced. He was grateful for anything to end the oppressive silence. When the television came to life, Steve endured a cacophony of raucous remarks as his visitor reacted to the team results.

Trying to ignore the catcalls, Steve opened mail that had gathered behind his front door. They had several hours to kill before setting off on their late-night mission; to the young executive, that seemed like a lifetime. He was exhausted and really wanted to take a nap, but he was not happy to leave his uncouth visitor to his own devices in his pristine flat. As the evening wore on, Steve asked his visitor whether he would like a Chinese takeaway meal.

The slob, who had spent the evening slumped in front of the TV, showed little appreciation for his host's generosity. When the food was delivered, the ingrate scoffed it as he sprawled on the couch, splattering morsels of egg fried rice around him. He flipped between television channels with complete disregard for Steve's viewing habits. After consuming the takeaway food, the brawny fellow belched and fell asleep in front of the television.

Steve felt an immense sense of relief when Anne arrived shortly before 'zero-hour'. His befuddled guest woke in a panic as his former skipper entered the room. "Stand by your beds!" she quipped, with a smile on her face. The disgraced artificer shot up as his naval training kicked in, and the fellow was half-standing before he recalled that Anne was now a civilian, with no authority to order him about. Comforted with that knowledge, the disgraced petty officer reverted to his cheeky-chappy persona as he slumped back onto the soft couch.

The way that Anne chuckled suggested that there was a growing affection between the pair, underpinned by running jokes. "All hands salute the Iron Lady!" quipped the artificer, rather tardily, as he wiped sleep from his eyes. This remark harked back to the time they served on the patrol boat, where Anne's admiration for the first female prime minister was a frequent source of banter on the lower decks. Anne took the provocation as a challenge.

"Who let that 'oily rag' out on deck?" she retorted in a spirited manner. Anne knew that the description 'oily rag' would infuriate the technician, who was proud of his mechanical skills, but her wide smile showed there were no hard feelings. Animated by their exchange, the pair barely acknowledged Steve, who was clearing up the detritus from the takeaway meal he had shared with his slovenly guest.

Lucy had been left behind to park her family car. When she reached the flat a few minutes later, she could sense a turbulent undercurrent. It was obvious that Steve was exasperated by the presence of two unwanted guests. "What a lovely view! The harbour looks wonderful at night," remarked Lucy in a friendly way as she tried to console him.

The flat overlooked the harbour, providing a view of twinkling lights along the waterfront. Neither of the earlier arrivals thought to remark on the panorama. After serving in warships that berthed in ports such as Hong Kong, Cape Town and Rio, they were blasé about such matters, so Lucy's observation helped to lighten Steve's sullen mood.

Lucy was in high spirits, relishing her role as 'wheelman' for the 'heist'. It was her task to ferry the gang to the boatyard and then collect them from a small harbour at Leighton Hollow when the operation was complete in the early hours of Sunday morning. The boarding party had some time to kill while they waited for Jackie to arrive with the duplicate keys that would give them access to the boatyard.

While Lucy was enjoying her role in the escapade, Steve was burning with indignation as he watched his smart, stylish flat turned into a pig sty by unwelcome and ungrateful visitors. To make matters worse, his efforts to prepare for the mission had gone unrecognised. In the past weeks, he had risked his fragile relationship with Jackie in support of their operation.

Jackie was to play a key role. The easier part was to organise a lock-in party for the navy trials team at the Feathers. The less palatable part involved luring the security guard away from his post and getting hold of his keys. This was only possible because she was friendly with staff at a prominent night club in the city centre. To pull off this stunt, Jackie cultivated a relationship with the security guard. This called for all her feminine wiles, because she loathed the guy.

After rebuffing his advances, Jackie dropped a hint that they could 'get to know one another better' at the night club late on Saturday night. This called for the gullible fellow to abandon his post guarding the boatyard. When Jackie arrived at the night club at eleven o'clock on the appointed night, she was provocatively dressed in a short skirt and fishnet tights. The brawny security guard was waiting and eager to see her. He stank of a pungent aftershave and his hair was slicked back with gel.

Jackie dragged him to the dance floor and during a slow, romantic number, she dissolved into his arms. "Is that a pistol in your pocket, or are you just glad to see me?" murmured Jackie suggestively, echoing the words of a Hollywood film star Mae West. The guard glowed with pride as they smooched.

But then Jackie pulled away from him in horror. "Ouch, you scratched me!" she yelped. The shrill cry drew angry looks from bar staff and fellow dancers. It was a reminder that the petite landlady had many admirers among the late-night crowd, and they would not be slow to defend her against predators. "Sorry, it's my keys," apologised the security guard as he looked down with a mortified expression at the bunch of keys in his bulging pocket, which spoiled the line of his tight-fitting trousers.

"Those keys will ladder my tights!" complained Jackie indignantly. Then she recovered her poise. "Why don't you leave them at reception?" she suggested with an affectionate kiss on his cheek. At first, the brawny guard was wary of parting with his valuables, but Jackie reassured him, saying the keys would be locked in a safe. To clinch the deal, Jackie handed over her own handbag for safekeeping. Fearing that he would lose the romantic mood, the guard relented.

"That's better," murmured Jackie in a comforting way as the pair returned once more to the dance floor. "We don't want anything to get between us." With that, the keys were spirited away to allow copies to be made by a skilled locksmith, who was one of the regulars at the Feathers. All this was carefully choreographed. The receptionist signalled to Jackie when the duplicate keys were ready. Jackie then needed an excuse to deliver the keys to the gang, who were waiting in Steve's flat.

With the duplicate keys cut, Jackie whispered in her partner's ear that she needed to return to the Feathers. "I need to chuck out the punters and put out food for an overnight lock-in party," she told her dancing partner. "It should not take too long." This part was true, so the story was convincing, but then Jackie set the trap with a seductive smile and pouting lips. "I should be back before the club closes and then we can spend some *special* time together. We can use a private room."

After that assurance, the pair returned to the reception desk where Jackie retrieved her handbag and the security guard regained his keys. Little did the security guard suspect that Jackie's handbag contained a duplicate set of keys for the boatyard. "What happens if you are held up?" asked the gullible fellow.

"Don't worry," promised Jackie. "I should be back before the club closes at one o'clock, but if I'm held up for any reason, lock yourself in the gents' toilet and wait for me. I've got a key to the club, so I can let myself in, and then we can party without being disturbed." The poor deluded fellow was so inflamed by lust that he swallowed the story hook, line and sinker. After watching the departure of his exotic dancing partner, the deluded fellow spent the rest of the session leaning morosely at the bar, waiting expectantly for Jackie's return.

There was no sign of the landlady as closing time approached. So, following her instructions, he locked himself in the gents' toilet. When the club was empty, he emerged from the dank chamber in the hope of an amorous encounter with his paramour, but the minutes turned to hours and Jackie failed to appear. It was not until the early hours that he realised he had been duped. The entrance was locked and barred closed and he did not dare use his mobile phone, fearing that this would tip his employers off that he had abandoned his post. It was not until the cleaners arrived at nine o'clock on Sunday morning that the shamefaced fellow was able to escape the building.

During that episode, Jackie returned to the Feathers, where she threw out the regulars and prepared for the all-night party, just as she had promised. But after that, the petite landlady headed round to Steve's flat to deliver the duplicate keys. The duplicates would allow the gang to enter the guard house at the boatyard, and then to gain access to a cabinet that held a set of keys for the *Normandy*.

There was a dissonant atmosphere in the flat as zero-hour approached. Lucy was chatting amicably with Steve in his well-appointed kitchen. The young bachelor spoke about his life in Plymouth, and Lucy listened in an appreciative way. The mechanic lolled on the sofa in front of the television, indifferent to all that was taking place around him, while Anne, the gang leader, paced impatiently by the front door, complaining about the late delivery of the keys. "*Where* is she? We will never make it at this rate," muttered the female naval officer.

When the doorbell finally rang, just before midnight, Anne threw open the door. "Have you got the keys?" she demanded gruffly, as though addressing a wayward pizza delivery boy.

"Yes. Here they are," answered Jackie demurely as she removed the heavy bunch from her handbag.

"We've been waiting for you," hissed Anne, with the unstated implication that Jackie was at fault for upsetting their plans.

Anne grabbed the keys and tried to close the door in their visitor's face. In a deft movement, Jackie extended her foot to prevent the door closing. The petite landlady was outraged at the ingratitude – it had taken all her guile to lure the security guard from his post and to persuade a locksmith to help them out, late on a Saturday night. "Steve gave me permission to use his flat!" she retorted indignantly. "I've left some belongings in the bathroom and I need to take them home." With that, she ducked past Anne with the agility of a scrum-half retrieving a rugby ball from a ruck.

Steve was distracted by his convivial conversation with Lucy when this row broke out, and was slow to react. But on hearing the commotion, he rushed to the front door, where he made vain efforts to calm the combatants. "Jackie has permission to use my flat," explained the young executive soothingly as Anne tried to waylay the petite, but deceptively tough, landlady. As Steve attempted to placate the female naval officer, Jackie sashayed into the living room with a beaming smile of triumph. Here, she introduced herself to the recumbent mechanic.

When Steve had resolved the situation at the door, he returned to the living room, where he was met with the troubling sight of Jackie chatting affectionately to the slovenly mechanic about a party. In a foolish effort to establish his mastery over his female friend, the young executive leaned over to peck her on the cheek. But the affectionate gesture was rebuffed – the petite landlady turned her head to avoid his embrace. To pour salt into the wound, Jackie pouted at the mechanic with a 'come-hither' look. The mechanic beamed back at the alluring creature.

Though small in stature, Jackie was tough as nails, and not someone to tangle with. After returning from the night club, the petite landlady was still wearing the short skirt and black fishnet tights she used to lure the security guard. The clothing accentuated the curves of her well-toned body. She responded to the animal magnetism of the brawny artificer by running her hand through her short-cropped bleach blonde hair to signal that she found him attractive.

"Wow!" exclaimed the artificer as he recovered his wits. "Where's the party?"

"We are celebrating at the Feathers!" replied Jackie flirtatiously. "The party should be in full swing by the time you get back tomorrow morning."

Anne was impatient to get underway and resented the female visitor's intrusion. So, stepping back into the living room, she silenced the artificer with a cold stare. In her haste, she failed to recognise the emotions that were swirling around the room. It was clear that she did not understand Jackie's role in their late-night mission. Commander Woods was responsible for her ignorance. All Anne had been told during her briefing was that 'the keys will be delivered at midnight'. The commander had made no effort to explain how that miracle would be achieved.

Lucy smiled wryly as she watched the unfolding human drama. It confirmed her instinct that Steve's fragile relationship with the wayward landlady was doomed to failure. So it pleased her to see that a rift had opened up between the pair. But, at the same time, she was troubled about her sister-in-law's aloof attitude towards the dashing young executive. In her obsession with the mission, her sister-in-law was in thrall to the obnoxious artificer. *She has failed to recognise Steve's good qualities*, Lucy mused.

Jackie was aware of the turbulent undercurrents as she made herself comfortable in the living room, but she feigned ignorance of the stir she had caused. Flaunting her cleavage and sexily stockinged legs, the petite landlady reclined on the sofa, cosying up to the leering mechanic. The mechanic was in heaven and showed little inclination to move. This infuriated their team leader. Anne was impatient to set off, and was peeved that her sidekick was distracted by the temptress. She had mistakenly believed that she had established a special bond with the brawny mechanic. It was only now that she realised that flirting was a way of life to the dissolute scoundrel.

There was little time to lose if they were to complete their mission before someone noticed the *Normandy* was missing from its berth. But like a stubborn mule, the mechanic failed to recognise the urgency. He was having a good time talking about the lock-in party and was reluctant to leave his cosy nook. The disgraced artificer had little real interest in their late-night mission, thinking that it would barely warrant his mechanical talents. They would have been stuck there all night had Lucy not stepped in to help her sister-in-law rally the troops. With their combined efforts, they finally managed to shift the stubborn fellow.

"Hope to see you at the Feathers when you get back," said Jackie with a suggestive smile as the burly mechanic hoisted himself unsteadily to his feet.

"You can bet on it," replied the mechanic with a wink.

The mechanic's enthusiasm for the mission had evaporated with his encounter with the seductive landlady. "I can't see the point of this caper," he muttered grumpily as Anne chivvied him towards the door.

The disgruntled fellow was further upset when Anne demanded that members of the gang should hand over their mobile phones. "We don't want anyone to trace our movements," she explained.

"Is that *really* necessary?" he asked with a scornful sneer.

Anne shepherded the reluctant boarding party to the car, and they set off to the boatyard. On their way, Lucy embraced her role as 'wheelman' with glee, but there was a sour atmosphere among her passengers. Anne was despondent. After the events in the flat, she was not sure that she could depend on the mechanic, and she thought that Steve would be 'little more than a passenger' on their mission. Steve regretted becoming involved in the stupid affair and wished that he had really been able to join Mark on his fishing trip.

Steve was tired and upset. The discomfort that he felt from Anne's offhand treatment was exacerbated by the jealousy he felt over Jackie's attraction to the swarthy grease monkey. But he pulled himself together, reminding himself that the future of the boatyard depended on the success of their late-night mission. So he clenched his teeth and buckled down to get on with the job. The artificer sat hunched beside him, sulking that he had been torn away from the alluring landlady and the fun of a 'lock-in' party.

As they approached the boatyard at Whitebait Cove, the boarding party donned balaclavas for disguise. This was Lucy's wheeze, based on films she had seen. She had purchased the garish headwear earlier that evening. The balaclavas were not really necessary, but Lucy thought that it would add to the drama. Anne issued flashlights to each member of the boarding party before the stepped from the vehicle. The initial phase of the mission went without a hitch, despite the fractious relationships within the gang.

The streets were deserted when they arrived in the small hamlet in the early hours of Sunday morning. It seemed that theirs was not the only subversive late-night mission. A fox slunk warily across the lane, intent on mischief. Lucy parked in a secluded spot close to the boatyard to allow the boarding party to alight without being seen. Then the three members of the boarding party sneaked up a lane to the vacant guardhouse and unlocked the door with the keys that Jackie had provided. Once inside, they found control buttons for the security gates and a set of keys for the *Normandy* stored in a cabinet.

Before moving on, Steve surreptitiously removed an embossed envelope from his jacket pocket and deposited it on the security guard's desk. This wheeze was dreamed up at one of the meetings in Fenchurch Street, but none of the other gang members knew about it. The ministry issue envelope was marked *Confidential*. It contained an official-looking document with the instructions: *The bearer has authority to move the prototype midget submarine to base X, where further sea trials will take place.*

The stationery had been purloined from the defence ministry and carried contact details of the ministry offices in Whitehall. It was signed by the 'First Lord of the Admiralty' with a flamboyant, but illegible, scrawl. It would not fool many people, but Felix believed that it would take time for investigators to establish whether it was genuine or not, given the labyrinthine nature of naval bureaucracy. This would give them a breathing space to cover their tracks.

With their keys, the boarding gang was able to pass unhindered through the wire mesh fence to the *Normandy*, which was moored at the quay. The gang split up after boarding the ship. Anne headed straight for the wheelhouse, where she familiarised herself with the navigation equipment; the mechanic headed to the emergency generator. Steve's only task was to release the mooring lines when they set sail. So, with nothing much else to do, he decided to take a look round the engine room. This proved fortunate.

As Steve stumbled into the bowels of the ship, the beam of his flashlight created eerie images among the pipes linking the equipment and machinery. The cone of light fell on a pressure gauge, showing that there was plenty of air to start the main engine. All seemed in order until he tripped over a small-bore pipe which seemed to have shaken loose on the side of the engine, so he stepped up closer to investigate.

When examining the small-bore pipe, he discovered that it led to the engine's 'turning gear'. This mechanism has a worm which engages with a gearwheel on the main crankshaft. On that particular ship, the crankshaft of the engine was directly connected to the propeller. The 'turning gear' could be used to lock the propeller shaft in position, or rotate it slowly, during maintenance. The gear is occasionally used in port to keep the bearings surface lubricated when the engine is left idle for long periods of time.

Steve's knee-jerk reaction would have been to reconnect the loose coupling, but he hesitated, recalling an incident that had occurred during one of his sea voyages. He knew that old machines tend to develop quirks that are only really understood by those who are familiar with them. He did not want to jump to the wrong conclusion. It was unclear to him whether the coupling had shaken loose, or whether it had been disconnected deliberately. To solve the riddle, he recalled a tip that he had picked up from his shipmates on the *Sea Ranger*.

After examining the mechanism, it became apparent that the small-bore pipe led to a sensor that detected whether the 'turning gear' was engaged or not. It would be hazardous to start the engine with the turning gear engaged, so he needed to check that the teeth of the worm wheel were jacked clear of the gearwheel on the crankshaft. His flashlight allowed him to peer under the floor plates to ensure that was the case.

Steve double-checked his observations, making sure that the 'turning gear' was firmly locked in the disengaged position. From these observations, he concluded that it would be safe to start the engine, whatever the reason the crew had for disconnecting the small-bore pipe. As he moved on, he heard the clatter of a diesel engine high above, and the machinery space was soon flooded with light. The artificer came sliding down the ladder shortly afterwards, with a triumphant expression.

The grease monkey was chuffed that he had been able to bring the ship to life by hand-cranking the emergency generator. He paid no heed to the young executive as Steve tried to explain his thoughts about the disconnected pipe and the turning gear. "You best get up on deck, *son*," barked the mechanic with a swagger. "I can handle the engines. You cast off."

After dismissing Steve, the grease monkey inspected the machinery space. He checked there was enough fuel in the tanks and sufficient compressed air for starting the engine.

Then he fired up the main generator and switched on the auxiliary pumps. As he made his way about the cramped machinery space, he belatedly recalled Steve's comment about a disconnected pipe. It was then that he noticed that the coupling on a small-bore pipe had come adrift on the side of the engine. With the instinctive reaction of a mechanic, he nipped up the joint with the wrench that he always kept in the back pocket of his overalls.

Having completed his preliminary checks, the disgraced artificer took hold of the starting handle and gave it a sharp twist. This action would normally admit compressed air to the cylinders in a controlled sequence to start the large diesel engine. But nothing happened. The engine did not react in any way, so he tried again. And again. But the engine showed no sign of life. The seasoned mechanic was not normally flustered, but he was rattled by the silence.

While the mechanic was messing around in the engine room, Steve was pacing impatiently around the deck, waiting for orders to cast off the mooring lines. The emergency generator was clattering away all this time and the living quarters were bathed in light. This raised fears that local residents would notice that intruders had boarded the ship. As he waited, he heard the occasional puff of released compressed air deep down in the engine room, but there were no other signs that they were about to move off.

After kicking his heels, he decided to climb up to the bridge, to see what was holding them up. When he reached the wheelhouse, he found their female team leader hopping from one leg to another in frustration. The mechanic was the focus of her rage. "What's going on down there?" she yelled into the telephone that connected directly to the engine room. Anne had served on many ships during her naval service and had never experienced a delay of this sort.

For a moment, Anne wondered whether the mechanic was playing the fool after being distracted by the 'painted trollop' who had delivered the keys to Steve's flat. She was still smarting over the way her new-found pal had leered at the 'party girl'. Anne was not usually given to such uncharitable thoughts, but the lurid images flickering through her mind were a sign of the stress she was under at that moment.

"What do you mean, the engine won't turn over?" she demanded angrily when the hapless mechanic finally answered the phone. "I thought you understood machines!" she added tartly, moderating her language when she noticed Steve entering the wheelhouse. "Looks as though the mechanic needs our help," she suggested in a slightly more charitable manner. Then she signalled for Steve to follow her, and the pair made their way down the steep ladder to the engine room. This was the first time that Anne had shown any appreciation for the young executive, but it did not last.

When the pair arrived on the floor plates of the engine room, they found the mechanic in a state of panic. As the grease monkey explained the problem to his team leader, Anne turned her back on Steve in a deliberate way as a sign that he could not help. Free to move around the cramped space, Steve noticed that the loose pipe coupling had been reconnected. *That might be the problem*, he mused.

When he attempted to draw the mechanic's attention to the pipe, he was snubbed. "Mind your own bloody business!" shouted the grease monkey, with a dismissive wave of his arm.

Steve was riled by the grease monkey's attitude and decided to take matters into his own hands. He wanted to disconnect the pipe to see if that would fix the problem, but lacked the tools. Then he spotted a wrench in the back pocket of the grease monkey's overalls. In an uncharacteristically aggressive move, he snatched the wrench and unscrewed the coupling. The mechanic turned in a threatening manner and raised his fist to punch the slightly built executive. But Steve stood his ground. "Give it another go!" he challenged, pointing to the starting lever.

The artificer had no intention of obeying the stuck-up prig, but Anne did not share his view on that occasion. "No harm in trying," she suggested in a conciliatory way. With that, the disgraced artificer lowered his fists and twisted the starting lever. Compressed air hissed through the valve, and the engine started to turn over. Then he twisted the lever to the next position, and the huge machine chugged into life. The grease monkey stood with a bemused expression, unable to comprehend what had taken place.

With the main engine running, there was no time to lose. Anne rushed to the wheelhouse to prevent the ship from breaking the mooring lines. The forward and astern movements of the ship were controlled from a single lever mounted on a panel at the centre of the bridge. The finely graduated controller sent out signals to regulate the throttle of the main diesel engine and the pitch of the propeller blades in a coordinated fashion.

Steve bounded up the ladder to the deck and released the mooring lines when he received a signal from the bridge. Once they got underway, Steve made himself useful, helping Anne with the navigation. They reached their destination without further incident. They berthed at a rickety jetty close to the abandoned village Leighton Hollow. To Anne's relief, they were met by a squad of men and a mobile crane. This gang had little difficulty lifting the midget submarine stowed on the rear deck of the ship, so there was no need to use the antiquated lifting gear. This part of the operation was organised by the Texan, who was working behind the scenes after relinquishing his role as project manager.

It later emerged that the Texan was friendly with the owner of a commercial haulage firm. The firm supplied mobile cranes. One of these monsters was able to lift the midget submarine in its launching frame off the rear deck of the supply ship in one go. The midget submarine was then spirited away on an articulated lorry to a warehouse at Portland, where it was to be stored before being shipped to a shipyard in the Netherlands. This work was arranged on an unofficial basis and the workmen were sworn to secrecy.

As soon as the midget submarine had been landed, the *Normandy* was moved to a nearby anchorage in Plymouth Sound. Once they had set the anchor and shut down the machinery, the boarding party prepared to abandon ship. Anne first switched on the satellite location beacon so the ship could be easily located by its owners. The boarding party then jumped into the ship's lifeboat and rowed to the shore. When they beached the lifeboat, they found Lucy waiting at the rendezvous point and she drove them back to Steve's flat at full speed.

With his long naval service, the late-night escapade had been at times an amusing but otherwise routine caper for the mechanic. "Now it's time to party!" he exclaimed in high spirits. He could not wait to get his hands on the alluring landlady. So Lucy dropped the 'grease monkey' off outside the Feathers public house, while the more sensible members of the gang continued on to Steve's flat. They were able to slip into the apartment block in the early hours of the morning without being observed by the nosy gossip on the ground floor.

After their arduous late-night operation, they needed to spruce themselves up. While Lucy was away in the bathroom,

Anne tried to mend fences with the young executive. Anne was impressed by the way the young guy had diagnosed the problem and started the ship's engine. The simple fix had not occurred to the 'grease monkey', despite his reputation as a mechanical genius. With time to reflect, she now regretted the offhand way she had treated the young executive. It was clear that she had badly misjudged him.

"How did you identify the problem with the diesel engine?" she asked in a friendly way as she extended an olive branch. Steve was taken aback by her amiable manner. It was the first time that he had seen the affable side of her character, but he was completely exhausted, having been on the go for more than twenty-four hours. So he replied in a mechanical way.

"I noticed the loose pipe connection when we boarded the ship, and came to the conclusion that it had been disconnected for a reason," explained Steve pedantically. "Your mechanic must have screwed it up when he saw it was loose. Something similar happened a few years ago when I was serving on a bulk carrier. An Indian greaser noticed a loose pneumatic pipe and screwed it up, and he did so without telling anyone. That mistake nearly caused a collision. Luckily, the chief noticed what had happened in the nick of time. It was a close-run thing!"

Anne followed the gist of the story, but she knew little about merchant ships and was not familiar with the vernacular. She was caught off balance, having forgotten in her haste to organise the mission that Steve had served at sea. This insight into his character surprised her. In her experience, ships' engineers tended to be brawny, larger-than-life characters. The slightly built young executive did not seem the type, somehow.

"You served at sea, then?" she enquired tentatively.

"Years ago, when I left school," he replied in a matter-of-fact way. "It was a crazy time!"

As they chatted, Anne warmed to the taciturn young executive. Before embarking on their escapade, she had judged him the sort of callow academic type she met at university.

But the engine room incident was evidence of his self-effacing nature and practical ability. *There's more to that chap than meets the eye*, she mused. As she reflected, she realised she had been dazzled by the boisterous 'grease monkey' and had failed to recognise Steve's attributes.

Lucy took her time washing her hands. She wanted to give the pair a chance to get to know one another, away from the malign influence of the mechanic. When she emerged from the bathroom, she was gratified to see that her sister-in-law was warming to the young executive. But there was no time to linger. It had been a long night and they all needed to sleep, but that moment was a pleasant interlude to conclude an exciting day.

"You are welcome to come and visit us when you have recovered," suggested Lucy with a smile as she bid farewell.

Steve did not place much importance on Lucy's invitation at the time. It seemed like one of those pleasantries that people often make to people that they have just met. But as he lay in bed, reflecting, he recalled the warm feelings he had experienced when chatting to Lucy in her kitchen. Up until that night, Steve had seen his apartment as a stylish bachelor pad. But the truth was, it had a sterile feel. The two down-to-earth women had made it feel like home.

Chapter 18

Steve in Bother, not Scotland

It was a great relief for the whole gang when the disgraced artificer jumped out of the car when Lucy dropped him off outside the Feathers on the way home from their late-night mission. The lusty mechanic could not wait to join the 'lock-in' party and continue his pursuit of the alluring landlady. It did not take long for him to regain his animal spirits once free of the censorious atmosphere inside the vehicle. The lusty fellow grinned, recalling the refrain as his rowdy shipmates set out for a trip ashore: "There's a rumbling in the pants department."

The front door of the Feathers was locked and bolted like Fort Knox, but there was a faint sound of music deep within the building. The mechanic hammered on the door with his fists, itching to join the fun. The stupid fellow had no idea that the 'lock-in' party was intended as a cover story for their late-night mission. The grease monkey was relieved to hear the sound of footsteps approaching the thick oak door, but his ardour was dampened by his reception.

Expecting to be greeted by the attractive landlady, he was instead met with the sight of a well-groomed male head poking around the half-open door. "What are you doing here?" demanded Commander Woods angrily.

"The landlady told me there was a lock-in party," replied the mechanic with a sinking feeling. The lusty guy was flustered, not knowing whether he should salute the distinguished officer.

"Did she indeed!" came the irate reply. The commander was annoyed to see the reprobate, fearing that the presence of the boarding party might undermine the carefully constructed alibi for his own men.

But the commander relented when the disgraced artificer explained that the submarine had been spirited away to a temporary store at Portland. After learning that the mission had been successful, the commander allowed the new arrival into the pub. But he did so with great reluctance, not wishing to undermine the rationale for the lock-in party, which was to provide an alibi for the trials team. "Stay away from the bar and keep quiet about what you have been up to!" he warned. The mechanic was left to kick his heels in a darkened room, separated from the bar. He was finally allowed to join the party an hour later.

When he emerged into the dimly lit bar, the grease monkey was disappointed that the petite landlady was nowhere to be seen. There were a couple of women – the skipper's wife and a girlfriend of one of the male guests – but otherwise the affair had the appearance of a dull all-male get-together. A group of men lounged around the bar, but the atmosphere was subdued, and it was not the sort of rowdy affair that normally takes place when naval ratings go on the razzle. There was no sign of the lusty chicks who managed to wheedle their way into parties on the lower decks.

The subdued atmosphere was explained by Jackie's absence. The landlady was normally the life and soul of the party, but her relationship with the pompous war hero had got off to a bad start. When Jackie returned from delivering the keys to Steve's flat, she met the commander for the first time, and the encounter did not go well. Jackie was fuming at the rude treatment she had received from the female naval officer and the lack of gratitude for her efforts. The commander tried to patch things up, but his clumsy approach only made things worse.

In his flat-footed effort to make amends, the commander failed to recognise the casual nature of Steve's relationship with the svelte landlady. He knew Steve was seeing someone and, in his old-fashioned way, assumed that the eligible young guy was 'courting' a woman. "Never mind, dear. I'm sure that Steve appreciates what you are doing. You never know, he might pop the question!" he remarked superciliously as he tried to console her.

Jackie erupted at this crass remark. It revealed the naval officer's neolithic mindset and lack of understanding of the real world. But the guy was a decorated war hero, so Jackie decided it was wise to hold her tongue. This was not something she was good at. So, to avoid making any further intemperate remarks, she took refuge upstairs in her living quarters. This allowed her to give the old warhorse a wide berth. "I'm waiting for the old buffer to beetle off!" she told a group of female friends who chose to join her isolation.

Although the commander was admired by the ratings, his presence put a damper on the normal boisterous fun of the lock-in party. The mood was further depressed by the absence of the alluring landlady, who was taking shelter above, so when the commander bid farewell, there was a sigh of relief from the entire party. Whoops, cheers and catcalls then erupted as the gaggle of women descended gracefully down the stairs from Jackie's living quarters. The music was turned up and partygoers took to the dance floor. As dawn broke, the party was buzzing.

Sitting on the sidelines, the mechanic watched entranced as Jackie glided down the staircase from her living quarters. The petite landlady was still wearing the short skirt and black fishnet tights that she had put on for the night club, her loose cotton blouse providing a tantalising glimpse of cleavage. As Jackie scanned the guests, she noticed the grease monkey sitting by himself. Their eyes locked, giving the impression she was in a frisky mood. The lusty guy could not believe his good fortune.

Jackie usually avoided alcohol, seeing it as an occupational hazard as landlady of a pub, but she kept a small stash of her favourite tipple for special occasions. Indignant at the way she had been treated by Steve and his naval colleagues, she decided it was time to break out the booze. As she sashayed over towards the dumbstruck mechanic, she signalled for the barman to bring over a bottle of bubbly. "You accepted my invitation, then," she murmured in a husky voice.

After taking the sparkling wine to a secluded corner, she asked her companion whether he would like to 'pop the cork' as she ruffled his hair in an affectionate way. The mechanic grinned at the hidden meaning. Other guests turned to watch the fun. The poor chap was overwhelmed. In his travels, the seasoned petty officer had been propositioned, but usually by women with some financial motive. This paramour seemed to find him attractive. She giggled at his jokes as they kissed and cuddled.

This was all an act. Jackie knew that Steve would hear of her amorous behaviour and that it would make him really jealous. 'Serves him right!' she thought malignantly. It was not long before the worldly-wise mechanic realised it was all a game. He was left frustrated when the sun rose, and Jackie reverted to her everyday persona of the hard-nosed landlady.

Jackie had another tough day ahead of her; she had to make sure that the bar was clean and restocked ready for opening time at midday. After disentangling herself from the artificer's octopus-like embrace, Jackie called time on the 'lock-in' party. The barman helped to steer the tipsy guests out into the deserted street outside. As the mechanic sobered up in the cool morning air, he remembered that he had left his rucksack in Steve's flat.

This was embarrassing because he needed to recover all his belongings before he could make his way home on the train. The grease monkey found Steve's apartment without difficulty because it was just a short walk from the Feathers, but there was no answer when he rang the door bell. Suspecting that Steve had fallen asleep, he hammered on the door and yelled. It was at that point that the frustrated guy recalled that Jackie had a key to the apartment.

The old lady on the ground floor was woken by the commotion and poked her nose out of her front door to see what was going on. She was just in time to catch a glimpse of a man leaving the building. The grease monkey was relieved to see that the lights were still burning at the party venue. It did not take long to attract the attention of a cleaner when he tapped on the window. The foreign worker spoke poor English, but the landlady was called in due course. Woken from her sleep, Jackie greeted the embarrassed mechanic with a cold, withering stare. She was suspicious of his motives. After a hasty explanation, she reluctantly agreed to accompany the befuddled fellow back to Steve's flat, to allow him to collect his things.

But then they encountered an obstacle. When they reached the entrance to the apartment block, they were confronted by the old woman on the ground floor. The feisty octogenarian was in high dudgeon. Although warned that Jackie might hold a party in Steve's absence, the old woman had been kept awake by the noise. "You young people have no respect!" she complained. "Coming and going at all hours and creating a disturbance. Mr Jones will hear about this when he gets back!" With that, she donned her hat and marched off indignantly, on her way to early morning mass.

The encounter amused the grease monkey and his companion. They chuckled merrily as the clambered up two sets of stairs to Steve's apartment. The episode rekindled Jackie's frisky mood. After knocking to check that the flat was empty, Jackie opened the front door with her key. In a jocular spirit, the mechanic offered to 'carry her over the threshold'. It was a feeble joke but, in a frisky mood, Jackie hooted with laughter as she was whisked through the door.

Jackie loved to visit Steve's stylish flat because it was an opportunity to enjoy comfortable surroundings and a stunning view without caring about housework. She spent so much time trying to keep her pub clean that she neglected her own living quarters. It made her feel despondent to spend long periods in the cramped, dreary rooms above the bar, with their drab decor so it was a great relief to visit Steve's spotlessly clean pad.

Sensing her amorous mood, the artificer took her gently in his arms. She did not resist. As they kissed, the Lothario's hands strayed down to unclasp her brassier strap. One thing led to another and before long they were stripping off their clothes on the double bed in the spare room. It was only the sound of a key in the door lock that prevented their relationship being consummated on the spot.

The grease monkey's passion was aroused by this time, and he was not in the mood to release his partner, but Jackie felt guilty. It was not so much that she regretted being unfaithful, as that she was abusing the trust of a good friend. So after disentangling herself from his octopus-like embrace for the second time that night, she threw on some clothes. She wanted to confront the flat owner with a modicum of dignity. Jackie later learned that Steve had slipped out of his flat to find a café that served breakfast. He had carefully timed his movements to avoid meeting his nosy neighbour on her way to Sunday morning mass.

Steve was shocked to see Jackie's dishevelled state. The landlady spent most of her life in the public eye and took pride in her appearance. But as she stood there, her false eyelashes had come adrift and her eyeliner was running in streaks down her cheeks. "What's going on?" he demanded angrily. This question scarcely needed an answer when the brawny grease monkey waddled out of the spare bedroom, eyes blinking, to see what was going on. It was an unedifying sight. The pallid figure was only wearing socks and hastily recovered underpants. Steve was outraged. "Collect your things and get out!" he yelled.

Unaware of Steve's relationship with the attractive landlady, the artificer was not prepared to budge an inch. He thought Steve was worried about the mess in his spare bedroom. "You know your trouble, mate?" he growled. "You should mind your own business!" Then seeing Steve's challenging expression, he moved forward, with fists raised in an aggressive stance.

Steve was boiling with anger. Jackie had gone too far this time in bringing a lover to his flat, but he knew he was no match for his swarthy opponent in a fistfight. So, quick as a flash, he leaned down and tugged at the end of the Turkish rug that lay on the polished wooden floor. The artificer, who had just trodden onto the other end of the rug, was sent flying. The poor fellow knocked his head as he crashed to the floor, and lay unconscious.

"You idiot!" cried Jackie. "What did you do that for?"

They were both too shocked to move, but sense prevailed as they surveyed the pudgy figure laid spark out akimbo on the floor. Jackie knelt down to check whether there were any signs of life. "Is he okay?" asked Steve fretfully.

"Yes, he's still breathing," she replied with relief as the grease monkey opened his eyes in a groggy manner. Together, they just about managed to wrestle the hefty body onto the double bed in the spare bedroom.

"What shall we do now?" asked Jackie with a note of distaste in her voice. The amorous mood had long since evaporated. She was now repulsed by the pale, corpulent invalid stretched out on the bed.

"You'll have to deal with this!" replied Steve masterfully. "You brought him here, so it's *your* problem. You need to call an ambulance. I can't help – I'm not supposed to be here." In all the excitement, Jackie had forgotten that Steve was supposed to be fishing in Scotland.

"Well, I can't stay," declared Jackie firmly. "I've got a pub to run."

After pondering their predicament, Steve figured out a crafty compromise. "We could call Anne," he suggested with an impish grin. That solution would settle a number of scores.

"Who?" asked Jackie.

"Anne Dexter," he repeated. "She's the naval officer who led our boarding party. You ran into her last night when you delivered the keys." That solution did not appeal to Jackie one bit. She recalled the 'stuck-up cow' who had tried to eject her from the apartment, and wanted nothing else to do with her.

"Why her?" asked Jackie doubtfully.

"She used to be this guy's commanding officer on a naval patrol boat," explained Steve. "They have a good working relationship."

"Well, you will have to organise it then," declared Jackie tartly. The landlady wanted to wash her hands of the whole messy affair.

"I'll call her and explain the situation," replied Steve helpfully, recalling that the formidable female naval officer was staying at Mark's house. That solution suited the petite landlady and so Steve picked up his mobile phone and dialled the number. When Lucy answered the phone, she was reluctant to wake her sister-in-law after her late-night escapade, but she quickly changed her mind when she learned what had taken place.

"There's been an accident!" exclaimed Steve in a desperate tone. "The mechanic has fallen over and knocked himself out."

"Have you called an ambulance?" asked Lucy anxiously.

"He's awake now, but a bit groggy. Jackie thinks that he's okay," replied Steve, evading the direct question. "We really need someone else to keep an eye on him."

It was an embarrassing affair and Steve was reluctant to explain the gory details over the phone. "Look, I think it's best if Anne comes over here," he pleaded. "Your sister-in-law knows the chap better than any of us, so she is the best person to look after him." This presented a bit of a problem because Anne had not brought her own car down to the West Country, so she had no transport.

"I'll have to bring her over," replied Lucy eagerly. The reason for this generosity was that Lucy was keen to find out more about the relationship between Steve and the racy landlady.

As she reflected on the call for help, Lucy began to read between the lines. *It's not so much what the young executive said, as what he did not say*, she mused. Lucy knew the grease monkey had attended a lock-in party at the Feathers, so it was reasonable to suppose that he had become inebriated, fallen over and injured himself. *But why was Steve evasive and why was Jackie unwilling to take care of the casualty? There's more to this than meets the eye*, she mused with impish glee. 'Perhaps my matchmaking plans will bear fruit after all.'

Lucy's enthusiasm for the mercy mission was not shared by her slumbering sister-in-law. Anne was tetchy when woken with news that the mechanic had been injured in an accident. "Bloody typical! I knew it was a mistake to involve that guy," she declared sourly as she wiped the sleep from her eyes. "He's been nothing but trouble!"

Meanwhile, back in Plymouth, Steve found himself in a real pickle as he waited impatiently for help to arrive. The young executive had been left to take care of the obnoxious guy after Jackie stormed off, washing her hands of the affair. This was not only unpalatable, but it also threatened to blow his 'fishing trip' alibi. To complicate matters, he needed to meet Mark on his return from Scotland, so he was immensely relieved when he heard a knock on the door.

When Steve admitted the rescuers, Lucy had little sympathy for the drunken invalid and she watched unfolding events with suppressed amusement. Her sanguine attitude was not shared by her sister-in-law, who was shocked to see the mechanic lying dazed on the bed. Anne was shocked by the sight and reacted instinctively, as her naval training kicked in.

"Why didn't *you* call an ambulance?" she demanded in a strident voice. Steve spluttered as he tried to explain the situation, but his efforts were in vain. Anne dismissed his excuses and picked up her mobile phone After punching 999, an ambulance was soon on its way. The self-righteous female naval officer might have been more considerate if she had taken the time to appreciate Steve's invidious position.

As they waited for the ambulance, the old woman on the ground floor was sauntering back from morning mass. The old woman was, of course, under the false impression that Steve was fishing in Scotland. So the young executive needed to slip out before she arrived home, to ensure that he was not spotted. Anne knew nothing of this because Commander Woods had failed to brief her about the fishing trip charade. Steve did not have time to explain the convoluted situation.

While they waited for the ambulance, Anne used her first aid training to make the grease monkey more comfortable in the spare bedroom. So, while the female naval officer was occupied in that way, Steve took Lucy aside and told her more or less what had taken place. Lucy chuckled at the story; she thought it hilarious that Steve had pulled the rug from under the boastful Lothario.

But they had little time to talk because Steve had to slip away before his nosy neighbour reached the apartment block. "You had better go!" hissed Lucy. "Don't worry. I'll try to sort it out with her ladyship." Lucy watched Steve scuttle out with some trepidation because her sister-in-law was, by this time, in full Nightingale mode. She feared Anne's reaction when she discovered that the young executive had gone.

Her fears proved justified. When she discovered that the young guy had left them to deal with the casualty, Anne shouted, "Bloody typical!" In the swirl of events, Lucy decided to wait for a more propitious moment to explain the reason for Steve's stealthy departure, although it meant enduring her sister-in-law's acid comments for the rest of the day.

The accident brought out an unpleasantly censorious side of Anne's character. While others might laugh off the incident, Anne reacted in a brittle and unsympathetic way to the comic situation. This character trait explained why she had remained single into her thirties. Lucy thought that an understanding partner would help her sister-in-law to chill out, and she hoped that Steve would be that person.

In a 'bossy-boots' mood, Anne insisted that they accompany the mechanic to hospital. This irritated Lucy, who had domestic matters to deal with. So, once they were satisfied that the injured man was being cared for, Lucy persuaded her sister-in-law to leave the medical staff to get on with their job. After all the excitement, the pair returned home by mid-morning.

Lucy could not afford to relax when she arrived home, because she had to collect her two boys from their grandmother. The boys created chaos when they arrived home, preventing Lucy telling her sister-in-law the full story. As a result of all this distraction, Anne failed to fully understand the rationale for the fishing trip charade.

Of course, Anne knew that her brother was on a fishing trip to Scotland as a wheeze to remove himself from the scene of the crime. But she had no idea that Steve had supposedly joined him on the same trip, because the commander had failed to brief her properly. So she was startled when Mark turned up later that afternoon, sitting in the passenger seat of Steve's sleek sports car.

But Lucy was unable to enlighten her bemused sister-in-law because of the chaos as the excited boys rushed to greet their father. Before Anne had a chance to vent her wrath about being left in the lurch with the invalid that morning, Steve set off once again, heading on that occasion back to the boatyard. Before the young executive departed, Lucy reminded him of the invitation.

"Why don't you come around for a meal this evening?" she suggested. She hoped that this would provide an opportunity to mend fences. But the young executive declined, saying that he had urgent issues to deal with at the boatyard.

It was not until the boys had gone to bed that the older

generation were able to sit down and chat about the crazy goings-on over the past few days. In a relaxed atmosphere, with a bottle of wine to create a mellow mood, they shared some of their experiences. By the time the wine bottle was empty, Anne had a better understanding of the motives for the fishing trip charade and some of the pressures that the young executive faced.

But Lucy and Anne said little about their late-night mission. They knew that Mark would be questioned about the disappearance of the submarine, even though he was in Scotland at that time that it went missing. They also knew that he was not very good at telling lies. So the less that he knew about their late-night escapade, the less he would reveal.

Chapter 19

Turmoil at Whitebait Cove

While the injured grease monkey was being stretchered to hospital in Plymouth early on Sunday morning, the sleepy community at Whitebait Cove was stirring into life. Few of the law-abiding citizens expected to find themselves at the heart of a police investigation as the church bells summoned the faithful to prayer. The little village was a dormitory for retired old folk, tucked away inland on a branch of the estuary, isolated from the main tourist routes.

In the past few weeks, the boatyard had been busier than usual with the comings and goings of people involved with the new security arrangements and the sea trials. All this was grist to the rumour mills for the gaggle of pensioners who gathered on the waterfront to gossip as they watched the *Normandy* sail from the yard each morning and return in the evening. But with the end of the sea trials, the community reverted to its normal somnolent character.

So the streets were deserted at breakfast time as Terry Smith whistled cheerfully as he cycled to relieve his colleague guarding the boatyard. On his way, the unsuspecting fellow stopped at the village store to buy a Sunday newspaper. It would be a long, boring day, with the yard closed and the sea trials completed. With little else to occupy him, the salacious tabloid rag would provide a welcome diversion during his twelve-hour shift.

Terry Smith was a reliable sort, but he was unhappy with his job and was on the point of resigning. His dissatisfaction stemmed from his distrust of Brian Squires, the man he was relieving. Squires was a heavy drinker and familiar face in the local pubs. On boozing sprees, he spread malicious gossip about his colleagues. The unsuspecting guard regarded Squires as unfit for security work. He could not understand why the owners of the security firm tolerated his wayward behaviour, and suspected that the scoundrel had a hold over them.

Brian Squires was normally snoozing or up to some mischief when he was relieved in the morning, so Terry Smith was not unduly alarmed to find the guard house locked and unoccupied when he reached the boatyard. The elderly guard used his own key to enter the wooden shack. Once inside, he noticed a sealed envelope lying on the floor and placed it on the desk while he went in search of his colleague. It did not occur to the unsuspecting fellow that anything untoward had happened.

When the unsuspecting fellow ventured into the boatyard, he noticed that the *Normandy* was no longer berthed at the quay. This did not worry him unduly. After all, the little ship was rarely at its berth when he arrived in the morning, because it had normally sailed for the day's sea trials. But Terry Smith was under the impression that the trials had finished the previous Friday. So, to check this was the case, he phoned the skipper's guesthouse.

When the skipper picked up the phone, he was befuddled after returning in the early hours of the morning from the overnight lock-in party. But when he had regained his wits, the old sea dog exploded. "Are you telling me that some bugger has nicked my ship!" he yelled. The skipper then threw on his clothes and raced off to the boatyard to find out what had taken place. In all the excitement, the sealed letter on the floor of the security hut was forgotten.

As he raised the alarm, the reliable security guard did everything by the book, reporting the ship's disappearance to the military and civil police, the coastguard and the port authorities. As an afterthought, he phoned Martin Beckwith at his North London flat.

This was a heated, and uncomfortable, conversation. The academic was incandescent with rage, bellowing down the phone at the hapless security guard. His fury at the loss of the ship was compounded by his embarrassment over the absence of the security guard, but what really troubled the academic was that the police were involved. A thorough police investigation would find out about his dodgy dealings.

His first frightening thought was that a debt collection agency might have sent bailiffs to recover the goods to compensate for money owed to contractors. The academic was aware that bailiffs sometimes use strong-arm tactics to recover goods but he quickly dismissed this thought, thinking it unlikely that bailiffs would commandeer a ship chartered by the navy.

As he calmed down, Beckwith reached the conclusion that the navy trials team were the culprits. It was pretty obvious that his adversary, Commandeer Woods, was playing tricks on him. So, after gulping down a coffee, he raced down to the West Country in his battered old saloon car. Skidding to a halt shortly before midday, Beckwith found the boatyard swarming with police and officials from the port authority. The military police had taken over guard duty by that time.

Some journalists were sniffing about, searching for a juicy story.

The dishevelled academic leaped out of the steaming vehicle and marched to his portable cabin, shouting abuse at anyone who crossed his path. Once ensconced in his cabin, he summoned the skipper of the *Normandy* for a dressing-down. Getting no sense from the 'daft old fool', the angry academic demanded to speak to the navy trials team. When the military police told him that the trials team could not be found, he smiled in a knowing way. Their absence confirmed his suspicion that his foes in the navy had hijacked the ship at the behest of Commander Woods.

As he reflected, Beckwith recalled the unhealthily close relationship that had developed between the navy trials team and the crew of the *Normandy*.

The navy team must have become familiar with the ship during their daily outings, he mused. *So it would not be too difficult for them to commandeer it*, he concluded. In his rush to condemn the navy trials team, it did not occur to Beckwith to consider any other suspects.

As the day progressed, the military police investigators made a breakthrough when they opened the sealed envelope that Terry Smith had found lying on the floor of the guard hut. The letter had been overlooked in all the confusion. Inside, they found an official-looking form typed on ministry stationery. Like most bureaucratic forms, it was divided into boxes, most of which were completed with codes and acronyms, so it was hard to decipher. One box stated that *The midget submarine is to be transferred to naval base X where further sea trials will take place*.

In another box headed Order Issued By were the neatly typed words, '*Special Logistics Agency (SPA)*. But the contact details for the agency were smudged and illegible. None of the military investigators were familiar with this particular branch of the military; but that was not altogether unusual. Few people have knowledge of every branch of the armed forces. The official-looking stationery was headed with contact details for the ministry in Whitehall.

When the military investigators dialled the number, they heard a recorded message saying that the ministry offices were closed for the weekend. The only named person on the form was the First Sea Lord, and no one had the courage to contact that eminent official. While there was some scepticism about the document's authenticity, it did look official, and it went some way to explaining the mysterious events. It also prompted a keen young police officer to search for the *Normandy* on the internet, much to the amusement of his older colleagues.

The bright young police constable was familiar with a website that tracks shipping movements, but the old lags scoffed at his gullibility. They knew that satellite tracking equipment could be turned off to hide the ship's position. "Do you really think that villains would leave the satellite beacon switched on?" scoffed one old lag. But to the embarrassment of the old cynic, the ship's position was clearly displayed. It turned out that the *Normandy* was moored in a regular anchorage, just a few miles down the estuary.

The discovery of his ship was a huge relief to the skipper, who was, this time, a sad and forlorn figure, pacing angrily about the boatyard. It took the old sea dog quite some time to round up his bleary-eyed crew, who were still suffering the after-effects of the all-night drinking party in Plymouth. It was a Sunday, and the crew had been promised a day off. But after a few sharp words, they grudgingly set off to recover their vessel. The crew found the ship's dinghy tied up to a jetty a few miles up the estuary, with the *Normandy* swinging at anchor nearby.

When the crew boarded the old rust bucket, they noticed that the midget submarine was no longer stowed on the rear deck. This did not surprise the skipper, given the discovery of the 'transfer document' in the guardhouse. It did not take the old sea dog long to get underway, and his ship was berthed back at the quay by teatime. The absence of the midget submarine seemed to give credence to the official-looking 'transfer document' that was posted through the guard hut door. But it was an embarrassing affair, nevertheless, and all were happy to play along with the notion that it was a bureaucratic cock-up.

All this confirmed Beckwith's suspicions that the navy trials team had stolen the midget submarine and hidden it somewhere along the estuary. They had probably done so at the instigation of their leader, Commander Woods. In reaching this conclusion, the academic figured that the commander wanted to sabotage the grand press launch that he had been planning. *A successful demonstration of the midget submarine in front of high-ranking officials would be embarrassing for the old warhorse*, mused the academic.

This theory seemed to fit all the facts; after all, it was quite plausible that the commander had dreamed up the phony 'transfer document'. But Beckwith kept this view to himself. It suited the artful academic to play along with the theory that the midget submarine had been moved for legitimate reasons. A thorough investigation into the loss of the submarine would reveal the academic's dodgy dealings. All he had to do was find the midget submarine. *That should not be too difficult*, he mused.

The investigation into the missing submarine was a chaotic affair, with confused officials milling about the boatyard, unable to decide whether it was a military, civilian or coastguard matter. The local police chief washed his hands of the whole affair as soon as he discovered that the *Normandy* had been chartered by the navy, but the navy did not have the resources to carry out a thorough investigation. As a maritime force, the navy only had a small pool of specialist criminal investigators.

In practice, the navy worked in cooperation with other branches of the armed services on terrestrial criminal inquiries. So, after lengthy discussion, it was decided that an army officer would lead the investigation. The ruddy-faced officer set up his headquarters in the portable cabin, which had only just been vacated by the navy trials team. It soon became evident that the corpulent fellow was more used to dealing with drunken squaddies than criminal activity, but he went about the investigation in a methodical way, nevertheless.

As investigating officer, he ordered his forensic team to search the *Normandy* for clues to identify the villains who had commandeered it. This proved to be a fruitless undertaking. The filthy wheelhouse was covered in fingerprints, including those of the naval trials team, who were regarded as prime suspects in the eyes of some. It was not possible to draw any useful conclusions from the time-consuming exercise. While the ship was being searched, the investigating officer interviewed Martin Beckwith.

This proved painful because the artful academic faced awkward questions about the absence of the guard and shortcomings of the security firm. In negotiating this minefield, Beckwith tried to distance himself from the decision to employ the security firm. Nonetheless, it proved an uncomfortable session. So the academic breathed a sigh of relief when the investigator turned his attention to the validity of the document found lying on the floor of the security hut.

The academic was keen to give credence to the document, thinking that this would give his people breathing space to track down the missing craft. The document would also distract the investigators from his dodgy dealings. So despite knowing that the document was fake, he did not admit it. "Our midget submarine performed much better than the navy expected," he remarked in a boastful manner. "It's quite likely that they want to put it through even more stringent tests. That is probably why the navy decided to move it to another base."

The corpulent army officer did not know what to make of it all. He had never heard of the Special Logistics Agency (SLA), the agency that had supposedly issued the transfer order. But then he had never heard of the Marine Special Projects Agency (MSPA). *Service life is full of acronyms that no one understands,* mused the battle-hardened veteran. He had little time for bureaucrats and was distrustful of the academic.

Reluctant to be drawn into that quagmire, he studied the document suspiciously. In doing so, he sniffed it like a piece of rank cheese as he held the paper to the light for inspection.

"Have you dealt with the Special Logistics Agency before?" he asked at length.

"Not as such," replied Beckwith equivocally, careful to avoid an outright lie.

"Do you recognise the contact details shown on the letterhead?" asked the investigator.

"Yes," replied Beckwith with growing confidence as the interview moved on towards safer ground. "That is the defence ministry building, where our headquarters are based." The investigator was pleased with that reply.

"So, if you share the same building, you should be familiar with the agency," he suggested hopefully.

"Well, not really," replied Beckwith doubtfully. "Many new agencies have been set up by the government in the past couple of years, and I don't know them all. We all share the same office building but don't speak to one another."

"Are you talking about a quango?" asked the puzzled investigator as he tried to get to grips with this labyrinthine military bureaucracy.

"Yes, that sort of thing," said Beckwith airily. With that welcome opening, he warmed to the topic and embarked on a long diatribe about the administrative structure of the armed forces.

The battle-hardened investigator had no desire for a lesson in bureaucracy and held up his hand to halt the academic. "So you think the document is genuine, then?" he asked in a blunt fashion.

"Well, nobody told me that the navy wanted to move the submarine for further sea trials," replied Beckwith hesitantly. But then he continued in a jaunty way, "But the document does look genuine. It has all the hallmarks of a naval order. That's what makes me think it is a bureaucratic mix-up."

In his effort to distance himself from responsibility for the security failings, Beckwith tried to give the impression of a modest person with little knowledge of naval affairs.

"The truth is that I have an academic background and I am not really familiar with naval procedures. But you know what Whitehall is like! The left hand doesn't know what the right hand is doing. It's probably best if you check with the Admiralty when they open for business tomorrow morning. They should be able to clear this up."

"One final question. Where is Base X?" asked the ruddy-faced army officer in an exasperated manner. "Sounds a bit fishy to me."

"Beats me," replied Beckwith with a sympathetic smile. "You know how the navy loves its jargon." The army officer had reached a dead end with the Whitehall offices closed, and no further leads. The search of the *Normandy* had been completed by this time, with no useful clues found. So he reluctantly acknowledged that his enquiries would need to be postponed until Monday morning when the Whitehall offices opened for business.

With the end of his interrogation, Beckwith returned to his cabin, where he remained closeted with his cronies for the rest of the day. The unwholesome gang spent this time scheming how he could recover the midget submarine and salvage their reputation from the unholy mess. As a first step, the academic printed a circular suggesting that an incident had taken place at the yard as the result of a 'bureaucratic snafu'.

When Steve arrived at the boatyard on Sunday afternoon, after dropping Mark off at his home, a smartly uniformed red cap checked his credentials and handed him the printed note. As the young executive parked his sports car, he noted with satisfaction that the *Normandy* was berthed back at the quay. *It did not take the crew long to track down their ship and return it to the boatyard*, he mused. He found it hard to hide his amusement at the yawning, empty space on the rear deck, where the submarine was formerly stowed under its tarpaulin cover. The printed note was a reassuring sign that Beckwith wanted to hush up the incident. The Fenchurch Street gang had anticipated that the academic would behave in that way. The note read:

To all boatyard staff, from Martin Beckwith of the Marine Special Projects Agency (MSPA), London,

On Saturday night, the media broadcast a news story suggesting that the offshore supply ship Normandy, which has been berthed at the quay for the past few weeks, disappeared from the yard without explanation. The story was false, and nothing untoward has taken place. We suspect that this story was planted in the media with malicious intent.

To set the record straight, the Normandy transported the prototype submersible to another military base over the weekend.

Some confusion arose over the ship's movements due to an administrative error. Statements have since been issued to the media to clarify the situation.

An investigation is currently taking place into the source of the leak. Staff are reminded that they are not allowed to speak to the media about naval matters. This is particularly important following some terrorist incidents in recent weeks. Discussion of security issues could have serious security implications. You are reminded that penalties under the Official Secrets Act and terrorist legislation include long jail sentences.

We are now actively seeking the source of this malicious leak, and wish to make it clear that we will not hesitate to prosecute anyone who releases classified information to the media without permission. All yard staff are asked to make themselves available for interview and assist with the investigation. Anyone who has information that could help us should come forward immediately.

After reading the note, Steve joined a group of gleeful yard staff gathered on the quay. These employees lived close to the boatyard and had returned to their place of work out of curiosity. News of the missing ship spread like wild fire through the close community and caused great merriment among the disgruntled workers. The loss of the midget submarine seemed a fitting retribution for the high-handed behaviour of Beckwith and his cronies.

After talking to his staff gathered on the quay, Steve learned that the yard had been in turmoil since early morning, when Terry Smith had raised the alarm. The young executive was soon able to piece together what had taken place. After the alarm was raised, the yard had been flooded with outsiders. Most had drifted away during the day, leaving a couple of red caps to guard the yard and a military investigator to work out what had taken place.

It seemed that the official investigation into the affair

had been scaled down after recovery of the *Normandy* on Sunday afternoon. The corpulent army officer believed the events could be explained by the absence of the security guard, combined with a bureaucratic blunder. The transfer note seemed to provide a plausible explanation. But the army officer needed to wait until Monday morning to sort things out with the ministry in Whitehall. There was no great panic.

Beckwith had done his best to shape this complacent view of the situation, in an attempt to divert attention from his dodgy dealings. After his interview, the artful academic spent the afternoon holed up with cronies in his portable cabin, devising cunning schemes to minimise the damage caused to his reputation by the embarrassing events. A stream of sinister-looking characters drifted into his portable cabin during the course of the afternoon. The first of these was a political advisor from Whitehall.

By the evening, the cabin was bursting with conspirators, including a couple of board members of the Marine Special Projects Agency, who owed him allegiance. It was soon clear that they had gathered together for a 'damage limitation exercise'. As Steve sidled past the cabin, a thug emerged to confront him. The emissary told the young executive to 'keep his mouth shut'. The guy's aggressive attitude was a sign of panic within the conclave. The need for caution was obvious – a press pack was circling the yard in pursuit of a juicy news story.

A shamefaced Brian Squires tried to sneak back into the guard house in the late afternoon to collect his things. The gullible fool believed the coast was clear because he had received news that the police investigation had been wound up for the day. But when he was spotted, the errant guard was hauled unceremoniously into Beckwith's cabin, where he received a thorough dressing-down. Squires was loathed by the yard staff because of the officious way he went about his work. Those gathered on the quayside listened gleefully to the commotion.

The staff gathered on the quay sniggered when a snatch of dialogue wafted their way. They listened entranced as the two board members called for Squires to be sacked, while Beckwith did his best to defend the miscreant. A bitter argument ensued. As a compromise, a story was cobbled together that the guard had abandoned his post due to the unexpected illness of an elderly relative. As tempers cooled, the voices became more muted, and yard staff were unable to follow the discussion.

It later emerged that the conspirators were trying to work out how they would recover the midget submarine. Beckwith needed to find the craft using his own resources after fooling investigators into believing that the transfer document might be genuine. "It should not be difficult to find the craft," observed the academic brightly. "After all, the mother ship was left moored quite near here so the midget submarine can't be that far away. There are only a few jetties where it could be landed." His confidence was not shared by his associates. The academic was worried that a thorough investigation would lead the authorities to look into his dodgy dealings. It was for this reason that he decided to play down the overnight events and give credence to the transfer document, which he knew to be false.

These actions had given him a breathing space to find the submarine and produce evidence that the navy trials team were responsible for pinching it. The academic believed that it would take the dull-witted military investigator several days to prove the transfer document was a forgery. That should be more than enough time to track down the submarine and nail his nemesis, Commander Woods. The only problem was that his cronies were high-minded 'left-wing thinkers' with little stomach for work or, indeed, getting their hands dirty. But, as always, Beckwith had another trick up his sleeve.

To achieve his aim, the artful academic intended to call in favours from an old pal called Jason Tyrone. The lawyer ran a small agency that investigated war crimes in long-forgotten campaigns. Tyrone employed retired police officers to carry out investigations in far-flung parts of the world. The agency did not handle high-profile cases in Iraq and Afghanistan and was little known to the public. It was threatened with the axe under the cost-cutting regime of the incoming government.

Tyrone shared Beckwith's jaundiced view of service personnel, and it would give him great pleasure to uncover the wrongdoing of a naval officer. A successful investigation would also help justify his agency's existence, so Beckwith was confident that his old pal would be able to provide an investigator to help him out. With the help of a private sleuth, they would be able to track down the midget submarine without undue difficulty. With luck, the private sleuth would also be able to collect evidence to convict Commander Woods of stealing the craft. After all, the submarine could not have been transported far in the half-day that had elapsed since the theft.

So confident was Beckwith of this crackpot scheme that he gave little thought to the role of the civilian police. The academic believed that the civilian police had enough work on their hands already, without worrying about military mishaps. This view was justified at first with the police chief's decision that the military police should handle the affair. But things took an unexpected turn when a plain-clothes detective, called Peter Fellows, became involved.

The plain-clothes detective was friendly with Steve after investigating a break-in at the boatyard some months earlier, so the sleuth was asked to keep an eye on things and liaise between the forces. The unassuming fellow was born locally and wanted to work at the boatyard when he retired from the police force, but his involvement was greeted with hostility by Beckwith's gang. A thuggish emissary from Beckwith's cabin warned the easy-going fellow 'not to impede the military investigation!'

After being given the cold shoulder by the military police, the easy-going fellow was glad to see a friendly face when Steve emerged from the office building. The young executive was on his way home. The warm sentiment was not reciprocated on this particular day; the detective was the last person he wanted to see. The young executive was exhausted after the late-night mission and did not relish the prospect of deceiving the sharp-eyed sleuth with the fishing story. Steve greeted the wily sleuth with a tired smile as he edged towards his mud-spattered sports car.

"You look exhausted!" observed the plain-clothes detective as Steve scrabbled to find the car keys in his trouser pocket, in the vain hope of evading his friend.

"I can't wait to get some shut-eye," replied the young executive, yawning in an ostentatious way. "We have just driven down from the Highlands. There was a major hold-up for roadworks at Spaghetti Junction!" As he clicked the remote lock, he pointed towards the salmon lying on the back seat to provide evidence of his fishing trip. Steve hoped that he could sneak away before he was drawn into a prolonged conversation. He feared that his friend would see through the fishing trip charade.

"Sorry to keep you from your bed!" replied the plain-clothes detective "but I would appreciate a quick word!"

Steve's blood ran cold with those words. He closed the half-open car door and turned back with a reluctant sigh. As they trudged back to the office building, Steve tried to make small talk about his 'catch' and the motorway hold-up. Once inside the foyer, the pair looked out with amusement at the portable office bursting with Beckwith's cronies.

"It's like watching ferrets fighting in a bag!" remarked the detective in a friendly, laconic manner.

After the break-in at the boatyard, the pair met up from time to time in the Feathers public house, where they were both regulars. Steve thought that Peter Fellows was a capable officer. He had been impressed by the way that he dealt with the break-in at the yard, but this only stoked fears that the wily sleuth would discover what he had been up to. He knew that while the unassuming fellow gave the appearance that he was absent-minded, his sharp eyes did not miss a thing.

As they chatted in the foyer, the plain-clothes detective scoffed at Beckwith's story that the loss of the midget submarine was the result of a 'bureaucratic snafu'. This suspicion made Steve uncomfortable, so the young executive tried to muddy the waters. The plain-clothes detective's sleuthing instincts were awakened by Steve's evasive behaviour. With his sharp, observant eyes, he had already noted some inconsistencies in the Highland fishing story. The salmon was, indeed, a handsome specimen. But it had the plump, well-fed appearance of a farmed fish, rather than the mean, hungry look of wild salmon. *Of course, anglers tell fibs*, mused the detective, *but Steve's comments about a motorway hold-up do not ring true either.*

Steve had rather foolishly parroted a remark that Mark had made about the long motorway queue caused by roadworks at Spaghetti Junction when he was travelling north at the beginning of the week. The young executive wrongly assumed that he had run into the same problem on his way south, but this was not the case. Mark had failed to tell his boss that the traffic cones had been removed on his journey home. The detective was aware that the traffic restrictions had been lifted. The wily sleuth noted these small errors but did not air his doubts.

Peter Fellows saw no need to probe the holes in Steve's story at that particular time, because he had no role in the investigation and did not wish to embarrass his friend. But he quickly surmised that the plump salmon was not the only 'fishy' business in the boatyard. It was clear that something sinister was taking place. What role Steve had in this he did not know, but he was curious to find out what was really going on.

As the boatyard was closed for business on Sunday, most employees learned about the mysterious weekend's events when they arrived for work on Monday morning. Staff members were each handed the circular describing the 'bureaucratic snafu' when they reported for work at the security hut. After the turbulent events on Sunday, the boatyard slowly returned to normal the following day. The military investigation continued in a half-hearted manner. As a matter of routine, staff members were asked to account for their movements at the time the *Normandy* went missing on Saturday night.

Steve could not report for work at the boatyard on Monday morning, because he was busy dealing with the dredging business in Torquay. Few people remarked on his absence – his ill health and fishing trip seemed to provide an explanation. His supposed ill health and trip to the Highlands with his deputy had been the subject of gossip for some days.

Chapter 20

The Shipmates are Introduced to the Dredging Business

While hordes of worried officials were scurrying around the boatyard on Sunday morning, trying to account for the disappearance of the submarine, Bill and Alex were cooling their heels at home, oblivious to the excitement. After their abortive reunion weekend, the pair of engineers had a week to kill before starting work for Steve in Torquay. With nothing else to do, Alex headed back to Glasgow while Bill returned home to West London. The pair were under the impression that their new boss was fishing in Scotland during the week.

Bill was glad of a short break before starting work for the slippery new boss. It was a chance to tidy the garden and sort out his paperwork, but it was a depressing way to spend the week. The house felt cold and lonely after his wife's premature death. So, to keep up his spirits, he kept his television set switched on for entertainment. This was how he first got wind of some mysterious goings-on in the village they had visited the previous weekend.

While loading his hatchback on Sunday morning, he was shocked to hear that a naval vessel had gone missing in the West Country. Curious to learn more, he searched the internet, where he found a posting with news that *Military police are investigating the disappearance of a naval vessel in a small harbour near Plymouth.* He wondered whether this could possibly refer to the ship they had visited during their boatyard tour. Bill tried to contact Steve to find out whether that was the case.

When he failed to receive a reply from Steve's flat or his mobile phone, the bean counter naturally concluded that the young executive was on his way back from Scotland. He didn't think it appropriate to send a text message, thinking that the young executive had enough on his plate. *We will find out soon enough,* he mused, so he tried to put the matter behind him as he set off on his journey. But the news nagged at the back of his mind during the tedious car trip, as did the ugly confrontation that had taken place during their tour of the small ship.

Bill arrived in Torquay in time for tea, but he did not meet his Scottish pal until breakfast the following morning. Bill was fast asleep when the cantankerous Scotsman arrived at the guesthouse in the early hours. When they finally met at breakfast, Alex was in a bilious mood after yet another frustrating train journey. Forever the diplomat, Bill wanted to avoid a squabble over the breakfast table. So, as they chatted, he made no mention of the disappearance of the ship.

After a hearty breakfast, the pair set off in Bill's hatchback, and it did not take them long to reach the parade of shops where Steve had rented an office for the dredging business. The parade was located on the outskirts of the seaside town. Bill drew into a small car park set at the end of the parade.

They found the freshly painted office at the top of a flight of stairs, above a bookmaker's shop. A sign with the insignia *Deepwater Dredging* was fixed to the door. The graphic style bore all the hallmarks of Steve's business at Whitebait Cove. Their young boss was busy shifting furnishings.

After a good night's sleep, the young guy had recovered from the weekend's excitement. With rolled-up sleeves, Steve looked more like a removal man than a thrusting executive as he welcomed them into the brightly lit room. Their new boss was setting out the desks as they entered; boxes of office equipment were strewn around the small room. Without being asked, Bill lent a hand, while his pal looked on with a sour expression.

The Scotsman was still in a grumpy mood after his frustrating rail journey and showed little inclination to help. Taking care not to antagonise the cantankerous Scotsman, Steve gave him a twenty-pound note and asked him to buy some coffee, milk and sugar for their tea break. The errand provided an opportunity for the young executive to have a private conversation with the placid bean counter. But this carefully choreographed plan was blown to shreds.

With Alex's departure, Bill felt free to speak about the news story that had been troubling him on his long journey down to the West Country. He was confident that his young boss would provide an explanation. "Did you see the news about the disappearance of a naval vessel?" asked Bill casually as the pair lugged a heavy desk across the floor.

That threw a spanner in the works. Steve was worried how his former shipmates would react when they learned about the somewhat unsavoury side of the dredging business. He hoped to gradually introduce them to the murky operation. But the news report had wrecked his 'slowly-slowly' plan. Unable to deny the news story, he decided to 'play dumb' for the time being.

"No. I missed that," he replied disingenuously. "I'm a bit out of touch. We were travelling from Scotland yesterday. What's happened?"

"There was a news report on the television. It was only a brief one, so I followed it up on the internet," declared Bill smugly. "A naval vessel has disappeared from a small harbour near Plymouth." The bean counter was chuffed that he was better informed than his cocksure young friend for the first time since they had met for their abortive reunion. "It was a strange coincidence," he remarked. "It sounded a bit like the ship you showed us round."

Steve looked startled. "Have you told Alex about the story?" he asked anxiously. The young executive's mind was racing as he was forced to revise his recruiting strategy.

"No," replied Bill cheerfully. "Alex was really grumpy this morning. His train was late and he has been swearing at the rail companies ever since, so I didn't think it wise to tell him about the missing ship. You know what he's like. He sees conspiracy theories everywhere! I thought that I should speak to you first."

"A naval vessel has disappeared, you say? That sounds worrying!" remarked Steve, feigning disbelief. "I better phone the yard to see what they know." With a worried look on his face, he stepped outside to make a confidential call on his mobile. The phone call was just a ruse to give credence to his cover story. When he stepped back into the office, he had figured out a new approach. He thought it best to play along with Beckwith's 'bureaucratic snafu' line of argument for the time being.

"It's just a storm in a teacup," explained Steve with a look of relief. "It seems that the guard went missing in the early hours of Sunday morning when the *Normandy* sailed. There were no records of the ship's movements, so the military police were called out. But the guys at the yard now think it's just a mix-up. People have got their wires crossed. It's the guard's job to keep a record of all the ships that come and go. It seems that the guard was called away to look after a sick relative. I've been in Scotland all week, and have not had a chance to talk to my staff. But nothing to worry about. It's all a big mix-up."

The episode put an end to Steve's plan to win Bill over while the two of them were alone in the office. It was also a waste of Steve's valuable time; there were many other urgent matters to deal with. The young executive was also worried how the cantankerous Scotsman would react to the news. "Best not to mention the news story to Alex," begged Steve. "It will just upset him. He tends to jump the gun. We don't want him to get the wrong end of the stick!"

Bill was surprised by this request. It all added to the impression that his slippery young boss was not being straight with them. It led the bean counter to feel uneasy about the business venture that they had been asked to join. There were a lot of unanswered questions. Why did Steve want to prevent Alex from finding out about a news story? What was the real purpose of the reunion? Why was there so much emphasis on confidentiality? What had really taken place at Whitebait Cove? But despite these fears, he decided to give the ambitious young executive the benefit of the doubt, for the time being.

When Alex returned from his errand, he noticed that most of the office furniture was still in the same position. Nothing had been moved in his absence. This led him to believe that they had been talking about him behind his back. But he had other things on his mind, expecting Steve to quibble over the money he had spent. In his normal cheeky manner, Alex had added packets of biscuits and snacks to the original shopping list. He was smugly satisfied when the cocksure young boss told him to keep the change. Once Alex had made three cups of coffee, Steve asked his former shipmates to gather around his desk.

With a serious businesslike demeanour, the young executive asked his new recruits if they had read the conditions of work that he had given them the previous weekend. The pair both retrieved the documents from their briefcases. "First things first," said Steve as Alex noisily munched a digestive biscuit, "I would like you to sign the forms. The agreement covers *one week's* consultancy work." He then drew their attention to the strict confidentiality clauses.

The Scotsman scattered crumbs on the form as he scanned it. Then he signed the document with a flourish. Alex's unusually docile behaviour upset the cautious bean counter, who was uneasy about the way events were unfolding. Bill was reluctant to admit it, but he hoped that his Scottish pal would ask some awkward questions about the dredging business, and spare him the task. There were points he needed to check before he became more deeply involved.

"You just want us to draw up a business plan for the business?" asked Bill cautiously.

"Yes. That's exactly what I'm expecting you to do *this week*," replied Steve. The reassuring words had a sting in the tail. "If you decide to stay on, we might need your help recruiting seagoing personnel, and we may need your expertise on other matters."

"Are we free to leave at any time?" queried Bill, who was becoming increasingly nervous about the whole situation.

"Well, no," replied Steve firmly. "I expect you to stay until the end of the week. That will give you a chance to understand our plans more fully."

Bill was reluctant to sign the form. The young executive could see that his former shipmate was bridling at the fence, and felt that he needed to tackle his fears head-on. He would like them both to join his team, but only if they put their heart into the job. So, facing the bean counter square in the eye, he delivered an ultimatum.

"You are probably wondering why I have been talking about secrecy so much. Well, the answer is that while the dredging company is legitimate, it will also act as cover for an undercover operation. The dredger will be used for covert surveillance operations along the coastline of the Horn of Africa. We need to keep that to ourselves because we don't want the bad guys to know what we are up to," he added sombrely.

Alex nearly choked on his biscuit as he reached across the table to grab the document he had just signed with his meaty fist. "Bloody typical! I should have guessed!" he exclaimed in an angry outburst. "You're a slippery devil! I knew it was a mistake to trust you! I'll have no part in this!" But it was all bluster. There was a tongue-in-cheek undertone in his abusive remarks. A faint smile suggested that he was having some fun at his pal's expense. It was almost as though the Scotsman had anticipated what Steve had to tell them.

This little act only added fuel to Bill's rage, just as the Scotsman had intended. The law-abiding bean counter was feeling decidedly queasy about the whole affair, and this revelation confirmed his worse fears. It raised worrying questions about the disappearance of the ship from the boatyard. The normally placid engineer felt that the young executive was walking roughshod over them and taking them for fools.

"You've abused our friendship," he growled through gritted teeth. "You think we are a pair of washed-up engineers who can be press-ganged into a cloak-and-dagger operation! Well, neither of us has military experience, and we know nothing of the secret services! Come to that, I've never stepped foot on a dredger in my life!"

Steve had anticipated an eruption of anger from the truculent Scotsman, but Bill's hostility to the operation came as a real shock. When he set out that morning, the young executive had hoped to win over the placid marine engineer to help smooth things over with his volatile Scottish pal. But that plan had gone awry when Bill raised the issue of the missing ship at Whitebait Cove. The young executive now faced an immense challenge to square things with both his rebellious former shipmates. He had no choice but to lay out the facts, in clear, blunt terms.

"Look, I know that I should have been more honest with you!" he admitted solicitously, "but you need to know that the dredging business is part of a major operation to protect merchant ships from hijackers. That is bound to involve risk, so there is no room for fainthearts. But there will be trained military people for the dangerous stuff. The dredger will simply be there to support them. We need a civilian crew to operate the dredger. We need someone to manage them. That's where you come in, so don't worry about the military side of the operation.

"All I'm asking from you, at the moment, is business advice. Then, if you decide to stay, we will need your help to recruit seagoing staff, but that's for the future. But all I'm asking from you this week is a business plan for a dredging business. That's a reasonable request, isn't it! So don't get so stressed. We can talk about the undercover side when I come back on Friday. You can bail out then if you don't like the sound of it, but please remember that you cannot talk to anyone about this!"

Steve then slid a dossier of papers across the table to Bill, who was sitting with a glum expression. "This is a dossier of information about the dredging business. You will see that it is a legitimate company. It will be listed in trade directories, and we will file annual accounts. So the business will be open to public scrutiny. We are negotiating to buy the dredger. If you decided to join us, Bill, you would be appointed as operations manager. You will report direct to me. I'm the managing director."

He then passed a similar package of documents to Alex with the comment: "You are being offered the job as Bill's deputy."

Alex's eruption was all bluff and bluster; the Scottish engineer was more than happy to go along with the young executive's plans. The bitter truth was that the Scotsman had little choice in the matter. It was difficult to find a decent job at his age; the alternative was to work on some foreign-owned rust bucket. The undercover side did not worry him in the least. After all, the military people would perform dangerous tasks in the hostile waters, he figured. But his pal's antagonism put the wily Scotsman in a strong bargaining position, so he used this leverage to clarify some points before taking the plunge.

"Let's be clear," asked Alex with the crafty expression of a poker player who has been dealt a royal flush, "you want us to stay until Friday. Then you will pay us for a full week's work, and we are free to go our merry way, with no comeback, no hard feelings?"

"It's not *quite* that simple, I'm afraid," replied Steve as he backtracked. He was relieved that one of the truculent pair was prepared to join the operation, but did not want to undermine his negotiating position. "During the week, I expect you to prepare a professional business plan. The plan must include an assessment of the ship we propose to buy and advice on how to run it. You must complete the business plan by Friday. That is your assignment. Provided that you complete that task, you will receive your pay. Then we will talk further, and you can make a decision whether you wish to stay on, or not."

Alex was reasonably happy with the offer. He could not see any loopholes. "Okay. I'll stay until Friday and complete your report, but don't blame me if I pack my bags and leave you after that!" he declared with smug satisfaction. The canny Scotsman thought he had got the best of the deal, and could not believe that the cocky young guy could be such a pushover.

Bill was not so easily appeased. The recently widowed engineer did not need the money and he was uneasy about the news story concerning the missing ship, but Alex's meek acceptance of the offer swayed his view. As he tried to make up his mind, he voiced his thoughts out loud. "Dredging could be an interesting business, so I'm happy to draw up a business plan. But I'm too old to start any cloak-and-dagger stuff and will probably leave you at the end of the week. Employers always paint an attractive picture when they offer you a job. Then they throw you to the sharks when you start work!"

"Well, you've got all week to think it over," remarked Steve impatiently. The young guy was finding his former shipmates' foibles tiresome, and he had many other pressing matters to deal with. "I hope the pair of you will stay on, but I'm not going to make false promises. It won't all be plain sailing. We managed to get along together on the *Sea Ranger*. Anyway, I've got to rush back to the boatyard. There is a bit of a flap on. Bill knows the score! So I'll leave you with that information dossier and expect your business plan at the end of the week. You can always contact me on my mobile. But if not, I'll see you here on Friday."

Before leaving them, Steve rushed down the stairs to his sports car and bounded back up to the brightly lit office with a box containing laptop computers and other bits and pieces of computer equipment. "Could you set up a web connection, Bill?" he asked. Then on a second trip, he returned with a box of manuals, which he handed to Alex. "You will find Class

The Shipmates are Introduced to the Dredging Business

Rules and information about dredging machinery among that lot," he explained.

Then turning to Bill, he added: "I'll leave you in charge," as he bolted out of the door, leaving his former shipmates looking at one another in astonishment. Neither of them knew what to make of their young boss's weird behaviour, but they gradually reconciled themselves to the situation and settled down to work. Bill busied himself setting up the internet connection while his Scottish pal studied the stack of technical manuals with a look of fascination.

Steve's mind was filled with conflicting emotions as he returned to the boatyard after the less than inspiring meeting. It had proved more difficult to deal with his former shipmates than he had anticipated. But he had more important things to worry about. The discovery that Jackie had been unfaithful was intensely painful and made worse by the fear that she might betray them. But on a positive note, they had acquired the midget submarine and things seemed to be going more or less in the right direction on that front. One good omen was that the yard was returning to normal after the turmoil of the previous day.

The red cap guarding the boatyard gate asked Steve to account for his movements in the early hours of Sunday morning. The perfunctory procedure was followed for each new arrival at the yard, and was no cause for alarm. But after the roller coaster of emotions over the past few days, the young executive found the question unsettling. Then his confidence received another knock when he ran into his old pal Peter Fellows once again. The plain-clothes detective was kicking his heels in the foyer of the office building.

Steve could not reveal what he had been up to earlier that morning, so he fobbed off his old friend with an excuse that he had urgent business in his office upstairs. The snub irritated the sleuth, who had an important issue to clear up with Steve. Refusing to take no for an answer, the plain-clothes detective offered to buy his pal a pint in the Feathers later that evening. Steve was flummoxed by this friendly gesture, knowing that it would appear churlish to refuse. So he agreed to the meeting, thinking that the delay would, at least, give him time to get his story straight.

After sidestepping the plain-clothes detective, Steve was at his wit's end when he stepped into his sanctum to find Commander Woods waiting. The commander was in an ebullient mood, believing that their weekend escapade had been a total success. "How did you enjoy your fishing trip?" he asked conspiratorially. The commander was cock-a-hoop that the midget submarine was now safely in their hands and that he had got one over on the loathsome academic.

The commander knew nothing of the problems that plagued the mission, or the fracas that had taken place in Steve's flat. "Yes, it was very pleasant, thanks," replied Steve tersely before continuing in an ambiguous vein. "We achieved all we set out to do!" With that, the young executive signalled they should talk on the balcony, where they would not be overheard. In a jolly mood, the preening naval officer peered through the brass telescope, smiling broadly as he admired the view, with sunlight sparkling from the choppy waters of the estuary.

"Beckwith was apoplectic!" remarked the war hero gleefully, oblivious to his friend's travails. "The blockhead suspects that our lads pinched his precious submarine and he is determined to prove it. But our lads were drinking in Plymouth until the early hours of Sunday morning. Beckwith did not buy that story, so the investigators are going to double-check the story with the landlady."

The commander thought the shenanigans were amusing, believing the investigators had set off on a wild goose chase.

After all, there were videotapes to prove that the navy trials team were present at a lock-in party at the Feathers when the *Normandy* went missing. So what was the problem?

Steve failed to see the funny side. The young guy knew that Jackie bore a grudge and might drop them in the mire. While Steve ruminated about these fears, the preening naval officer rambled on, oblivious to the undercurrent. "Our friend is creating a smoke screen to conceal his failures," remarked the commander with suppressed mirth. "He needs to explain why the guard abandoned his post. So the blighter is trying to cover his tracks! Does he really think people will believe his absurd story about a bureaucratic snafu?"

"I don't think he has any choice!" replied Steve thoughtfully. The young executive did not want to rain on the commander's parade until he had a clearer idea of the problems they faced. As he pondered the situation, he pulled a piece of paper from his pocket. He read the note carefully, looking for hidden meaning. When he had finished his scrutiny, he asked whether the commander had spoken to Beckwith.

"That's the strange thing," replied the war hero. "He hasn't spoken to me. In fact, he has been avoiding me. But he has spoken to my men."

"Why do you think he's avoiding you?" asked Steve.

"No idea," replied the commander grandly. "We've been at daggers drawn since I started on this project. So he must suspect that I'm responsible in one way or another. My guess is that he wants to put the screws on my guys, hoping they will give the game away."

"Perhaps he's scared of you," suggested Steve, tongue in cheek.

"That could be!" replied the commander vainly. "He bullies people that do not stand up to him. But you know the old story – behind every bully lies a craven coward."

Steve did not really believe the academic was a coward – and thought that the commander was a fool to underestimate their adversary. "Well, I suppose we had better face the music!" he sighed in a resigned manner. "We need to confront the guy and put our stories on the record. The sooner the better."

Stepping back inside his office from the balcony, Steve punched Beckwith's number into his office phone. The call was promptly answered by Simon, the administrator. Steve apologised for his absence that morning and asked to speak to Martin Beckwith. After a brief exchange, the young executive replaced the handset with a bemused expression. "Our friend has gone home to London!" he spluttered in disbelief. "He's not expected back until next week, and the military police have been told to wind up their investigation."

This was puzzling. Why had they abandoned the investigation before finding the submarine? As they pondered that conundrum, it did not occur to either Steve or the commander that the artful academic would employ a private detective. Relieved that the investigation had been wound up, the commander saw no need to linger in the boatyard.

As far as the preening naval officer was concerned, the mission had been a total success. Not only was the midget submarine now in their hands, but the investigation had been called off. All was well. The commander was amused that his adversary had scuttled back to London, where he would, no doubt, be skulking, trying to figure out a way to save his career.

"Well, there is nothing left for me to do here – the boarding party has been disbanded," he announced complacently. "So I'll leave you in peace." With that, he swaggered off to the naval base, leaving Steve sitting down to eat a sandwich and brood over his predicament. Steve had bought the sandwich while filling his sports car at a petrol

The Shipmates are Introduced to the Dredging Business

station on his way back from Torquay that morning. The crusty egg and bacon sandwich was one of the few comforts in a difficult and disturbing day.

With his stomach satisfied, the young executive began to take stock of his situation. The mission had gone more or less as planned, he mused. The yard staff had swallowed the fishing trip story. The military investigator seemed to accept that all the trials team were boozing in the Feathers in the early hours of Sunday morning when the midget submarine had gone missing. But the plan had started to unravel with the fracas at his flat.

As he looked at events from a wider perspective, it dawned on him that he was caught in an inter-departmental dispute that could easily have been resolved in a civilised manner. The events had been blown out of all proportion as the result of a feud between two egotistical men.

On the one hand, there was the commander with his well-groomed grey hair and neatly trimmed beard. His distinguished military record included a citation for bravery when he had led a party to remove an unexploded bomb lodged deep within the bowels of a frigate during the Falklands conflict. There was no doubt that he was a competent seagoing officer, but his detractors saw him as vain and arrogant.

His protagonist, Beckwith, was a pacifist at heart. The academic ridiculed the naval officer as a tired old 'warhorse' and spiced his conversation with aphorisms such as 'lions being led by donkeys'. His contempt for the military boosted his popularity in left-wing circles, but it was foolish to underestimate the man.

The young executive had sought no part in their feud, but he had been press-ganged into a crazy caper to purloin the midget submarine nonetheless. The future of the boatyard depended on the success of the mission. The crazy operation had put his relationship with Jackie in jeopardy. There was also the possibility that he would face criminal charges.

The meeting with the plain-clothes detective later that evening might prove his undoing – it all depended on Jackie. Would the capricious landlady corroborate his story, or betray him? What if the observant plain-clothes detective learned about the fracas in his flat? It would not take him long to figure out what had really taken place. As he reflected on these matters, he felt an increasing sense of resentment at the smug attitude of the naval contingent. They had little to lose if the plot was uncovered, he reflected sourly, but his livelihood and freedom were at stake.

Chapter 21

Detective Smells a Rat

If Steve had bothered to speak to Peter Fellows on his return to the boatyard, it would have spared him a lot of heartache. The plain-clothed sleuth did not want to quiz him about the disappearance of the midget submarine. The sleuth wanted to ask his friend about some industrial waste that had been found at a fly-tipping site. There were signs that the waste was linked to the boatyard. The plain-clothes detective was not investigating the loss of the submarine.

There had been an outbreak of lawlessness over the weekend, and the police were overstretched. That was why the police chief wanted to leave the boatyard investigation to the military. It was only a sense of curiosity, and a long association with the boatyard, that led Peter Fellows to take an interest in the boatyard incident on Sunday. While not involved in the investigation, he retained a liaison role. But after being given the cold shoulder by the military police and the rogues' gallery gathered in Beckwith's office, the plain-clothes sleuth was investigating an apparently unrelated fly-tipping incident.

The incident had been reported at a disused quarry in Leighton Hollow in the early hours of Sunday morning, which was, by chance, shortly after the *Normandy* went missing from Whitebait Cove. No connection was noted between the two incidents, at first. A fly-tipping incident would not normally warrant the attentions of the police, but the overworked force took a particular interest in the disused quarry because a notorious gang of hoodlums used the secluded spot for their illicit activities. Among their many crimes, the gang was suspected of stealing valuable material from Steve's boatyard.

The prospect of nailing the Murphy gang had persuaded the police chief to deploy a forensic team to the fly-tipping site. The plain-clothes detective was keen to pursue this investigation. He was irked by his failure to convict the gang for the break-in at the boatyard and this was a chance to make amends. So he set off, early on Monday morning, in an ebullient frame of mind. When he arrived at the remote location, the forensic scientists were sifting through a pile of industrial waste that had been dumped over the weekend. They hoped to find clues that would finally allow him to convict the hoodlums.

Leighton Hollow was a deserted hamlet on the far shore of the Plymouth estuary. It was tucked away in rolling hills, in an area rarely visited by tourists, and was approached by a coastal road. The coastal road ran parallel with, but set back from, the shoreline. The land between road and the water's edge was designated as a nature reserve. Most of the land inland of the road belonged to the military and was used for training.

The hamlet had been evacuated during the war to provide a training area for the Normandy Invasion force. All that remained were the foundations of buildings. Many local people worked in the quarry, which lay abandoned. The quarried material was shipped from a jetty that remained in place. While the jetty had a ramshackle appearance, it was structurally sound and was used by the military from time to time.

The coastal road turned inland as it approached the deserted hamlet and then climbed a ridge that stretched back from a headland. A rough dirt track lane branched off the coastal road to the disused quarry and its jetty. The narrow entrance to the quarry lay on the right-hand side of the dirt track. High, rough-hewn walls surrounded a horseshoe depression of the quarry to conceal illicit activity. Further down the dirt track lane, a nondescript corrugated iron shed stood at the head of the jetty. The building was the only evidence of human occupation. The shed provided a base for management of the vast swathe of military land that lay inland and was used for gunnery practice.

The plain-clothes detective parked his car by the forlorn-looking structure while the forensic team were busy sifting evidence from a heap of industrial waste that had been dumped during the weekend in the horseshoe-shaped quarry. There was little he could do to help with the painstaking forensic work, so he sought out the range warden, who had reported suspicious activity in the early hours of Sunday morning. He found the warden in a shabby office, set in one corner of the corrugated iron shed.

"Morning, Harry," said the plain-clothes detective as he greeted his old friend. Their paths had crossed on many occasions, although the military training ground lay, technically, outside the jurisdiction of the local police. "It seems that the Murphy boys are up to their tricks again! Was it you who raised the alarm?"

"Yes. I phoned your lads," replied the range warden with a weary nod. "I thought that it might be an exercise. They sometimes organise a show without letting me know." The warden lived close by and his home had a fine view of the estuary, but the quarry was hidden from view by a ridge that ran inland from an intervening promontory.

"So, what made you suspicious?" asked the plain-clothes detective.

"It was the din they were making. They were behaving like a bunch of clowns," explained the warden with a frown. "Lights were blazing for anyone to see in the early hours of Sunday morning. It was all crash-bang-wallop. That's not like our guys. The squaddies behave in a disciplined manner. It kept me and the missus awake until the small hours. The gang didn't seem to care if anyone knew what they were up to."

"Why didn't you call in the red caps?" asked the plain-clothes detective, believing that the army should enforce the law on its own property.

"They are not really interested in what goes on here," replied the warden dejectedly. "They are too busy rounding up drunken servicemen in the city centre, in the early hours of Sunday morning."

"Don't suppose you could see what they were up to in the quarry?" asked the plain-clothes detective hopefully. The warden shook his head.

"You could have taken a look!" suggested the plain-clothes sleuth with a cheeky grin. This was a provocative suggestion. The last time the warden confronted intruders at this desolate spot, he had been assaulted and left injured. After the attack, he was left lying on the ground for thirty minutes while he waited for an ambulance to turn up.

The plain-clothes detective had been diligently recording all the range warden's comments in his notebook, and snapped it shut as he prepared to depart. "Is there anything else you can tell us?" he asked as an afterthought.

"Well, there were a couple of unusual things," replied the

warden as he sucked his lip in a thoughtful way. "The first was a ship acting rather strangely. The ship passed close to our house before all the hullabaloo kicked off last night. It was sailing outside the normal shipping channel."

"Can you describe the ship?" asked the plain-clothes detective in a methodical way as he reopened his notebook. This was a bit of a coincidence, given the disappearance of the *Normandy*. The detective's sleuthing instincts were awakened by this remark. It was remarkable that none of the military police had picked up on this piece of intelligence, he mused.

"Well, I'm no expert on ships," replied the warden uncertainly, "but it was a stubby little thing with its cabins all bunched up in the bow. There was some cargo on the rear deck, covered by a tarpaulin."

The detective was able to call up an image of the *Normandy* on the screen of his mobile phone. "Is that it?" he asked. It was an old image taken many years ago, showing the offshore supply vessel shortly after it was built.

"Yes, that sort of thing," replied the warden uncertainly. "I didn't get a good look, so I'm not absolutely sure. We watch a lot of ships passing up and down the estuary, but this one caught my attention because it strayed out of the normal shipping channel."

"Did it land at the jetty?" asked the detective hopefully.

"Can't be sure," replied the warden. "It might have done, but the jetty is hidden by that ridge over there, so I couldn't see it."

"You said there were two things," prompted the detective.

"Oh yes," replied the warden, after pausing for a moment to think. "I said that the intruders were making a real din – shouting and carrying on. But there was an odd noise and I didn't recognise it at first Then it occurred to me that someone might be using a power saw."

"Have you told anyone else about this?" asked the detective.

"No," replied the warden. "You are the first to ask me any questions."

"Do you mind keeping this under your hat for the time being?" begged the plain-clothes detective, who thought there was more to the sighting of the *Normandy* than met the eye. After bidding farewell to the range warden, the plain-clothes detective went to see how the forensic team were getting on. They were still sorting through the heap of industrial waste lying on the floor of the disused stone quarry. He made no mention of his conversation with the warden as he focussed his attention on finding evidence to convict the Murphy gang.

The forensic team were cock-a-hoop when they found paper documents linking the dumped material to the Murphy gang. But the precise source of the material was unclear. At first, it looked as though an industrial boiler had been broken up for scrap. But as they sorted through the rubbish, the boffins became increasingly confident that the material was related to one of the scrap metal thefts that had been reported in the area. There were signs that the villains had been disturbed while sorting the stolen material because some valuable copper pipes, couplings and an unusual diverter valve were left behind. The diverter valve had a serial number that could be traced.

Strange metal chips were later found embedded in the mud and this led one of the boffins to speculate that the power saw had been used to cut a large metal structure into manageable chunks. This confirmed the range warden's observation, but the plain-clothes detective chose to keep that knowledge to himself for the time being. Peter Fellows had taken a particular interest in the scrap metal thefts since the Whitebait Cove break-in. So, on the off-chance that the usual diverter valve could be traced back to one of these incidents, he sneaked a look in the evidence bag. He noted down details of the unusual component while the forensic guys were taking a break.

As soon as the plain-clothes sleuth arrived back in the police station, he phoned the maker of the diverter valve and was amazed to learn that it was supplied to the boatyard at Whitebait Cove. This crazy coincidence was a major breakthrough and cause for celebration. It also cast doubt on the industrial boiler theory, as speculated by the forensic guys. It was at that point that the plain-clothes sleuth set off for the boatyard to find out more of the history of the unusual valve. That was why he wanted to talk to Steve, who had access to the firm's records. All this also pointed to some connection with the disappearance of the midget submarine.

With this hot lead, the plain-clothes detective arrived at the boatyard shortly after lunch, when the sleuth was disappointed to learn that the young chief executive had not arrived for work. This was a huge disappointment. He had no desire to discuss his findings with the military investigator or with Beckwith's cronies, who had given him the cold shoulder the previous day. So he kicked his heels in the office foyer waiting for his friend to return. Then to add to his frustration, Steve gave him the brush-off. It was only with reluctance that the young guy agreed to meet the plain-clothes detective in the Feathers.

With exciting news to impart, the plain-clothes detective felt peeved as he killed time waiting for the evening meeting in the Feathers. With nothing else to occupy him at the boatyard, he returned to the police station in a sour mood. Here, he leafed idly through incident reports for the past weekend, and was intrigued to find a report about a man who had been injured during a fracas inside Steve's apartment building, in the early hours of Sunday morning.

This incident pricked his curiosity and led the plain-clothes sleuth to reflect on his friend's wayward behaviour. The sleuth realised that he had become so obsessed with his mission to nail the Murphy gang, that he had lost sight of the strange events at the boatyard, so he took out his notebook to refresh his memory. The most recent entry concerned the range warden's sighting of the *Normandy* close to Leighton Hollow.

On the face of it, that did not prove anything. After all, the *Normandy* would have to pass that headland to arrive at the anchorage where it was discovered on Sunday morning. So the sighting did not add much to their knowledge of the ship's movements. But why had the ship strayed outside the main shipping channel? Had it really berthed at the rickety old jetty? As he pondered that possibility, his mind drifted to the inconsistencies in Steve's story about the fishing trip. *What is Steve up to?* he mused as he waited impatiently for the evening meeting.

Peter Fellows had arranged to meet Steve at seven o'clock. So, with plenty of time to spare, he wandered round to the apartment block where Steve lived. This was, after all, only a short detour on his route to the pub. After talking to some of Steve's neighbours, he headed on to the Feathers where he read the paper and enjoyed a pint of real ale while waiting for his friend to arrive. The plain-clothes sleuth normally looked forward to these interludes, but on this occasion his pleasure was marred by the offhand reception he received from the landlady, who slopped beer into his glass in a hostile manner.

As a serving police officer, he was not the most popular regular in the pub, but he was usually greeted warmly nonetheless. The immaculately made-up landlady normally had a twinkle in her eye. The plain-clothes sleuth was envious of Steve's close relationship with the petite blonde. But that night, the landlady looked tired; her make-up had the garish look of a washed-up entertainer. All this led the plain-clothes detective to suspect that her washed-out appearance had something to do with the fracas at Steve's flat.

Although he was aware of inconsistencies over the fishing trip story, the sleuth had not yet joined up all the dots. It had not yet occurred to him that Steve might be involved with the disappearance of the midget submarine, or that he was in league with the foxy landlady. That was too far-fetched for him to contemplate.

Steve regretted accepting the invitation to meet the plain-clothes detective in the Feathers, fearing that Jackie would let the cat out of the bag. He considered wheedling his way out of the meeting but dismissed the thought, knowing that it would only create more suspicion. His sense of foreboding was intensified by the weather. It was a stormy day, so he popped home to collect a raincoat before setting off on the final leg of the journey to the Feathers on foot.

When Steve stepped into the bar, it was clear that Jackie was seething with rage about the way she had been treated by their gang. While the bedraggled figure stood dripping rainwater onto the copper bar, the petite landlady pointedly ignored him and chatted in an animated, but forced, way with another customer. The bar staff followed her lead and gave the young guy a cool reception.

Jackie made a barely perceptible signal and one of her staff sidled over to serve the unwanted visitor, who had been left standing like an outcast. Steve's order for low-alcohol lager was served in a grudging manner. To compound Steve's discomfort, his order was met with disdainful looks from the real-ale buffs assembled at the other end of the bar. The young executive had to watch his alcohol intake because he was driving his sports car later that evening. Jackie watched this cruel scene with a spiteful expression as she cosied up to her newly favoured customer.

Steve was relieved when he spotted the detective nursing his pint, sitting at a corner table. He was glad to escape the icy reception at the bar as he carried his glass over to the table. But it was like jumping from the frying pan into the fire because he now faced the sleuth's probing questions. But he did have one card up his sleeve. In accepting the invitation, Steve warned that he was visiting some friends later that evening. This provided an excuse to duck out if the going got tough.

Sitting quietly in the corner, the detective, meanwhile, pretended to read his newspaper as he watched all these shenanigans out of the corner of his eye. The frosty reception confirmed his suspicions that Jackie was involved in the commotion at Steve's flat in one way or another. The plain-clothes detective knew that Steve was jealous of Jackie's many admirers.

One plausible explanation was that Steve had concocted the fishing trip story so that he could spy on his unfaithful female friend. Jackie might have found out about it. That would explain why the petite landlady had treated the young guy in such a cold manner. But he intended to tread lightly. After all, it was a delicate personal issue, and he did not wish to upset his pal too much.

"Strange goings-on at your yard yesterday," observed the detective in a laconic way, as Steve removed his dripping raincoat. The detective could hardly ignore the incident, but that was not what he really wanted to talk about. "My boss has told me to steer clear and leave the investigation to the red caps." The wily sleuth watched his friend as he settled down at the table, curious to know what was really going on.

Steve mumbled something incoherent. He made a big show of shaking his raincoat to hide his embarrassment at being snubbed at the bar. "I think your boss is right," he declared at length, as he took his seat alongside his old friend. "It sounds like a typical military foul up. People have got their wires crossed somewhere along the line. Beckwith seems to think that the navy took his midget submarine away for some more sea trials." Steve did not want to be drawn into the debate. He was walking on eggshells, not wanting to deceive his friend about his nefarious activities at the weekend.

"Yes. I saw the note," replied the sleuth in a cryptic way, as he tried to gauge his friend's reaction. "But I don't believe it." The detective wondered why his friend had swallowed Beckwith's 'bureaucratic snafu' story. After all, the two men were hardly close friends. Instead of replying, the young executive made a great show of flapping his rain-soaked overcoat to hide his discomfort.

"There is another story doing the rounds," speculated the detective in an attempt to smoke out the truth. "Some people think it's an insurance scam. There is a rumour that he cannot afford to pay his contractors and that the navy doesn't want to charter his submersible. If that's true, then he is up the creek without a paddle, but an insurance claim would solve his problems."

Sensing a trap, Steve poured water on that notion, hoping to put a stop to the debate. "That sounds pretty far-fetched," he replied in an offhand way. "I'm not Beckwith's greatest fan, but I doubt that he would stoop to that!"

It was a great relief to the young executive when his friend changed tack. "Anyway, thanks for coming – I can see you are busy!" remarked the plain-clothes detective as he got down to business. "There was another reason why I wanted to talk to you. Do you remember the Murphy gang? We think they broke into your boatyard. Well, we've been on their trail for years. We think they are responsible for a whole spate of scrap metal thefts."

Steve nodded eagerly, relieved that they had moved onto safer ground. "Yes. I remember. Why are you telling me?" he replied. "I remember that you suspected the Murphy gang but could not prove it."

"Well, we had a bit of a breakthrough," declared the detective triumphantly. "The range warden at Leighton Hollow noticed some suspicious activity on Saturday night. The land is used by the military for live firing exercises, so it is strictly out of bounds to the public." The plain-clothes detective went on to describe his visit to Leighton Hollow that morning. At first, Steve found the words reassuring because it suggested that the police had fallen for the phony scrap metal story, which was part of their cover-up plan.

But as the conversation progressed, the young executive became uneasy; it was a reminder that his friend was a relentless, terrier-like investigator. Steve recalled his friend's furious outburst when he learned that the prosecution had been abandoned. "I will nail those buggers before I retire, even if it kills me," declared the sleuth at that news. This raised fears that in his relentless pursuit, the plain-clothes detective would discover what had really taken place at the weekend.

"How do you know it's the Murphy gang?" asked Steve innocently, to muddy the waters.

"The fly-tipping incident has got all the hallmarks of those villains," replied the detective decisively. The detective's cheeks flushed red as he relished the forthcoming battle with the thuggish gang. "They got the better of us last time, but this time we'll nail them!"

"Why are you telling me?" asked Steve lamely. The young executive was starting to regret their half-baked efforts to deceive the investigators. He was also feeling guilty about their crazy escapade at the weekend. He had no wish to get on the wrong side of the plain-clothes detective, particularly when he was roused. The guilt he felt left him with a dry throat.

"We've been keeping an eye on the army training ground for months because the Murphy gang uses the disused quarry for illicit activities," continued the detective in an unstoppable tirade. After kicking his heels all afternoon, the detective needed to let off steam. "Well, our efforts have paid off! The range warden reported a rumpus in the early hours of Sunday morning. At first, we thought the gang was fly-tipping. But now we think they were cutting up a large steel structure into manageable chunks, for easier disposal."

"There were signs that the gang were disturbed before they finished the job, and so they left some evidence behind. Our forensic boys have been sifting through a pile of waste, looking for clues as to where it came from. They are trying to track down the history of bits and pieces they found," continued the detective. "It might just give us what we need to nail the rascals."

"We found a diverter valve among a tangle of pipes, couplings and bits and bobs. It was an unusual item and I made a note of the maker's name and serial number. The forensic team also found chips of some unusual material – not the sort of material that you would expect to find in industrial waste. The chips are being analysed in the lab."

"That's interesting, but why are you telling me?" asked Steve nervously. He was becoming increasingly alarmed by the detective's gung-ho attitude towards the investigation.

"Our forensic people work slowly – it's like watching paint dry!" explained the detective in an excitable manner. Then seeing that real-ale buffs were listening to their conversation, the plain-clothes detective moderated his tone. "Anyway, I phoned up the valve maker to speed things up," he continued in a hushed voice. "Please keep this under your hat. It's contrary to our procedures and could land me in hot water.

"They told me that the diverter valve was supplied to *your boatyard*. That was a real coup! So, I need to find out what the valve was used for. If it's part of the haul the gang stole when they broke into your yard, we might have the evidence to prosecute them."

"Sounds like a good lead!" said Steve with feigned enthusiasm. In a way, it was good news because it showed the police had picked up on the trail of false clues that had been planted at the disused quarry. But in laying the false clues, they had failed to take account of the detective's obsession with scrap metal theft. Steve wondered how long it would take the wily sleuth to figure out what had really taken place. There was the fracas at his flat to worry about. With deception upon deception, Steve bitterly regretted deceiving an old friend.

"It would be really helpful if you could tell me what the diverter valve was used for and when it was supplied to the yard. It will save me going through the normal rigmarole," continued the plain-clothes sleuth in a more moderate manner. At that point, the sleuth retrieved a slip of paper from his pocket that carried the details of the diverter valve, and handed it to Steve.

"That could take a few days," replied Steve disingenuously as he played for time. "I will get someone to check our records and get back to you." In truth, Steve knew the valve's history perfectly well. The diverter valve had been planted during their late-night caper, as part of a false trail of clues.

Although the plain-clothes detective spoke about the Murphy gang in an excitable way, he had other thoughts on his mind. In a cool, almost unconscious way, he was observing his friend's reaction to their conversation. There was a reason for this. He was curious to see whether his pal would raise the subject of the fracas at his flat, or try to conceal it. The wily sleuth knew that Steve was up to something and he intended to play his cards close to his chest until he knew what was really going on.

In the belief that he had fulfilled his side of the bargain, Steve wanted to slip away before he revealed anything incriminating. "Well, if that's all you wanted, then I'll be on my way," he remarked.

But before he could escape, he was waylaid. As he prepared to rise to his feet, the detective leaned towards him. "Something you need to know. Beckwith has hired a private detective to track down his submarine!" whispered the detective conspiratorially.

After thanking his friend for the tip-off, Steve returned his glass to the bar. The kind gesture was repaid with a venomous stare from the petite landlady. It was obvious that she was still seething with resentment. The detective watched the little drama from behind his newspaper. "Mind how you go. We don't want to see you in A&E!" remarked the detective as Steve returned for his coat. Relieved to escape an interrogation, and tired from the weekend's escapade, the young executive failed to see anything sinister in the remark.

After successfully negotiating what could have been a dicey situation, Steve waltzed from the Feathers with the light tread of a reprieved man. The meeting had gone much better than he anticipated. Jackie had not betrayed him, and the plain-clothes detective had not asked him any awkward questions about the disappearance of the submarine. He naively assumed the strange farewell remark was friendly advice to wrap up against the stormy weather, so he felt quite chipper. It was only later that the undertones of the remark came back to haunt him.

After leaving the plain-clothes detective reading the paper in the Feathers, Steve drove to Mark's home where he had been invited for an evening meal. He wanted to see Mark to make sure they were all singing from 'the same hymn sheet'. They needed to get their story straight about their imaginary fishing trip to Scotland. When he arrived at the family home, he was disconcerted to find that Anne was staying with her brother. This made things a bit awkward at first, but Lucy managed to smooth things over.

After a pleasant evening, Steve drove home and began to see light at the end of the tunnel, for the first time in many weeks. After sleeping soundly, he ate a hearty breakfast. *Things are going our way at last,* he thought as he munched the scrambled eggs on well-buttered toast. That was a rare, if unhealthy, treat. *We have acquired the submarine and that will unlock finance for the boatyard,* he mused, with considerable satisfaction. The dredging business presented an exciting new challenge.

But Steve's sense of well-being evaporated when he bumped into his nosy neighbour as she slouched outside the front door, puffing on a rolled-up fag. Still dressed in a tatty dressing gown and slippers, the old woman spoke to him in a low, husky voice of a smoker, with a harsh working-class accent. She made a habit of waylaying people as they passed by her flat on the ground floor. The self-appointed 'gatekeeper' managed to combine an earthy humour with prudish morals when she conversed with her fellow residents.

Steve was used to her tirades about unruly neighbours, overflowing bins, noisy parties and other matters that troubled her. It was never an easy passage. In high spirits, on this occasion, Steve trotted out rehearsed patter about his fishing trip as he tried to inch his way towards the sanctuary of his sports car. But the old woman stood steadfast, barring his way. "We had some excitement on Sunday morning, you know," declared the busybody. "An ambulance was called and some fellow was taken off to A&E!"

"Yes. Jackie told me," replied Steve with a boyish grin as he tried to edge further down the path. This was a delicate subject and he did not want to be drawn into discussion of the affair.

"Did she tell you the police came around yesterday morning asking questions?" she added with a sly glint in her eye. That stopped Steve in his tracks and caused him to recall the plain-clothes detective's apparently friendly remark about A&E.

"Did the police officer give his name?" asked Steve, adopting a more sympathetic demeanour in a vain attempt to butter up the old dear. The old woman grimaced as she searched her memory.

"He did give a name – but I've forgotten it. My memory is not what it was!" replied the old busybody with a chuckle. "It was a funny name – like that posh bloke who wrote a TV programme about a country house."

"Fellows?" suggested Steve with a sinking heart.

"That's it!" replied the old woman with the triumphant expression of someone who had just passed a gallstone. "Julian Fellowes! No, that's the writer. But something like that. Nice chap, though. I invited him in for a cup of tea." That seemingly innocent remark was like a punch in the gut to the young executive. Steve knew that a 'cup of tea' with the old woman tended to involve a long diatribe about problems in the apartment block. It meant that the detective would be aware of the character of his fellow residents.

More worryingly, it also meant the detective was aware of the fracas, and raised a question about why he had not raised the subject during their, apparently, friendly conversation in the Feathers. Could it be that the plain-clothes detective suspected that Steve was lying about the fishing trip? If that was the case, it would not take the wily sleuth long to work out what had really taken place over the weekend.

When he finally reached his sports car, Steve's optimism was replaced by deep foreboding. His future, and that of the boatyard, was in jeopardy if the plain-clothes detective found out that he was responsible for the disappearance of the submarine. That would imperil the cash injection to the boatyard at the very least. That would be a disaster. The cash flow problems had become even more severe with the end of the sea trial that had been funded by the navy, but it raised even greater concerns. Steve might face criminal charges, for all he knew.

In the meantime, the young executive faced the unpalatable task of dismissing a number of loyal employees. This was a tough job at the best of times, but he was exhausted after the weekend caper. On top of everything else, the young executive needed to set up a dredging business. It was becoming clear that their plans were unravelling. The plain-clothes detective was on their trail. Steve's worried demeanour when he arrived at the boatyard did, at least, support the story that he was suffering from ill health.

Locked away in his office, the young executive reflected on his predicament. His situation made him intensely angry. Steve had never been enthusiastic about the plot to purloin the midget submarine, believing that the whole matter could have been handled in a grown-up way. He had been pressganged into joining the foolhardy mission. *That IS water under the bridge*, he told himself. He had to work out how he could extract himself from the mire.

The plan to purloin the midget submarine had been devised by the Admiral with the help of the commander and his accountant, Felix. The master plan incorporated some crafty moves to deceive investigators. The first wheeze was the phony transfer document that was left at the guard hut. The aim of that was to delay and confuse the investigators.

That part of the plan had worked better than anticipated. The investigators had been distracted by the document and persuaded to scale back the investigation.

The second wheeze was to lay a trail of false clues, leading investigators to believe that the midget submarine had been landed at Leighton Hollow, where it had been broken up for scrap. The false clues were designed to suggest that the Murphy gang were responsible for this act of desecration. On the face of it, this had been successful. The plain-clothes detective was already asking about the history of the diverter valve found in the pile of waste. His investigation would show that the valve could be directly linked to the midget submarine.

So, looked at from the navy's perspective, everything seemed to be fine. But the navy plan did not take account of the vagaries of civilian life. Looked at from Steve's perspective, the plan was unravelling fast. His fears centred round the fracas that had taken place in his flat and the risk that Jackie might betray them in revenge for the shabby treatment she had received from the naval contingent.

It was now clear that his friend, the plain-clothes detective, knew about the fracas in his flat in the early hours of Sunday morning. With his ear to the ground, it would not take him long to piece together what had really taken place. So, with the plans starting to disintegrate, Steve needed to take some steps to halt the rot. He needed to speak to Commander Woods as soon as possible. In a phone call, they agreed to a meeting beside Drake's statue on Plymouth Hoe later that evening.

The commander did not visit the Plymouth naval base very often, so when he did, he made a pilgrimage to the Hoe, to reflect on naval history. On this occasion, the decorated war hero reflected on Drake's victory over the *Armada*. This was a topical subject because papers had recently been unearthed to suggest that the Spanish fleet was defeated because the nobleman in charge refused to disobey instructions from the king of Spain. Drake, on the other hand, was free to adapt his plans to suit the unusual weather conditions.

As the commander pondered this subject, he started to appreciate why the Admiral adopted a *laissez faire* approach. In his campaign to acquire the midget submarine, the old fox gave his subordinates freedom to follow their instincts. This approach to naval life was an anathema to the more traditionally minded naval officers, but it had been successful on this occasion. They had achieved their objective.

The commander believed the mission had gone smoothly. The midget submarine was now hidden in an abandoned naval base near Portland Bill, while the bewildered military police were floundering around trying to figure out whether a transfer document was genuine. Given the success of the mission, the war hero was puzzled as to why Steve wanted to see him.

From what the commander had heard, Steve had not distinguished himself during the late-night escapade. To make matters worse, the young executive had got into a scrap with the disgraced artificer. When he added it all up, the commander suspected that Steve was getting cold feet. The commander's disdainful view was reinforced when his young friend arrived looking tired and nervy.

It was hardly surprising that Steve looked worried. The plot was unravelling because of his fragile relationship with Jackie. This made things particularly difficult because Steve had no wish to discuss his personal affairs with the unsympathetic father figure. So he faced a difficult conversation. The pair greeted each other rather coolly as they stepped out across the parade ground to admire the harbour.

Leaning on the stone balustrade, they looked an unlikely pair. The commander wore a formal three-piece suit, with a blue serge overcoat, while the young executive was stylishly dressed in jeans and a leather jacket. As the pair watched a frigate glide by, the older man explained how the clean sloping surfaces of the warship were designed to reduce its radar profile.

While Steve braced himself to tackle some sensitive issues, the commander pontificated about the problems these 'all-electric' warships suffered. It was a topical subject at the time. The problems had been aired by the Commons Defence Committee a few weeks earlier. After this small talk, Steve broached the sensitive issues that worried him. "Did you hear about the trouble at my flat on Sunday morning?" he mumbled awkwardly.

The young executive would have preferred to sweep the whole incident under the carpet, but that was not possible because the plain-clothes detective knew what had taken place. He had no choice but to admit the whole messy affair to this unsympathetic father figure.

"Yes," replied the commander with a broad smile. "Anne told me all about your brawl when she phoned me." This was disingenuous. News of the brawl had, in fact, spread like wildfire around the Plymouth naval base. As it happened, the commander was somewhat impressed that the diminutive young executive had prevailed against the burly artificer. He saw nothing unusual in this sort of behaviour for any red-blooded male.

"Well, I didn't want to mention it," said Steve, "but it is going to cause us problems."

The commander did not think that a petty squabble between members of the boarding party would have any bearing on the success of their mission. "*Why?*" enquired the war hero sharply.

"One of the police detectives knows that the artificer was injured in my flat," replied Steve.

"Was that the chap who was hanging around in the foyer of your office?" asked the war hero disdainfully. The commander was contemptuous of the police, feeling that the modern force was a bunch of softies, obsessed with political correctness.

"Yes. His name is Peter Fellows and he's a good friend," explained Steve. He went on to tell the commander about the dealings he had had with the plain-clothes detectives during the break-in at the boatyard. "Don't be fooled by his laid-back appearance," concluded Steve.

"He is a tenacious investigator. A real terrier!"

"How did he find out?" asked the commander absent-mindedly as he stood admiring the view and sniffing the sea air with a look of contentment. He was not unduly concerned about this piece of tittle-tattle.

"The hospital reports suspicious injuries to the local police," explained Steve doggedly. "It's routine procedure."

"Does the detective know that you caused the injury?" asked the commander as he began to take the matter seriously. After all, Steve's involvement in the brawl would blow a hole in his cover story about the fishing trip to Scotland.

"No. The detective doesn't know that I was involved, and I doubt the artificer will point the finger," replied Steve.

"So, what are you worried about?" retorted the commander magisterially as he reverted to his musings about naval history.

"The brawl is not our only problem," grumbled Steve in a hangdog way. "The detective is also investigating reports of suspicious activity at Leighton Hollow in the early hours of Sunday morning. It won't take him long to put two and two together." Steve then embarked on a description of the detective's dogged character and his fragile relationship with Jackie.

The commander did not pay too much attention to the tittle-tattle. As far as he was concerned, their team were in possession of the midget submarine, and the young executive would receive his investment. So what was his problem? Of course, there would be some fall-out from their weekend mission. But it was unlikely that they would get into trouble, provided they all stuck to their stories. There was no point in worrying until things happened. So, while Steve bleated on, his mind was elsewhere.

As he stared out into the harbour, the commander began to ruminate, once again, about Drake's victory over the *Armada*. One lesson from that battle was that subordinates should be free to adapt plans to suit the circumstances, he mused. "Look, Steve," he remarked at length, in an effort to console his highly strung companion, "I can see that you are worried about all manner of 'what-ifs'. So, just tell me what you think we should do to solve the problem."

Glad that he had finally got the attention of his distinguished friend, Steve laid out a plan that he had been hatching for some time. "I want to confide in the detective and explain what we are up to," said Steve firmly.

The commander did not like that at all. "Can we trust him?" he asked sharply. This question would not have been necessary if the commander had bothered to pay attention to his young friend's lengthy diatribe about the detective's virtues.

"He's a good friend and wants to work at the boatyard when he retires from the police force," replied Steve earnestly. "*I trust him*. He does not care too much about promotion, unlike the rest of the bunch of jobsworths who work in CID. He has been helpful in the past and cleared up some problems – petty theft, vandalism and such like. He appears relaxed, but he does not miss anything and can be as tenacious as a terrier. He keeps nagging away at a problem until he solves the case. A bit like Wycliffe." The reference to a TV detective from a bygone era reflected the nostalgic taste in television they both shared.

"You say that he might join you at the boatyard. Can you offer him a job on the condition that he keeps his mouth shut?" said the commander bluntly.

"He's still got six or eight months to serve in the police force before he is eligible for his pension, so he has to keep his nose clean," replied Steve cautiously. "I don't think that he would be influenced by the offer of a job. One thing drives him. He is determined to arrest the Murphy gang before he retires." Steve did not want to overplay his hand. There were risks in confiding in the plain-clothes detective and risks if they did not. So, in reality, it was a no-win situation.

"It would be a serious mistake to deceive him," concluded Steve forcefully. "You've seen how quickly he learned of the incident in my flat. He did not say anything about that when we met at the Feathers. He plays his cards close to his chest. I have no idea what else he knows. If we try to fool him, he could side with Beckwith and that would land us in a real mess!"

The commander knew that Steve was a reluctant member of their team and that their efforts would be undone if Martin Beckwith discovered what they were up to. But he also looked at their escapade from the somewhat blinkered viewpoint of a naval campaign.

"I think you are too worried," remarked the commander in a somewhat more conciliatory tone. "We may have bent the rules a bit, it's true, but we have acted in good faith and not done anything seriously illegal. The truth is that our friend Beckwith has more to lose than we do. After all, he was responsible for the security of the *Normandy* when it went missing.

The commander did not believe it wise to confide in a serving police officer and suspected that the young executive had got cold feet. It was also possible that Steve's friendship with the detective had swayed his judgement. But recalling lessons from the *Armada*, he decided to hand the matter over to his superior officer. "Look, I'm not comfortable with your idea – but let's see what the Admiral thinks," he conceded grudgingly.

The commander put Steve's proposal to the Admiral when he returned to his naval base in Portsmouth the following day, but his garbled account of their discussion on the Hoe did not convey the subtle points that Steve had made. This did not trouble the old fox, who was well informed about what was going on and was able to read between the lines. His immediate reaction was that the young executive had jumped the gun.

Unknown to Steve, or the commander, the Admiral was working behind the scenes on a scheme that would allow them to claim legal ownership of the midget submarine. But the plan called for stealth and patience. They all had to hold their nerve and wait for the plan to reach fruition. When quizzed about the plan, the Admiral rubbed his nose and mumbled in a barely audible way that 'possession is nine-tenths of the law' with a crafty expression, and no further explanation.

During their conversation, the commander reminded the Admiral of the lesson from Drake's victory over the *Armada*. "It's important to allow your subordinates freedom of action," he declared. The old boy was swayed by this. But he was still reluctant to confide in the local police force and so he set out certain provisos. "Steve can confide in his friendly detective about the dredging operation, provided that he does *not* mention the midget submarine," declared the old fox.

The commander added another caveat when he passed on the Admiral's instructions to the young executive. "I've spoken to the Admiral and he's happy for you to confide in your friendly detective, but he does not want you to tell him the whole story," remarked the commander. "You can tell him about the undercover dredging operation but do *not* mention the midget submarine. One more thing. The Admiral thinks that you should offer the guy a job with the dredging company, rather than the boatyard."

The commander had dreamed up this restriction by himself but thought that the suggestion would carry more weight if it were attributed to the Admiral. It was one of the most sensible contributions that the old warhorse made to their plans because it provided a plausible reason for inviting the plain-clothes detective to visit Steve's dredging business in Torquay. It would also explain why they wanted him to keep his mouth shut.

Although Steve felt hamstrung by the restrictions, he reluctantly agreed to comply. So he invited the plain-clothes detective to the dredging office on the following Friday, when he was due to brief his former shipmates. This would allow him to explain the undercover role of the dredging business to the plain-clothes detective and to his old shipmates at the same time. It would allow him to kill two birds with one stone.

By this time, Steve was having difficulty dealing with all the deception. The joint meeting would save time and ensure that they all received the same story, but the briefing would be a delicate task to handle. To complicate matters, Steve feared that his former shipmates would be unsettled by the presence of a serving police officer. They were already nervous about the undercover nature of the operation, and this might be the straw that broke the camel's back.

When he phoned Peter Fellows the next day, Steve asked whether his friend wanted to work in his new business venture when he retired from the police force. But he did not make a firm promise. The plain-clothes detective was hesitant. The prospect of a new job in the future was not enough in itself to persuade the detective to take a day off work, but it was a chance to find out what his pal was up to. So, after mulling it over, he accepted the offer, to satisfy his curiosity.

"I would appreciate it if you would keep quiet about my new business venture for the time being," begged Steve when the detective accepted the invitation. "The yard workers are worried about their jobs as it is, and we will have a riot on our hands if they get wind that I'm setting up another business." He then passed on the information that the detective requested.

"By the way, that diverter valve you found at Leighton Hollow was fitted to the midget submarine that went missing over the weekend," remarked Steve, in a matter-of-fact way.

"We checked our records and it was definitely fitted to the submarine. Bit of a coincidence!" The remark was met with astonished silence.

"That's *really* interesting," replied the startled detective at length. "I wonder how it got to Leighton Hollow."

There was a small snag with the proposed meeting because the plain-clothes detective was unable to use a police vehicle for an unofficial journey. So Peter Fellows asked his friend to pick him up from the mainline railway station at around ten o'clock. This suited Steve fine because the car journey would give him an opportunity to win over his pal before facing his truculent shipmates.

Steve needed an ally because the pair were proving a bit of a handful. He hoped they had used the week to produce constructive proposals for the embryonic dredging business, but he was not overly optimistic. The pair had seemed rebellious when he left them after the stormy meeting on Monday. The presence of the detective would stir up more discontent, no doubt.

Steve's startling information about the diverter valve

was an intriguing development in the case of the missing submarine. Curious to follow up the lead, Peter Fellows paid another visit to the range warden, to see what else he could tell him about the events in the early hours of Sunday morning. The range warden greeted him cheerfully.

"Got your man?" quipped the warden teasingly. The pair both shared the hope that the fly-tipping waste would yield up clues to prosecute the Murphy gang.

"No, bit of a setback," replied the plain-clothes detective dejectedly. "It's a bit more complicated than we anticipated."

"Why is that?" asked the range warden.

"Remember the ship you told me about?" asked the plain-clothes detective. "You said it was behaving in a strange way." The detective waited as the warden searched his memory. The range warden had not given the matter much thought since their conversation on Monday.

"You mean the ship that strayed out of the normal shipping channel on Saturday night?" queried the range warden.

"Yes, that's the one," replied the plain-clothes detective. "Is there a possibility that it landed its cargo at the jetty?"

"It could have done," replied the range warden, who was slightly irritated at having to run over the same old ground. "There was something stowed under a tarpaulin on the rear deck, as I told you before. But I didn't see the ship again, so I don't know whether the cargo was unloaded. It's not possible to see the jetty from my house, so I can't really help you. Why is it so important?"

"Well, we found a component in the fly-tipped waste that was fitted to a midget submarine that was stowed on the rear deck of the *Normandy*," explained the detective.

"The midget submarine has gone missing, so we wondered whether it was offloaded at the jetty."

"You've lost a submarine?" remarked the range warden in

a jocular manner, hooting with laughter at the incredulous suggestion.

"It's a long story!" replied the embarrassed plain-clothes detective, who did not want to be drawn into speculation about the bizarre incident. "But please let me know if you can think of anything else that you saw that night."

"All sounds mysterious!" observed the range warden, with suppressed mirth.

Chapter 22

A Botched Investigation

While Steve was agonising over his predicament, Martin Beckwith was facing a crisis of his own. The disappearance of the midget submarine was acutely embarrassing, and it focussed unwelcome attention on his dodgy dealings. To add to his woes, his enemies were spreading a rumour that he was engaged in an insurance fraud. While he bolstered his defences against this onslaught, the artful academic took shelter in his Whitehall bunker, but he received little sympathy from others in the office building.

In the immediate aftermath of the heist, Beckwith did his best to encourage the view that the disappearance of the midget submarine was a bureaucratic 'snafu'. This deception was made possible by an official-looking document found lying in the guard hut. The document seemed to contain orders for the submarine to be moved to another naval base. The academic knew the document was false, but it suited his purpose to pretend otherwise. This provided a window of opportunity to track down and recover the missing submarine.

The academic was certain that the navy trials team had purloined the submarine; the team were, after all, familiar with the *Normandy* and its cargo. *They were most likely acting on orders from Commander Woods*, he concluded, so it should be quite easy to track down the missing craft. After all, the *Normandy* was found moored just a few miles down the estuary and there were only a handful of potential landing sites.

But the military police were no help in this endeavour, because they were chasing their tails, trying to find the source of the official-looking document. This suited the artful academic because it diverted them from his dodgy dealings. So he was caught up in a web of lies and deception of his own making. To resolve this conundrum, the academic sought assistance from a private detective, provided by one of his cronies; a lawyer called Jason Tyrone. The lawyer maintained a pool of ex-police officers to investigate war crimes in long-forgotten overseas campaigns. It so happened that the lawyer was familiar with the submarine project and Beckwith's feud with the navy.

This plan started well enough when Beckwith phoned shortly after Sunday lunch to ask for Tyrone's help in tracking down the submarine. The phone call was well timed because the lawyer had just returned from sharing a lunch engagement with a female colleague. The pair shared a love of fine dining. The legal colleagues had shared a meal of slow-roast pork with roasted vegetables, accompanied by Chilean red wine. The main course was followed by a deconstructed rhubarb crumble and custard.

When Tyrone answered the phone call, he was savouring the perfectly cooked food and was in an unusually mellow and benevolent frame of mind. The lawyer sympathised as his friend provided a slanted version of the events that had taken place that weekend. "After all my efforts to provide the navy with a groundbreaking new submarine, one ignorant old warhorse sets out to undermine me!" he whined. "The sea trials were a complete success. Far better than anyone expected. But do they show appreciation? No! Instead, they kick me in the bollocks!

"That old warhorse resents my ability. He is determined to prevent me from demonstrating the submarine to naval top brass, so he arranged for his trials team to commandeer the new submarine. They have probably hidden it somewhere in the estuary. The commander has tried to obstruct us at every turn, so the demonstration would have been a huge embarrassment for that old dinosaur."

In a mellow mood after his lavish lunch, Tyrone found it an amusing tale, even though it sounded a bit far-fetched. "Surely that's a matter for the military police!" he replied jovially.

"They are useless!" replied Beckwith peevishly, knowing that his friend shared his jaundiced view of the armed forces. "They have even accused me of stealing my own creation!" It was a shared antipathy towards the military that created a bond between the two like-minded men.

British troops had mistreated members of Tyrone's family during the Irish Troubles and the lawyer would never forgive them for it. The bullying behaviour of the soldiers towards his brother had inspired the lawyer to prosecute wrongdoing in other theatres of war. But his agency was restricted to long-forgotten conflicts, and the lawyer had ambitions to take on higher-profile cases in Iraq and Afghanistan. In the back of his mind, Tyrone hoped that Beckwith would use his political influence to help him expand his agency. If he could show that the navy had misbehaved at Whitebait Cove, the academic would have to return the favour.

"As it happens, I can send a man down tomorrow," offered Tyrone in a grand gesture after his sumptuous lunch. "You know that my wings have been clipped by some right-wing headbangers who feel sorry for their chums in the armed forces, but I do have a spare man on my books." The lawyer was referring to a pool of investigators. These (mostly) retired policemen were available for overseas assignments at short notice.

The gesture was made in alcohol-fuelled bravado and Tyrone began to have second thoughts as he sobered up. When he woke with a clear head the following day, he bitterly regretted his recklessness. The magnitude of his folly became clear when he discovered that his friend no longer wielded political influence. There was also a practical problem, because he was unable to provide an investigator until the middle of the week, at the very earliest.

Tyrone was reluctant to admit his mistake, so he instructed his secretary to field his friend's increasingly frantic phone calls. In trying to fob off his old pal, the lawyer only made matters worse. The stalling tactic only served to further enrage the academic. So, when they spoke on Tuesday afternoon, his friend was primed to explode. By that time, Beckwith's behaviour was a hot topic of gossip among the bright young crowd who gossiped in the reception area outside Beckwith's cubbyhole.

Beckwith's spartan, neon-lit cell opened onto the dowdy reception area on the third floor of the crumbling, stone-clad, colonial-style building. The reception area was a hive of activity in the morning, but it came to resemble a social club when senior officials set off for their long luncheon engagements. With little work to occupy the young folk during the afternoon, the reception became a nest of gossips. To this bright young crowd, the disappearance of the midget submarine was a source of amusement. They watched the academic's volatile moods and intemperate behaviour with glee.

The young crowd noted the academic's chipper mood on Monday morning, after being promised a private detective by his friend Tyrone. Then they sniggered at his increasing despondency as the private detective failed to materialise. The hours passed and nothing happened. By Monday afternoon, Beckwith was in danger of losing it. He made repeated phone calls, but his calls were met with bluff and evasion.

"Sorry, Mr Tyrone is busy at the moment, but I'll pass on your message," replied the personal assistant in a polite, clinical and efficient way. The following half-dozen calls were met with a similar evasive response. After returning from their long lunch break, the gallery of young folk watched from the reception area as the academic banged his desk in growing frustration. Beckwith was in an untenable position, with his entire future dependent on finding the midget submarine.

When he finally got to speak to Tyrone on Tuesday afternoon, he was fit to burst. By that time, his intemperate actions had attracted a substantial audience of bright young office workers. "You've let me down... you... Irish bastard!" raged the indignant academic as his face turned an unhealthy shade of puce with rage. "Where is your bloody investigator? I've tried to phone you dozens of times since Monday morning! Got no reply! Where have you been?"

"I'm sorry about the *small* delay," replied the lawyer in an emollient fashion. He spoke with the measured tone that he habitually adopted with his legal clients. His detached approach to the matter was in marked contrast to the enthusiasm he showed after his lavish Sunday lunch. "Something came up, and my investigator was needed elsewhere."

"So, when can we expect your man?" barked Beckwith.

"Or woman!" corrected the lawyer pedantically.

"Yes, yes," retorted Beckwith impatiently.

"I'll do my best to find someone tomorrow," replied Tyrone smoothly.

"That's too late! The trail's gone cold!" bellowed Beckwith. "You promised that you would send *your investigator on Monday morning!*"

"Hang on a moment!" replied Tyrone. The smooth façade slipped away as he set out his tanks to defend his position more aggressively. "When you phoned me *out of the blue* on Sunday, I said that I would *try* to send an investigator on Monday. But I don't carry my records around in my head. It turned out that my *man, as it happens,* was needed on another job. I'm sorry that things did not work out as you hoped, but you are not the only one facing problems."

"You've let me down, Jason!" bawled the angry academic. "The navy has stolen my midget submarine and you have not lifted a finger to help. You made a promise to send an investigator *first thing on* Monday morning. I was banking on it. Now you are trying to wriggle out of it. I shan't forget this!" Mention of the missing submarine, and the pain of his embarrassment, drew hoots of sneering laughter from reception. The loss of valuable military equipment made him a laughing stock among the fun-loving group.

"I'm truly sorry if there has been a misunderstanding," replied Jason as he resumed his polished legal tone. "When I said I would *try* to help you, I meant it."

The lawyer was spared the tirade of invective that followed his comment after replacing his receiver. When he realised that no one was listening, the academic hurled his handset at the wall. His antics reverberated around the Whitehall office building, and the commotion caused his young audience to collapse with mirth. One cheeky member of the group peered into the academic's bleak cell to see what was taking place. "It's a bloody conspiracy. They are all ganging up against me!"

mimicked the wag as he reported back to his pals. The loss of the submarine was the source of ribald humour for the rest of the working week.

Beckwith's words served their purpose, however. Tyrone was stung by the sharp rebuke. The lawyer knew that his friend had a nasty, vindictive streak, and would not take kindly to being slighted, even though he did not weald much political power. Beckwith could exact revenge for his failure. So, somewhat reluctantly, the lawyer called an investigator, called Hugh Malone. The former police detective lived in Bristol and was waiting to receive a visa for a foreign assignment. The visa application was delayed by some bureaucratic foul-up, so Malone was free to take up this small assignment in the West Country.

In the course of their phone call, the investigator was told to drive to Whitebait Cove, where he was to search for a submarine. The private detective was told to liaise with the military police at the boatyard. When he learned that an investigator was on his way, Beckwith's rage abated somewhat. Feeling guilty about his remarks, he phoned his old friend to apologise, but Tyrone refused to answer the call. "I want nothing more to do with that odious prat!" he remarked to his personal assistant. The young folk in the reception area noticed an improvement in Beckwith's mood, but the lanky academic remained a laughing stock.

Beckwith was caught in a trap of his own making. If he accepted that the submarine had been stolen, it would initiate a major police investigation. That would expose his dodgy dealings and lay him open to public ridicule. But if he delayed reporting the theft, it would undermine any insurance claim he might make. So it was absolutely vital that the midget submarine be found as quickly as possible. To ensure this happened, the academic set out clear instructions when he finally spoke to the private sleuth. "Your first priority is to find the submarine," he instructed. But Malone had his own ideas and was nobody's patsy.

Malone was pleased with his assignment to the West Country, thinking that it would make a pleasant change from his normal assignments. It would also give him freedom to use his well-honed detective skills, free of interference from the armed guards who normally accompanied him in the lawless third-world hellholes where he normally worked. The armed guards were supposedly provided for protection but, in practice, their role was to manipulate the inquiry. Their presence intimidated witnesses, who might embarrass powerful political figures.

When he arrived at Whitebait Cove, the private detective familiarised himself with the lie of the land by speaking to the seasoned red cap who was standing guard at the gate of the little boatyard. The world-weary serviceman was contemptuous of the army investigator who was leading the inquiry. "The idiot thinks the transfer document is genuine!" observed the red cap. His raised eyebrow suggested they needed their heads examining. The red cap did not believe the official story for one minute. "Your job is to get Martin Beckwith off the hook!" he added sardonically.

Malone chuckled to himself as the red cap recounted the tale of bungling and confusion when the *Normandy* disappeared from the quay. The sleuth knew that his demanding new master would not take kindly to this account of affairs. So, to sugar the pill, he reported his findings in a monotonous voice when he phoned Beckwith in his Whitehall lair, late on Wednesday afternoon.

"I arrived at the boatyard at 14.37 hours," explained the private sleuth in the stilted way that some police officers give evidence in court. "The military policeman guarding the gate told me that the offshore supply ship *Normandy* was no longer berthed at the yard. It had sailed to the North Sea the previous day. The naval trials team were not present at the yard. They returned to their naval base on Monday. So I was unable to interview any witnesses about the weekend's events."

Beckwith had been waiting impatiently for this call, expecting rapid developments. But the academic became increasingly angry and frustrated as the private detective droned on. "You might have made some progress if you had driven down on Monday," he observed acidly. "I'm not interested in what's happening at the boatyard now. *I want you to find the midget submarine!* That shouldn't be difficult, even for you! There are only so many landing places in the estuary."

"I did speak to a yard employee called Mark Dexter," he remarked hesitantly. "It seems that he used to be in charge of boatyard security."

"Yes, I know who you mean!" exploded Beckwith irritably. "What did *he* have to say?"

"Not much. He was in Scotland when your submarine went missing," admitted the private sleuth lamely.

"So, you have *no idea* where the submarine has been landed!" observed Beckwith, with a contemptuous sneer.

Stung by the comment, the private detective searched his memory for something worthwhile to add. "The chap guarding the yard made an interesting comment," observed the private sleuth as an afterthought. "Apparently, a police detective has been investigating an incident at a place called Leighton Hollow." It later emerged that after his visit to Leighton Hollow, Peter Fellows had spoken about the army training ground during an idle conversation with the red cap at the gate, but had not explained the reason for his visit to the abandoned village.

"Did you say Leighton Hollow?" said Beckwith in a hopeful tone. This was a revelation for the academic, who had spent hours studying maps of the estuary in search of landing sites for a small submarine. But he could not recall the name Leighton Hollow.

"Yes, Leighton Hollow," confirmed the investigator hesitantly. "You won't find it on the map because the village was abandoned years ago. It seems that the land was requisitioned by the government during the war and was used to train our troops for the Normandy Invasion. The army maintains it as a training ground. It is tucked away on the estuary and is out of bounds to the general public. Few people know about it."

"Bingo!" cried Beckwith excitedly. "You need to get over there straight away. See whether the navy has hidden the submarine close by."

"Okay. I'll drive there tomorrow," replied the private sleuth with lukewarm enthusiasm. After his conversation with the red cap, the private sleuth realised that it was his job to clean up the mess created by this disreputable academic. The private detective had grown cynical about the assignment.

"The *sooner* the better," demanded Beckwith forcefully as he waved the handset in the triumphal manner of a footballer who has scored a winning goal. His antics were viewed gleefully by those gathered in the reception area.

"Are you still there?" enquired Malone, who was puzzled by the strange buzzing noises emitting from his mobile phone.

"Uh, yes," replied Beckwith as he regained his composure and retrieved the handset from the floor on the other side of his desk.

The private detective continued hesitantly, with another afterthought. "The yard employee that I was talking about – Mark Dexter – is a navy man. But he knows quite a lot about the shipping industry. He asked whether you have reported the loss of your submarine to the 'shipping casualty register'. I don't know what he meant. I have never heard that term before. But those are the words he used. I thought you should know."

After his heartening conversation with the private sleuth, Beckwith was confident that his submarine would be found at Leighton Hollow the following day. In a jubilant mood, and with little else to do while he waited for the detective to report, he carried out an internet search on the phrase 'shipping casualty register'. The term had a nice ring to it, he thought. As he followed the various links, another phrase, 'missing presumed lost', caught his attention. The academic recalled the use of that phrase to describe the disappearance of an Argentine submarine close to the Falkland Islands. This research forced him to acknowledge that shipping accidents had a particular nature, because there are rarely any witnesses.

As he continued his search, he was reminded that in days gone by, the loss of a ship was only recorded when the vessel in question failed to reach its destination. In today's world, a radio distress signal is usually sent when a ship runs into trouble. But that is not always the case – the bulk carrier *Derbyshire* sank before a radio warning could be sent. The fate of that vessel and her crew was only discovered when an underwater survey was carried out at great cost.

The disappearance of an Argentine submarine occurred without warning. The alarm was only raised when the submarine failed to make a routine radio signal to the naval base, but there was no other evidence that it had been lost. It later emerged that some US warships detected a large explosion close to the submarine's last reported position, but that was the only clue to the submarine's fate. As he mused, he reflected on the coincidence that their own submarine was 'missing presumed lost' within days of the Argentine submarine.

It seemed that the shipping world had developed its own casualty reporting system over the centuries. It seemed that the first step, in this archaic system, was for the owner to post a notice in the casualty column of a shipping newspaper to say that a ship was overdue. Then as time passed and the ship failed to appear at its destination, the fate of the ship would be discussed with insurers. This might lead to agreement that the vessel was 'presumed lost'. An insurance claim would be made for 'total loss' of the ship and its cargo.

As the academic delved deeper, he began to wonder whether the idiosyncratic nature of the marine casualty reporting system could be used to his advantage. Beckwith started to wonder whether he could use this drawn-out procedure to provide additional breathing space to track down the midget submarine, without the need to report that it had been stolen. The thought that he could benefit from this archaic system caused him to smile with satisfaction. It would allow him to get one over on the smug public school boys who dominated the marine insurance industry.

So, the academic summoned his sidekick, Simon, and they sat down together to compose a suitably worded missing ship report for publication in a shipping newspaper. The notice was to be a low-key statement which was technically accurate but ambiguous, so that it could be interpreted in many different ways. Beckwith wanted to put the loss on record but obscure the more embarrassing aspects of the affair.

After following his boss from the Plymouth project office to Whitebait Cove, Simon now occupied an open-plan office on the same floor, where he attempted to stay aloof from the young folk who were poking fun at his boss. He was the last member of the Portsmouth project team to remain loyal to his master. It did not take Simon long to draft a notice suitable for posting in a shipping paper. The notice read:

A prototype submersible went missing in the Plymouth Estuary in the early hours of Sunday 19 April 2018. The submersible was unmanned at the time of its disappearance and there were no human casualties. A search is currently underway to locate the submersible in the surrounding waters.

After arranging for the notice to appear in the shipping papers, Simon then mailed a copy of the notice, with a covering letter, to the insurers. The correspondence was produced in a sloppy way that suggested it had been thrown together in a hurry. The post code was omitted and the letter (accidentally) failed to mention the number of the insurance policy. It was hoped that these omissions would delay the response and provide a breathing space for Beckwith to locate the midget submarine. All this was, in short, a carefully calculated ruse to gain more time.

As he set off home from the Whitehall office that evening, Beckwith felt a warm glow of satisfaction from the day's achievements. They now had a strong lead regarding the submarine's whereabouts, and the 'presumed loss' ruse would give them time to finish their search. The private detective was due to visit Leighton Hollow the following day and, so, with any luck, the whole mess would be tidied up by the end of the week. Beckwith keenly anticipated the detective's report from the army training ground.

When he arrived at the office on Thursday morning, Beckwith paced impatiently, waiting for the private investigator to report back. There was also an air of anticipation in the reception area where the young folk were gathered. Many of the carefree bunch were habitués of West End night clubs, with busy social lives. They regarded Beckwith as an aging rue and figure of fun. They made many jokes about the 'man who lost a submarine'.

When Malone phoned shortly before midday, silence descended on the reception area as the young folk craned their necks to hear what was taking place. This conversation would be the main source of gossip for the rest of the day. "How did you get on?" asked the academic with keen anticipation. But his enthusiasm was not reciprocated by the caller on the other end of the line.

As in the earlier call, the sleuth related the facts in the dull, monotonous tone of a dull-witted police officer giving evidence at a trial. He described the geography of Leighton Hollow and the restriction on public access to the army training ground. Beckwith sat tapping his fingers on his desk in frustration. When he could no longer contain his impatience, he shouted: "Yes, that's all very well – but did you find our submarine?"

"Well, yes and no," replied the private detective ponderously. He had some disturbing news to impart and did not wish to deviate too far from his planned narrative.

"What does that mean, *yes and no?*" demanded Beckwith testily.

"It seems likely that your submarine was landed at Leighton Hollow," replied the private sleuth cautiously. This comment ignited an explosive reaction. Waving his arms in triumph, the tall, spindly academic bounced up from his seat like an uncoiling spring. The audience in reception sniggered at his antics.

"Where is it now?" demanded Beckwith.

"We are not sure," admitted Malone somewhat sheepishly. Then after a pause the sleuth made a clumsy attempt to appease his disgruntled client. "A plain-clothes detective called Peter Fellows knows what's happened to it." The supposedly conciliatory remark had the opposite effect to that intended.

It gave the impression that Beckwith was being given the runaround by the local police, and that sent the academic into orbit. Beckwith's blood was up and he was determined to get to the truth.

"Are *you telling me* that a local plod knows where the submarine is hidden?" demanded the academic incredulously.

"Yes. That seems to be the case," replied Malone hesitantly. As soon as the words slipped from his mouth, he began to regret the injudicious remark. He realised, rather belatedly, that he had put too much faith into a conversation with the range warden at the army training ground. The truth was that he had not met, or even spoken to, the police detective in question.

"Why won't he tell you?" demanded Beckwith.

"Well, it's complicated," replied Malone as he tried to backtrack. "I think it's best if you speak to the detective yourself." This unsubstantial response fed Beckwith's paranoia, leading him to suspect the private detective was involved in a conspiracy to torment him.

"I'm coming down to sort this out!" barked the academic decisively. "I want to see you and this Peter Fellows at the boatyard at five o'clock. Somebody is going to pay for this!"

"I'm only too happy to meet you at the boatyard, sir," replied the private sleuth obediently, "but I can't vouch for Peter Fellows. But I'll get in touch with him and ask him to join us at five o'clock."

"*You do that!*" retorted the academic. The unfolding drama was watched gleefully by the audience of young folk gathered in the reception area. They watched as the academic collected up his things and marched off in high dudgeon.

Gripped by an all-consuming rage, the academic had forgotten that he had travelled to work on the London underground that morning, leaving his car at home. He did not have time to return to his North London flat to collect his car, so he was forced to return to the office to arrange for a hire car at Plymouth station. His embarrassment at this *faux pas* was the source of further merriment in the reception area.

Without further delay, the academic dashed to the Waterloo terminus to catch an express train heading towards the West Country. Despite 'staff shortages', he reached Plymouth in good time. After racing through the country lanes, he arrived at the boatyard car park to find workmen removing the temporary office used by the navy trial team. Fortunately, the cabin used by his project team was still in place but, by that time, it had been stripped of all its furnishings.

When he burst into the cabin, slightly late for the scheduled five o'clock meeting, he found Hugh Malone chatting in a relaxed way with Peter Fellows. The pair were reminiscing about their service in the police force while they shared a cup of tea. The pair occupied the only chairs in the cabin. Lost in their own thoughts, they made no effort to find their visitor a seat, and paid little attention to the interloper.

Their disrespectful attitude fuelled Beckwith's paranoia further. The academic was, by this time, tired and emotional after the rushed journey and was certain that the pair were plotting against him. A chilled silence descended on the spartan cabin as the conversation petered out. After an embarrassed pause, the errant sleuths looked up sheepishly. They wore the forced smiles of beaten dogs acknowledging their master. Red in the face, the academic let fly with both barrels. "You are not paid to sit round drinking tea!" he growled through gritted teeth.

The recalcitrant underlings reacted sullenly, somewhat heartened by the fact that it was the academic who was late for their meeting. In other circumstances, one of them would have risen to welcome the weary traveller, and offer him a chair. But, irked by his intemperate manner, the detectives remained stubbornly in their seats while the lanky academic hovered over them, spitting bile. "Can someone tell me what is going on?" demanded Beckwith testily.

"You asked to see Peter. Well, here he is," replied Malone, like a dutiful servant.

"Well, perhaps *Peter* can tell me what happened to *my* submarine," demanded the academic with a sarcastic undertone. The word *Peter* was spoken with a sneer to suggest that the pair had developed an unhealthily close relationship. Any vestige of goodwill was thrown away with that derogatory remark. That was unfortunate because the plain-clothes detective was prepared to be helpful, if approached in the right way. Instead, he clammed up.

To follow the crucial exchange that followed, it's necessary to look back at the police investigation whose aim was to find evidence to convict the notorious Murphy gang. The investigation was set in motion by a report of fly-tipping at the gang's secret hideaway at Leighton Hollow. The forensic team were then mobilised to sift through the rubbish, in the hope that a link could be found to the gang. Little did they know that this was a false trail of clues, carefully laid by the navy team.

When they found some planted evidence, the police were able to obtain a warrant to search scrap yards linked to the notorious gang of thugs. When the police searched the yards, they found a number of components that were directly linked to the missing submarine. This was another part of the false trail of clues laid by the navy team. These discoveries led the police investigators to speculate that the submarine had been stolen by the Murphy gang and broken up for scrap.

Accepting that bizarre version of events, the police superintendent assembled a team of detectives to collect more evidence to convict the gang. This was time-consuming because the forensic work had to be carried out in a painstaking way to provide cast-iron evidence. The investigation had to be carried out under a cloak of secrecy, to make sure that the criminals did not abscond before they were arrested.

In other circumstances, Peter Fellows would have played a central role in this activity. After all, a conviction of the notorious gang would be the crowning achievement of his career. But he resisted the temptation to join the hue and cry, sensing that something 'did not smell right'. *The evidence looks too good to be true*, he mused. A number of issues muddied the waters for the wily sleuth, not least inconsistencies in the Scottish fishing story and questions about the fracas in Steve's apartment block.

So the plain-clothes detective distanced himself from the team who were building the case. When he expressed his reservations to fellow officers, they scoffed, and it was not long before he found himself ostracised. But swimming against the tide, his doubts about the guilt of the Murphy gang mounted with each passing day, but he was put on the spot when the private sleuth summoned him to meet Beckwith. This placed him in an awkward position because he was in no mood to share his private thoughts with anyone.

"*Mr* Malone tells me that you visited a place called Leighton Hollow and that you know where our midget submarine is hidden. Would you care to elaborate, *Peter?*" demanded Beckwith in a particularly condescending manner.

"That's not how it works, sir!" growled the plain-clothes detective. "*We* ask the questions!"

The academic was taken aback by the effrontery of this insignificant local plod. The remark added further fuel to his paranoia and he reacted instinctively. "You should be aware that I have some powerful friends," he declared pompously as he fixed the plain-clothes detective with a steely glare. "You will end up chasing litter louts if you don't cooperate!"

The detectives could scarcely restrain their mirth at this crass remark. They were both familiar with the phrase from television police dramas, but neither of them had heard anyone use the phrase in real life. It added to the impression that the academic had a sense of entitlement that he did not deserve. But having made his point, the plain-clothes detective thought it unwise to further provoke the prickly individual.

"We are all public servants," replied the plain-clothes detective in a conciliatory tone. "But we need to follow the rulebook. In reply to your question, I have no idea where your midget submarine has been taken. My visit to Leighton Hollow was in connection with another case. Sadly, I am not at liberty to divulge what I learned during the visit."

"What do you mean – *another case?*" replied Beckwith, throwing his arms up in exasperation. "Malone told me that you had information about the midget submarine."

"As I said, I am not at liberty to discuss the other case," replied the plain-clothes detective resolutely.

"Well, I'll just have to speak to your superiors, won't I!" declared the academic, knowing that his bluff had been called.

"You do that!" replied the plain-clothes detective calmly.

Beckwith stepped out of the portable cabin into the car park, to make his call without being overheard. After a couple of minutes, he returned and handed his mobile phone to the plain-clothes detective. "Your boss wants to speak to you!" he remarked with a smug expression. The plain-clothes detective took the mobile and answered yes or no as he received a torrent of invective from headquarters. Beckwith watched this with the satisfied smile of a Cheshire cat, believing that the detective was being reprimanded.

A Botched Investigation

"Well, are you prepared to tell me what you know?" demanded Beckwith spitefully.

"Yes, I am," replied the plain-clothes detective with a look of defeat. But then after a pause, he added: "But you may not like what you hear!"

"Well, spit it out, man!" barked Beckwith impatiently. He could not wait to hear where the submarine could be found.

"As I said before," explained the plain-clothes detective in a formal manner, "we do not normally speak to the public about ongoing investigations. That is especially true in this case, where we are still collecting evidence against some notorious villains. But my superior officer has instructed me to cooperate with you, so I am passing this information on in the strictest confidence. Here is what I know.

"We've been keeping an eye on the military training ground at Leighton Hollow for some time because it's used by the Murphy gang for their criminal activities," explained the plain-clothes detective in a formal manner. "The gang believe that the training ground lies outside the jurisdiction of the civilian police. But they are wrong. We work in close cooperation with officials who manage the training ground. They keep us informed of what is taking place.

"The range warden phoned to report some suspicious activity in the early hours of Sunday morning," continued the plain-clothes detective ponderously. Beckwith's face lit up at this remark in the expectation that he would soon learn where his midget submarine had been found. "Some police units were sent to investigate," continued the plain-clothes detective in the same dull monotone.

"The villains had vanished by the time our units arrived. But they left behind a large pile of industrial waste in a disused quarry – the gang is known to use the quarry for fly-tipping. So a forensic team were sent over to sift through the waste material to look for envelopes, papers or any other clues to the source of the waste material. This will allow us to prosecute the gang for scrap metal theft and fly-tipping.

"Our forensic team think the gang must have been disturbed by our police raid, because they left some valuable items behind. There were some copper pipes, valves and odd pieces of equipment. At first, the team thought that it was the remains of an old industrial heating boiler. Tyre tracks suggested that it was a major operation involving several heavy goods vehicles. There were also metal chippings to suggest that a power saw was used to cut up steel plates.

"It took the forensic experts most of Monday to sift through all the waste, but in the process, they found documents linked to the Murphy gang. They also found some rather unusual valves. Each of the valves carried a maker's name and serial number. So they have been bagged as evidence, along with samples of the metal chips. The forensic team will get in touch with the valve makers and they will analyse the metal chips in due course. It will take a few days to complete all the tests."

In making these comments, the plain-clothes detective said nothing about the suspicions that these components could be linked to the midget submarine. So, believing that he was being told a shaggy dog story, Beckwith showed signs of increasing frustration. After all, Malone had suggested that the local policeman knew the whereabouts of the midget submarine. *So what was all this piffle about fly-tipping and scrap metal?*

"Look, I'm trying to be patient," commented Beckwith through gritted teeth. "But I'm really not interested in fly-tipping, local thugs or humdrum rural crime. We have enough crime in London without listening to your trivial problems in this backwater." Then turning towards the private sleuth, he continued: "Malone tells me that you know what has happened to our midget submarine. Is that true, or not?"

The private detective wished the ground would open beneath his feet, feeling guilty that he had dropped his new-found friend in the mire. His injudicious comment about the submarine had the potential to destroy any rapport that had been created with his fellow detective. In the few minutes since meeting together, the pair had shared amusing anecdotes about their police service and a bond had been established, but they had refrained from discussing the events that had taken place at the weekend.

Peter Fellows was angry that he had been forced to show his hand and, in revenge, he turned his fire on the private sleuth. "Don't put words into my mouth!" he rebuked his new-found friend. "There is *some* evidence to suggest that the submarine *might* have been landed at Leighton Hollow. That is all!" Then in another wave of anger, he continued challengingly. "Who told you that I know what happened to the midget submarine? It was not me!"

The detectives were at cross purposes. Malone kicked himself, realising that he had jumped the gun when making his phone report to his demanding client. "The range warden told me that you know what happened to the submarine," he pleaded sheepishly as he shuffled his feet with embarrassment. Beckwith raised his eyebrows in exasperation. The plain-clothes detective fixed Malone with an acrimonious stare, adding to his discomfort.

After taking a breath, Malone began a convoluted story, his face red with embarrassment. "When I visited Leighton Hollow yesterday, the range warden came by in a jeep and warned me that I was trespassing on a restricted military training area," he explained. "The warden told me that a live firing exercise was about to start and that I should leave straight away. But as I left, he mentioned that he had spoken to you." At that point, Malone turned accusingly towards the plain-clothes detective before continuing. "The warden told me that an unusual valve was found near the jetty that might be *linked to the submarine*."

This was an embarrassing revelation for the plain-clothes detective, who did not want to be drawn into that line of discussion. While the theory that the Murphy gang had stolen the submarine and broken it up for scrap was accepted by colleagues at the police station, the plain-clothes detective did not want to be associated with it. "It looks as though our wires have crossed," he replied evasively as he desperately tried to distance himself from the rash remark he had made to the range warden. "I was investigating a fly-tipping incident at army training ground. Nothing else. My visit had nothing to do with the disappearance of the submarine."

"So why did you mention the midget submarine to the range warden?" challenged the private sleuth, who did not want to be accused of misleading his client.

"As it happened, I visited Whitebait Cove earlier that day. The disappearance of the midget submarine just came up in conversation," replied the plain-clothes detective as he tried to backtrack. But he did so in an unconvincing way.

In his paranoid state, Beckwith exploded at these confused and contradictory accounts of what had taken place. It was now apparent that he had raced down to Whitebait Cove on a wild goose chase. All the pair of dunderheads had discovered was that the midget submarine *might* have been landed at the army training ground at Leighton Hollow, nothing more. The midget submarine had obviously been spirited away by the naval trials team. So, why all this talk of fly-tipping, scrap metal, range wardens and army training grounds? It was a smokescreen to conceal their incompetence, he surmised.

A Botched Investigation

"You are a pair of clowns!" bawled Beckwith contemptuously. "Get off your backsides. Get down to Leighton Hollow and find our submarine! It can't be that difficult! But in four days you have not made any progress at all!" Then turning to Malone, the academic continued: "This has been a complete waste of time, so don't call until you have something worthwhile to report!"

This impetuous comment alienated the detectives. If he had acted in a considerate way, he would have won the pair over. They would have been useful allies to find a way out of his nightmare. Instead, he flounced off, leaving the recalcitrant detectives chuckling like naughty schoolboys who had been caught scrumping apples.

"You dropped me right in it!" remarked the plain-clothes detective, but the mocking smile belied the recriminatory nature of his words. The reason for his good humour was that he had misrepresented his police chief's instructions. When the plain-clothes detective picked up Beckwith's mobile phone, the police chief asked whether anyone else could overhear their call. When he received assurance that no one else was listening, his manner changed.

"Seems that you have ruffled some feathers, Peter," remarked the police superintendent. "Our friend can make life difficult. I don't know what you are up to, but I trust your judgement. I'll back you. But *please try to keep that maniac off my back.*"

Given free rein, the plain-clothes detective decided to conceal his private thoughts. Although he had described the fly-tipping incident in detail, he refrained from mentioning the sighting of the *Normandy*, or that a component had been found linked to the missing submarine. But this left the plain-clothes detective with a difficult balancing act nevertheless. He wanted to get at the truth but needed to shield the police chief from the irate academic.

Malone could tell that his fellow detective had only told Beckwith part of the story and he was keen to winkle out the facts. "So, what did the range warden really tell you?" he asked with a cunning smile.

Peter Fellows took some time before answering; he did not know how far he could trust his new-found friend. By this time, the wily sleuth suspected that people were playing games and trying to mislead the investigators. *Should I tell him what I suspect?* he mused.

"You probably know that the midget submarine was stowed under a tarpaulin on the stern deck of a ship called the *Normandy*, which carried out the sea trials," explained the plain-clothes detective in a thoughtful way. Malone nodded in agreement. "Well, the range warden spotted the *Normandy* near Leighton Hollow in the early hours of Sunday morning. A short time later, the ship was later found abandoned a few miles down the estuary. When the crew recovered the ship, the midget submarine was no longer on the rear deck."

"So, the midget submarine *must* have been landed at Leighton Hollow," surmised the private sleuth with an excited gleam in his eye.

"We can't say *that* for definite, because the range warden could not see the jetty," replied the plain-clothes detective cautiously. "But he did notice that the ship strayed outside the normal shipping channel, which suggests that it *might have* berthed at the jetty. There are also tyre tracks to suggest that a mobile crane was used to lift something heavy onto the jetty. So, there is a lot of circumstantial evidence that the submarine was landed there. We also found a component in the fly-tipping waste near the jetty that was fitted to the submarine."

"So why didn't you tell my client what you had found?" asked the private sleuth with a puzzled expression. The plain-clothes detective looked thoughtful before answering,

A Botched Investigation

as he pondered how much he should reveal. From their first meeting, it was clear that the pair of detectives had shared values. Both men had an inquisitive and independent nature. After weighing up the risks, Peter Fellows decided to level with his counterpart.

Pointing to the boatyard's stylish office building, the plain-clothes detective spoke about the background to the case. "This boatyard is run by a young guy called Steve Jones, who is a good friend," explained the plain-clothes detective. "We first met when I was investigating a break-in at the boatyard. During the raid, we believe the Murphy gang stole some valuable material to sell as scrap metal. That's typical of the crimes they commit. The gang runs a couple of scrap yards which allows them to sell on the material.

"We think they are responsible for a whole string of scrap-metal thefts. On one occasion, they tried to steal some electrical cables from the railway tracks. They bit off more than they could chew with that job. One of the gang members suffered an electric shock. They left the injured man behind and we arrested him, but he refused to implicate the ringleaders." The detectives chuckled at this story of blundering incompetence.

The plain-clothes detective then spoke about the diverted valve that had been found and other odds and ends of evidence. As the plain-clothes detective spoke, Malone put together the new information with what he already knew, to reach the obvious conclusion. "So, you believe the Murphy gang commandeered the ship, landed the midget submarine at Leighton Hollow with a mobile crane and broke it up for scrap," concluded Malone with a flourish.

"Well, that's likely to be the conclusion when the forensic people complete their report," responded the plain-clothes detective with a sphinx-like inscrutable expression.

"But you don't believe it," challenged the private sleuth.

"I don't have any views," replied the plain-clothes detective enigmatically.

"You know something different?" observed Malone provocatively.

"Might, or might not," replied the plain-clothes detective teasingly. "One thing I can tell you, you could write a book about the hostility between the project team and the navy boys." The plain-clothes detective went on to describe some of Beckwith's scams, garnishing his tale with anecdotes about the dodgy security firm employed to guard the quayside, and suspected links between the firm and the notorious Murphy gang.

After their conversation, Malone realised that his counterpart had a thorough grasp of the situation. It was clear that Peter Fellows knew the area and understood the murky politics surrounding the midget submarine project. While the assignment was a pleasant break from the rigours of life in a war-torn African nation, Malone realised that he had little to contribute and might as well leave the foot-slogging to his new-found friend.

"Well, let me know how it all turns out," remarked Malone cheerfully. "Sounds like an interesting story. But, sadly, my assignment ends tonight. I'm flying to an African hellhole next week."

"Good luck with that!" sympathised the plain-clothes detective.

When the private detective submitted his report, it concluded that the whereabouts of the midget submarine were unknown, but noted that a pile of industrial waste had been found in a disused quarry at Leighton Hollow, linked to the missing submarine. This seemed to support the theory that the submarine had been landed at Leighton Hollow, where it was broken up for scrap. No mention was made of the range

A Botched Investigation

warden's sightings of the *Normandy*. A copy of the report was sent to the sleuth's boss, Jason Tyrone, and a second copy to the Whitehall office of the Marine Special Projects Agency.

Shortly after the report was dispatched, a police task force prepared to swoop on the Murphy gang. The forensic team had, by this time, established that the metal chipping found at the disused quarry consisted of a rarely used titanium alloy that had been used for the construction of the hull of the midget submarine. Similar chippings had been found at a scrap yard operated by the Murphy gang. It was believed that this provided enough evidence to prosecute the ringleaders of the Murphy gang for fly-tipping and theft of the midget submarine.

Chapter 23

Steve Briefs His Team

After the sea trials and the turbulent weekend events, the boatyard returned to its normal somnolent character. But this did not make life easier for the yard boss. The business was short of cash and the order books were bare. The staff believed that their boss had returned from a fishing trip while recuperating from a heart attack. They little suspected that he was responsible for the disappearance of the midget submarine. The story of ill health explained his testy behaviour. Steve's sour mood was hardly surprising, given his predicament.

At the boatyard, the young executive faced the prospect of laying off staff, chasing up bills and implementing economy measures. While dealing with these unpalatable matters, the plot to commandeer the submarine was rapidly unravelling. The plain-clothes detective was now hot on his trail. With all this weight on his shoulders, he was barely able to find time to deal with his fledgling dredging business. As he prepared for the Friday meeting with his old shipmates, Steve felt guilty that he had not been able to answer Bill's increasingly desperate phone calls.

Apprehensive about the meeting with the truculent pair, the young executive set out before dawn to ensure that he arrived at the office in good time, before his reluctant recruits. This would allow him to see what they had been up to during the week. With all these worries, the world seemed a grim place as he made his way slowly through the suburbs of Plymouth. His mood lightened as he joined the dual carriageway heading out of the grim city. Cruising in his sports car, his heart lifted as he watched the sun rise on a glorious spring morning.

When he reached the open countryside, the young executive sat contentedly behind the wheel, admiring the counterpoint between the growl of the fast-spinning turbocharger and the rhythmic beat of the high-performance engine. The machinery performed with the sparky precision of a well-oiled Swiss watch. There was little traffic as he drove on between gently rolling slopes covered by newly tilled fields. The green shoots of barley sprouting from geometric drill lines promised a plentiful harvest to come later that summer.

In this bucolic scenery, it was easy to put his *travails* behind him. The young executive felt a surge of adrenalin as he reflected on the excitement of challenges to come. With all his cares, it was easy to lose sight of his objective. The dredging business was, of course, just a small part of a philanthropic scheme to protect seafarers from hijackers. Their intention was to hide the purloined midget submarine on board a dredger. The dredger would then be employed on a port project in the Horn of Africa. This would allow them to keep an eye on criminal hideouts along the lawless coastline. If all went well, the Dutch corporation would reward his weekend mission by injecting capital into the boatyard.

Others were procuring a suitable vessel at that very moment. The young executive hoped that his former shipmates would manage the conversion to house the midget submarine in a secret compartment onboard the dredger. But it was touch and go whether the truculent pair would cooperate, because he had lied and misled them about the nature of their mission. The pair had acted skittishly after learning of the undercover nature of the operation. To make matters worse, Steve had not spoken to his new recruits since introducing them to the business on Monday morning. So he was, naturally, apprehensive to see how they had settled in.

As he approached the outskirts of the seaside town, Steve felt some sympathy for the ill-matched pair, cooped up together in the charmless office for a week. It was a depressing room, with old-fashioned neon lamps and characterless walls painted with cream emulsion. The north-facing sash window looked out over rickety rooftops and drab garages. The subdued daylight gave the room a clinical feeling. He tried to picture the claustrophobic atmosphere as the pair worked together.

But these concerns were dispelled when he entered the office to find his new recruits had brightened up their spartan workspace. He could barely recognise the room that he had left behind on Monday. He was cheered to see pictures hung on the walls. This was an optimistic sign that his former shipmates had settled in for the long haul.

Steve was particularly pleased to see a framed photograph of the *Sea Ranger* on her maiden voyage. This suggested that his former shipmates treasured pleasant memories of the old rust bucket. On the opposite wall, there hung an artist's impression of a suction dredger, showing the pumps, hoppers and internal workings. The pictures gave the impression that his new recruits had entered into the spirit of the venture. The furnishings had been neatly arranged.

The four desks had been moved to form two separate workstations. These workstations were set out, one behind the other, on the right-hand side of the room, looking from the door. Each workstation was formed of a desk projecting from the wall with the second desk set at right angles at the end, to form an 'L' shape. A comfortable swivel chair provided easy access to the encircling work surface. A computer was placed on each of the outer desks.

A bookshelf stood opposite the workstations, on the left-hand side of the room. The shelves were stuffed with manuals. A corridor between the workstations and the bookshelf led to a conference area, where a hardwood table was surrounded by chairs. Another, smaller, table in the corner supported a kettle and all the ingredients for making tea and coffee. This table was covered in crumbs and half-finished packets of digestive biscuits. One of the workstations showed similar signs of lax housekeeping, with scattered documents threatening to cascade onto the floor. It was not hard to guess the culprit.

The workstation nearest to the door was neat and tidy, by contrast with a framed photo of a well-groomed middle-aged woman and other items laid out with geometric precision. That workstation bore all the hallmarks of Bill's fastidious nature. It was obvious that the untidy workstation was occupied by the cantankerous Scottish engineer. So, while there were some dispiriting signs of discord within the ranks, there were also heartening signs that the pair had settled into the spirit of the operation, concluded Steve.

Steve's musings were interrupted with the sound of high-spirited banter as the old-timers clambered up the stairs at the start of their working day. Bill was poking fun at Alex for wearing his heavy weatherproof jacket in the warm spring weather. This long-running joke had been one of the few sources of humour during their abortive reunion weekend. Steve guessed that the high spirits could be explained because the pair were 'demob-happy'.

This was a familiar emotion for those working away from home for long periods. Steve recalled that many of his shipmates used the term 'channels' to describe the roller coaster of emotions that gripped the crew towards the end of a long voyage. The clock seemed to stand still as the ship crawled towards its final port with the crew counting off the hours before freeing themselves from obnoxious colleagues. Mariners are confined together like battery hens twenty-four hours a day, seven days a week, for months on end. It calls for enormous strength of character to tolerate the irritating habits of one's shipmates. This can lead to outbursts of aggression in the final hours as pent-up grievances boil over.

The banter evaporated, and an icy chill descended as the pair burst into the office to find themselves confronted by their new boss. Distrust of the slippery young executive was the one factor that bonded the mismatched pair of engineers. It was clear that the former shipmates got on each other's nerves, cooped up in the claustrophobic office, just as Steve feared. Bill berated the Scotsman for his slovenly habits. Alex responded by teasing the bean counter for his fastidious nature.

Disdain for their former shipmate was one thing that united them. The pair thought that the shy youngster had morphed into a manipulative con artist with a chameleon-like character. Bill was particularly angry that his phone calls had gone unanswered. So it was hardly surprising that Steve received a cold reception. Trying his best to ignore the hostility, the young executive asked his new recruits to sit round the conference table. The truculent pair grudgingly complied as

Alex made a barely audible comment about 'who pays the Piper?'

"Nice pictures," observed Steve cheerily, in a valiant effort to break the ice. "Who found them?"

"Found them in a bric-a-brac shop," replied Alex in a grumpy manner. While the Scotsman's churlish response was a warning that Steve faced a tough time to win the pair's respect, it was also a useful reminder that the Scotsman was passionate about collecting marine artefacts. Bill remained silent during the exchange, staring straight ahead of him in a defiant fashion.

The bean counter was spooked by the undercover nature of the business and feared that they had been tricked into joining a shady operation. After a distinguished career, he did not want to damage his reputation. So, to maintain a clear conscience, he played things strictly by the book. Steve had asked him to produce a business plan for a dredging business, and that was precisely what he had done. No more, no less.

As the pair faced their boss, Bill had the dejected appearance of an award-winning chef who was forced to work as a hamburger-flipper in a greasy spoon café. During his career, he had planned business schemes for large international corporations. The bean counter had now been reduced to working for a tin-pot outfit involved in some murky business. With a sigh, the bean counter removed a glossy document from his briefcase and thumped it onto the table. He did so with an embarrassed air.

This was the all-important document that they had been hired to compile, but he was not proud of it. The stylish cover went some way to concealing the paucity of the information contained within. The first section of the slim report looked at the prospects for a dredging business in the North Sea. This was followed by some technical and financial analysis, but it was flimflam.

Bill knew that the business plan was a work of fiction. "I've done my best, but there are *many unknown factors*," declared the bean counter with suppressed fury. "Some of the figures are little more than guesswork. I tried to contact you *many times!*" Bill had spent much of the week trying to contact his new master to clarify some points about the proposed business. His failure to do so caused him enormous anger. Steve could appreciate his former shipmate's anger. He felt guilty about his failure to respond.

"I'm sorry that I did not reply to your calls," admitted Steve contritely, "but I've been a bit busy." After flicking through the neatly bound report, the young executive could see that the report painted a pessimistic picture of a dredging business in the North Sea. It was typical of the well-intentioned but useless reports that gather dust in the archives of big organisations. The figures presented with the aid of spreadsheets, pie charts and tables made for grim reading.

The document painted a bleak, but honest, view of the dredging industry in the North Sea at that time. While it was couched in professional jargon, the conclusion could be summed up with the words: 'It would be financial suicide to set up a dredging company at this time'. Few people would be surprised at this view. It was common knowledge that North Sea contractors were struggling to survive as a result of a slump in the price of crude oil.

When Steve asked whether Alex shared his friend's pessimistic view, the question struck a nerve. The cantankerous Scotsman looked daggers at the bean counter. It was clearly a contentious point. Despite the friendly banter when they arrived that morning, the enforced confinement had created animosity. The Scotsman was contemptuous of his colleague's timid approach to their task. So, as Bill plodded on in a dutiful way, the Scotsman went his own way, refusing to take part in what he regarded as a pointless exercise.

The Scotsman thought that they had been sent on a wild goose chase. *No one in their right mind would want to establish a dredging company in the North Sea at that time*, he believed. If the business was to succeed, they would have to look for work in other parts of the world. So, instead of wasting time on a futile exercise, he went in search of new ideas that might give their embryonic business a competitive edge. A heap of conference papers and technical reports was evidence of his thinking.

This research work suited the mechanically minded engineer down to the ground. He was fascinated by machines. But his fascination with machines did not extend to other areas of technology. He had no understanding of electronics, though he was a dab hand at operating personal computers when it suited him. His friends thought that he had been born in the wrong era, and that he would have made his mark as an inventor in the nineteenth century.

But his love of machines was not the only characteristic he shared with engineers of the Victorian era. Like his heroes, Stevenson and Brunel, the Scotsman had a cavalier attitude towards cost and deadlines. To make matters worse, he performed his work in a chaotic and disorganised manner. It was little surprise, therefore, that he had failed to finish the assigned task by the Friday deadline. But the documents littering his desk were, at least, evidence that he had not been idle. To justify his contribution, Alex dumped the contents of his briefcase onto the conference table.

"You might find an answer in this lot!" grunted the Scotsman. Steve looked askance at the torrent of paper as it cascaded onto the table. He had neither the time nor the inclination to go through the ill-assorted confetti, but neither did he want to alienate his cantankerous new recruit. So he accepted the gift in gracious spirit.

"I can see that you are getting on top of the job!" remarked Steve euphemistically. Watching from the sidelines, Bill noted the sarcastic undertone with malign pleasure.

Although the Scotsman had not bothered to sort the conference papers and magazine articles into a logical sequence, his views were made clear with Post-it notes and scrawled comments drawing attention to significant points. The young executive viewed the assortment of paper with the sour expression of someone who had found a mess behind the toilet bowl. His initial instinct was to consign the whole stinking pile to the nearest waste bin.

Out of innate politeness, Steve leafed through the jumble of papers, but he did so in a half-hearted way. Watching proudly from across the table, the Scotsman chipped in from time to time to draw Steve's attention to a particular item of interest. Steve was about to abandon this pointless exercise when he noticed a magazine article discussing port projects on the east coast of Africa.

"No point in looking for work in the North Sea," remarked the Scotsman with a knowing air. "You need to look further afield."

That was not only an astute comment, but it was an insightful critique of Bill's flat-footed approach to their assignment. What really impressed the young executive was that he had not mentioned the Horn of Africa to his former shipmates. He feared that they would shy away from becoming involved in the strife-torn region. He planned to introduce them to the risky side of the venture in a gradual way. "Why did you mention East Africa?" he asked curiously.

"It's the land of opportunity," replied Alex rather grandly. "That article describes some port projects in Mozambique,

Kenya and Ethiopia. That would be a good place for us to look for work. There are not many contractors in that part of the world."

"Did you mention that to Bill?" asked Steve in an upbeat way.

"Aye! But he was nay interested!" growled Alex as he reverted to his Scottish brogue to emphasise the point. The older engineers stared at each other in a hostile way.

It seemed that Alex had picked up a reference to East Africa as if by osmosis. But while impressed by the Scotsman's insight, he despaired of his chaotic methods. This was why he wanted to recruit the ill-matched pair. If he could combine the Scotsman's ingenuity with Bill's administrative skills then they would make a formidable team, but he needed to bang their heads together to achieve that outcome. It was still too early to reveal that a port project in East Africa lay at the heart of the undercover plans.

Their conversation was cut short at that critical point because Steve had to pick up the plain-clothes detective from the mainline station. The plain-clothes detective could have taken the branch line that ran into the seaside resort, but it would have been an awkward journey and Steve hoped that a substantial car journey would give him a chance to sound out the plain-clothes detective. So, gathering up his things, he told his former shipmates that he had an errand to run and would be back in a short while.

This was the last straw for Bill. The fastidious engineer was fed up with Steve's fly-by-night behaviour. The seeds of distrust had been sown during their so-called reunion, when the slippery young guy snared them into this dodgy dredging business. Bill's disdainful view of his former protégé was also coloured by their angry encounter with the tall bearded guy at the end of their boatyard tour. That episode had amused him at the time, but the affair had taken on an ominous character when the brash young guy failed to provide a plausible explanation for the mysterious weekend events at his boatyard.

Bill might have looked on things in a favourable way if the young executive had been straight with them, but the young guy dodged and weaved and it was impossible to pin him down. To add to Bill's unease, he had heard rumours that Steve's boatyard business was on the brink of bankruptcy, so he decided that it was time to make a stand. "How do we know that you are coming back?" demanded Bill sharply.

The petulant tone of the remark enraged Steve. Over the past days, he had had to cope with an undercover mission, a rift with Jackie, the fracas in his flat, a nosy neighbour, a police inquiry and an ailing boatyard. He was juggling too many balls. Although he had misled his former shipmates, he had treated them in a decent way, offering them interesting and well-paid work. All these suppressed feelings burst to the surface, creating a ferocious backlash.

"Sorry, Bill. What exactly *is* your problem?" he exclaimed as the rage and frustration that had been brewing all week finally boiled over.

"You said that you would pay us if we completed the business plan, and then we were free to go," replied Bill petulantly. He was taken aback by the young executive's fierce reaction.

"Yes. I *did*," replied Steve impatiently.

"Well, we've completed the business plan, and now we expect you to honour your side of the bargain. When are you going to pay us?" retorted Bill defiantly.

This petty-minded accusation hit a nerve. Bill had pushed his luck too far. Steve struggled to contain his wrath. "When I come back!" growled Steve, with a look of exasperation.

Alex chuckled as he watched the set-to gleefully from the sidelines. "Steam pressure rising fast, and the boiler is about to blow!" he murmured in a barely audible but comical tone. The Scottish engineer was content with his work and was relaxed about the undercover nature of their operation. He was confident that there were legitimate reasons for the undercover plan, and that they would learn about them in due course.

The cantankerous Scottish engineer had taken a perverse pleasure in needling his pal. As Bill fumed about their elusive boss over the past week, Alex goaded him, adding fuel to the fire with tales from his extraordinary adventures on foreign-owned ships. The Scotsman had a fund of anecdotes of bribery, theft and corruption. He mocked the fastidious bean counter, accusing the 'Softy Southerner' of leading a sheltered life.

Though the bean counter was undermined by his Scottish colleague, he stood his ground and repeated the question. "How do we know you are coming back?" he demanded angrily. "We can never get hold of you. You never answer your phone!" The young executive was at his wits' end by this time and did not have time for any more of that nonsense.

"I can't believe that you said that, Bill!" exclaimed Steve angrily. "After all the time we've worked together, you accuse me of trying to fiddle you. But if that is what you think, then you can clear off, for all I care. I'll send your money next week. But I can't deal with you now! I've got to pick up someone from the station." With his blood boiling, he could not resist ending his tirade with a spiteful jibe. "As it happens, he's a plain-clothes detective. He is coming for an 'off-the-record' chat. If you are prepared to wait, you might learn what is really going on."

Despite his affection for Bill, Steve was not prepared to put up with his timorous approach to their embryonic mission. Their operation would obviously involve a degree of risk; there was no point in denying it. But then seafaring was risky, by nature. The last thing he wanted was a faintheart who would let them down when the going got tough. They had to trust each other. So he issued an ultimatum.

"You've finished your work, so you are free to leave right now. It's up to you." Then he continued ominously. "This business won't be easy and we may need to bend the rules a bit. So we need to know whether you are prepared to support us, or not. I would like you to stay. But if your heart is not in it, it's best if you go. Once you sign up, you must stay with us to the bitter end!"

Steve made no effort to sugar the pill when he uttered that tirade, thinking that his ultimatum would serve as a loyalty test. The pair had bridled at the undercover nature of the business at the start of the week, so he feared they would jump ship when they learned that a plain-clothes detective was to join them. It was something of a relief that Alex took it all in his stride. The Scotsman did not seem unduly troubled by the cloak-and-dagger nature of the business and seemed content with the work. The 'Softy Southerner' was the weak link.

At least he has given us a straight answer, for once, thought Bill. The tough ultimatum had actually served to reassure the cautious bean counter. But he nevertheless remained fearful of the unchartered waters that lay ahead. The placid bean counter saw himself as an honest and law-abiding citizen and he did not wish to risk his hard-won reputation. On reflection, he regretted his accusation that the young executive was a cheat.

"I'm sorry, Steve, but I've finished the work you set us," said Bill apologetically, pointing to the glossy report that was now lodged in Steve's briefcase. "But I am getting too old for cloak-and-dagger stuff. And I don't fancy getting a criminal record! You should have been honest from the start. You still have not told us what happened to the ship that was berthed in your yard. Why is the detective coming to see us? Does he suspect that we are involved?"

"The detective is not going to interview you," replied Steve testily. "You are not criminal suspects. Nobody is going to arrest you! It's just a friendly 'off-the-record' chat." With that, the young executive looked at his watch and realised that he would have to rush to catch the train. This was not the time to argue; neither did he want to make rash promises just to keep the cautious engineer aboard.

"Look, Bill, I know you think that I have acted in a high-handed way, but events are moving fast at the moment. I hope that you can join us – it's a worthwhile job – you may help to save people's lives – but we need to trust each other." Then echoing the commander's comments the previous evening, "Put it this way. We are not planning anything seriously illegal, but we may bend the rules a bit. So if you can't cut the mustard, now is the time to bail out.

"Anyway, I must rush to the station," he continued firmly, before Bill had a chance to raise any more questions. "Talk it over with Alex, and if you decide to stay on, I hope to see you when I get back in an hour's time. But if you decide to head back home, there will be no hard feelings, and perhaps we'll meet again in happier times." Not knowing whether he would see the pair again, he shook hands with his former shipmates and dashed from the office.

As he left the office, Alex shouted after him: "I'm with you, son. I've had some run-ins with the authorities in my time, and they don't scare me."

On his journey to the station, Steve pondered the attitudes of his former shipmates and was fascinated to see how their attitudes had changed since the reunion weekend. But when he analysed it, he could see that each of them had acted in character. Bill had been friendly and cooperative at the outset, but he was easily spooked. Alex was initially suspicious, but once engaged in the mission, he was bold and prepared to enter into the spirit of the adventure. *I think Alex is hooked, but Bill might slip away*, he mused.

Peter Fellows was sitting on the London-bound train while Steve was involved in that heated exchange. The well-respected detective was approaching retirement, and he could afford to do things his own way. Watching the unfolding events from the sidelines, the plain-clothes detective liked to keep his thoughts to himself. Although he was a conscientious police officer, he was looking forward to his retirement. He wanted to escape from the hoodlums and riff-raff whom he encountered in the course of his police work.

The prospect of working for Steve when he retired was an attractive prospect, so he was looking forward to learning more about the new business he was setting up. It would be an added bonus if Steve chose to unburden himself about the mysterious events that had taken place at the boatyard over the past few days. After his encounter with Beckwith, he suspected that it was part of a conspiracy. The case was intriguing. A satisfying puzzle to end his police career.

There was some hard evidence to suggest that the submarine had been stolen by the Murphy gang and broken up for scrap. His police colleagues believed that theory, and conviction of the Murphy gang would have been the crowning achievement of his career, but the sleuth believed that something far more sinister lay behind it all. His reluctance to toe the party line set him at odds with his fellow officers.

This was not the first time he had been ostracised in the canteen, but it was uncomfortable for the old-timer nevertheless. It would be a relief to get to the bottom of this mystery. While the plain-clothes detective was having these thoughts, Steve was on his way to collect him from the station. The young executive drove cautiously through the suburban side streets. Despite the turbo-charged power at his disposal, he observed the speed limit, much to the annoyance of the hot-headed driver following in his wake.

The speeding ticket issued during the fishing charade was the only traffic violation he had received since moving to the West Country five years earlier. But when road conditions permitted, he enjoyed putting his thoroughbred sports car through its paces. On those rare occasions, he handled the machine with skill, thanks to an advanced driver training course organised by the sales dealership.

Peter Fellows was waiting patiently by the kerb when Steve arrived at the mainline railway station. As the six-foot-tall sleuth coiled himself into the bucket seat of the low-slung vehicle, Steve asked whether he would mind if they took a detour on their way to the office, so he could show off the performance of his car. The plain-clothes detective enjoyed the adrenalin rush of high-speed 'shouts' and was fascinated to find out how Steve's sport car measured up to the top-of-the-range saloons employed by their traffic division. This was the first time he had ridden in a thoroughbred sports car.

As they set off, he was not overly impressed by the vehicle. The doors were flimsy and the interior had a spartan feel. It did not measure up to the comfortable saloons used by their traffic division. The vehicle lacked proper sound insulation. The engine rattled, stuttered and coughed as they pulled away from the kerb. Each pothole made its presence felt through the seat of his pants. As they bounced down the road, the detective asked Steve whether there was any more news about the disappearance of the midget submarine. Steve shook his head as his words were drowned out by the road noise.

Peter Fellows' disillusion with the thoroughbred vehicle was dispelled when they reached a patch of desolate moorland on their roundabout route to the office. "Tighten your seat belt," warned Steve as they topped a rise. The vantage point showed the road was clear of traffic. The sinuous tarmac snaked out before them on the descending slope. Steve kicked down a gear and hit the throttle. The turbocharger howled, forcing air through polished valves into the fast-revolving engine. The plain-clothes detective was thrown back into his seat as the car surged forward.

Racing towards a tight bend, the tail of the rear-engine sports car swung out wildly. The lanky detective grabbed the dashboard and crouched low in his seat, preparing for disaster. But, by some miracle, they rounded the corner unharmed. The young executive controlled the tail-end skid with the élan of a rally driver. As they drove on, Steve reverted to his normal pedestrian pace. The sleuth had little idea that this was a regular stunt that Steve used to soften up his clients. He found that people were much more amenable after being treated to a 'white-knuckle ride'.

The sleuth was exhilarated but also impressed by his friend's modesty. Others boasted of their driving skills, but Steve had never mentioned it. The detective's eardrums enjoyed a welcome respite when they stopped at a railway crossing. When his ears stopped ringing, the plain-clothes sleuth asked why his friend had become involved in a dredging business. "It's a humanitarian mission and that is where I need your help," replied Steve mysteriously. "I'll explain more when we reach the office," he added as they resumed their rackety progress.

As the sports car came to a stop outside the office, Steve warned the detective what to expect. "You will meet a couple of my old shipmates in the office. They are helping me to set up the business; making financial plans, and so forth." As they climbed the stairs, he explained that he had met the pair while serving as an engineer apprentice on a ship called the *Sea Ranger*. The detective was still shaken up by the roller coaster ride from the station and was not really concentrating on what his friend was saying. When they entered the brightly lit office, Steve was relieved to find that both his former shipmates had decided to stay on.

While Steve was collecting the plain-clothes detective from the railway station, his former shipmates were trying to decide whether they would stay with the business. There was a sharp difference of opinion. Bill wanted to go home. He was spooked by the undercover nature of the operation and disturbed by news emanating from the boatyard. His Scottish pal was, by contrast, sanguine about the undercover aspects and he was keen to stay on. But he did not want to do so on his own. So he used his wiles to assuage his pal's fears. While he waged his subtle campaign, there was a truce in their fractious relationship.

In their day-to-day banter, the bean counter was the butt of Alex's jibes. But beneath the bravado, the Scotsman knew he needed Bill's support to survive in a cut-throat commercial world, so Alex toned down his belligerent patter and adopted an uncharacteristically kindly attitude towards his friend. "It won't be much fun for you to return to an empty house," remarked Alex sympathetically as he cajoled his pal. After many considerate exchanges, Bill was persuaded to stay on.

With Bill's surrender, the truce was forgotten as far as the Scotsman was concerned. To rib his fretful pal, the Scotsman made the 'bee-burb' sound under his breath to imitate the siren of a police car when Steve arrived with the detective in tow. "Don't worry, Bill. He is not here to arrest you! Well, not yet!" he teased. The plain-clothes detective did not know what to make of the Scotsman's bizarre remark; the poor chap was still dazed from the helter-skelter car journey. Steve used all his diplomatic skills as he tried to smooth things over.

"I've known Peter for many years," he explained smoothly as he introduced the new arrival to his former shipmates. "He investigated a break-in at the boatyard and we've been friends ever since. Peter is retiring in six months and is thinking of joining the dredging business. So, if it's all right with the pair of you, I would like him to sit in on the briefing. It will help him understand the 'humanitarian' side of the business." Bill winced at the word 'humanitarian', noting the cynical use of the public relations term. He now regretted his decision to stay.

The young executive then pointed to the picture of the *Ocean Ranger* and described how they had served together on the venerable old ship. He related a couple of short anecdotes from their voyages and described the part his former shipmates might play in the dredging business. Alex thought that the cocky young executive was painting an overly rosy view of their relationship and so he decided to throw a brick into the pool.

"Steve invited us both down to a reunion at the boatyard," remarked the Scotsman in an apparently friendly way. Then with a wicked look, he plunged in the dagger. "After looking round the offices, we climbed on a wee ship that was berthed at the quay. But we could not stay on board. An angry fellow with a beard ordered us to leave the ship. Seems that our friend here did not have permission to board the ship!"

"Thank *you*, Alex," said Steve through gritted teeth as he struggled to control his temper. Bill was shaken from his reverie by that remark. Some troubling rumours were swirling around the boatyard, and the ever-cautious engineer was worried about their implications. *Typical! Why did the bloody Scotsman have to bring that up!* he brooded. But he held his tongue. Sitting beside him, the Scotsman grinned at his friend's unease.

Struggling to maintain order, the young executive shepherded his disparate team into the chairs set out at one end of the conference table. The young executive then morphed into a college lecturer as he unfurled a flipchart hanging from an easel standing under the window at the far end of the room. Steve had prepared some simple charts and sketches to help with his presentation. To the surprise of his audience, the first illustration was a graphic showing the size of the naval fleet of navy over the years.

"Like going back to school!" remarked Alex jovially. Despite irritation at his indiscreet remark, Steve was grateful that the capable Scottish engineer was starting to show enthusiasm for their operation. He was mindful of the way that Alex flounced out of the Feathers pub at the mention of submarines and the navy.

In drawing up his presentation, Steve faced a difficult balancing act. He needed to explain the covert surveillance role of the dredging business without mentioning the disappearance of the submarine. In time, he would reveal what had taken place, but only after some delicate legal matters had been resolved. Until then, he needed to take care how much he revealed about their weekend caper to the plain-clothes detective.

Once he was satisfied that they were all paying attention, Steve began his presentation. "You will know that over the past years, a fleet of warships has been protecting ships from pirates in the Indian Ocean. The operation has been successful, but the warships are now needed for other roles." He went on to talk about the range of challenges facing the navy all around the globe. "Some naval planners believe the new aircraft carriers have placed an intolerable strain on the navy's budget," he added as a provocative aside.

Alex had become restive. "We know all that! What's it got to do with dredging?" he asked.

"I'm coming to that, Alex," replied Steve patiently. "Just bear with me.

"During the war, shipping companies worked closely with the navy," continued Steve. "You will all be aware of the role the Merchant Navy played in times of conflict."

"Yes. And a fat lot of thanks they got!" replied Alex derisively. The Scotsman was angry that the vital role played by merchant seamen in the Arctic convoys was not fully recognised. It was one of his many hobby horses.

Steve looked at Alex sharply, daring him to continue. "There has been a long history of cooperation between merchant shipping and the armed forces, as you will all know," continued Steve pompously. "You might recall the part the *QE2* and *Atlantic Conveyor* played in the Falklands. Fighter aircraft flew from oil tankers during the Atlantic convoys."

"Britain is not the only country where the navy works with commercial shipping," observed Alex argumentatively. "The Russians use trawlers for surveillance work."

"Thank you, Alex! That was a useful observation," replied Steve in a more friendly tone. As it happened, the interruption *was* a useful contribution, on that occasion. "Our business will operate along similar lines," continued Steve. "We will run a commercial company, but we will provide a base for military personnel." The detective nodded his head. He was beginning to appreciate Steve's obscure reference to the 'humanitarian role' of the business.

"Our dredger will act as a 'decoy ship' – are any of you familiar with that term?" asked the young executive. The three members of the audience shook their heads, each with a slightly bewildered expression.

"Some old cargo ships were fitted with concealed weapons during both the First and Second World Wars. The ships appeared defenceless and easy prey. They were used to lure enemy submarines to the surface. The submarine commanders did not like wasting a torpedo on a defenceless ship, so they would surface to attack with a deck gun. When that happened, the innocent-looking decoy ship would bare its teeth."

Then to illustrate the point, Steve handed a copy of the day's newspaper to the detective. The paper carried an obituary of a German U-boat commander who sank a decoy ship called the *USS Atik* off the coast of the United States during the Second World War. The decoy ship put up a valiant fight and forced the submariner to fire one of his last torpedoes to sink her. After this short aside, to give them a chance to read the obituary, Steve continued.

"Anyway, a branch of the navy wants us to convert a dredger to act as a base for covert surveillance in pirate-infested waters off the Horn of Africa. When we have completed the conversion work, we expect to win a contract to dredge a channel to a new container port project in the region. Our ship will provide a base for special forces. The scheme is jointly funded by the government, shipping and insurance industries. It's all part of a scheme to protect merchant seamen.

"Our vessel will dredge channels to a new port. But while it is operating, it will provide a base for special forces to reconnoitre the coast and keep an eye on the pirate gangs. Our job is to support the undercover operations, so we obviously need you to keep quiet about what we are up to. If the role of the dredging company was made public, our cover would be blown, and the whole scheme would be a waste of time. I hope that explains why we place so much emphasis on confidentiality in your employment contracts. We will operate on a 'need-to-know' basis. That means, in practice, that you will only be told what you need for your work. But this is technically a civilian operation, so we are not covered by the Official Secrets Act."

Bill was becoming agitated by what he heard. "You don't seriously expect me to work in pirate-infested waters?" he enquired nervously.

"If you accept my offer, you will look after the business side of things, from this office," replied Steve. "I would expect you to recruit the seagoing staff and look after the commercial aspects of the business. I would like Alex to oversee the conversion of the dredger and act as engineering superintendent. That will probably mean spending time at a shipyard on the continent. So you won't be expected, either of you, to work in risky waters. But remember that expats work in many dangerous places."

"You can say that again!" chipped in Alex to boast about his various scrapes in lawless regions. "We once berthed in a rat-infested slum near Karachi. Gangs sneaked on board and nicked anything that was not bolted down. They attacked us when they went ashore." Steve was not amused. He looked at the Scotsman sharply to cut his diatribe short. He had better things to do than to listen to him reminiscing.

"What I was going to say," continued Steve patiently, "is that expats work in dangerous parts of the world *without getting into trouble*. Big corporations are able to protect their staff. They employ professional security people. We will do the same. People with military training will be hidden on board, so that our vessel will have the appearance of an innocent dredger. But it will be able to defend itself, don't fear!"

Alex was nettled by the put-down and was determined to get his own back, so he raised his hand in a jokey display of deference. "Yes, Alex!" barked Steve impatiently. "Have you got some other pearls of wisdom?"

"Well, I was thinking that you could hide a midget submarine on the dredger," suggested the Scotsman with an impish grin. Unspoken questions about the missing submarine had hovered over the room since his indiscreet remark about the unauthorised tour of the *Normandy*. The cantankerous fellow was fully aware of the inflammatory nature of his comment, even though it was delivered in an off-the-cuff manner. This was his crafty revenge for the young executive's snide put-down.

The exchange placed Steve in an extremely awkward position. He had gone to great lengths to avoid mentioning the midget submarine up to that point. He could not discuss it until the legal ownership was resolved. After all, they were technically guilty of theft. But he had been assured by the Admiral that they would acquire legal ownership of the submarine within a few days. Once that legal process was sorted out, Steve would be free to discuss the midget submarine with his recruits. But until then, he had to keep schtum.

"Do you think so?" replied Steve, adopting a poker face as he played dumb. "What had you in mind?"

"A wee submarine, like the one you showed us last weekend, could be hidden away in one of those big hoppers," observed Alex with a cunning expression as he pointed to the cut-away sketch hanging on the wall. "The hoppers have underwater hatches to drop material onto the seabed. A little submarine could be launched through the hatch without attracting too much attention."

Noting Steve's unease, Bill could see that the observation had hit its target. He pretended to play a trumpet fanfare as he watched his Scottish pal's chest swell with pride. The young executive squirmed with embarrassment. He was in an invidious position. Until given the green light, he needed to deny that they possessed a submarine. But playing dumb was alien to his nature. The impetuous Scotsman had let the cat out of the bag and so Steve needed to disband the meeting with all speed.

"That's an interesting idea, Alex!" remarked Steve in a disjointed way to show that he was flustered. "I'll pass on your idea to the navy. There is a meeting in Portsmouth in a few days to discuss the operation. You are welcome to attend, if you decide to stay on. But please keep that idea to yourself for the time being. Remember, secrecy is key to our success, so don't go about discussing your idea with anyone else."

Peter Fellows tried to suppress a smile as he watched all this from the sidelines. It was confirmation of his theory that his friend was up to no good, and that the disappearance of the submarine was part of some conspiracy. A murky picture was starting to emerge. The tentacles of the conspiracy seemed to extend in all directions. But the sleuth could not piece all the elements of the story together in the hot-house atmosphere of the antiseptic office. He needed time and space to mull it all over.

The plain-clothes detective also felt some sympathy for his friend as the young guy flailed about trying to extract himself from a morass of lies and deceit. He did not wish to make his friend's life more difficult by asking awkward questions in front of strangers. So, to spare embarrassment, he raised an unrelated issue to change the subject and divert attention from his friend's plight. He intended to ask his probing questions when they were alone, later that day.

"Could you explain how I will fit in?" asked the detective in an absent-minded way. He spoke as though he were lost in his own thoughts, oblivious to the underlying tensions in the room. "You know that I have never been to sea, unlike the rest of you," he added modestly.

Steve breathed a sigh of relief. The detective's soft-ball question allowed him to escape from the quagmire. Grabbing at the lifeline, he addressed the simple question in a more fulsome manner than it warranted. "You will play a key role, providing administrative back-up from this office," he replied with renewed confidence. "It will be a challenging job. You would be responsible for purchasing supplies and forwarding them to the ship. You would make travel arrangements for the crew, important jobs like that. Basically, you would support Bill and Alex." In this exchange, Bill and Alex were excluded from the conversation.

"That sounds interesting, but surely there are people better qualified than me," observed the plain-clothes detective.

"Well, yes," replied Steve, "but don't forget this is an undercover operation. We are only going to employ people we can trust. People we *know*."

"Well, I could give it a go," said the plain-clothes detective gamely, "but you know that I'm not available for six months."

"Don't worry about that. That timescale should fit in well with our plans," replied Steve encouragingly. "It will take more than six months to convert the dredger. You will not be needed until the dredger is ready to sail for East Africa." The ploy to change the subject achieved its aim with Alex sidelined but, denied the spotlight, the Scotsman's peevish expression was that of a small boy whose ice cream has been snatched from his hand.

Alex did not have the slightest interest in administrative work, so he yawned ostentatiously to show his disdain for the way the discussion was heading. "Sorry, are we keeping you up?" teased Steve.

Bill joined the hue and cry. "An administrator is just what we need," observed the bean counter, pointing scornfully at the papers spilling from the Scotsman's desk. "You need help keeping your papers in order," added the bean counter spitefully.

The plain-clothes detective had only played along with Steve's line about the admin work to save his friend's face. He had no intention of accepting an administrative post, and nor did Steve intend to offer him that kind of work, but both had acted in unison to prevent Alex making any more intemperate remarks. Alex had behaved like a bull in a china shop and showed a reckless lack of discretion.

With Alex silenced for the time being, Steve called a break for lunch. Looking at the plain-clothes detective, he asked: "Unless there is anything else you need to know, I will drive you back to the station and let these reprobates enjoy their sandwiches." With that, the young executive jumped up and grabbed his coat. "Don't worry, I'll be back in an hour," he promised as he bowled out of the office with the plain-clothes detective in tow. The bewildered pair were left to mull over what they had heard.

The plain-clothes detective was in a thoughtful mood as he clambered into Steve's sports car for the return journey back to the railway station, but he was unable to probe further because the road noise prevented them talking when the car was moving. But when they finally pulled up outside the railway station, he took the opportunity to quiz his friend. The sleuth hoped that Steve would come clean about recent events, in return for his own insights.

"Thought you might be interested to know that I spoke to Martin Beckwith and his private detective yesterday," commented the detective as he unbuckled his seat belt and prepared to extract his lanky frame from the low-slung vehicle.

Steve's ears pricked up at this valuable nugget of intelligence. Rumours had swirled around about a bad-tempered confrontation. The reason for the discord in Beckwith's portable cabin was the subject of intense speculation among the yard staff, so he was keen to hear the inside story.

"Oh yes. What did he have to say?" remarked Steve nonchalantly. The young executive had been taciturn during the journey, preparing for awkward questions about Alex's remark.

"Beckwith drove down to the yard in the belief that we had found his midget submarine at Leighton Hollow," remarked the plain-clothes detective with the trace of a smile. He hoped this would provoke a reaction. But Steve played it cool. The pair were dancing on their tiptoes, circling like featherweights in the opening round of a boxing match. This opening gambit was like the first feint. Neither was being open and honest.

"Had you?" asked Steve with a slightly teasing inflection. In reply, the plain-clothes detective shook his head with a look of incredulity.

"What on earth gave him that idea?" continued Steve curiously. The detective's remark had provided the young executive with a valuable insight into Beckwith's thinking, and justified Steve's decision to confide in his old friend.

"His private detective gave him that impression," explained the detective. "Hugh Malone, that's the private detective's name, has been sniffing around the army training ground. He found out that I was investigating an incident there. So Malone phoned his client with a half-baked story. The pair of idiots put two and two together and got five!

"It was a misunderstanding. You remember me telling you about the fly-tipping at Leighton Hollow? For some reason, Beckwith got the impression that we had found his submarine. I refused to tell him anything at first. Fly-tipping is none of his business, but the arrogant sod pulled strings and the superintendent ordered me to tell him what I knew.

"The silly fool went ape when I told him that I was investigating a fly-tipping incident. The guy accused us of wasting his time. Of course, some of my colleagues believe the two events are linked. They believe that the Murphy gang stole the submarine and broke it up for scrap. That is what Malone is going to put in his report. But Beckwith doesn't believe that for a minute."

"Does the private detective *really* believe that the gang broke up the submarine for scrap metal?" asked Steve with an assumed air of disbelief. Maintaining an incredulous expression, the young executive watched his friend's reaction with gimlet eyes. It was important for him to know whether his friend had fallen for their false trail of clues. In their verbal joust, neither of the men were laying all their cards on the table.

"Malone has only just arrived in the West Country, so he has not had time to track down the submarine," replied the plain-clothes detective evasively. "He just parroted the view of some of the other detectives in our station. But Beckwith won't buy the scrap metal story. He is convinced that the midget submarine is hidden somewhere along the coast. He is desperate to find it."

As he tried to assimilate all this, Steve wondered just how much the plain-clothes detective had read into Alex's indiscreet remark about hiding a submarine in the hull of their dredger. "Do you believe the scrap metal theory?" he asked provocatively.

"Haven't a clue," replied the plain-clothes detective noncommittally as he stared into his friend's eyes, trying to fathom out what was going on. "That's what some of my colleagues think. They are planning to raid scrap yards belonging to the Murphy family to see if they can find evidence to link them to the disappearance of the submarine."

"You have your doubts, though?" suggested Steve. The plain-clothes detective's poker face gave no indications of his thoughts. Steve was sorely tempted to reveal the truth, because he did not like to deceive an old friend. But his lips were sealed until the Admiral had sorted out the legal ownership of the craft. He was still waiting for the green light. So, instead, he settled for an oblique remark.

"One thing we do know is that the diverter valve you found at Leighton Hollow was fitted to the midget submarine," continued Steve as he prepared to drive away. That hint was not very much help, because it simply confirmed what the forensic team already knew.

"So, you think we should pursue that line of inquiry …?" asked the plain-clothes detective as he stepped onto the pavement.

"It's probably best if you let your colleagues track down the scrap metal thieves and take credit for arresting them!" suggested Steve, to save his friend from making a monumental blunder. The ambiguous comment was enough. It confirmed the plain-clothes detective's views that there was more to this affair than met the eye.

With that, the dashing young executive accelerated away, leaving his bemused friend standing in a cloud of dust. It had been a weird meeting, reflected the plain-clothes detective, but it confirmed his view that Steve was involved in a major conspiracy whose tentacles extended in many directions. The meeting forced him to reassess his views about the Scottish fishing trip and the fracas at his flat. Until now, he held the view that these events were related to Steve's unstable relationship with the alluring landlady. The meeting dispelled that view.

Unlike many of his colleagues, Peter Fellows did not rush to judgement. He believed that you could sometimes learn more from what people did not say than from what they did say. The truth could probably be found in Steve's awkward response to Alex's indiscreet remark about the midget submarine, he mused. The detective was starting to perceive the vague outline of the bigger picture, but he needed to sleep to digest what he had learned that day. It would be foolish to leap in with accusations before assimilating what he knew. But the day had shown one thing. While his friend was obviously bending the rules, there were clear signs that he was doing so for honourable reasons, so he did not want to create too many waves.

After dropping the detective off at the railway station, Steve ruminated as he returned to face his truculent employees in the dredging office. In recruiting his old shipmates, he felt like a drover trying to coax unruly sheep into a pen. It was hardly surprising that they balked at his orders, because they did not know what was really going on. In time, they would realise they had been treated fairly. In the meantime, he needed to impose some order on the fractious pair.

Steve's first challenge was to deal with Alex. His indiscreet remark about the submarine, in front of the detective, had nearly let the cat out of the bag. The cantankerous Scotsman had acted like a marauding bull. Steve could not tolerate this sort of behaviour, so it was now time for him to lay down the law.

The young executive understood that the pair squabbled while incarcerated together in the claustrophobic office; this made it hard for them to cooperate. Alex was content with his lot, but he took delight in goading his cautious colleague. His mischievous nature had nearly undermined the operation that morning. But his colleague was little help. It was obvious that

Bill fretted about the stories emanating from the boatyard at Whitebait Cove.

So how could the young executive persuade the fractious pair to cooperate? He normally adopted a relaxed management style at the boatyard in contrast to the authoritarian regime of his predecessor. Sam Wheeler ruled the boatyard with a rod of iron, but Steve gave his staff freedom to make their own decisions.

As he reflected, Steve reluctantly acknowledged that while this enlightened approach was effective at the boatyard, it was not an effective way to manage this wayward pair. So the young guy decided to lay down the law, even if it cost him their friendship. He did not have the time or patience to coax them. True to form, the young executive found Bill and Alex arguing when he returned to the office.

"Excuse me!" shouted Steve as he encountered the bickering pair. "Please remember that I'm your boss and pay the bills, so show me respect!" The pair were taken aback by their new boss's aggressive stance. They had difficulty accepting that the youthful cadet had morphed into an executive. "I'm *not* happy with what you have achieved. The truth is that you did not complete the task I set you. So I'm going to retain half your pay!" he declared. The sharp reprimand was like an irate schoolmaster condemning the whole class to detention.

"I knew we couldn't trust you," remarked Bill petulantly. "I have finished the task you set us." The Scotsman nodded in agreement, showing solidarity with his pal, for once.

Steve fixed Bill with a steely gaze. "Okay. You did complete a business plan. It was a flashy document. But you assumed that the dredging business would be restricted to UK waters. If you had listened to Alex, you would have considered business prospects in other parts of the world, beyond the North Sea."

"Well, we did not know that you planned to work in Africa," whined Bill. "You only told us that today!"

"That's not really the point. What I'm trying to say is that you failed to work together as a team," remarked Steve sharply. "You live in your own little worlds and bicker all the time. If you work for me, you will have to cooperate for the common good."

After learning of the financial difficulties at the boatyard, Bill thought this was a crafty ruse to allow the slippery young guy to welch on their agreement. "When do we get our money, then?" he asked with a sarcastic edge to his voice.

"You get half now, and the other half when you have finished the job next week," replied Steve masterfully.

"Who said we will come back next week?" retorted Bill. He was amazed at the young guy's effrontery.

"It's up to you!" replied Steve firmly. "You have not distinguished yourselves this week. There are plenty of other people with your background looking for work." With no further ado, he passed each of them an envelope containing their half-pay. As the pair spluttered with impotent rage, the young executive calmly collected his belongings and made a graceful exit. His tough negotiating position was a shock for his former shipmates. They thought that they were doing their young friend a favour, but it now seemed it was the other way around.

Steve's words served to crystalise the envy and distrust that the pair felt towards the young upstart. This was a watershed moment in the relationship that would sweep away any semblance of friendship among the trio of engineers, but Steve's draconian action served its purpose. His old shipmates were both chastened and bonded by hatred of their new master. But like beaten dogs, they grudgingly accepted that they would return to the dredging office the following week.

Chapter 24

Tweak his Tail

After his abortive trip to the West Country, Beckwith scuttled back to London and went to ground in his Whitehall bunker with his enemies in hot pursuit like a pack of braying hounds. But the angry academic attracted little sympathy from the buzzy young folk gossiping in the reception area. This buzzy young crowd had become accustomed to Beckwith's temper tantrums, but the volcanic eruption that greeted Malone's report came as a shock, even to these hardened observers.

There was a view that the sleazy academic was suffering from paranoid delusions. That view was confirmed by the titanic outburst when Beckwith read the report's tentative conclusion, that his submarine had been broken up for scrap. "Any half-wit can see that the navy team stole the submarine," yelled the purple-faced academic as he punched the wall to relieve his fury. This ugly scene was met with gales of laughter from the audience in the reception area.

Matters went from bad to worse when Jason Tyrone sent a

brief, impersonal message saying that he had completed his side of the bargain, in respect of the Whitebait Cove investigation. Though couched in legalese, the wording gave the impression that the lawyer wanted no further dealings with the washed-up academic. This left Beckwith with a desperate sense of impotence, but it was a mess of his own making.

The academic had dragged his heels over reporting the theft in the belief that he could find the midget submarine without getting the police involved. But his gamble had backfired in spectacular fashion. The private sleuth's report concluded that the submarine had been stolen and broken up for scrap. This presented an insoluble conundrum. How was he to explain his delay in reporting the theft, if the conclusion was correct? With a sense of resignation, he asked his trusty sidekick, Simon, to bring him the insurance policy file.

As he flicked dejectedly though the pages, he learned that the Texan had arranged an insurance policy to cover loss of the submarine during the sea trials as one of his final acts as project manager. His spirits lifted as he turned the pages and came across some paperwork that seemed to offer a way out. The documents suggested that the insurance policy had been arranged through a shady insurance broker.

The correspondence suggested that the Texan project manager had an unhealthily close relationship with the insurance agent. One letter referred to complimentary tickets for a rugby match at Twickenham. An imprint of a handwritten message was barely legible on the file copy. But when he examined it closely, the message read *Thank you for the pleasant outing.* This brought a smile to the academic's face. It was just the sort of back-scratching relationship that the academic fostered with his own suppliers.

This revelation suggested that the Texan was not the Boy Scout that he pretended to be. The correspondence painted a different picture, revealing that his predecessor had a venal streak, like his own. As he dug further, he found a couple more scruffy handwritten notes that suggested his predecessor was in cahoots with a guy called Felix who was loosely attached to the insurance agency. It seemed that this fellow was an independent marine consultant, so the academic decided to call the guy to sound him out.

Artful dodges picked up on the mean streets of North London had helped Beckwith to prosper in the morally dubious *demi-monde* of politics and public affairs. He planned to use these dark arts to win this corrupt consultant as an ally, but it called for all his wiles. The scale of the challenge became evident when the academic received a cool, guarded reception to his introductory phone call. But when he mentioned the Texan by name, the marine consultant's attitude softened and he let his guard down. Beckwith was soon on cordial terms with the consultant, and they arranged to meet in the Whitehall office.

A sharply suited businessman arrived promptly at nine o'clock the following morning in the reception area of the Whitehall office. On being ushered into Beckwith's cubbyhole, the visitor did not waste any time before settling down to business. "My name is Felix Sikorski," he declared in a clipped Polish accent as he withdrew a shipping newspaper called *Lloyd's List* from his briefcase. He leafed through the pages with deft fingers, until he came to the casualty notice that had been composed by Simon, the office administrator.

"We follow up casualty notices in the shipping papers. I assume that this one relates to your midget submarine?" observed the dapper visitor as he turned the paper round and carefully placed it in front of the bemused academic. The no-nonsense approach threw the academic. It upset his plan to tiptoe around the delicate aspects of his predicament. Beckwith was acutely embarrassed that the submarine had been pinched from beneath his nose, and wished to cloud the matter with all manner of diversions.

The academic rapidly changed his strategy. "Could you explain your role?" he asked, to size the man up. This gambit was effective, because the bumptious visitor was only too happy to blow his own trumpet, and this gave the academic an opportunity to rethink his whole approach.

"I'm an *independent* marine consultant," replied the visitor with the first hint of a smile, to soften the angular features of his face. It was clear that the fellow took great pride in his independent status. "No two jobs are the same. My work can be really exciting. I recently tracked down a stolen ship in the Far East. It was a torrid tale. There followed the sort of sales pitch that a consultant employs while seeking a new client.

"The crew were a mutinous lot. After murdering their captain, they sent a message to say they were abandoning the sinking ship. But they had actually sailed the old rust bucket to a backwater in Bangladesh. When they arrived, the crew sold the vessel and fled with the proceeds. We managed to recover the ship, though. It was not easy because she was sailing under another flag. The new owners had painted her a different colour and had given her a new name, but we managed to track the ship down nevertheless."

As he spoke, the sharp-suited visitor gave the impression of a Pinkerton detective in the Wild West. He painted a colourful picture of a buccaneering industry, confirming views that the academic had gained from reading the specialised shipping papers. The words opened up an exciting new world, full of opportunities, to the credulous academic.

Beckwith had learned quite a lot about the shipping world in the past few days. He was able to do that because Simon had taken up an introductory offer to the specialist shipping paper *Lloyd's List* when he placed the casualty notice. The offer provided a free subscription to the otherwise costly newspaper for a couple of months. This allowed Beckwith to follow the events that take place on the high seas every day. It was a revelation that put his own *travails* in perspective. One story described events that harked back to the *Mary Celeste*.

A seaworthy cargo ship was found washed up on the shore in the Far East without any sign of crew or why it was abandoned. It later emerged that the ship was being towed to Bangladesh, where it was to be scrapped. It seemed that the tug abandoned the ship when the towline snapped in stormy weather. The tug master failed to report the incident. This was typical of the outlandish events that take place on the high seas on a regular basis.

"Pretty interesting work!" remarked Beckwith admiringly. The academic was won over by the dapper businessman, admiring his intoxicating tales and cavalier attitude to life. So, throwing caution to the wind, he decided to trust the mysterious guy. After all, he was in a deep hole and there was little to lose. Pointing to the paper lying on the table between them, he let down his guard. "Our midget submarine has not been found," admitted the academic with a rueful expression. "Who pays for your services?"

"Each job is different. Sometimes we receive a 'finder's fee', and on others we charge a percentage of the insurance settlement," replied the smart-suited consultant in his clipped, businesslike way. "It varies, depending on the work involved. It is open to negotiation."

"So, if we asked for your help to find it, you would not want any cash up front?" asked the academic with a cunning expression. This was an important consideration because the coffers were bare.

The dapper consultant smiled encouragingly. "We are normally paid by the insurers as part of the settlement. Fees vary. It all depends on the work involved. We'll need some more information about your loss. My team should be able to handle the work because things are a bit slow at the moment. We don't take on every case we're offered."

The sales pitch rang true because much of it was true. The visitor did carry out marine consultancy work and he was involved in the recovery of a cargo ship, although his role in the case was slightly exaggerated. The consultant's dapper appearance and professional air gave his polished words a ring of authenticity. Little did Beckwith suspect that his visitor was responsible for his plight. Beckwith was clutching at straws and swallowed the bait hook, line and sinker. "What do you need to know?" asked Beckwith hesitantly.

"The casualty notice doesn't provide much detail," replied the sharp-suited consultant in a reassuring way as he perused the newspaper page laid out on the desk. "Can you tell me any more about what took place?"

The notice was, indeed, vague. It had simply been a ruse to gain time to find the missing craft. But, to get the visitor's help, he needed to be a little more open. *How can we achieve that without revealing embarrassing aspects of the case?* he mused.

While he was pondering that conundrum, he noticed, with a start, that Malone's report, with its unpalatable conclusion that the submarine had been stolen and broken up for scrap, was lying on top of his in-tray. Fortunately, his visitor was distracted by raucous laughter in the reception area at that particular moment, so the academic slipped a piece of paper on top of the offending document in a surreptitious way. This sleight of hand did not go unnoticed by the sharp-eyed visitor, however. The marine consultant had noticed the contentious report on entering the office and had a pretty good idea of its contents.

Relieved that a potential disaster had been averted, the artful academic then proceeded to paint a grandiose picture of his place in the world. In doing so, he followed in his visitor's example. "Some years ago, we set up the Marine Special Projects Agency to improve the efficiency of warship procurement. You may have heard of us," he declared with the pompous air of an elder statesman. He then trotted out a well-oiled sales pitch describing the aims and achievements of his new agency. In the course of this diatribe, he dropped the names of powerful political figures, to give the impression he was a person of some consequence. This flimflam was a smokescreen to divert attention from his embarrassing predicament.

"We were asked to build a midget submarine using a novel form of propulsion. It will be used by the navy for submarine rescue operations," he continued smoothly. With that, he handed over a glossy brochure describing the groundbreaking project. "It's the first time that fuel cells have been used for propulsion of a British submarine," he boasted. "Sadly, the naval officers were out of their depth with this new technology. They were unsure of the technology and wanted to test the performance of the prototype before accepting it for rescue work, so they provided a team to carry out sea trials from Whitebait Cove in the West Country.

"The prototype was launched from a supply ship called the *Normandy* during the sea trials. After transporting the prototype to the trials area, the ship returned to berth at the quay at Whitebait Cove each evening. The trials were a *great success*. They ended last Friday. But then the supply ship sailed without warning from the berth and was found some miles down the estuary. The submarine was no longer on board. There is some confusion about where the submarine was landed."

The sharp-suited visitor recorded the bizarre story in his notebook, in a noncommittal fashion, with the air of a diligent professional. "Have you any idea where they took the midget submarine?" he enquired politely, after reading though his carefully written notes. This query touched a sore spot, causing the academic to speak rashly.

"I know what happened to it!" replied Beckwith angrily. "The navy trials team sneaked on board the *Normandy* in the early hours of Sunday morning. Then they sailed down the estuary and landed our midget submarine somewhere along the coast. Probably at one of their naval bases. They did it out of spite!" The outburst was a sign that the academic could no longer contain himself, believing he was the victim of a conspiracy.

"That sounds a bit far-fetched. Why on earth would they want to do that! Surely, they could arrange the transfer of the submarine through official channels," observed the sharp-suited consultant sympathetically. His saccharin expression benefitted from experience of amateur dramatics.

The injustice led Beckwith to speak in an injudicious way. "The navy is jealous of our agency," he declared peevishly. "The naval officers are envious because the trial was a great success. They were determined to find fault with our new propulsion system, but it performed better than predicted. They were proved wrong! We also demonstrated that complex projects can be completed on time and budget," he blustered. "Their projects always overrun," he added with a disdainful sneer.

"So, you believe that the disappearance of the submarine was a navy plot to discredit your new agency," suggested the smart-suited visitor in a supportive manner, giving the appearance that he was swayed by Beckwith's views. "But can you prove that?" he added quizzically.

"Well, we haven't got any proof, but if you join up the dots you don't need to be Sherlock Holmes to see what is going on," replied Beckwith defiantly.

"Perhaps it was stolen by professional thieves?" suggested the smart-suited visitor as an afterthought. With that, the consultant gathered his belongings, giving a clear sign that he had no further interest in the matter.

"That's ridiculous," blurted out Beckwith, fearing that the capable consultant was about to abandon him. The visitor's behaviour caused him to wonder how much more he knew. If he was to keep the conversation alive, he had to lay more cards on the table, he surmised. "Some people believe the prototype was stolen by thieves and broken up for scrap," he reluctantly admitted, "but that is a load of nonsense in my view!"

"That sounds plausible," responded the smart-suited visitor thoughtfully as he paused his departure. "Scrap metal thieves have stolen all sorts of valuable equipment. Thieves have stolen power cable. There have even been reports of villains stealing the brass plaques from war memorials."

"I'm sorry. It does not make sense to me," replied Beckwith defensively, saddened that yet another person was prepared to accept the bizarre theory. "The hull of the submarine is fabricated from titanium. It would be impossible to sell rare material like that."

"Perhaps. But they could take the titanium abroad," speculated the visitor as he, once again, picked up his coat in preparation for his departure. "Anyway, it sounds like a fascinating case. Let me know how you get on." This final remark was made in a throw-away manner, as though it was a matter of little interest. The gambit worked. Beckwith was in a bind, and he was now forced to show how desperate he was.

"We would be extremely grateful if you could track down the midget submarine," begged the academic in a pleading voice towards the fast-retreating figure. The desperate plea achieved its aim. The visitor slowed and turned back to face the academic.

"We'll need more details if we are to investigate it properly," observed the smart-suited consultant doubtfully.

"No problem. Only too glad to help," replied Beckwith with relief as the visitor walked briskly from the office. "I'll ask my assistant to assemble a dossier and we'll email it to your office," he added to the retreating figure. When he settled down to reflect, Beckwith felt satisfied by the way the meeting had gone. The tide was changing. It was just possible that the capable guy would carry out an investigation for free. The marine consultant might succeed where Malone had failed.

But that was not the only reason for his satisfaction. The academic needed an insider to steer him through the treacherous waters of the insurance market if he was to make a claim. He intended to befriend the consultant, and win him over as an ally. *This should not be too difficult,* he mused. After all, the file suggested that behind the honest façade lay a venal individual who was open to a bribe. All he had to do was find a chink in his armour. This was just the sort of challenge that he relished.

Beckwith spent the afternoon closeted with Simon, compiling a dossier that, supposedly, outlined the weekend's events at Whitebait Cove. But the dossier was carefully slanted to downplay the theory that the craft had been stolen by scrap metal thieves, and it skipped over details of security failings at the boatyard. Instead, the document focussed on facts that pointed to the guilt of the trials team. The conniving pair did their best to discredit the notion that the navy trials team had spent the night at a 'lock-in' party. This was described as a 'flimsy alibi'.

Felix smiled wryly when he read the concoction in his office the following day, pleased to see that the academic had behaved just as expected. No mention was made of the videotapes that showed that all those involved in the sea trials were all present at the 'lock-in' party at the time the *Normandy* went missing. But there was another reason for his satisfaction. In focussing his attention on the navy trials team, who were the obvious suspects, the academic was blind to other possibilities.

Watching the artful academic extract himself from his predicament was like watching a fly repeatedly batter its head against a pane of glass, not realising that a window was open nearby, mused Felix. The fly could see the outside world and was determined to head in that direction, heedless of the impenetrable barrier that lay in its way. The little creatures seemed unable to learn from their mistakes.

When he had had time to absorb the dossier's contents, Felix returned to Whitehall for a showdown with the academic. As before, Felix did not waste time on pleasantries and got straight down to business. "I've been in touch with the local police, and they have been most helpful," he observed with a sinister smile. "They also told me that the security guard was absent when the *Normandy* went missing on Saturday night.

"Some components from your midget submarine were found at a disused quarry on an army range in Leighton Hollow," remarked the consultant in a brisk, businesslike way. "That seems to support the theory that the submarine was brought ashore and broken up for scrap. The police are looking at possible links between the security guard and a gang of hoodlums."

The academic knew he had been rumbled. "You obviously have access to information that has been withheld from us ordinary mortals," replied Beckwith, playing for time, as he tried to figure out how to play his dapper visitor. It was a tricky balancing act because he had to find a way to justify his dossier and win the friendship of the dapper visitor at the same time.

"I *did* hear a rumour that the security guard might have taken a *short* break," remarked the academic, as though searching the far recesses of his memory. "The military police were a bit vague about the security failings, but it is the first time I've heard that the security guard *abandoned* his post. That is a very *serious* accusation indeed. It shines a different light on the affair. Perhaps there is truth in the scrap metal theory after all!"

The dapper consultant listened to this litany of deceit and lies with a courteous air. "Well, I'm sure that your insurers will honour a claim if the submarine was stolen," he observed sympathetically. "We could help you with the insurance claim. Marine claims tend to be a bit complex. Nothing is clear-cut, so there is generally room for negotiation. We would be only too happy to assist you."

Up until that point, Beckwith had refrained from making an official report of the loss of the submarine in the belief that the craft would be found. After all, a report would make him a national laughing stock and throw light on his dodgy dealings. But it had become clear that the game was up and he would have to report the loss through official channels. Like a drowning man desperately clutching on to drifting wood, the academic believed that an insurance claim was his only hope of survival. A successful insurance claim would, at least, allow the Marine Special Projects Agency to stay afloat.

The smart-suited visitor was well aware of the academic's agonising dilemma and was playing his adversary trick for trick. So, to entice the academic further into the spider's web, the dapper visitor used euphemisms such as 'marine casualty' and 'presumed loss' to ease the pain. The respectable ring of these terms would allow Beckwith to save face. The success of their plan depended on persuading the academic to accept the loss of his midget submarine without stirring up too much trouble.

"How do we proceed with a claim?" asked Beckwith with a greedy gleam in his eye.

"Marine casualties are rarely black and white cases," explained the dapper consultant with a pompous man-of-the-world air. "When a ship is lost at sea, the owner will have no evidence of what has taken place and so *we professionals* use the term 'presumed lost'. The loss is then a subject of negotiation between the different parties. We strive to get a good deal for the owner. We can do this because we have a good relationship with the insurance syndicates and the 'Names' who are exposed to the liability."

Then as an aside, the dapper consultant lowered his voice. "Many of the Names have more money than sense, you know!" he confided with a disdainful expression. "So we are in a good position to negotiate the best settlement on behalf of the owner."

These comforting words had the desired effect. Beckwith was seduced by the authentic nautical terms, little suspecting that the legal jargon was being used on this occasion to bamboozle him. It would be some time before he learned that the Good Samaritan was, in fact, part of the gang who had stolen his midget submarine.

"You said something about taking a percentage of the settlement?" observed Beckwith with an avaricious twinkle in his eye. The phrasing of this question suggested that the academic was resigned to the fact that the submarine would not be found. An insurance settlement was his only way out. It would allow him to salvage his agency and perhaps rebuild his career. He had little choice; his enemies were gathering like vultures around dead meat. With this visitor's help, he could rise like the Phoenix from the fire.

"Yes. We normally receive a small percentage of the final insurance settlement, so it's in our interest to maximise the claim," replied the sharp-suited consultant reassuringly. "We will write to you with our terms." The academic breathed a sigh of relief that there was no need for an upfront payment. He was also gratified that this canny professional would be working on their behalf. While many pitfalls remained, Beckwith was starting to see a light at the end of the tunnel.

"Will the police become involved in an insurance claim?" he enquired nervously. This issue had been keeping him awake at night. Further police investigations into the murky events at Whitebait Cove might uncover his dodgy dealings.

"It all depends," replied the smart-suited visitor evasively. The marine consultant then embarked on a rambling diatribe about maritime affairs, touching on the International Maritime Organization (IMO), the role of coastguards, class societies and Port States inspections. The flimflam was a smokescreen. The marine consultant had no more desire to involve the police than the person sitting opposite him. To ingratiate himself with his visitor, Beckwith pretended to listen respectfully, but he had difficulty grasping the point that the dapper consultant was making.

When Felix finally paused for breath, Beckwith aired his concerns in a more direct manner. "Do we need to report the theft to the police?" he asked bluntly. The smart-suited consultant reacted with the distaste of someone who had stepped on mess in the street. The look suggested that this was a gross oversimplification of a highly complex issue. But after composing himself, the visitor nodded as though addressing a backward child.

"Well, if you put the question *like that*, the answer is *no*. As you know, you must report vehicle theft to the police, but those rules do not apply to marine claims in quite the same way."

The smooth sales pitch persuaded Beckwith that he should place his insurance affairs in his visitor's capable hands, and they proceeded to negotiate the fee payable on settlement of the insurance claim. After customary haggling, the dapper consultant agreed to pursue the insurance claim in return for ten percent of the final settlement. With that thorny issue resolved, they said farewell as new-found friends. The consultant promised to report on his progress.

When the marine consultant phoned Beckwith a couple of days later, he had some bad tidings to report. "I met the lead underwriter yesterday. It was not a pleasant experience. He was shocked that it's taken so long to report the submarine's loss. There were other issues that worried him," explained the marine consultant in funeral tones. "The lead underwriter was really mad! We need to meet with him."

Beckwith had steeled himself for some difficulties, and the consultant's remarks were no worse than anticipated. With the benefit of hindsight, his failure to report the loss of the midget submarine had been a massive blunder. "We could have handled matters better," he admitted to his new-found friend. As a defence for his actions, he harked back to the early stages of the investigation, which had been total chaos. "Did you tell him about the confusion over whether this was a civil or military matter?"

"No," admitted his new-found friend. "I was waiting to speak to you first – we need to agree our strategy."

"Well, perhaps we could discuss it over lunch. My shout!" suggested Beckwith, hoping that his generosity would further ingratiate him with his new-found friend. This was the routine that he normally adopted for delicate situations. During years in the *demi-monde* of politics and public relations, he had honed skills that allowed him to influence events with lavish entertainment.

With his jaundiced view of human nature, he was confident that the uptight consultant would have his fair share of vices and foibles. *Most people can be bought. You just need to find out what they want* was the rule he lived by. This view was justified by the handwritten notes about the complimentary tickets in the project files, which suggested that his new-found friend was not quite as honest as he seemed.

In his heart, Beckwith believed that the insurance industry was 'institutionally corrupt', like much of the corporate world. As a student, he had penned many articles on that theme for socialist publications. His view of the insurance industry was largely based on scandals from the 1980s when crooked underwriters hoodwinked gullible Names into investing in doomed syndicates. But though passingly familiar with the scandals, he knew little of the measures that the industry had taken to clean up its act.

The dapper consultant might present himself as an upright and virtuous citizen, but I would not mind betting that behind the honest façade, he's as bent as a nine-pound note, mused the academic. This was a fair assessment. The urbane accountant was indeed a cunning and deceitful operator. But, on this occasion, Beckwith was the prey.

"That would be most welcome," replied the marine consultant in an emollient way, in reply to the luncheon invitation. "It's not often that I am invited to lunch these days. The authorities have clamped down on free entertainment, you know."

Beckwith was gratified by the response. *The old magic is still working*, he prided himself as he set about finalising their dining arrangements

The pair met the following day outside an Italian trattoria in the West End of London where Beckwith was a regular customer. An attractive waitress, in a short black dress, greeted the academic with a hug before ushering them to a corner table in the dimly lit Mediterranean-themed dining room. While perusing the menu, the marine consultant refused the offer of a glass of wine, insisting that he 'had to keep his wits about him.'

On hearing that his most favoured customer's guest was abstaining from wine, Luigi, the flamboyant proprietor, strutted over to their table to remonstrate. "Please, sir. You must try our vino. It is brought specially from the family vineyard in Tuscany," he explained. The proprietor spoke with the sort of thick Italian accent that Mediterranean gigolos adopt when chasing girls from the colder climes of northern Europe. But the marine consultant was not to be swayed.

When the proprietor had moved away, Beckwith smiled and leant towards his guest and whispered conspiratorially: "Don't take any notice of that chap. The sales patter is just for gullible tourists. Luigi has never been to Italy! I doubt if he has ever been further than Southend. He was born just down the road from my flat in Islington. His father came to this country after the war and used to run the local chippy." Then after revealing this confidence, he continued more loudly. "The wine is wonderful. You have to try it!"

That amusing aside broke the ice, and in the ensuing light-hearted chatter, the marine consultant relented and accepted a large glass of wine. As the meal progressed, it became apparent that the dapper fellow did not have a head for alcohol. As the *spaghetti alle vongole* was served, the pair exchanged knowing smiles as the voluptuous waitress leant over to provide a provocative view of her cleavage.

Beckwith's guest became garrulous as they finished the first bottle of wine and started on the second. Slang expressions began to pepper the Polish émigré's impeccable English grammar. Beckwith felt smugly satisfied that he had breached his guest's uptight façade. With his tongue loosened by alcohol, the Pole began to reminisce about his family's *travails*.

With tears in his eyes, the dapper consultant told a story about obtaining false identity papers that allowed family members to escape from the evil clutches of the Soviet Union.

The academic listened respectfully to the harrowing tales, little suspecting that much of it was fabricated. The stories did contain some element of truth, but the facts were greatly embellished to create an impression of a man-of-the-world.

In an attempt to match this story, the academic spoke of a close relationship with a respected left-wing journalist called Edward Pearce, whose obituary happened to appear in the paper that day. This was an artful wheeze because Beckwith had only met the journalist once. *But you cannot check the facts with a dead man*, figured the academic.

After speaking of his imaginary dealings with the illustrious journalist and sadness at his demise, the academic passed a copy of the paper to his guest and pointed to an amusing passage. The obituary quoted a passage from one of the journalist's best-known articles: *Some elements of the trade union movement look upon a profitable section of the economy much as certain sorts of Manchester United supporters view a nice new railway carriage after an away defeat.*

The consultant laughed uproariously at the passage to give the impression that he had sympathy for the academic's political view. To bolster the warm mood, Beckwith made sure that his guest's glass was kept topped up while barely sipping from his own glass. The academic refrained from speaking about his family background, but he did let slip that he disliked his boarding school. As they settled back in their seats, at the end of a sumptuous meal, sipping their balloon glasses of brandy, the conversation turned to the insurance industry. They chatted in an amiable way.

The marine consultant spoke of his disdain for his fellow insurance professionals, much to the academic's delight. The marine consultant spoke about the Names who had been left penniless by ruthless operators during the Lloyd's of London scandal of the 1980s. "I don't have any sympathy for them," growled the now inebriated consultant. "Those fools did not know what they were getting into. Most of them inherited more money than they knew what to do with. They did nothing to earn their wealth. So it served them right!"

Warming to his guest, Beckwith felt that he had found a kindred spirit; an intelligent man who shared his disdain for the establishment, little suspecting that he was being played like a fish. As they waited for the bill, Beckwith broached the subject of the insurance claim. "How do you think we should approach the claim?" he asked casually, although nervous about the expected response.

"Have you told me all the facts?" asked the marine consultant thoughtfully. This was a delicate subject, given the difficulties that the marine consultant had outlined during their phone call. "There's nothing more that I should know?"

"You seem to know more than me," replied Beckwith fawningly. The academic figured that his guest would be flattered that he had a greater knowledge of what had taken place than he – flattery was always an effective tool in his experience. Playing dumb, it now suited the academic's purpose to go along with the theory that the submarine had been stolen and broken up for scrap. That theory would justify an insurance payout, after all.

"The authorities have been cagey about what went on, and the navy have been no help. It's been nothing but confusion from the start. Our dossier has set out what we know. But who knows what really took place?" He made this comment in an airy way to explain why his dossier failed to mention important facts, such as the absent security guard. There was no mention of the private eye's investigation. "We really need your help to unravel the mess."

"Then, if you are happy, I think you should leave me to sort out your insurance claim," suggested the marine consultant in a jaunty manner.

The upbeat tone caught the academic off balance; he was prepared for tough negotiations. "Are you *sure* you have enough information to work with?" he asked sceptically. "You didn't sound very hopeful when you phoned me yesterday." He wanted to make sure that his new-found friend could deliver, because his salvation now depended on an insurance payout.

The well-oiled marine consultant pondered the question then he framed his reply in a way that played directly to the academic's prejudices. "Don't concern yourself with the underwriter's reaction," replied the dapper guy in words slurred by drink. "They always balk at the first approach. It's part of the game, but he will cave in at the end. Leave it to me. You have to approach these old school tie types in the right way." Then he added conspiratorially, "Butter them up and you can achieve anything. The people I deal with spend most of their time snoozing in the gentlemen's clubs. They don't know what time of day it is. It's easy to bamboozle them. You just have to go about it in the right way."

Beckwith couldn't believe his good fortune. It seemed that his guest would bring him salvation, with little collateral damage. His overriding fear was that an intense police investigation would reveal his crooked dealings. As he savoured his good fortune, his guest leaned towards him in a comradely way. With a cockeyed expression from a surfeit of alcohol, the consultant recounted anecdotes of corruption in the insurance market. The academic greedily assimilated the stories, wondering how he could exploit the rotten system. "How does that affect us?" he asked avariciously.

Most of the anecdotes were fabricated nonsense, but there were a couple of true stories that gave his narrative credence. The true stories dated back to the scandals of the 1980s. Measures had since been taken to clean up the market. Many of the irregular practices had now been outlawed, but the academic was only too happy to believe that there was widespread corruption.

"The market depends on trust, but it's a two-way street, you know," proclaimed the marine consultant grandly, with the slurred speech and false sincerity of the inebriated. "Our clients must trust syndicates to pay their claims." The meal seemed to have created a bond between them, as often happens when drunken strangers fall into conversation in a bar.

"As I said, the marine insurance market depends on trust," confided the consultant after pausing for a fit of coughing, "but here is the rub – not *everyone* is honest!" With that dazzling insight, the consultant adopted a cunning expression to give the impression that he was a venal and corruptible character. "The rich people who put up the money haven't got a clue about the risks they insure. They follow the lead underwriter without asking awkward questions. But the lead underwriter *can be influenced*."

"I'm starting to get the picture!" replied Beckwith with a knowing wink. This was familiar territory to the academic, who employed all manner of tricks and wheezes to influence people and achieve his aims. "So, we need to persuade the *lead underwriter* to accept our claim," he added with a cunning expression, to make sure that he understood the full implications of the inside information.

"All the Names will follow suit," declared the tipsy consultant with a satisfied air as he flourished his balloon glass and drained the last dregs of brandy from the bottom. "The money men will follow their leader like a little flock of sheep." The marine consultant illustrated the point by scissoring his fingers across the table, in a comic display.

"But *how* do we persuade the lead underwriter?" asked the academic curiously. The academic was reluctant to pay a bribe, and that was the only solution he could conceive. Such a crude tactic would compound his problems, so he was relieved by the broker's imaginative response. It confirmed his belief that they were kindred spirits.

"I handle reinsurance business," whispered the broker as he suppressed a belch. "I can hand out lucrative reinsurance business to the syndicate who insured your submarine. So, all I have to do is hint that I'll take my business to another syndicate and he will settle your claim without too much trouble. It's a dog-eat-dog world!"

The academic had little knowledge of 'reinsurance', but he was aware that it played a significant part in the insurance scandals of the 1980s. So the words had a ring of truth. Believing that he could trust his new-found friend, Beckwith decided to place his faith in the stranger. As they collected their coats, the pair agreed to meet the lead underwriter the following day to pursue their claim. The academic left the restaurant with a spring in his step, not only hopeful that his claim would be settled, but also wondering whether marine insurance might present another opportunity to feather his own nest.

When setting up their meeting, the dapper consultant suggested that it would be best if they visit the lead underwriter in his Hampshire home. "We will be able to speak more freely away from his City office," explained the consultant. Beckwith readily agreed to this suggestion. Once the academic had been picked up from Guildford railway station, the pair drove on to the Hampshire village in the marine consultant's modest saloon car. It was a pleasant journey on a late-spring day, with trees coming into bud.

Beckwith felt a surge of optimism as they cruised through the road tunnel on the dual carriageway from London. It was the first time that the academic had seen the newly opened tunnel, and he was impressed by the attractive landscaping.

The academic was looking forward to the meeting with relish. *This will test my wits*, he mused happily.

The plan of campaign was for the marine consultant to lead the discussion, with Beckwith providing covering fire from the sidelines. His blood pulsed as adrenalin surged through his veins. As they approached their destination, the marine consultant issued his final words of wisdom: "Play it by ear. But leave the talking to me!"

As they arrived at the old rectory, the academic was disappointed to find that the lead underwriter was, in fact, a genial old buffer, pottering around in his greenhouse. He felt like a heavyweight boxer psyched up for a twelve-round bout only to find himself matched against a six-stone weakling. Their host greeted the new arrivals in a friendly way and arranged for his housekeeper to serve them tea in the sitting room while he washed his hands. The old buffer reappeared after a few minutes wearing a pullover with holes in his elbows, presenting the image of an absent-minded professor.

It soon became clear that the marine consultant was on friendly terms with their host. This did not worry the artful academic unduly. Remembering that they were to 'butter up' the underwriter, Beckwith asked their host politely: "Did you serve in the navy?" This was rather an obvious question, given the naval mementos hanging around the sitting room. There was a photograph of a young naval officer in uniform on the mantelpiece, with pictures and paintings of naval scenes decorating the walls.

"Yes. We saw a bit of action," replied the scruffy old buffer in a modest way – the wily old fox made no mention of his rank in the navy. "Felix values my experience. That's why he asked my views about insuring your submarine. By the way, I must congratulate you. I understand that your submarine employs a new form of propulsion. The word is that it performed exceedingly well. Well done! We need more people like yourself!"

Beckwith was about to reply that similar technology had been used by German shipyards but checked himself when he recalled the quip *Don't mention the Germans* from the TV series *Fawlty Towers*. Basking in the praise, he was brought back to earth with a bump. "Pity that you have lost it!" remarked their genial host. The words were delivered in a jovial way with impeccable timing. The marine consultant could barely keep a straight face. The acid put-down was a warning that while their scruffy host might look like an absent-minded old coot, his mind was as sharp as a razor.

Beckwith's quick wits had allowed him to fend off bullies at boarding school. In later life, his verbal skills were honed by debates with political opponents. But to prevail in argument, he needed to hold an ace up his sleeve. Sadly, he was out of his depth on this occasion. He had approached the meeting in a complacent way, believing the lead underwriter to be an 'upper-class twit'. As a result, he found himself strangely defenceless in the benign surroundings.

The academic had been lulled into a false sense of security by the marine consultant's patter during their lavish meal in the Italian trattoria. It had not yet dawned on the credulous academic that his new-found friend was in league with their genial host and they were out to fleece him.

"So, what can we do for you, *Mr Beckwith?*" asked their apparently genial host in a polite but predatory way. The unnervingly direct approach was at odds with their host's eccentric appearance.

Beckwith expected the marine consultant to field that awkward question; after all, he had promised to take the lead in the discussion. But the dapper consultant excused himself, murmuring that he had eaten something that upset him. "I need to find the little boys' room," he added. Left to fend for himself, the academic played for time, waiting for his newfound friend to return. But this expectation was dashed when he heard the marine consultant laughing and joking with the jolly housekeeper in the kitchen. It was then that he realised that the guy was a turncoat who had abandoned him. The academic suddenly realised that he had been thrown to the dogs.

"Well, we want to talk to you about an insurance claim for the midget submarine. You see, it disappeared after the sea trials at Whitebait Cove," stuttered the academic with a dry mouth and uncomfortable look of embarrassment. He struggled to recall the marine jargon that the consultant had used during their friendly meal at the Italian restaurant. His only real hope was that his new-found friend would return to rescue him. But there was no let-up in the chatter in the kitchen, and little sign that the marine consultant intended to extract him from his awkward predicament.

"What exactly do you want to know?" asked the scruffy gardener sharply, as though he were addressing a dunce.

"Well, you have probably heard that our midget submarine was 'presumed lost' after the sea trials at Whitebait Cove," mouthed the academic. Those unnatural words stuck in his throat.

"What on earth is that supposed to mean?" asked his host with an incredulous expression.

"Well, there was some doubt over what has happened to our midget submarine," replied Beckwith with a defeated expression. "There was some confusion over whether it was a civil or a military matter."

"I've never heard such tripe," replied his host in a crisp, no-nonsense manner. "We know the *Normandy* went missing in the early hours of Sunday morning while the security guard was absent from his post. We know the security firm was incompetent. We know that the police have a theory that the submarine has been broken up for scrap. We know your agency is in financial difficulties. We know you owe money to your contractors and are unable to repay your bond holders. Now you want an insurance payout to bail you out."

The normally silver-tongued academic was left speechless. All his shady dealings had been exposed in one pithy statement. It was as though his scruffily dressed host could gaze into the inner recesses of his soul. The artful academic felt like a poker player who had carelessly exposed his hand while trying to bluff an opponent.

"Don't try to deny it!" continued their host calmly as the academic squirmed, struggling vainly to frame his reply. "We know what you have been up to, young man!" Then after a pause to allow his words to sink in, the Admiral continued in a conciliatory fashion. He had achieved his objective and had no wish to humiliate his visitor further. "We might be prepared to settle your insurance claim, however, but on our terms."

Beckwith had been on an emotional roller coaster since learning of the disappearance of the midget submarine, with his hopes raised, only for them to be dashed again, so he was suspicious of the Admiral's olive branch. "What's the catch?" he growled, like a cornered animal. He did not have to wait long for an answer.

"I've drafted out the terms for you," replied the Admiral briskly. He handed over a neatly typed document setting out terms for an insurance settlement.

The insurers have been advised that the submersible vehicle built by the Marine Special Projects Agency (MSPA) went missing at the conclusion of its sea trials as a result of security failings as the Whitebait Cove boatyard. The whereabouts of the submersible are unknown at present, but agreement has been reached with the insurers that the craft will be declared a 'total loss'. The insurance claim will be settled on the following basis.

1. The insurers will reimburse all outstanding debts with contractors and suppliers for construction of the submersible.
2. The insurers will reimburse all loans due to bond holders.
3. The Marine Special Projects Agency will be reimbursed for any legitimate expenses involved in design and project management of the submersible.
4. In return for those payments, the insurers will have the right to take possession of all, or parts, should the submersible be recovered at a later date.
5. Neither party should instigate a police investigation into events leading to the disappearance of the submersible.
6. This is a confidential agreement whose contents must not be revealed to third parties.

After his apparent betrayal, Beckwith could not believe the generosity of the offer. The settlement would allow him to salvage his agency and retain some dignity, although the payout did not reflect the full value of the midget submarine. This was a small price to pay, because the fifth clause would put an end to the bothersome police investigation and the confidentiality clause would enable him to evade awkward questions.

In any event, he was in no position to haggle because the Admiral obviously knew what was going on and could blow the whistle on his chicanery. Though he had a weak hand, it was not in his nature to accept the first offer. Beckwith recalled that the marine consultant would charge a fee for arranging the settlement. It was not clear how this would be paid. "One small thing. This does not mention the fee for the marine consultant," he observed meekly.

"There is no broker's fee. Felix lied to you about that," replied the Admiral blithely. "He works for me." Then after a pause, he continued cheerily. "Anyway, take your time to think it over. Call me when you are ready to sign. I'll be outside." After delivering the *coup de grâce*, the old fox shuffled off to join the pair who were happily chatting about village affairs in the kitchen.

Beckwith knew that he had been deceived by his newfound friend. But with the prospect of a handsome settlement, he was prepared to overlook the duplicity for the time being. It was an uncomfortable situation, but he knew the game was up. Revenge would wait for another day. When he looked at his watch, he was staggered to discover that he had only been in the house for thirty minutes. The marine consultant had been chatting in the kitchen for most of that time.

The academic looked daggers at the marine consultant as the duplicitous guy sauntered casually back into the sitting room, without the slightest remorse. Then to add insult to injury, the cheeky fellow offered to drive the academic back to the railway station as though nothing had happened. Beckwith had no wish to share a long car journey with the scoundrel, but he had no other form of transport. So he grudgingly accepted the lift.

As the Admiral bid them farewell, he looked at Beckwith and remarked: "You don't remember me, do you?"

Beckwith racked his brains but could not recall meeting the eccentric old buffer. "Can't say that I do," he replied.

"I was a sixth form prefect when you arrived at school," declared the old fox jauntily. Then with a deadly serious expression, he continued. "Let me give you a piece of advice, young man. If you want to get on in the world, it's best to be straight with people. You play fair with others, and they will play fair with you." Beckwith did not know what to make of that strange remark and put it down to senility, but memories of his boarding school flooded back as he ruminated on his way back to London. The truth of what had happened started to dawn on him.

Chapter 25

Portsmouth Outing

Oblivious to the tussle taking place behind the scenes over legal ownership of the midget submarine, Bill and Alex returned to the charmless office with the grudging manner of whipped beasts. While the pair felt cheated by their young boss, the emotion was tinged with guilt that they had failed to complete the assigned task in a professional way. While the pair got on each other's nerves, they were united in distrust of their slippery boss.

By docking their pay, Steve had established his authority over the pair, but he had done so at the cost of their friendship. This created a chilly atmosphere as they settled down to produce an improved business plan in accordance with Steve's instructions. The new plan would discuss international dredging prospects away from the North Sea. Chastened by the pay cut, Alex knuckled down to help his pal.

Bill was totally bemused by their situation, but Alex had a pretty good idea about what was going on. When he heard that the midget submarine had gone missing from the Whitebait

Cove boatyard, it had not taken him long to put two and two together. It was obvious to the Scotsman that the submarine was to be installed in the dredger. The only thing that puzzled him was why their young boss did not come clean and admit it. *The young laddie is making a fool of himself,* he mused. *He should have been straight with us.*

In his mischievous manner, Alex made no effort to enlighten his pal. This job was more important to the Scotsman than he was prepared to admit. With failing health, he had poor employment prospects. Over the past few years, he had been forced to work on foreign-owned rust buckets. This was bad enough, but his employment prospects were now blighted by unnerving stories about the emergence of a virus in China.

This was not yet a cause of concern in the West, at that moment, but the far-sighted Scotsman perceived storm clouds on the horizon. Unlike his pal, the Scotsman did not have a generous occupational pension. With meagre bank savings, he faced a bleak future. So the prospect of guaranteed work in his home country was a godsend, and he was prepared to endure almost any indignities to retain his position.

While Alex had his differences with the bean counter, he knew that he could not survive in a commercial world without his friend. The capable Scottish engineer had little understanding of finance and found the subject intimidating. That was the reason why he persuaded Bill to stay. But even so, he could not resist teasing the bean counter from time to time.

With greater cooperation, the mismatched pair rubbed along, and by the end of the second week, they had produced a greatly improved business plan. In completing this new plan, Bill incorporated Alex's technical knowledge in a condensed form. When they presented this new plan to Steve, their new boss was impressed and, in gratitude, he reinstated their original pay agreement.

But the harmony between the pair evaporated at the start of the third week when they were summoned to a meeting in Portsmouth. Alex demanded to know why the meeting could not take place in Torquay and he was indignant when Bill failed to support his protest. Then to add insult to injury, Bill refused to use his car. The prospect of yet another awkward train journey was too much for the cantankerous Scotsman. Alex was fed up with the crumbling rail system and ever-present threat of strikes. When Alex heard the term 'industrial action' on the news, it was like a red rag to a bull. "Industrial inaction, more like!" he would scoff.

Unlike his pal, Bill looked forward to the Portsmouth outing, seeing it as an opportunity to do some sightseeing. The bean counter had never visited the famous naval city and was keen to see the tourist attractions built to celebrate the millennium. An added attraction was that it would provide an opportunity to visit some of the historic pubs in the Old Town. The use of public transport would allow him to enjoy a pint or two.

The pair got on each other's nerves from the moment they started their long and frustrating rail journey. After changing trains at several draughty, windswept stations, they finally arrived at their destination. The dilapidated terminal projected out into the harbour to provide a tantalising glimpse of ships through grimy windows. When they emerged onto a newly paved terrace at the exit to the station, they were barely on speaking terms. While Bill was travelling light, his pal was weighed down with a heavy briefcase packed with documents.

Alex broke the silence to express his admiration for a historic iron-clad warship moored on the wharf opposite. "That's what I call a ship!" he declared. "Steam and sail. Belt and braces. They knew how to build decent ships in those days!" This was a subtle dig at his pal. The fractious couple often argued about the merits of steam and diesel. Alex was proud of his 'combined ticket' which allowed him to serve as chief on both steam and diesel ships. Bill was only qualified to take charge of the machinery on diesel ships. So the Scotsman rarely missed a chance to rib his pal on the subject.

"That old tub is not a patch on the *Victory*," retorted Bill, stung by the reference to steam propulsion. "Look at it. The warship does not have any character. Just a couple of stubby funnels sticking out of the deck. No deck houses. It hasn't got any interesting features, except the figurehead and a little bit of carved wood around the captain's cabin. Anyway, it's never proved itself in battle." The terrace was plastered with advertisements hailing the *Victory's* achievements, though the venerable old sailing ship lay out of sight, within the dockyard.

"The *Victory* is not all it's cracked up to be," replied Alex scornfully. "The Admiralty wanted to turn it into a prison hulk, and would have done so if Napoleon had not threatened this country." Bill did not rise to this bait. He knew better than to challenge the Scotsman about nautical history. Alex spent most of his spare time studying the subject and could be a crashing bore on the subject, so they tramped sullenly around the station entrance to a pedestrian tunnel that led towards a modern shopping complex. The area was dominated by the Spinnaker Tower.

"That's another eyesore," observed Alex sourly, knowing that his pal wanted to visit the attraction later that day.

This time, Bill could not resist the temptation to respond. "You wouldn't recognise good architecture if it smashed you in the face," remarked the bean counter testily. "It is a tribute to the sailing community," continued Bill as he pointed to the modern, bread loaf-shaped building that housed the America's Cup challenge.

The fractious pair made their way past fashionable clothes stores and restaurants, and then crossed a newly renovated swing bridge over a channel linking a chain of seawater basins. Brightly coloured boats for children were moored in one of these basins. Alex chuckled with satisfaction that he had got under his pal's skin. "Hoot, man! It's nothing but a tourist trap!" he teased. "Portsmouth is a dump. Just look at it," he sneered, as he ostentatiously surveyed the nondescript buildings that lined the dock road. By this time, Bill was heartily fed up with his colleague's sniping.

"Don't wait for me when we've finished our meeting this afternoon," he growled spitefully. "Make your own way home, you old grouch." Bill could see that some parts of the island city were run-down, but it did not detract from his enjoyment of the newly remodelled waterfront and its fashionable attractions.

As they trudged along, Bill was fascinated to watch the myriad ferries, warships and harbour craft dodging round the bustling waterway. A pastel green ferry shuttled across the harbour entrance. Its catamaran hull skidded sideways in the surging current. As they approached the Isle of Wight terminal, a slab-sided ferry churned up the water as it reversed into its berth to deposit its cargo of vehicles. The vessel seemed top-heavy to Bill's eyes. The route took them past a gated residential area, to another group of wharves and docks.

The fractious pair trudged on in silence as they reached the Camber Basin, where fishing boats jostled in the shadow of the stylish new building that housed the America's Cup team. As they approached the Spice Island promontory, Bill consulted the sketched map that Steve had given them. The pair followed directions to the Admiral Bligh public house, where the meeting was to take place. Bill wondered why the term Admiral was used. He thought that the crew had mutinied against Captain Bligh, and promised that he would look into it.

Following the sketched map, they found the historic establishment in a cobbled lane set back a short distance from the seafront. The pub's name was emblazoned in gold gothic script on a wooden sign hanging above the front door. The quaint old building was tastefully renovated. A notice hung on the door with the single word *Closed*, so they knocked on the latticed stained glass window to attract the attention of the cleaner.

When they were admitted, they made their way along a passageway with cosy nooks set on either side. The stairs at the end of the passageway led up to a plainly decorated room. An old-fashioned slide projector was set beside a lectern at one end of the room, with a screen on the wall behind. Chairs were laid out around a beer-stained pine table running down the centre of the room. Pads of paper were laid out on the table in preparation for their meeting. One person had arrived before them.

Tim Wesley was sitting at the beer-stained table, reading a newspaper. The young designer greeted Bill with a friendly nod, but he turned away when he saw the sweating Scotsman trailing behind. "What a hole! I can see why the crew mutinied!" joked Alex as he burst into the room with his briefcase. Tim raised an eyebrow at the feeble attempt at humour. The young designer had not forgiven the Scotsman for his boorish behaviour in the Feathers during their abortive reunion weekend. The young designer was also contemptuous of Alex's scruffy attire.

The Scotsman was swaddled in his weatherproof jacket and was puffing with exertion from lugging his heavy briefcase from the station. After collapsing onto a chair, Alex burrowed in the briefcase and removed a pile of technical documents.

Tim continued to read his newspaper, ignoring the Scotsman and showing little inclination to speak to anyone. When Steve breezed into the room a few minutes later, the chilly atmosphere started to thaw. The young executive was trailed by Commander Woods.

The commander was dressed in a casual naval uniform, with gold-striped epaulettes fitted to the shoulders of his otherwise plain navy blue pullover. Steve made the introductions. "The commander is in charge of our mission," explained the young executive. "Sorry that I had to call you to Portsmouth, but the rest of the team are based here." Alex glowered at the remark and continued to thumb through a stack of technical documents, ignoring his young boss.

As a stream of casually dressed folk drifted into the room, they formed a group around Steve and the commander near the lectern. The new arrivals clearly knew one another and they paid little attention to those sitting at the table. As Bill and Alex sat like outcasts, a smartly dressed businessman sat down beside them. Acknowledging his neighbours with a polite but curt nod, the dapper businessman removed documents from his briefcase, which he proceeded to study.

The commander stepped out of the room for a couple of minutes before returning to call the meeting to order. After asking everyone to take their seats, he introduced the newcomers in a formal way. With the preliminaries concluded, he called for the curtains to be drawn. As the light faded, a picture appeared on the grimy screen showing a cylindrical object mounted on its trailer, surrounded by straw bales and farm machinery in a ramshackle old barn.

"As you can see, we are now in possession of the midget submarine which we need for our covert surveillance work," he announced with a theatrical flourish. This remark was met with whoops of applause, suggesting that this news was long awaited and keenly anticipated. But this enthusiastic response was not shared by Bill, who was absolutely flabbergasted. The bean counter had been impressed by the midget submarine during their tour of the boatyard, but now the craft looked forlorn in the grubby agricultural setting.

Bill was disgusted that the craft should be treated with so little respect. It also confirmed his suspicion that their young boss had twisted the truth and misled them. At best, Steve had been 'economical with the truth' during his presentation. It justified his concerns about the dodgy nature of the dredging business. The commander was aware of Bill's fears and had prepared a short motivational speech in an attempt to allay them. The opening part of this speech was aimed squarely at the newcomers.

"The aim of our mission is to protect merchant seamen in pirate-infested waters," declared the commander in a pompous way. He went on to describe harrowing hijacking incidents and the debt of gratitude that seafarers owed to international naval fleets. "The naval operation has been a great success, but the warships are needed elsewhere and so now the shipping industry will have to pick up this burden," he continued. The next slide was a diagram showing how the midget submarine would be hidden within a compartment of the dredger.

Having set out the lofty aims of their mission, he admitted that acquisition of the midget submarine had involved skulduggery. "We have bent the rules a bit, but we have not done anything seriously illegal," he assured them. "We have put noses out of joint, but when the dust settles, the acquisition will be viewed as an 'inter-department transfer' as far as the authorities are concerned. So we now have a valuable surveillance asset and we can forge ahead with our mission." He concluded this statement with another theatrical flourish: "It's a noble cause!" Several members of the team banged the table to show their appreciation at the commander's words.

Alex was still bristling with resentment at being summoned all the way to Portsmouth and sat idly doodling on the pad of paper as the commander spoke. He was unmoved by the pompous speech, having already figured out what was going on. The Scottish engineer simply wanted to get on with the job. It was only when Steve started to speak about their dredging company that his interest started to perk up.

Steve went on to speak about an international project to develop a commercial port to bolster the fledgling economy of this war-torn region in the Horn of Africa. It was hoped that the port would help revive the local economy, allowing the government to bring law and order to the region. If all went to plan, their new company would dredge a channel into the new port. Alex's ears pricked up when Steve went on to speak about their plans to buy a dredger.

In the course of his lecture, Steve explained that they would be able to use the dredger in other trouble spots around the globe. "It will provide a base for security people and will complement the naval efforts in those areas," he explained. He went on to describe cases of piracy in West Africa and the Indonesian Archipelago and the war clouds gathering over the Strait of Hormuz. As there was a need for dredging in those parts of the world, they would have no difficulty finding work for the vessel. After that, Steve explained how the business was organised.

"The undercover work will be carried out by former members of the armed forces," he explained. "The dredger will provide a base for the undercover team while it carries out commercial work. The vessel will be managed from an office in Torquay. We have already appointed managers." He pointed towards Bill and Alex. "We expect to recruit seagoing staff in the coming months, and hope that the commercial work will allow the company to become self-financing. I shall be acting as chief executive for the time being, and some of you might be asked to become non-executive directors."

He then turned towards the dapper businessman, who had been sitting with a sour expression during the proceedings. "Felix is our shipbroker," announced Steve genially. "Perhaps you can add a few words?" The prickly financier took offence at this introduction. It was true that he was acting as a 'shipbroker' on this occasion. But as the Admiral's aide and confident, he felt he played a much more significant role in the operation. He had, for instance, devised the scheme to wrest ownership of the submarine from Beckwith's grasp.

"I was asked to find a suitable vessel," explained Felix in the brisk, impersonal manner of a lawyer who had been asked to defend a guilty client. "We have scoured the market and found a suction dredger laid up in Rotterdam. The owners have gone into administration and the receiver is keen to sell the ship, so we should be able to buy her quite cheaply. It is overdue for a class survey, and work will need to be carried out to make her fully seaworthy." He then passed copies of the ship's particulars to everyone sitting at the table.

"Thanks, Felix," said Steve in a supercilious way as he returned to the lectern.

"So, the next step is to survey the ship, and this is where you come in, Alex," declared the young executive. The unkempt Scotsman squirmed in his seat, embarrassed to be thrust into the spotlight. "You have been studying the dredging business, so I would like you to fly to Rotterdam next week with Frank Cooper. Frank is a skilled draughtsman. He retired a couple of years ago but does some freelance work. You may be interested to know that he designed the launching gear for the midget submarine – so he's the ideal person for this project. The commander will introduce you later."

With that, the commander made his apologies, saying that he had duties to attend to at the naval base. On his way to the door, he signalled for the Scotsman to follow him. Alex scrabbled up his papers, donned his waterproof and shambled off in the commander's wake. The unlikely duo descended to the ground floor, where they found a naval rating drinking tea and finishing a crossword puzzle. It seemed that the commander had access to a staff car in Portsmouth, and this rating was his driver. The navy rating was ratty after being disturbed, having almost completed the puzzle, but he grudgingly shepherded the pair towards the staff car.

With the commander's departure, the atmosphere in the room became more relaxed, with people sharing jokes about the wheezes used to acquire the submarine. This cheerful mood was not shared by the dapper businessman, who smouldered with a stony expression while sitting bolt upright at the table. It was obvious that he harboured a grievance. As the team members drifted away, Steve sauntered over to find out what was troubling him. When the young executive opened his mouth, the financier vented his spleen.

In an opening salvo, the financier poured scorn on the 'schoolboy antics' the team had used to acquire the midget submarine. "You will end up in jail!" he growled. Although slightly built, the prickly man could be threatening when roused. The wiry figure pinned Steve into a corner, waving his finger and demanding to know why his achievements had not been acknowledged. Bill and Tim shuffled about; uncomfortable witnesses to the ugly scene.

The volcanic eruption led Steve to suspect that the commander had slipped away early to avoid the man's wrath. "Sorry, Felix. We did not have time to discuss your role in the operation," replied the young executive nervously. The sharp words forced Steve to view their situation with fresh eyes, and he started to regret the triumphant tone of the meeting thus far. "Everyone has done a marvellous job," he declared as he tried to placate the angry man. "We can push ahead with our plans thanks to your efforts."

Steve's confusion was understandable because he had only met Felix briefly at the Admiral's house when he had been press-ganged into joining the mission. The young executive knew nothing about the episode where Beckwith was persuaded to hand over ownership of the submarine. "I've used up a lot of goodwill to sort out *your* problems," growled Felix. "Most of the time I have been flying by the seat of my culottes."

Steve was unsure whether this was a slip of the tongue or a pointed reminder that the Polish businessman was fluent in many different languages. Pinned up against the wall with a finger wagging in his face, Steve tried to defuse the situation with humour. "Pants! Not culottes!" he observed in a light-hearted manner.

"Pants, trousers, slacks or culottes, all the same! You know what I mean!" growled the wiry Polish guy in response. But the humour did have a calming effect. Steve's assailant relaxed his grip, allowing him to gulp some air. But in a torrent of words, the dapper guy proceeded to complain about the amateur way that the whole operation was being run. "Where is your business plan?" he demanded angrily. "How do you expect me to raise finance without one?"

With similar gripes, Bill decided to step in and put in his two pennies' worth. In making his point, he imposed his bulk between the pair of featherweight combatants. Sitting on the sidelines, Tim did not wish to be drawn into the argument, and he sidled away with a shamefaced expression.

"I'm sorry, Steve, but I agree with this gentleman," asserted Bill in an unusually forceful way. "From a business perspective, the whole operation is a mess. We've had to use guesswork. There's no proper planning, no budget, nothing! You know that I was in two minds whether to stay with you. Well, I'm only prepared to stay if you are prepared to answer my questions and give me the authority to run the operation in a professional way."

After his painful experience at the Admiral's home, Steve knew that the Polish guy could be difficult to deal with, but he was shocked when Bill stabbed him in the back. This was unfair. After all, he was not the architect of this mission; he was simply following the vague orders of a shadowy group of shipping people. The young executive was under enormous pressure, trying to set up the undercover business while trying to salvage the boatyard. He was utterly exhausted.

"Please keep out of this, Bill!" barked the young executive. "You have only just started with our team, and you only know part of the story. You do not fully understand all the challenges we face. So please mind your own business!"

Turning back to face the dapper businessman, he took a deep breath and spoke as calmly as he was able: "You are right. We do need a proper business plan. That is why I recruited Bill and set up an office in Torquay. I'm sorry it has taken so long, but we are making some progress. But no one has given me clear directions and I have many other things to worry about."

Felix did not allow the young executive to finish his defence. "That's all very well," he retorted, "but you have had months to sort this out, and yet we are still waiting for some proper estimates. I have been told to look for a dredger, but you can't tell me how much we can afford to pay. We need hard facts. How much will the dredger earn? How much will it cost to operate and what revenue can we expect from the dredging work?"

"You have your problems," countered Steve. "I have mine, but please remember that my boatyard has provided all the cash for the dredging business so far." He went on to explain that he had paid the office rent and wages for his two recruits using the petty cash from the boatyard. This took the steam out of the attack.

"Okay. I'm prepared to pay your out-of-pocket expenses, but you must give me some *accurate* cost estimates," conceded the disgruntled financier.

Steve balked at this. He would not have final cost estimates until Alex had inspected the ship and discussed the modifications with the shipyard. This could take several weeks. The young executive could not afford to wait that long – it would cause him severe cash flow problems. "I need the cash before the end of next week. Otherwise, discrepancies will show up in the books," argued Steve.

Felix was heartily sick of excuses and doubted that Alex's trip to Rotterdam would produce the necessary information. But he controlled the purse strings, and so he was in a strong bargaining position. After some horse trading, they finally agreed that Steve would receive a proportion of the cash straight away. The remainder would be held back until Steve handed over a properly costed business plan.

While Steve was left to deal with the irate financier, the commander was cruising to the naval base in his staff car, accompanied by Alex. The staff car pulled to a halt as it approached the imposing brick gateway to the sprawling naval establishment. The red cap stepped out of his booth to check the commander's papers and led Alex into the guardroom to issue him with a visitor's pass. After passing through the gates, they made their way to a nondescript brick building, where the draughtsman Frank Cooper was working at a drawing board. The skilful draughtsman was seated in an alcove beside the commander's glass-partitioned office.

Frank Cooper was a corpulent figure, with a shock of silver hair and bushy eyebrows which extended outwards to give him the appearance of a wise old owl. His bulbous stomach was jammed against the base of the drawing board, suggesting he had a sedentary lifestyle. But he could be agile, when needed, despite his physical bulk. When called to sort out a problem, he would leap from his stool with the grace of a gazelle. He had enjoyed an impressive career with prestigious companies and was much in demand for freelance work, but he chose his assignments with care. He was only prepared to work on interesting assignments with people he found agreeable.

Frank Cooper had developed a good working relationship with Commander Woods, and the decorated naval officer enjoyed listening to the old-timer's anecdotes about the early days of gas turbine propulsion of warships. The commander greatly valued the draughtsman's skills and had recommended him for the job of designing launching gear for the submarine rescue vehicle. But when Beckwith took over the project, he sacked the old-timer, saying that he was not in tune with the modern digital world.

After making the introductions, the commander went about his naval duties, leaving the two veterans chatting amicably. Alex quickly developed a rapport with the old-timer, recognising a kindred spirit. As they shared yarns, the draughtsman invited his new-found friend to the canteen. When they surveyed the food on offer, both scornfully ignored the healthy options and tucked into plates stacked with traditional stodgy grub.

When they returned to the office, Cooper outlined the history of Beckwith's submarine rescue project, describing the trials and tribulations. The old-timer peppered his narrative with scornful comments about the 'air-headed academic' who had sacked him. As the tale unfolded, Alex came to appreciate the navy's reservations about using a fuel-cell propulsion system for rescue operations. Alex listened to his new-found friend with respect, but he did not show too much interest in the internal politics.

The Scotsman became animated as the conversation turned to their forthcoming visit to Rotterdam to inspect the dredger. Alex was looking forward to the trip. His interest in dredging technology had been fired by his research over the past couple of weeks, and this was the first chance to see dredging machinery for real, but their amiable discussion was interrupted when Steve turned up.

The draughtsman greeted Steve jovially. The pair had become friends while working together in the early stages of the submarine rescue project. Alex resented the intrusion, not trusting the slippery young executive. The Scotsman was further irritated when Bill and Tim pushed their way into the small cubicle. The young executive had given the pair a lift from the pub, with Tim squeezing his small frame into the cramped space behind the seats of the sports car.

Bill was in a fractious mood, uneasy about the way things were going. But the good-natured draughtsman had a calming effect, and they settled down to discuss the dredger conversion project in a constructive manner. In their discussion, they were able to refer to drawings of the midget submarine and its launch system. Tim had purloined these documents from the portable cabin that Beckwith occupied in the car park of the boatyard. He had posted the illicit material to Frank Cooper a couple of days earlier.

The draughtsman had been studying the drawings before Alex arrived, earlier that day. "It's interesting to see that they have adopted my design," remarked the corpulent fellow with a satisfied expression. It gave the old-timer pleasure to know that the arrogant academic had adopted his 'old-fashioned' designs after sacking him.

While this discussion created a convivial atmosphere, Alex was piqued by the loss of his new-found friend's undivided attention. He had little interest in the midget submarine and wanted to talk about the dredger. He felt sidelined. With hurt feelings of the odd man out, he extended an olive branch to Bill during a lull in the conversation. "Have you sorted out your financial problems then?" he asked as a conciliatory gesture.

"We've made a start, Alex," replied Bill pleasantly as he reciprocated Alex's efforts to repair their fractured relationship. "I've had a chat with the financier and I have now got a clearer picture of how funds were raised, but we still need to sort out a proper financial plan. It all really depends on what you find when you inspect the dredger next week." Alex nodded absent-mindedly. In truth, he had only asked a question out of politeness; he could not care less where the money came from.

Alex was spared the need to make further comment when Commander Woods arrived to join the group. The old warhorse looked a bit sheepish and avoided Steve's accusing look. If he was honest, the commander would be forced to admit that he used his 'naval duties' as an excuse to avoid a confrontation with the prickly financier. The pair had been at odds about how they would acquire the submarine. Although the commander had prevailed, it was Steve who bore the brunt of the financier's displeasure.

The commander owed the young executive a debt of gratitude. "Sorry that I had to leave early," apologised the commander with a guilty expression, "but I needed to catch up with my official duties," he added disingenuously. "Thanks for dealing with Felix! He has done a magnificent job. But he does try my patience!"

"Felix was a bit excitable," replied Steve euphemistically as he looked towards Bill for confirmation. "He did calm down when I promised to sort out the business plan. In the end, he agreed to cover some of my out-of-pocket expenses. We have promised to provide some cost forecasts in return." Then looking towards Alex and the draughtsman, Steve continued. "These two need to inspect the dredger in Rotterdam, so they need to make their travel plans. It's important that they get that organised."

After completing his duties, the commander was in a relaxed mood and asked if anyone fancied a drink back at the Admiral Bligh pub. Steve and Tim declined the offer, saying they had to start their long car journey back to Plymouth, but Bill was keen to take up the offer. This was an opportunity to experience night life in the Old Town. The outing would also allow Alex to chat to his new pal. So the fractious pair put their differences aside and booked into a budget hotel nearby. With that, they climbed into the commander's staff car, and they set off in high spirits. What adventures would they face in the future?